THE
DEMON'S
COVENANT

Also by Sarah Rees Brennan

The Demon's Lexicon

THE DEMON'S COVENANT

SARAH REES BRENNAN

SIMON AND SCHUSTER

A simon pulse book

Simon Pulse and its colophon are registered trademarks of
Simon and Schuster UK Ltd.

First published in Great Britain in 2010 by Simon and Schuster UK Ltd
A CBS COMPANY

First published in the USA in 2010 by Margaret K McElderry Books,
an imprint of Simon & Schuster Children's Publishing Division.

Copyright © 2010 Sarah Rees Brennan

Simon & Schuster UK Ltd
1st Floor, 222 Gray's Inn Road
London WC1X 8HB

This book is a work of fiction. Names, characters, places and incidents are either the
product of the author's imagination or are used fictitiously. Any resemblance to actual
people living or dead, events or locales is entirely coincidental.

A CIP catalogue record for this book is available from the British Library.

ISBN: 978-1-84738-290-0

1 3 5 7 9 10 8 6 4 2

Printed by CPI Cox & Wyman, Reading RG1 8EX

www.simonandschuster.co.uk

FOR CHIARA – my best friend, and the best thing I ever found in a library

1

Magic on Burnt House Lane

"ANY MINUTE NOW," RACHEL SAID, "SOMETHING TERRIBLE IS going to happen to us."

The area around Burnt House Lane was deserted at this time of night. The cracks in the pavement that Mae hardly noticed by day had turned into shadowy scars along the cement, tracing jagged paths that led into the dark of yet another dead-end alley. They peered down into the alley and made the silent mutual decision to walk on extremely fast. Mae was in the lead.

"Come on, this is an adventure."

Rachel muttered behind her, "I'm pretty sure that's what I just said."

Mae had to concede that this might not have been one of her better ideas. She'd just wanted something different now that she was finally able to leave the house, something a little exciting, and a party in an empty warehouse near Burnt House Lane had seemed the perfect plan.

A streetlamp above slowly winked its single evil orange eye, and night swallowed them at a gulp. The light sputtered back on with a grudging crackle and night spat them up, but by then Rachel and Erica had both walked into Mae's back and were huddling together.

Rachel was shivering. "I think this may be the worst situation I have ever been in."

"Don't be an idiot," said Mae. "I've been in much worse situations than this."

She shivered and thought of the knife sliding in her sweaty grasp, the terrible resistance as she had sunk it into skin. She remembered the blood on her hands.

Rachel and Erica didn't know anything about what had happened last month. They still thought she'd run off to London with her poor misguided brother on some crazy impulse.

Her mother thought that too, which was why Mae had been grounded for two weeks, picked up outside school in Annabel's car like one of the younger kids who ran from school to car, frantic to exchange one cage for another.

Mae closed her eyes, more desperate to escape than any of them, and the dying streetlamps and broken lane faded away. She remembered bright lanterns flooding the forest with gold, dancing with an edge of danger so she wasn't sure if she was sweating from exhilaration or fear, and black eyes on hers.

She'd seen magic. And now she'd lost it.

She wasn't thinking about that, though. She was finally out for the night and she was going to have a good time. She was going to see Seb, and she wasn't going to think about anyone else.

There was a clatter and movement in the shadows. Mae jumped and Erica grabbed her arm, five sharp fingernails biting like a small scared animal.

"It's fine," Mae said loudly, more to herself than her friends. She'd walked around Burnt House Lane after dark hundreds of times. She'd never been scared before. She wasn't going to start being scared now just because she knew exactly what could be watching.

Mae walked on, keeping her stride measured and sure, and nothing followed them that she could hear.

"There's nothing to worry about," she told Erica. "Nothing."

They reached the next alley and saw the warehouse where the party was being held, its windows streaming steady yellow light. Erica took a deep breath, and Mae grinned.

"See," she said. "What did I tell you?"

"Sorry I got freaked out," said Erica, who had not said a word all this time, who was always the angel on Mae's shoulder saying, "Sounds great!" while Rachel on the other said, "We're all doomed." "I know the Lane's safe enough, really. After all, Jamie hangs around here. Can't really see Jamie strolling through a crime den."

She laughed, and Rachel on Mae's other side did too, both of them towering over Mae in their heels, fear melting away in the light.

The warehouse suddenly looked a lot less inviting.

"Jamie's been hanging around the Lane?" Mae asked. "Since when?"

Jamie hadn't been grounded. Annabel had assumed Mae was responsible for the whole thing, and Mae had let her. It wasn't as if they could tell anyone the truth.

Mae had taken the blame and waved Jamie out of the house every night for weeks. He'd said he was going to the library to study; after all, it was his GCSE year, and the tests were coming up soon.

She didn't know why she'd believed him. He'd lied to her before.

Erica looked uncertain about how Mae would take this, but she said, "Tim's seen him around there almost every night for weeks."

Erica's boyfriend Tim was in Seb's gang of guys, who weren't Laners but liked to hang around Burnt House Lane anyway. The Lane was mostly just kids messing around, but far too many of those kids thought hassling Jamie was a good time.

Wandering Burnt House Lane after dark . . . Jamie did not take chances like that. She always told him he needed to take more risks, have a little fun, and Jamie always smiled his lopsided smile and said that he felt he got all the danger he needed in his life eating school lunches.

Mae thought about the very real danger Jamie had been in, less than a month ago. She thought about seeing a black mark on Jamie's skin and hearing two strangers tell her that her baby brother was going to die.

She could hear the music coming out of the warehouse by now, not calling to her and promising her magic, but steady and reassuring as a heartbeat. She wanted to have fun with her friends again, to find Seb and see where that was going. She wanted to return to her normal life.

And she would, as soon as she knew her brother was safe.

"You guys go ahead, I just need to check something out."

Mae had already sprinted a few steps away, so when she looked back her friends were superimposed against the light and music, staring at her with identically wide eyes.

"You just need to check something out in the pitch dark, in a dodgy part of town?" Rachel asked.

Mae didn't need to be told it was dangerous. If it was dangerous for her, it would be twice as dangerous for Jamie, and every minute she spent talking was another minute he could be getting deeper into trouble.

"You're barely even wearing a shirt! What are you going to do if a mugger jumps out at you, flash them?"

"That's the basic plan," Mae told her, and ran.

Mae had walked around Burnt House Lane at night plenty of times before, stumbling out of clubs with a guy who always turned out to be less interesting in the light of day. It was different now, alone with the night air running cool sharp fingers along her bare shoulders, her whole body tense. The moonlight was casting spiderweb graffiti on already scrawled-on walls and the night was full of potential danger.

People who thought it was funny to write "Gaz was here" on the walls might think it was funny to hurt Jamie. Mae was almost stumbling in her hurry through the night, so intent on her search that she put her foot into a slimy puddle. The plastic bag half-sunk in the dirty water clung to her laces as if it was a drowning swimmer. She shook her foot until it slipped off and into its watery, oily grave.

As she shook, she heard a boy's voice say, "Crawford?" and she turned, wet shoe squishing as she ran towards an alley.

Lurking in alleys around the Lane, Mae thought in outrage. What did Jamie think he was doing?

She was mad about his stupidity right up until she turned the corner and actually saw him: skinny, small, his blond hair standing up in spikes that didn't make him look any taller. Jamie always seemed a little fragile, and he seemed a whole lot more fragile when he was backed against an alley wall, staring up at three taller boys. The alley looked forlorn, the walls dirty and the dented, lopsided bins leaning against one another like drunks. It looked like the perfect setting for some petty crime.

Then she recognised the other boys.

Apparently Seb McFarlane wasn't waiting to dance with Mae in the warehouse. Instead he'd decided it would be better fun to corner her brother in an alley.

The other boys were two guys she knew vaguely, part of a crowd who liked to smoke behind the bike shed and grab at clubs without asking.

Seb was tall, dark, and a little dangerous, but he never grabbed. Mae had really thought he was a possibility.

Now he was stalking towards Jamie, and Jamie was shrinking away, and the only possibility in Seb's future was the possibility of being bitch-slapped by a girl.

He wasn't that close to Jamie yet, so that meant Jamie had backed into a wall all by himself. Which was just like Jamie.

"Out here all alone?" Seb asked. "You sure that's good thinking, Crawford? What if you get into trouble?"

Jamie blinked. "That is a concern. I'm glad I have you big strong men here to protect me!"

Seb shoved Jamie hard. "Your helpless act isn't convincing me."

"I don't know," another boy said lazily. "I think it's pretty convincing, myself."

The two boys Mae didn't really know just seemed bored and ready to mess around, which wouldn't have been a problem; Mae could have strolled in and made it all seem like a joke until she could whisk Jamie out of there. It was different with Seb, his big shoulders set and his voice intense. He seemed angry.

"It's an act," he insisted. "And you should drop it. Or . . ."

6

He leaned in, very focused, his eyes sharp and his voice soft. "Maybe I'll *make* you drop it."

Jamie swallowed and spoke, his voice equally soft. "I think I'm beginning to understand. Are you, um," he said, and grinned suddenly, "are you hitting on me? Because I don't know how to tell you this, but you're not really my type."

Seb stepped away from Jamie as if he'd just been informed Jamie was radioactive. "You're not funny," he snapped. "You're just pathetic."

Jamie kept grinning. "I like to think I'm maybe a little of both."

Seb's face twisted and his hand moved, clenched in a fist. Mae moved too, but her wet shoe slid and she almost fell. Her heart was beating hard with surprise and rage, absolute rage, because to keep Jamie safe she had killed someone – she kept remembering the knife and all the blood and that magician's surprised face – and now this stupid boy dared touch him. Why didn't Jamie do something?

That was when she felt the warm hand at the back of her neck. It was a light clasp, as if a friend or a boyfriend were passing by and wished to alert her to their presence, fingers trailing over the delicate skin. The talisman she wore tucked in her corset flared into life, pain bursting like a small star against her skin. She found she could not move, not even to shiver. She was held frozen in place, like a butterfly gently caught between two fingers and then abruptly transfixed by the cruel steel point of a pin.

Her heart was beating harder than ever, loud in her ears and in her enforced stillness. She thought and almost thrilled to the thought: magic. Magic here, magic in Burnt House Lane, when she had thought it would never enter her life again.

She felt a presence brush by her and heard a voice ring out in the night close to her ear, almost echoing her own thoughts.

"Jamie," said Gerald, "why don't you do something?"

The last time Mae had heard that voice, he'd been promising to come back for their lives.

Seb and the other boys turned their heads and stared, the tension in their bodies easing as they took in the sight of Gerald. He was hardly an awe-inspiring sight, Mae remembered, though all she could see of him was a blue shirt and sandy hair going in every direction.

She recalled the mild, freckled face under the sandy hair; the shy voice, the sweet smile, and those clever, watching eyes.

Gerald lifted a hand, and the lid of a bin rose and spun in midair like a ninja's star, missing one of the boys by an inch and striking sparks off the wall.

"Funny how these freak winds happen," he observed in his friendly way.

The boy who the bin lid had almost hit took several steps back. Gerald gestured easily and the lid rose again, quivering in the air.

A slow, small creak came from the darkest corner of the alley. Even the boy being menaced by the airborne bin lid turned his head to see the rusty old drainpipe peeling itself from the wall.

The bin lid was pinwheeling in the air now, a blur of silver. The drainpipe was bowing towards them, tall and thin, looming out of the night like a spindly, starving giant who had finally spotted food.

Gerald laughed indulgently, as if he was showing them all a trick, as if he'd just produced doves from his sleeve rather than killer drainpipes.

"Run," he suggested.

Two of the boys exchanged frantic looks, their eyes swivelling from Gerald standing in the alley entrance to the drainpipe, and then back again.

"Don't bother Jamie any more," Gerald advised. He stepped back, politely motioning for them to go through.

The two boys ran. They didn't even notice Mae standing frozen and furious to one side.

Seb did not move. For a moment Mae thought he was frozen by magic as she was, his hand still lifted to deliver Jamie a blow that would never land. Then he let his hand fall.

"Did I fail to make myself clear?" Gerald said, with an edge to his voice now. "When I said run, I meant you, too."

"I'm—" Seb began, and shook his head. "Sorry. I'm sorry. I – right."

He bowed his head to Gerald. Mae saw him shoot a dark look under his lashes at Jamie.

Jamie gave him a little wave. "Don't let the alley hit you in the ass on your way out."

Seb looked like he wanted to answer, possibly with a blow, but then he cut a swift look back at Gerald and stepped slowly away. He passed Gerald, making for the alley entrance.

He did see Mae. For a moment they looked at each other, his scowling face smoothing out. He looked as if he wasn't quite sure what to do, and in the end he did nothing, just backed uncertainly away.

She'd deal with him later.

In the alley Jamie raised a hand and the spinning of the bin lid slowed. It was held still and suspended for a second, and then it flew with extreme force at Gerald.

Gerald caught it easily and nodded thanks, as if Jamie were a squire who had just tossed his knight a shield.

"Yes, like that. Why do you allow them to hassle you when you can just do something like that?"

"Because I don't have to," Jamie said shortly. "They're idiots, but that doesn't mean I want them hurt or scared. And I don't need you to scare them either. There was no need for all that! I have to live here, you know."

"No, you don't."

Jamie batted his eyelashes and laughed. "Oh yes, take me away from all this. You don't listen."

"It's you who doesn't listen!" said Gerald. "You're a magician."

"No, I'm not."

"It's not a choice," Gerald said. "You were born a magician. It's in your blood, and you think you can just stay here in this dull little life, being persecuted by dull little people, when you could be so much more. I could teach you."

Jamie smiled, so much more at ease with a murderous magician than with school bullies. He spread his hands wide and stepped away from the wall. Gerald was taller than he was, but he didn't look at all threatening.

He looked protective. They looked comfortable together.

"What could you teach me?" Jamie asked, a dimple flashing in his right cheek next to his earring. "Do I need to learn a secret magician handshake? Do I need to learn to do finger wands?"

Gerald burst out laughing. "I—" he said, and seemed somewhat at a loss. "I don't know what you're talking about."

"Like a finger gun, but only magicians get to do it," Jamie explained, grinning and shifting his schoolbag on one shoulder. He swished one finger in a dramatic circle, making a swooshing sound to accompany the gesture.

"We don't use wands," said Gerald.

"Don't think that wasn't a crushing blow for me."

Gerald laughed again and ducked his head, shoving his hands in his pockets. "C'mon," he said. "I want to show you something."

"Well, that sounds ominously nonspecific," Jamie remarked. "How could I refuse?"

They fell into step casually, as if out of long habit. Gerald grabbed the bag that was always sliding off Jamie's shoulder and adjusted it. Jamie murmured something that made Gerald grin.

When they were leaving the alley, Mae thought that Jamie would see her, but Gerald said, "Look," and pointed.

As Jamie looked up, the night over Burnt House Lane was torn like a veil. The air shimmered, and the broken road was paved with gold, and the whole world was magic.

"That's just an illusion," Jamie said while wonder still held the breath caught in Mae's throat. He hesitated and added, "How did you do it?"

"I'll show you," said Gerald. "I'm going to show you everything."

The light faded slowly, like honey dripping off a knife. Jamie still had his face upturned to the sky, mouth open, as Gerald led him away with one hand at the small of his back.

The magician brushed by Mae and suddenly she could move, as if she was made of ice and his touch was hot enough to change her to water.

She fell to the ground like a puppet with its strings abruptly cut, gasping and trying to think, trying to make a plan for a situation she would never have believed possible.

She'd always believed there was more to the world than school and clubs and the life Annabel wanted her to live. And she'd found out that there were people in the world who could do magic, people who sold magical toys in Goblin Markets and magicians who called up demons that could do almost anything. For a price.

The last time she and Jamie had seen Gerald, he'd just become the leader of the magicians' Circle that had given Jamie a demon's mark. The Obsidian Circle had almost got Jamie possessed by a demon, an evil spirit that would use his body until it crumbled from the inside out. The Circle had almost killed Jamie. Gerald had certainly killed countless others.

Now here he was in Mae's city, acting like her brother's best friend. And Jamie had told her nothing about it.

She was in over her head. They needed help.

She struggled up onto her hands and knees, and then sat up. She was leaning against a filthy brick wall in the wrong part of town with no trace of magic left.

She dug out her phone and called Alan.

When he answered she jumped, because he was screaming above high wind and the sound of a storm.

"Hello?"

"Alan?" she said, staring up at the calm, empty sky above her head. "Where are you?"

On the other end of the line there was an echoing snarl of thunder.

"Mae?" Alan yelled, and there was silence.

The sound of the storm had just stopped abruptly, not as if it was dying away but as if someone had thrown a switch and turned off the sky.

Mae realised she was trembling. "Alan, what's going on?"

She could hear Alan properly now, his low, sweet voice more remarkable over the phone than it was in person, when it was hard to notice much about it other than that it made you want to do whatever he asked and believe whatever he said. There was a warm undercurrent to it, as if Alan was happy to be talking to her.

Of course, that was the way he talked to everyone.

"Nothing's going on. Is something wrong?"

Mae swallowed and tried to sound calm and assured, as if she wasn't running to him begging for help. Again.

"Jamie's mixed up with a magician."

There was a pause.

Then Alan said, "We're on our way."

It was long past midnight by the time Jamie got back. Annabel was still at the office, because she liked being there more than being at home, and Mae had been sitting for hours in the music room with her head in her hands.

She'd thought this was over.

As soon as Jamie looked at her he came rushing to her, sinking to his knees between hers and taking her hands in his.

"I thought you were going out tonight. Did something happen at school? Are the teachers not understanding your unique and rebellious spirit? Did you kick some guy in the biology textbook again?"

Mae smiled at him with an effort. "Things are fine at school. Though now you mention it, no teacher does understand my unique and rebellious spirit at all. Where have you been?"

"Out," Jamie said. Mae saw the unease plain on his face. She supposed she should be thankful her brother wasn't an accomplished liar, wasn't like Alan, but seeing him dodge her question made Mae feel sick. "C'mon, get up."

Jamie sprang to his feet and turned on their sound system. He ran through their CDs and put on a waltz. She laughed and shook her head at him, and he beckoned to her.

"Come here."

"Nope," said Mae. When Jamie grabbed her hands and tugged her gently to her feet, she laughed again and let him.

He stepped back and spun her so the lights of the chandelier and the white walls formed a dazzling blur before her eyes, as if the walls had turned to light and were turning with her. These days Mae kept imagining magic.

For a moment it was as it had always been between them, him and her against the world. This big stupid house felt just like the house they'd had before Annabel and Roger split up: oriel windows, parquet floors, and Jamie and Mae being loud and silly enough to drown out the echoing expensive silence.

"So where did you learn to dance?" Jamie asked, starting the game.

"I learned to dance in a cowboy bar in the Old West," Mae told him. "The boys could shoot the neck off a bottle at a hundred paces, but my moves were too dangerous for them. Eventually the sheriff ran me out of town."

Jamie dipped her so her hair touched the floor. This smooth move was slightly spoiled when he almost over balanced and dumped her on her ass. He staggered and she grabbed hold of his shirt, using it as leverage until she was standing on her own two feet again.

Mae caught her breath and waggled her eyebrows. "Where did you learn to dance, sailor?"

"Oh, I learned to dance wearing a lace frock at Madame Mimsy's exclusive seminary for young ladies. They thought I was a good girl," Jamie said cheerfully. "Wrong on both counts."

He had a hand under her elbow, careful, as if he was afraid she was going to fall again. After a few moments of silent dancing, he said, "Is anything wrong? I feel like there's something you're not telling me."

Mae took a deep breath and heard the door creak open.

She and Jamie separated and turned to face their mother.

Annabel Crawford was as small as Mae and Jamie, and thin because she never ate anything but salads; her hair was lemon blonde and her eyes very pale green, not like emeralds but like old-fashioned soap. She would have seemed washed-out and easy to overlook except for how polished she was, always perfectly put together with her hair so glossy it looked lacquered. Somehow that lent her an icy lustre that was more noticeable than colour, and she was actually almost impossible to overlook.

"James," she said, her hands folded in front of her. "Mavis. Did you have fun tonight?"

Her cool gaze travelled over Mae, making Mae acutely aware that her jeans were slimy from falling in that alley. Annabel probably didn't like the corset top with the black lace and the pink ribbons that spelled out ALL WRAPPED UP IN ME either.

Mae lifted her chin. "Yeah, it had everything I ask for in a party. Hard drugs. Casual sex. Ritual animal sacrifice."

"Dancing," said Jamie, and advanced on Annabel with intent. "Would you like to dance, Mum?"

Annabel looked as if she would prefer to eat dirt, but she put her perfectly manicured hands in Jamie's anyway. When they started to dance, she caught him a nasty blow with one of her high heels.

Mae was pretty sure it wasn't the actual dancing that was tripping her up. Annabel loved sports as much as Roger did, so much that they'd forced Jamie and Mae to take a million classes, though only the dance lessons had stuck. It was spending time with her kids that Annabel was having trouble with.

Ever since Mae and Jamie had returned from what Annabel thought was a cry-for-help mission of mad truancy to London, Annabel had been trying to spend quality time with them. She wasn't very good at bonding, but that didn't matter to Jamie. He was eating it up with a spoon.

Mae appreciated the thought, especially since Roger's response to the whole affair was to decide that Mae and Jamie needed a more settled environment, and cancel all visits to his place. But Mae got along just fine without parental supervision. Annabel didn't need to strain herself.

"Where did you learn to dance?" Jamie asked playfully.

"Er, I took ballet lessons for several years," Annabel responded, and got Jamie again with her heel.

Mae went and sat on the window seat of the bay window, hands clasped around one slimy knee.

When the magicians had put a demon's mark on her brother, she'd killed one of them to get it off. Almost every night since then she had woken remembering the shocking heat of blood spilling over her fingers. She'd lain awake feeling the ghost of that warmth, looking at her clean hands painted grey by the dim light, remembering.

She wasn't sorry. She would have done it again without a second's thought, but tonight she had been helpless and had seen Jamie laughing with the magicians' leader.

Jamie came to stand beside her when the song was done, a warm presence at her side. Mae pressed her cheek against the night-cold pane of glass.

"So is there?" he asked quietly. "Something you're not telling me?"

"Maybe," Mae told him. "We all have our secrets."

2

A Demon in View

Nɪᴄᴋ ᴀɴᴅ Aʟᴀɴ ᴀʀʀɪᴠᴇᴅ ᴛᴡᴏ ᴅᴀʏꜱ ʟᴀᴛᴇʀ. Mᴀᴇ ᴛᴏᴏᴋ ᴛʜᴇ ᴅᴀʏ off school to welcome them back.

By now she and the secretary had almost made a game of this.

"Hello, this is Annabel Crawford. I'm afraid Mavis simply can't come in today," Mae said in a flawless imitation of her mother's voice, perfectly modulated and reeking of both tennis and law courts. "I fear she caught a chill at one of the soirées we so enjoy attending."

"Really. I hope it doesn't turn into strep throat, like it did the last time the college held a rave."

That was when Mae saw the battered car pull up outside the gates. They'd got a new car since the last one had been abandoned on Tower Bridge, but she knew it was them.

It didn't look like a vehicle for people who knew magical secrets. It was blue and scarred, and the brown tracery of age webbed across the door on the driver's side reminded Mae of the lines in the corners of an old man's eyes. The car was framed in the black and gold gates, and a sycamore tree was dropping yellow star shapes on the battered roof. To anyone else's eyes the view from her window would have seemed utterly ordinary.

The passenger door opened and Mae saw Alan emerge, moving stiffly, sunlight catching the gold gleams chased through his dark red hair.

She realised she was clutching the phone too hard. She switched it to her other hand and tried to flex her fingers; they seemed to want to stay curled in the shape they'd formed around the phone.

"Um, yes! I've been coughing and coughing," she said randomly into the phone.

"I'm sorry?" said the secretary, very dry. "I thought this was Mrs Crawford."

"I think I may have caught what Mavis has," Mae told her, and coughed. "Those soirées are hotbeds of disease. Excuse me. I have to go."

She missed when she tried to hang up the first time, then gave her hand a betrayed look and hung up like a reasonable human being. The intercom buzzed, and she smacked the button to open the gates without looking at it. She was still staring out of the window.

Alan limped towards the front door. The limp was the first thing she'd noticed about Alan, back when he was just a boy working in her local bookshop who went pink every time she spoke to him. It was only a small halt in his step, he didn't let it affect him much, but he also let people see it because the limp made him look harmless. It was the perfect camouflage, because it was real.

Alan's brother followed him, always walking one step

behind or one step in front, either guarding him or watching his back. Mae didn't think it would ever have occurred to Nick to walk alongside anyone: he would've thought being beside someone just for company was pointless.

Nick never looked harmless. He never tried.

Alan's limp seemed much worse when Nick was near him. Nick moved like river water in the night, in sinuous flowing movements the eye always registered a second too late. He had a grace that was terrible to watch: he moved, and a voice in your head whispered that if he went for your throat, you wouldn't even see him coming.

Mae could feel her heart beating too fast and her cheeks burning. She was furious with herself for being such an idiot.

She went downstairs and told herself with every step that she was fine, that she had called them because she needed help, that she hadn't particularly wanted to see either of them. She prepared a number of calm and practical things to say.

When she opened the door and saw their faces, she forgot them all.

She and Jamie had lived with them for over a week; their faces were as familiar to her as old friends', but she hadn't seen them since the day she'd killed someone and they'd found out the truth about Nick. They looked different to her, new even though they were familiar, and she felt new as well, as if she'd been broken apart and put back together with the pieces not fitting quite right. They were real. It was all real, that world of magic so different from the world of Exeter. They were a part of magic and danger and the blood she woke remembering every night.

"Hi," she said, and opened the door to let them in.

"It's good to see you again, Mae," said Alan, and gave her a hug.

She was startled not so much by the gesture as by how it felt. It made her recall her first impression of Alan, when she'd seen a skinny but sort of cute redhead with kind eyes behind wire-rimmed glasses and thought that he seemed nice, harmless, and not at all her type.

She knew better now, but there was still a moment of complete cognitive dissonance when he put his arms around her. He looked like one thing and felt like quite another.

His chest and arms were surprisingly hard, lean muscle against her hands, and under his thin T-shirt he was carrying a gun. Mae felt the shape of it press briefly against her stomach.

Alan wasn't harmless. He didn't mind if she knew it.

For a moment she didn't even think to return the hug, just stood there frozen. He'd started to pull away by the time she curved a hand around his shoulder, and there was an awkward instant where she grabbed him and he stepped back in too close and then they both stepped away too quickly.

She wasn't expecting a hug from Nick. She didn't even get a hello.

He leaned against her door with his arms folded and nodded at her. When she suggested they come inside he followed them into the sitting room, always one step behind, carefully shadowing his brother.

Mae couldn't stand how ridiculous and off balance she felt, and took the desperate measure of being her mother's daughter and playing hostess. "Sit down," she said, and pinned a smile in place like a badge. "Can I get you guys anything? Juice? Tea?"

"I'd love some juice," said Alan.

Nick shook his head.

"What, you don't talk any more?" snapped Mae, and wanted to bite her tongue out.

"I talk," said Nick, his mouth curving slightly. "And I see you still pester people."

He had a deep voice that reminded Mae of a fire; a low, dangerous sound that crackled occasionally and made you jump. Listening to Nick talk was like seeing Alan walk. It was always obvious there was something wrong.

"It is one of my favourite activities," said Mae, and went to get Alan some juice.

When she came back, she found Alan sitting in an armchair by the fireplace like a proper guest. Nick was roaming the room as if he was a feral dog she'd shut up in the house and he was searching for signs of danger and getting ready to bolt. He was stooped over the grand piano and he looked up, not startled but wary as she entered the room. Mae took a quick, instinctive step back and her free hand found the doorknob, her palm suddenly sweaty against the cool juice glass.

She'd always been a little jolted when she met Nick's eyes, and it was worse now she knew why. His gaze was steady, his eyes not the windows to any soul but to another world, a world with no stars or moon, no possibility of light or warmth.

Then he looked down at the piano keys and was again simply the best-looking guy she'd ever seen, with lashes lying feathery on high cheekbones, a sooty shock of hair such a dense black that it didn't shine but always looked soft, and a full mouth that should have been expressive but somehow never was.

"Do you play?" she asked, and felt stupid and enraged. She never usually felt stupid.

"No," said Nick in that low, emotionless voice. She thought that was all he was going to say, since he was always careful with words, acting as if he had a very limited supply and might run out at any moment. But he added, "Alan used to. When we were kids."

"Ages ago," Alan put in, his voice very light. "I was also on the football team and I played the guitar. But where I really shone was my work on the tambourine."

He didn't say that that had been before their father died and before Alan had been crippled, when they'd had money. Mae held on tight to the doorknob and felt embarrassed by her whole house.

"We could get a piano," Nick said.

"And what, keep it in the garden?" Alan made a soft sound, almost a laugh.

"We could get a bigger place. You could play the piano. You could play football. We can do anything we like—"

Mae had never heard Nick's voice show feeling, but she had heard it show danger plenty of times. He didn't shout, but sometimes everything went silent when he spoke and his voice sounded louder, like the slide of a knife from a sheath in a sudden hush.

She remembered Nick's voice sounding like this one night when he'd whirled and hit his brother. And she remembered Alan coolly pulling a gun.

Alan's voice cut Nick off.

"No, Nick. You can't." He turned away from his brother and focused on Mae. "Mae, come here – thank you – and tell me what exactly is going on with Jamie. What magician is he mixed up with? What's going on?"

And Mae found herself sitting in the armchair across from Alan, her hand curled, as if still around the glass Alan was now holding, and feeling at a loss and almost annoyed. That was the thing about these two. It wasn't that she didn't like them. She did, but she didn't feel in control around them. She wanted to feel in control.

"Gerald, of course," she almost snapped. "He said he'd come back for us and he has. Only I didn't know he'd come back, and it's – it's pretty clear that Jamie's been meeting him and not telling me. I saw them, and they seemed like they were friends. His damned Obsidian Circle tried to kill Jamie a month ago! I don't know what he's doing, what kind of hold he might have over Jamie, and I don't understand anything."

So she'd gone running to them. Again.

Mae clenched her hands into fists and looked away from them both into the empty grate. She hated feeling so useless.

She wasn't looking when the door burst open and Jamie's voice rang out, saying, "Mae, are you really sick – oh."

Mae twisted around and saw Jamie held still by surprise in the open door, one hand clinging to the door frame. His expression of concern was fixed on his face, as if he'd absentmindedly left it there even though he was done with it, and Mae felt suddenly and unexpectedly angry with him.

He was much more scared to see Nick than he'd been to see Gerald. And no matter what Nick was, he'd done nothing but help them.

"Hey, Alan," Jamie said, a real smile touching his lips but not staying long. "Nick. Wh-what's going on?"

You're busted, that's what, Mae thought, feeling about eight years old and meanly pleased to see her little brother in trouble. She turned to Nick, to tell him – to show him – that she knew what they owed to him, that she wasn't scared.

When she looked at Nick, she saw him draw his sword.

It was so bizarre that for a moment Mae forgot to be angry. This was her home: the shiny cold floors, high ceilings, and white walls that looked like blank pages were no setting for swords and sorcery.

Despite everything she knew, Nick still looked like part of the normal world. He was wearing jeans and a T-shirt. He shouldn't have been wielding a sword, but he was. The blade was bright and steady in his hands, held with casual expertise, and he walked forward softly as a stalking cat and lifted his sword with each step until the edge was held against Jamie's throat. For an instant Mae thought that Nick wouldn't stop.

He did stop.

"In trouble again, Jamie?" Nick asked. "Seems to be a hobby of yours. And I'm getting pretty tired of cleaning up your messes. I think last time was enough, don't you?"

Jamie swallowed, his Adam's apple brushing the sword edge.

"I can see the magic all around you," Nick continued, his voice sinking further. "Who gave that to you? Or should I be asking what you did to get it? Mae's been telling us all about the company you're keeping these days. Maybe I should have saved myself some bother and let the magicians cut your throat when I had the chance. They would have done it, you know."

Jamie tried to speak and had to clear his throat before he could. "I know. And I'm not—"

"Don't lie to me," Nick snarled. "I don't like it."

Nick took a step forward, just slowly enough for Jamie to

take a step away. His back slammed up against the door, and Nick had him trapped.

"That's enough!" said Mae, jumping up, but before she could move towards them the moment changed.

Jamie suddenly didn't look scared, didn't look uncertain. He tilted his head and fixed Nick with a long, calm look. Then he reached up and caught the blade gently between his palms. Mae looked at the back of Nick's head and wished for a frantic moment that she could see his face, until she remembered that even if he was about to slice Jamie's hands open, his expression would not show one trace of emotion.

Nick's body was held taut, either to attack or defend.

Jamie closed his eyes.

Between his hands the sword flew apart like a dandelion clock that had been blown on. It dissolved into a hundred glittering points of steel that fell in the air around both boys, fading as they fell until they were nothing more than dust motes, visible for an instant in the light from the bay windows.

"I'm not a magician," Jamie whispered. "I'm not. I know what I owe you all. I know that both of you could have let me die, and I know that if Mae hadn't killed a magician for me I would've died. You've all done more than enough for me. I didn't want to be a burden any more. I wanted to be able to handle this myself!"

"Let him go, Nick."

Mae looked back instinctively at the sound. Alan was leaning forward in his chair; he hadn't made the slightest effort to get up. She looked at him and realised his body had been held in the same taut lines as his brother's.

He had not spoken in that tone of low command until he'd heard Jamie say that he wasn't a magician.

Nick gave no sign that he'd heard Alan. The hilt of his vanished sword was still in his hand, and he tossed it high up into the air like a toy.

The day was so bright that the light of the chandelier seemed pale and irrelevant, but it caught the sword hilt with a sudden particular gleam. The gleam spread, became a ray of light that looked almost like a sword, and when the hilt hit Nick's palm the light had become steel. The sword was whole.

"Do you think I need a sword to kill you?" Nick asked softly.

"No," said Jamie in a shaky voice. "But you didn't have to threaten me."

"Let him go now," Mae ordered.

Nick didn't pay any more attention to her than he had to Alan.

"I wasn't threatening you. I was menacing you. You threaten people with words," Nick said. "I prefer swords."

He stepped back then, sliding his restored blade into the sheath he kept strapped to his spine, under his T-shirt.

"And that one is my favourite sword," he added, turning away from Jamie and heading for the window. "Don't mess around with it again."

He braced himself against the casement, one leg up on the window seat and his face turned a little away from them all. Jamie slumped against the door, looking massively relieved, and of course immediately said something ill-advised.

"You and swords," he remarked brightly. "Compensating for something?"

The corner of Nick's mouth curved upwards a fraction. "No."

He apparently didn't feel the need to say anything else, but the slight sign of amusement relieved the tense atmosphere a little. Mae took her seat again, and Jamie went over and sat on the hearth rug between Mae and Alan's chairs, curling himself up small and leaning closer to Mae's chair. She reached out and touched the ends of his spiky hair, and he smiled at her.

"Now that we're done menacing each other with swords, I feel it's time for social pleasantries," Jamie announced. "How've you been, Alan?"

"I've been all right," said Alan. "What's going on with Gerald, Jamie?"

"He hasn't hurt me," Jamie told them very quickly. "He came to me after school about – a couple of weeks ago. I was scared, but he didn't hurt me, and he said he wasn't going to. He just wanted to talk to me. I didn't want to, but what else was I supposed to do, go running to Mae after everything she'd done? Call you guys?"

"You could've called," Alan assured him. His voice was warm enough to strike a grateful smile from both Jamie and Mae.

"Oh yes," Nick said. "Call anytime. I love to chat."

"He really did just want to talk. I didn't want anyone else to get involved. I didn't want to risk Mae getting hurt," said Jamie. "It's not that I trust him. I don't trust him. I know he hurts people, but he was being reasonable. All he asked was for me to hear him out, and I thought that if I did there was a chance he'd just go away."

"You should have known magicians only want one thing," Nick said. Jamie abruptly flushed scarlet. Nick smirked and went on, "To recruit you for their magical army of darkness."

Jamie nodded cautiously. "I said no. I'm still saying no. It's all under control."

"Yeah, it's all totally under control," Mae burst out. "I saw you in that alleyway, and your new friend froze me before I could say a word or move a muscle. Like someone getting their dog to sit or pressing pause. Like I was a thing."

Jamie looked at her with wide-eyed concern, but Mae wasn't ready to forgive him yet. She looked away and her eyes found Nick, still standing apart from them all, still looking out of the window. His thumb was casually hooked in the loop of his jeans, and as she looked at his hand resting against his thigh, she noticed something new: he was wearing a silver ring. She could see there were shapes carved in the silver but not what they were, and she was a bit surprised. Nick had never struck her as the jewellery type.

Like it mattered. Like she'd ever really known anything about him at all.

"I'm sorry, Mae," Jamie said in a small voice. "He doesn't really think that – that non-magical people are as important as magicians. It's not his fault, exactly. He started doing magic when he was really young, and his family was terrible to him about it, and then the magicians came for him when he wasn't much older than ten and he was so grateful, he felt so rescued, he believed everything they believed. It doesn't mean—"

"That he's a bad person?" Nick asked. "He kills people. Now I'm no expert, but doesn't that make you a bad person?"

Jamie glared at Nick. "You've killed a lot more people than he has. What does that make you?"

"Not a person," Nick murmured, not sounding particularly interested. "Surely you remember."

There was a short and extremely uncomfortable silence.

"If you're not a magician," said Alan, quiet and thoughtful, to all appearances entirely unconscious that anyone might be feeling the least bit awkward, "then how did you just do magic?"

"I've been practising," Jamie admitted. "Just a little. Gerald's been teaching me some things." He paused. "I'm sorry. I won't – I won't do it any more."

Jamie looked guilty, and it broke Mae's heart, even if she was angry with him. He'd been born with these powers, and he'd hidden them from everyone for years. He'd even hidden them from her, and she hated that. She resented him for lying to her and making her feel stupid, and at the same time she hurt for him when he talked about doing spells as if he'd committed a crime.

Mae wanted to tell him he didn't have to stop, but she wasn't about to encourage this connection with Gerald.

Nick did not look terribly concerned about Jamie's dilemma.

"I can sense the magic on you. This isn't the trace of some little tricks you've been trying out. This is the real stuff." He tilted his head, considering; Nick always seemed thoughtful rather than worried when people were afraid. "If you haven't been doing any big magic," he continued softly, "then someone's cast a powerful spell on you. Curious about that at all?"

Jamie turned a nasty shade of white.

"Seems like your pal Gerald can't be trusted," Nick concluded. "I for one am shocked."

"Let's not start panicking when we don't know for sure what's going on," Alan said reasonably. "It might be nothing. Not that I'm inclined to trust Gerald myself, which is why I thought it might be best to come back to Exeter and stay for a while until we do know what's going on."

"I think it might be best to kill them all," Nick said.

At the same time Jamie said, "You don't have to do that for me."

Alan decided that he was going to respond to Jamie. "It's not a problem. We're used to moving around, we want to help, and besides, the company's good here." He sent Mae a small smile. "Plus, it might be nice to settle somewhere for a while. Maybe Nick could even make some friends."

Nick scowled out of the window. "I have friends in Exeter already. I have – those people, you know, they hang around outside the bike sheds, they're always hassling Jamie."

"Those are some awesome dudes," Jamie muttered. "Don't let them get away."

"You might try remembering just one name," said Alan sharply. "Since they're such good friends of yours."

Mae straightened in her chair. She had never heard quite that tone in Alan's voice before.

"Fine then," Nick snapped, and directed a dark glance Jamie's way. "Hey, Jamie. Want to be friends?"

Jamie looked extremely startled. "Um," he said, and went a bit pink. "Um, all right." He paused and added, "Friends don't menace friends with giant terrifying swords, okay?"

Nick snorted. "Okay."

"See, Exeter's working out well already," Alan said, sounding a little amused, and Mae thought she might have been imagining the note of tension in his voice before. "Jamie? Do you think you could make an appointment to see Gerald?"

Mae wondered if Jamie knew some sort of spell to get in touch with the Obsidian Circle, or if possibly Gerald had carrier pigeons.

"Well, sure," Jamie said. "I have his phone number." He hesitated for a moment and then said uneasily, "What – what are you planning to do to him?"

Gerald didn't think that normal people were as important as magicians. He killed normal people and fed them to demons in order to get more magic, and still Jamie could seem worried about him, as if Gerald really was a friend.

Of course, Nick and Alan were her friends, and she knew what they were.

She'd thought of Nick as more than a friend, once, and she'd imagined that perhaps he felt the same way about her.

She had been wrong about that. All he'd been interested in was using her to spite his brother.

It didn't matter that Nick had never cared. Mae had been interested when she'd thought he was a gorgeous guy whose strangeness she'd put down to the effects of living on the run from magicians. She wasn't still interested now that she knew he was a demon, put into the body of a baby by the Obsidian Circle magicians and raised human, but a demon all the same; something otherworldly that preyed on her kind. It would be impossible.

She tore her gaze away from Nick, dark and silent at the window, to the friendly face of the guy who'd raised a demon and set him loose on the world.

"I just want to talk to him," Alan said soothingly, eyes on Jamie's face. "For now."

3

Messenger at the Gates

MAE DECIDED TO SKIP THE END OF HER LAST CLASS SO SHE could get her break-up over with. She told the maths teacher that she had to go to the bathroom "kind of urgently", and Mr Churchill told her to go with a look on his face that said he wished he was teaching in an all-boys' school.

She made her way over to the new building, a stucco bungalow tucked in between the bike sheds and the playground where the GCSE class took art. The bell rang as she approached, and the other kids poured out, Jamie included, as if education was lingering in the classroom like a deadly airborne virus.

Seb didn't emerge. He was really keen on art, she knew, and probably finishing up a project in there. She would have to go in after him.

Mae really was not looking forward to this.

She didn't want to be with anyone who hurt her brother, but wanting to be with Seb had been an escape from longing for the lights of the Goblin Market, for all the bright and dangerous colours of magic in the air. She'd been so relieved to want something normal.

Mae hadn't been doing well, the first few days back at home. She would just be sitting in class and suddenly she would feel panicked, as if there were eyes on her, magicians about to swoop down on them, demons coming. She'd been sitting in English and found her hand going for a knife that she didn't have, the knife she was keeping in her sock drawer and trying to forget about.

She'd gone out and sat on the loose gravel, back against the peeling wood of the bike sheds, and then she'd seen him.

He had his back to her but was turning, and Mae saw his dark fall of hair, the broad shoulders and long legs, even the knife-straight nose in profile, and she felt her heart start to beat in a dangerous rhythm. She'd thought, He came back.

Then he'd turned properly and she'd seen Seb's clear green eyes, the colour of leaves with sunlight streaming through them, and his bright smile.

Nick could never smile like that.

"Hey," he'd said, a little awkward, coming to her side quickly but scuffing the gravel, as if he wanted to give her the impression he was reluctant about it. "It's Mae, isn't it? Crawford's sister?"

"Yeah."

"You okay?" he asked, and then looked mildly embarrassed. "I mean, is there anything I can do about you obviously not being okay?"

"Not really," Mae told him honestly.

"Would it help if I stood around uselessly, not knowing what to say?"

"Yeah, actually," Mae said after a second's thought. "Would you mind?"

"Not at all," Seb said, and the smile flashed out again. "You want useless, you have come to the right guy. I can be useless for hours at a time. Weeks even. I'm currently closing in on a month of being totally useless, which is by way of being a personal best."

"Congratulations."

They didn't say much else, but he stayed with her. She glanced up at him a few times, and he smiled uncertainly down at her, and they both kept leaning against the bike shed until the bell for their next class rang.

The next day she and Erica had run into Erica's Tim and Seb together, and Mae had given him her best smile and asked, "How are you? Still useless?"

Seb had flushed slightly. "Pretty much."

"Keep it up," said Mae, and left with Erica starting to grin beside her. Since then Seb had been hanging around a little, and everyone, Mae included, had assumed it was just a matter of when Annabel would let Mae out of the house.

She'd been happy about it, but she didn't need anyone who was going to hassle her little brother.

Mae squared her shoulders, pushed open the door to the arts building, and heard Seb's voice begging.

"Please. Please don't send me away."

Mae reached behind her to pull the door closed as softly as she could. Seb's back was to her, the phone to his ear. He was holding it with white knuckles, so tightly she thought it might break.

"Yes," he said after a moment, breathless and desperate. He sounded much younger than he was. "Of course. I promise. I won't ever do it again."

He let out a deep breath that tore raggedly in the air.

Too soon for the person on the other end of the line to have said much, he added, "I'll do anything you want!"

Time passed in the space of two more husky breaths, and then he said, hushed, "Yes. Yes, thank you."

He snapped the phone shut, and then let his forehead rest against it.

"Hey," Mae said behind him. "I'd say I couldn't help hearing, but – I really could have. I was just shamelessly invading your privacy. Are you okay?"

Seb spun around, going white beneath his summer tan.

"Yeah," he said shakily. "Yeah. I was just talking to my foster parents."

Mae had known vaguely there was something going on with Seb's home life, that he moved around a lot, but she hadn't known there were foster parents.

"They all right to you?"

"Yeah," Seb said again, a little less shaky this time. "Better than all right. The last few sets, not so much, but this lot have the works. Great people. Good food. The right address even: they live on Lennox Street."

He had given her one brief, appalled look when he turned around and then looked down. For a moment he could occupy himself putting his phone in his pocket, but that left him staring at his empty palms. He kept his head down, tugging at a long sleeve. The cuff was a little frayed.

He always wore long sleeves, Mae realised with a jolt. He could be hiding bruises or even scars.

"They heard about me hassling Crawford," Seb said, low. "They weren't pleased. I was – I was scared they were going to send me away. And you saw me do it, I know that. You're here to tell me to get lost."

Mae forced herself to stop thinking about all the possible horrors in Seb's past and concentrate on what she knew for sure. She knew whose side she was on.

"Yeah," she said, in a much softer voice than she'd planned.

"I won't do it again," Seb burst out. "I'm not saying that to make you change your mind. I mean it. I've never hit him. I swear. I keep telling myself I have to stop, but he just gets right up my nose."

"You're not winning me over with this line of argument, I've got to tell you."

Seb pulled on his sleeve again, threads coming away between his fingers. "It's just – I remember things like learning to fight with a broken arm, learning to keep my head down, and I see Crawford walking around as if life is easy, running his mouth off at every opportunity, and I get furious. And I always – I get the feeling that he acts like that because he has some secret he's able to hide from everyone; that when he makes all his jokes and acts helpless, he's laughing up his sleeve at us."

Mae took a moment to be extremely alarmed by Seb's powers of observation.

"Jamie doesn't have any secrets from me," she said carefully.

Seb's shoulders hunched inwards a bit. "It doesn't matter," he said. "It's no excuse. I know that. I always know, as soon as I calm down. And now I've let the people I live with down, and I let you down too. I – I'm sorry. I won't do it again. And I understand if you don't want to be around me any more."

He finally looked up from his sleeves, giving her just one apologetic glance before he turned and started packing his pencils and his large green sketchbook into his bag. Mae took a step closer to him, and then another.

Seb looked very startled when he turned around and found her beside him.

She gave him a small smile. "Look," she said. "If you bother my brother again, well . . . maybe they'll find your body one day. When exploring deep space. Bits of it, anyway."

Seb laughed a little nervously and took a step backwards and away from her.

"And I'm not going to date anyone who behaved the way you did," Mae went on. "But – you were nice to me when I was having a tough time, and you've had a much worse time of it than I have. I'll still be your friend. And I'll see. Sound fair?"

Seb gave her that smile, beaming like a child. He looked happy and young and terribly handsome. On an impulse Mae reached out and took his hand. He started but let her keep it.

"I'd like that," he said. "To be friends."

"Wise decision," Mae told him. "My beat-down would not have been at all sexy. I was just going to pulverise you and leave you a broken, sobbing wreck of a man."

They went towards the door, hands still linked.

Mae told herself not to feel guilty. She wasn't lying. She did like Seb, and she did want to be there for him if his home life was horrible. He'd reached out to her when he barely knew her; she owed him that much.

He knew Jamie had a secret, and he'd seen Gerald doing something inexplicable. It was only reasonable to keep an eye on him.

She wasn't going to feel guilty for looking out for her brother.

Mae pushed the door open, walking half a step before Seb, and the afternoon sunlight struck her full in the face, the yellow wash of rays blinding her for a second.

It was possible that she didn't want to be totally unattached now the Ryves brothers were back, and so what? Mae should feel good about that. For the first time in her life, she was choosing to stay out of trouble.

The light in her eyes faded, dwindling into bright spots dancing in front of her eyes. Then she blinked and all she saw was Jamie, who must have seen her going into the building and waited for her to come out. He was staring at her and Seb's linked hands.

"Hey," Mae said as she saw the slow sweep of disbelief, with fury following, across his face, and realised what this must look like to him. "Hey, Jamie. Wait."

Jamie didn't wait. He didn't even speak. He kept that stunned, betrayed gaze on her an instant longer, and then turned and ran.

When she dropped Seb's hand and ran after her brother, she rounded the corner of the school and found that he'd vanished.

Just like that. Like magic.

Mae searched for Jamie for about an hour before she gave up, went home, and ran up the stairs to find her mother in the parlour having tea with a messenger from a magicians' Circle.

"Uh," said Mae, quick-thinking and brilliant as always.

Annabel was gleaming with polite determination to be a perfect hostess, pale and avid as a very polite ghoul.

The messenger for the magicians' Circle looked far more normal. She had dark hair and a smart suit, but Mae could imagine her in jeans and a jumper, being a normal mother. Except then she tilted her head and Mae saw her earrings, circles with tiny knives inside them, real knives with needle-sharp points.

Alan had explained that circles with knives inside were a sign magicians had their messengers carry, promising death to anyone who interfered with them.

Mae had always thought that jewellery should make a statement.

For this one, though, she didn't need the jewellery. Mae had seen her before. Nick and Alan had drawn weapons at the very sight of her, and she'd smiled, her red-lipsticked businesswoman's mouth forming a smile that was just a little too calm, just a little too close to cruel, and said, "Black Arthur says that now's the time. He wants it back."

At the time, Mae had not even known who Black Arthur was or what he wanted. She did now.

She did not know the woman's name.

Annabel blinked at her twice, a motherly Morse code for, Well done, you barged in on me and my guest like a bull longing for a new china shop.

"This is my daughter, Mavis," she said apologetically. Whether she was apologising for Mae's sudden arrival or Mae's pink hair was unclear. "This is Jessica Walker, Mavis. She's a colleague of mine looking for planning permission from the board."

"I have a client who wishes to expand her interests to Exeter," said Jessica Walker, the magicians' messenger, and smiled with a hint of teeth. "We've met before, haven't we, my dear?"

That smile was an obvious challenge. Mae suddenly found calm in her sea of panic and smiled back.

"Have you?" Annabel asked.

"Certainly," said Mae, matching Jessica's cool, amused tone.

"I met her and a group of her friends when they were interviewing me for an extra-curricular project," Jessica said. "Do you know the Ryves brothers? Sweet boys."

"I don't believe so," said Annabel slowly, a pin-scratch line appearing between her silvery brows.

"Mavis struck me as a very promising girl," Jessica continued, twinkling at Mae. "School's almost out," she added. "Have you considered doing an internship? My client could use an extra pair of hands, and it would look terribly good on your CV."

"I hadn't thought about it, but maybe it would be interesting," Mae said, and Annabel looked briefly startled and pleased.

Not while the messenger was looking at her, Mae was glad to see.

"If it wouldn't be too much trouble," said Jessica, almost absently, "could you possibly get me another plate of that delicious shortbread?"

Annabel smiled, facade as perfect as the glaze on good china, and said, "Of course."

Her mother rose, smoothing her dove grey skirt, and left the parlour. Mae came in, scuffing the creamy carpet deliberately, making it clear that she was at home here, that she was facing down her enemy on her own turf.

Then she sank into the chair opposite the magicians' messenger, still warm from her mother's body, and said, "Does the Obsidian Circle have a message for me?"

"What makes you think it was the Obsidian Circle who sent me?" Jessica Walker asked smoothly.

It hadn't occurred to her before, but of course there were

other Circles. And of course, they might take an interest in Jamie.

"Whichever Circle sent you," Mae said, keeping her voice even, "I'd like to know what they want."

Jessica crossed her legs with a rasp of silk stockings. "My, you have learned a lot, haven't you? When I saw you in April, I don't think you had the faintest idea what was going on."

"Yeah, I catch on fast."

"What do you know about messengers, Mavis?"

"It's Mae," Mae snapped.

"Like Mae West?" Jessica inquired, and did not wait for Mae's nod. "Let me guess. You've heard we have the power to be magicians, but instead of killing people ourselves, we serve the magicians so they will dole out power to us. Like a magical weekly wage. Does that strike you as likely?"

"How d'you mean?"

"A great many messengers would be all too ready to kill for our own power," Jessica said softly. "The fact is, we do not have enough capacity for magic to bind the demons and set them loose on chosen victims. We were born with only the barest maddening trace of magic in our veins. Not enough. Not nearly enough. You do know it's hereditary, don't you?"

Nick had thought he was a magician, being Arthur and Olivia's son. Gerald had talked about having a magical ancestor.

Mae hadn't actually considered it before, but she said, "Sure."

"It goes underground in some families, and turns up when magic is forgotten, like stumbling on lost treasure. You didn't find treasure. Do you never hate your brother," Jessica murmured, "for being the one born with all that shining magic as his birthright?"

"No," said Mae.

"He's going to be very good," Jessica continued as if Mae hadn't spoken. "That's why Gerald is being so careful with him. He's going to stand in circles of fire and command storms one day. He's going to wear a ring. And you can dance up a demon just a little better than the other dancers in the Goblin Market. Do you think that's fair? Do you never want power of your own?"

Mae forced her mind to go slowly over what Jessica was saying, to be methodical and pick out the important details. The fact that she might have a drop of magic in her blood after all wasn't important.

Not compared to the fact that the magicians clearly had a spy in the Goblin Market, if they knew how she danced. Probably more than one.

"I never hated my brother," said Mae. "That was your question, wasn't it? And I answered it. Never did. Never will. I love him."

"And does he love you enough to share power with you?" Jessica asked. "He could, if he were a magician and you were a messenger. If he wore a sigil and you wore a token, you could have all the power you wanted."

"If I persuaded Jamie to join the Obsidian Circle, you mean."

"Not necessarily. But Gerald Lynch is a very brilliant young man."

Mae rolled her eyes. "I'm sure."

"You know the sigils the magicians wear?" Jessica asked. "Brands that feed them power and mark them as belonging to a particular Circle. They're a little like demons' marks, in a way. Power bleeds through."

Mae remembered Olivia pulling down her shirt to reveal

the black sigil of the Obsidian Circle on her white skin. Nobody who wears this mark is innocent, she'd said, her pale eyes glowing like a hungry animal's.

Gerald and this woman sitting so calmly in her mother's parlour wanted to put a mark like that on Jamie.

"Word on the street is that Gerald's invented a whole different kind of mark," Jessica said. "Some people say more than one, but I don't believe that. The one everyone is talking about is based on the Obsidian Circle's master ring. Thorned snakes eating their own tails. If it's true, that would be power worth serving." Jessica's lips curved, the knives in her earrings ringing out faintly, like wind chimes. "Could be power enough to take on a demon."

Mae curled her fingers tight into her palms and forced herself to keep smiling.

"So you're here to frighten Jamie into joining?"

"I'm here to watch you both," Jessica said. "And perhaps give you a little advice on your best course of action."

Annabel came through the door, walking like a cat in her towering heels.

"Have you two been having an interesting conversation?" she asked.

She shook her head as Jessica got up to help her with the tray, murmuring that it was not at all necessary, and Jessica leaned against the back of Mae's chair. Mae's spine felt as if it wanted to crawl out of her skin and hide down the front of her shirt, but she refused to let herself turn around, even when Jessica was so close her breath was ruffling Mae's hair.

"Very interesting. I do hope that Mavis will consider the internship," the messenger said, and she touched Mae's hair with one hand.

The gesture must have looked casual to Annabel, even affectionate, but it was such a shock that it felt like an invasion. Her fingers were just a little too tight in Mae's hair as she spoke, her calm voice the way Mae had heard it months ago, too close to cruelty.

"I will be sure," said Jessica Walker, "to keep in touch."

She did not stay long after that. When she was gone, Annabel offered Mae a cup of tea. Mae shook her head.

"If you took an interest in law," Annabel said, "it would make me very hap—"

"You can't ever let that woman in the house again," said Mae.

"Don't be ridiculous, Mavis!"

"Annabel," Mae said, "I – when I knew her before, I can't talk about it. It's private. But she was terrible to friends of mine. She scared me badly. I don't trust her. I don't want her here, or – or around you."

"It seemed like her client's custom might be a valuable asset to the firm," Annabel said slowly, and Mae's heart sank.

She was usually able to persuade people, to make them see things her way, but it had never worked with Annabel.

"When you and your brother disappeared," Annabel began.

"Oh, not this again!"

"Hear me out, Mavis. When you disappeared, I was very—" Annabel cleared her throat. "I was very distressed. I realise that your father has pulled away a lot from you both in recent years, and I have been absorbed in my work and not compensating for the loss. I regret that."

"Um," Mae said. "Okay."

"If you two ran away under the impression that I would not care," Annabel said, "I did. And while your behaviour was extremely reckless and irresponsible, I know I was at fault as well. If you wish me to turn away this client for your peace of mind, I will. I should cut back on my work anyway, and – we should make an effort to eat together."

Annabel was probably just saying this because she felt she had to, because she didn't want the girls down at the tennis club to gossip about her delinquent children, but she'd said that she would turn the magicians' messenger away all the same. Mae was so relieved she wanted to cry.

"All right," she said. "It's a deal."

She thought of something and fumbled at her neck, untying the cord that held her talisman in place. If the magicians had sent a messenger to visit her mother, they could send demons.

"Could you wear this, Annabel?" she asked, getting up and holding it out. "To seal the deal," she added, and gave Annabel a smile she hoped would be convincing.

Annabel looked pleased at the gesture and absolutely horrified by the necklace, which looked like a huge dream catcher, gleaming with bones and gems.

"Thank you, Mavis," she said bravely, tying it on and tucking it immediately under her blouse. "It's very unique. Does it have any . . . occult significance? I know you like that kind of thing."

Annabel probably classified anything from reading horoscopes to outright Satanism as "that kind of thing", but she was being terribly good about this. Mae went behind her mother's chair and then leaned down and circled her shoulders with both arms, giving her a brief squeeze.

Annabel's back went rigid, but she put a hand on Mae's arm, so Mae couldn't tell if she was embarrassed or pleased by the gesture.

She let go, but before she did she whispered into her mother's ear, "It keeps away bad dreams."

She remembered that in the night, when she dreamed that her father was at the window, saying that he was sorry and he loved them and he wanted to come home. Mae didn't open the window because she knew better than to believe her father, even in a dream, and then there were ravens at her window, there was a storm, there was something waiting outside for her and it was angry.

She woke up dreaming of a thunderclap loud enough to splinter the sky, and found herself lying in a bed full of broken glass.

The window was shattered. There was nothing outside but the night.

Mae went downstairs and made herself some coffee. It was fine, she told herself. She was fine. She could get a new talisman from Alan today.

She sat there with her coffee going cold until Jamie came downstairs. His face hardened when he saw her.

"Didn't hear you come in last night," Mae said. "Where were you?"

"Where d'you think?" Jamie asked. "Gerald says he'll meet us all after school."

"Oh he does, does he?" Mae inquired. "And it took you the whole evening to make the appointment?"

Jamie went red. "I can hang around with whoever I want," he muttered. "You are."

It hurt that he was ready to be angry without letting her explain; it hurt that he'd kept what was happening with Gerald from her, and kept the magic from her before that. Mae held her coffee cup tight.

"Yeah," she said. "Guess I am."

4

Asking the Wrong Questions

Y OU'RE QUIETER THAN USUAL," NICK REMARKED.

He was the one driving to the graveyard. Alan was sitting relaxed in the passenger seat beside him, body stretched out long and loose, without the tension his shoulders always held when he was driving. He'd said hello when they first got in, then seen their faces and fallen tactfully silent.

This was the first time Nick had spoken.

"Sorry," Jamie muttered to the window.

"Don't be sorry," Nick said calmly. "I kind of like it."

They went around a curve in the road where red brick houses stood almost in line, old and leaning against one another like rusty tin soldiers.

Mae looked at Jamie, but he kept staring out of the window, arms crossed tight over his chest and his profile tense. He didn't even glance at her.

"So why are you being quiet?" Nick demanded.

"Why, concerned about my feelings?" Jamie snapped.

"Yeah," Nick said. "You know me. I fret."

47

"I thought that demons weren't supposed to lie," Mae said.

"We don't," said Nick, his hands light on the wheel and his voice even. "But I am in full possession of the amazing power of being sarcastic."

The silence after Nick spoke sounded very strange to Mae, and for a moment she could not work out why. Then she realised that it would normally have been filled with Alan's soft laugh, loving if not always approving, and making Nick's humour seem less grim to everyone else.

The silence continued until Jamie spoke again.

"Do you remember Seb McFarlane, Nick?"

"Yeah," Nick answered warily.

"What did you think of him?"

"You're lucky I remember his name," said Nick. "Expecting me to have an actual opinion on the guy is going too far. Is he why you're being all quiet?"

Jamie was quiet some more.

"I'll deal with him," Nick said at length.

The offer was so unexpected that Jamie straightened from his sullen slouch as sharply as if someone had just applied a jolt of electricity to his spine.

"I don't want you killing anyone for me!"

When Nick pulled over, Mae thought for a second he was angry, and then she realised they had reached their destination.

The graveyard was close to home, on the edge of the St Leonard's district where Mae lived. It was set in sunken ground on the left side of the road, and they had to pass it and park in someone else's drive. There was a stone gargoyle set in the side of the house, looking with solemn surprise over at a red brick rise of flats.

Mae twisted her head and looked out of the back window. Tucked between road and graveyard was an alley that contained bricks, dustbins, and several waiting magicians.

"I'm not going to kill anyone." Nick turned off the car engine and then slid a cool, amused glance back at Jamie. "Well," he added, and smiled slowly, "not for you."

They had to scramble over a low wall on their way. Mae slid her foot into a crevice between the stones and then jumped off the wall. Jamie sat on it and threw his legs over, feet feeling tentatively for the ground. Nick took the wall in a bound: he barely seemed to register it except that he stopped once he was over and held out a hand to help his brother.

"I'm okay," Alan said, with his face turned away from his brother and his good knee up on the wall. He set his teeth as he heaved his bad leg over, and they all saw him wince.

Mae just smiled at him and pretended she hadn't noticed. He looked startled, and then smiled brilliantly back.

It was a good smile. It didn't make her feel better about the fact that she had to go and see the man who had bespelled her helpless. Mae shoved her hands in her pockets, and they all walked down the grassy rise, together but not united, towards the magicians' alley.

The magicians looked very united. There were two standing behind but close to Gerald, as if they were trying to be at his back and by his side at the same time. Mae recognised the short, grey-haired woman, Laura, but not the guy at Gerald's left. He was young, with a brown buzz cut. He looked as if he might be in his early or mid-twenties, not much older than Gerald himself. Both of the other magicians looked very serious.

Gerald was smiling. His smile lit up the little alley with its grey bricks and cracked concrete floor. For a moment the whole situation seemed normal. For a moment it seemed like they were all friends.

"Hi, Jamie."

"Hi," Jamie said, low.

"I didn't really get the chance to say hi before you paralysed me last time," said Mae loudly, to show she wasn't afraid.

Gerald looked at Mae, and when his eyes met hers she remembered Gerald as she'd first seen him, tied to a chair and playing the victim. She remembered pitying and almost liking him.

"I am sorry about that," he said. "But I'm glad to see you all here."

"Why's that?" asked Nick, voice rumbling in his chest as if at any point human words could transform into a growl. "Did you miss my little face?"

He'd gone to sit on a fallen chunk of wall, leaning his arms on his spread knees and staring around at them all with baleful eyes. Gerald glanced at him, shivered, and looked away.

Jamie moved a little closer to Gerald. He'd stepped forward before when Gerald spoke to him, and now he stood in a place almost exactly balanced between the two groups.

Gerald smiled at him and turned his gaze to Alan.

"You wanted to see me? Here I am," he said. "In return, I wondered if you could do something for me."

Alan held his gaze calmly. "What's that?"

"I wanted to speak to you," said Gerald. "Alone."

Sudden shadow blotted out the sun. Mae threw back her head and looked at the sky, where storm clouds were being born, tendrils of darkness writhing and spreading across the expanse of deep blue.

The threads of cloud were already black as ink, as if someone were inscribing threats and promises on the sky in a strange language. Mae looked down and into shadow-dark eyes.

Nick whispered, "What do you want with my brother?"

"I would prefer to keep that between us," Gerald said mildly. "I intend him no harm. Though you can drop that pretence of being an almighty protector right now, Nick. I know why you're here."

"Because you're messing with Jamie," said Nick.

"Exactly," Gerald responded. "And you don't want anyone else having a claim on him. Not when you have a use for him yourself."

Nick frowned and popped his wrist sheath with what seemed to be sheer absent-mindedness. A gleaming silver switchblade appeared between his fingers, the hilt carved with strange symbols Mae couldn't make out. Nick fiddled with it without looking at it. He was still looking at Gerald.

"I wasn't aware Jamie had a use."

"Oh please," Gerald said, a note in his voice that sounded genuinely incredulous. "We're all perfectly aware of how handy a pet magician would be for a demon. And here he is, tailor-made for you. He's young, he's impressionable, he's got real power, and he already owes you a debt. As soon as you had an excuse, you rushed down here to offer protection and friendship. It all fits."

Nick gave a sharp bark of laughter. Jamie stood stricken.

He looked back over his shoulder at Nick, eyes wide and doubtful, and Mae could practically see the memory of yesterday passing through his mind as it was passing through hers.

Hey, Jamie. Want to be friends?

"No," Jamie said slowly. "You've got it wrong, Gerald. Nick's not like that."

"Everyone's like that, Jamie," said Gerald, his voice gentle, as if he didn't want to tell Jamie this harsh truth. "Everyone wants power."

"I have enough," Nick said. Then he smiled, sudden and wild. "Or do you want to try me?"

"I wouldn't make any threats, demon," Laura said. "Do you have enough to protect your human allies every moment of the day? Watch your tongue when you talk to our leader. Some night when you're asleep we could come into your house and tear the human boy apart in his bed."

The whole sky went black. The magicians went flying backwards, Laura and the stranger hitting the wall so hard it was clear Nick did not care if they broke. Gerald hit the ground.

Nick was on his feet and towering over Gerald in one movement.

"You can't do anything if I kill you all now," Nick told him, his voice echoing and rolling like thunder.

He lifted a hand, and Gerald made a thin sound, as if Nick was wielding an invisible sword and slicing into him. He was pinned and struggling desperately on the earth. Nick laughed.

Jamie dived forward and caught Nick's wrist. Nick whirled around, lifting Jamie off his feet for a moment.

"Whose side are you on?" he roared.

"The side of not wanting anybody to get hurt!" Jamie yelled back.

"So not mine," snapped Nick. He shoved Jamie clear across the alley and into Mae.

Mae caught his weight, even though it made her stagger, and held on even though he struggled, her arm tight around his heaving ribs. Nick spun back to where Gerald lay, and the wind howled. The other two magicians were scrambling to their feet, Laura looking pale with pain, magic starting to shimmer between their palms. Over the wall Mae could see grey tombstones poking out of the earth like a leering mouth full of broken and decayed teeth. She could see Nick's face in profile, the hungry swing of his eyes from face to face, like the swing of his sword when he was fighting. She didn't know what he was going to do.

She had entirely forgotten that Alan was there. She remembered with a vengeance when he limped forward, grabbed a handful of thick black hair, and pulled Nick's head back. A small, wicked knife glinted in the shadowed space between Nick's shirt collar and throat.

Nick drew in a short, sharp breath and went still.

"Stop that," Alan said in his ear. "They came here to talk to Jamie. How do you think Jamie will feel if you slaughter them all?"

Nick made a low snarl of protest that Mae guessed did not indicate deep concern about Jamie's emotional state.

"She said—"

"Don't listen to her," said Alan. "Listen to me. Stop. Now."

The thunder made a low complaining sound and died away. Alan stepped back and slid the knife into his pocket, then reached out and offered Gerald a hand up. Gerald took it.

Nick went over to the wall and leaned his forehead against the grey bricks, teeth set. The clouds were slipping away slowly; the dark fingers of the storm curled around the sky as if they did not want to let go.

Mae felt much the same, but she released her hold on Jamie. He stumbled a few paces towards Gerald.

"I'm sorry," he began. "I didn't know – Alan said he only wanted to talk."

"And I do," Alan agreed calmly. "I apologise for Nick's behaviour."

"I apologise for Laura's," Gerald told him, voice just as smooth and friendly. They stood clasping hands for another moment. They both had blue eyes, Mae noticed: Alan's dark and Gerald's light and bright. Alan's crinkled behind his glasses as he smiled, and Gerald smiled back. "I have no intention of harming anyone," he assured Alan. "All I want is a word in private."

"I'll give you a word in public," Alan said, still smiling. "No."

Gerald blinked. Alan dropped his hand and stepped back.

The storm was clearing fast out of the sky now, clouds spiralling as if they were going down some unseen drain. Nick was leaning against the wall with his arms folded over his chest.

"I wanted to talk," Alan went on. "This is what I have to say: leave Jamie alone. Get out of Exeter. Or I'll turn your Circle over to Celeste Drake."

Gerald kept smiling, betraying no more than he had by that first blink, but Laura went a little pale.

"I'm not scared of Celeste."

"No?" Alan asked. "You should be. You're the leader of the Obsidian Circle now, aren't you? I'm sorry, I hadn't thought. Should we be using a title for you now? As a mark of respect?"

"Yes, I'm the leader," said Gerald. "And no. I thought—" He flashed a rueful smile at Jamie, and Mae was outraged to see Jamie smile hesitantly back. "Well, I didn't think Black Gerald sounded exactly fearsome."

"New leader," Alan observed. "You're very young. You lost about half your Circle when you lost your leader. You've been losing more since then, your best people leaving for more stable Circles. You're desperately trying to recruit new magicians. And the Aventurine Circle is out for your blood. What do you have going for you, Gerald?"

"You have no idea," the strange magician said hotly, "what he can do. He—"

"Ben, be quiet!" Gerald snapped.

The stranger – Ben – looked embarrassed and bowed his head, flushing faintly pink. Mae looked at him and remembered what the messenger had said about Gerald's new mark.

"I think my best people have stayed with me," said Gerald, and there was a firmness about his tone that made Mae understand for a moment why people might be loyal to him: there was a substance to him that she hadn't seen in Black Arthur, terrifyingly and deliberately impressive though he'd been. "And I could mention that you don't have anyone left on your side but a demon that could turn against you at any moment, Alan – but I'm sure you've been thinking about that yourself."

"I'm on his side," Mae snapped.

"A demon that could turn against you at any moment, and a human girl who can't do magic or fight," Gerald corrected himself. "Not an impressive list of allies, but that doesn't matter. I don't mean you any harm, Alan. Nor do any of my Circle. You don't need to be worried."

"Oh, I'm not," Alan said blandly.

"I do not intend to leave Jamie here among people who do not understand him and will turn on him in a moment when his secret slips out. Which it will, someday. Someday very soon. He's strong. Do you think his parents will react well once they know what he is? He belongs with his own kind!"

"I don't think Jamie asked for your help," Alan pointed out.

"Did he ask for yours?" Gerald countered. "He is a magician. His welfare is my concern. It is none of your business, and I will certainly not leave one of my own completely at the mercy of a demon!"

"That's sweet," said Nick. "The fact that you've put a spell on Jamie makes it not terribly convincing, but apart from that small detail, I found it a really touching speech."

Gerald's eyes went to Jamie.

"Hey," he said. "You know I wouldn't hurt you, don't you?"

Jamie looked down. "I don't know."

That was when Laura threw a spell at Jamie, sudden as lightning springing between them, magic rising like a pet bird from her palm. It streaked through the air, swift and bright. Mae ran forward and knew the brilliant deadly thing would strike before she could get to him.

The magic bounced off Jamie and earthed itself harmlessly in the ground at his feet.

Jamie jumped back all the same, and Mae found him catching her hands, grip desperate for a moment until he remembered himself. Then he stepped away.

"Thanks, Laura," he said unsteadily. "I always wondered what a tiny heart attack would feel like, and now I know. Very refreshing!"

He was still shaking a little. Mae's hand itched to grab him again, to hold him and keep him safe, but he'd already turned away from her.

Nick left his place leaning against the wall and stalked forward. He didn't attack anyone, but he put himself in front of Jamie, blocking him from the magicians' line of sight.

"What was that for?" he asked, very soft.

Alan answered him, his arms folded and his gaze on Gerald.

"It was a demonstration," he observed. "The spell on Jamie is a protection spell. It means no magical attack can touch him."

Nick turned and looked at Jamie, face unreadable.

"It's strong," he tossed over his shoulder at Gerald. "Where did you get power like that?"

Jamie was staring at Gerald, looking helpless and lost. Gerald gazed steadily back at him. His face was open and almost sweet. He looked like someone you could trust.

Nick's motives for helping Jamie had been seriously called into question. Jamie thought Mae had betrayed him. And then on this day of all days, someone had come through for him, and it had to be a magician.

"You don't need to know that," Gerald answered. "All you need to know is that I have enough power to take care of my own. And I will. Always." He nodded at Jamie. "Next time I'll come alone. I hope you will too."

Jamie nodded once. It was a nervous movement, and might even have been involuntary. He might not have meant it.

He might have, though.

"Ben, Laura," said Gerald, and they turned with him as he moved to go. He passed Nick by without a glance, as if he couldn't see him at all.

Then he stopped, his magicians flanking him, at the mouth of the alley.

"When you're ready to talk to me, Alan," he called out, "let me know. I can help you."

5

Getting the Wrong Answers

"THAT'S SETTLED, THEN," ALAN SAID ONCE THE MAGICIANS WERE gone. "We turn them in to Celeste Drake tomorrow."

"What will she do to them?" Jamie asked in a small voice.

Alan did not answer him directly, which was answer enough. "I gave him a chance to leave."

"No, you threatened him!"

"What do you want, then?" Nick demanded abruptly. "You want to be a magician? You want them to stick around in Exeter, maybe end up killing someone you know? Hey, how about your sister?"

Jamie glared at Nick. "Of course not. I just wish that there was some way besides murder or threats, or – I wish there was some kind of box I could check marked 'none of the above', that's all! You saw what happened when Laura cast that spell. You know Gerald's trying to protect me."

"And now he has a hold over you," Alan said. "You're grateful to him. You don't think he wasn't counting on that?"

Jamie hesitated. "It was a lot of trouble to go to, just so I'd be grateful."

"Yes," Alan agreed simply. "A lot of trouble. He must have killed several people to get that kind of power. And he could break it any time."

"I could break it now," Nick offered. Jamie turned and stared at him, and the corner of Nick's mouth turned up slightly. "But I won't."

Jamie smiled back, a little hesitantly.

Nick crossed the distance between him and Jamie before Mae could move, and pulled a knife on him.

"Why bother?" he asked Jamie lazily. He touched the skin of Jamie's throat lightly with the blade. "The spell will only protect you from magic. Gerald's not protecting you, he's protecting his recruit. Any other Circle tries to recruit you by magic, they won't be able to. Anyone needs to kill you . . ." He tossed the knife up into the air and caught it, playful and casual as a man flipping a coin. "It would be so easy."

Mae grabbed Nick's arm and he whirled on her, then caught himself and stood looking down at her with his pulse thudding against her palm and the knife still in his hand.

She lifted her chin. "Oh, put that away."

Nick put it away. "Just making a point."

"Yes, I took your point," Jamie muttered. "Right up against my throat."

Mae looked away from Nick and walked quickly towards the wall, scrambling over it and trying so hard to make the climb look easy that she skinned her elbow as she did so. She pretended it didn't sting.

Nick did not try to help Alan over the wall this time around. He stood with his hands clenched into fists in his pockets as they all waited for Alan to get over on his own.

"I wasn't trying to hurt you," he told Jamie suddenly.

Mae reached out and touched Nick's shoulder. Her hand brushed muscle, braced and tense under her palm, for a moment. Then he shied away from her and glared.

She smiled as if this reaction was perfectly normal. "Sometimes when you pull knives on people, they get this impression that you're going to hurt them, and then they're completely terrified. Crazy, I know!"

"Okay," said Nick. He turned to Jamie and popped his left wrist sheath again. "Look."

Jamie backed up. "Which part of 'completely terrified' did you translate as 'show us your knives, Nick'? Don't show me your knives, Nick. I have no interest in your knives."

Nick rolled his eyes. "This is a quillon dagger. That's a knife with a sword handle. I like it because it has a good grip for stabbing."

"Why do you say these things?" Jamie inquired piteously. "Is it to make me sad?"

"I didn't have you cornered," Nick went on. "You could've run. And this dagger doesn't have an even weight distribution; it's absolute rubbish for throwing. If I had any intention of hurting you, I'd have used a knife I could throw."

Jamie blinked. "I will remember those words always. I may try to forget them, but I sense that I won't be able to."

"Good," said Nick. "Like I said, that spell won't protect you, and you have a habit of getting into trouble. You need to know things."

There was a long pause, during which Nick eyed Jamie in what seemed to be a critical manner. Jamie eyed Nick in what seemed to be mortal fear.

"Do you want to learn how to use a gun or a knife?" Nick asked abruptly at last.

"Ahaha," Jamie said. "No?"

Nick raked a cold glance up and down Jamie's body, as if he was planning to skin him. "Well, you're too scrawny to be any good with a sword."

"I prefer to think of myself as slender," Jamie told him.

Nick gave Jamie a blank look, then said, "Come on. I'll drive you to my place and teach you how to throw knives."

"What!" said Jamie. "Why?"

"Because I am a sweet and caring individual who is truly concerned about your welfare," Nick drawled. "You coming?"

Jamie glanced at him and at Alan, and carefully did not look at Mae. It occurred to her, with a painful little shock in her chest, that Jamie didn't want to go back home with her.

"Okay."

Jamie didn't want to be around her, and Nick hadn't asked her to come. Mae had a vision of them all just getting into the car and driving away, leaving her by the side of the road. Then she turned and looked into Alan's eyes.

"Do you want to come and take a walk with me?" he asked. "I know you must have some questions."

His blue eyes were steady and so dark they looked like deep waters, like you could fall into them for miles.

"I do have a few questions," said Mae.

"Okay, so here's my first question," Mae said as they walked back to the city centre. "Who the hell is Celeste Drake?"

"She's the leader of another magicians' Circle," Alan said. "The Aventurine Circle. I don't really know much about it; her Circle never hassled us much. As magicians' Circles go, I believe they're not the worst. Not much interested in power squabbles, and a higher number than in most Circles have real uses for their power. I think Celeste herself is a doctor, and I know one of the Circle has a special interest in using magic for fighting; the time we heard that was the one and only time Nick has ever been inspired to do magical research on his own. There are a couple of historians who use scrying bowls to see the past."

"Well, speaking as a feminist, I'm glad that women can lead – uh, groups of unspeakable magical evil."

"Yes," Alan said gravely. "It'd be shocking if the evil magicians were sexist. For one thing, that would mean they were stupid, and having stupid enemies would be a terrible blow to my manly pride."

Mae laughed at him for being a goof and Alan grinned back at her, easy and charming. She elbowed him gently, and he didn't break stride.

"So why are we feeding Gerald to the Aventurine Circle in particular?"

"I still have a few contacts in the Goblin Market," Alan said. "Word is that Celeste's looking for him. I imagine it's to express her displeasure about the Obsidian Circle invading her turf when they came chasing after Nick. Her Circle's based in London, you see."

"And moving's difficult for them," Mae said. "Territory's a big deal."

"Every circle a magician ever draws is a reflection of the one circle of stones their group is named after. The sigils they wear link into the same circles, and bind them to each other. Some magicians' Circles have their circles buried in the ground, some of them hidden in plain sight as old druids' circles. They all guard them with their lives. And they hate the thought of another Circle coming near theirs. Black Arthur didn't ask Celeste's permission to move his Circle into her city. He took what he wanted and planned to crush anyone in his path."

"That was kind of Arthur's way."

Alan nodded. "It's left Gerald in a complete mess. A lot of magicians have left his Circle and taken different sigils. He had to move back fast, he's recruiting desperately, and one of the big Circles is after his blood for trespass. And it's all very convenient for us."

Mae touched her new talisman. "The messenger who came to see me said that Gerald might have invented something like a second sigil. A mark to give him more power. How much stronger is the Aventurine Circle?"

"Don't worry," said Alan. "They're strong enough."

They passed under the shadow of the trees that marked their entrance into the north side of the city. Alan glanced up at them, the branches heavy with their dark green summer armfuls.

"These used to be called dancing trees."

Mae smiled. "I didn't know that."

Alan's smile flashed back at her, brighter than the red, setting sunlight that sifted through the leaves and glanced brilliantly off his glasses. "Yes, they used to hang people in them and leave them up in the branches. Sometimes in pieces. Then in the wind the pieces would—"

"Okay, I get it," Mae said hastily.

"Oh," said Alan in a different voice. "Sorry about that. I just thought it was interesting."

Mae wondered if that was how Alan dealt with terrible

and frightening truths, how he dealt with Nick: by making even nightmares come to life a subject of intellectual curiosity.

"Wouldn't it be more convenient," she began instead, "wouldn't it be simpler, rather than getting in touch with this Celeste woman, if Nick just dealt with Gerald and the others?"

Her shoes hit cobblestones as their conversation crashed into silence. She kept walking; after the first glance she looked at the sandstone walls and not Alan's tightly controlled face.

"How do you think he'd deal with them?" Alan asked at last, his voice a thread strung taut enough to snap.

"Well," Mae said, and thought of her own hands covered in hot blood. The words died on her lips.

Alan said it for her. "He'd kill them all."

"They're murderers."

"They're not my concern," Alan answered. "Walk me through this plan of yours. So we ask Nick to kill them all. He does it. Mind you, I'm not entirely certain he could do it."

"I thought demons were the ones with all the power," Mae said. "That's why magicians give them innocent people to possess and destroy, isn't it? I thought that was the whole point of demons."

They went right down another narrow street, this one with shop fronts fitted into the old sandstone buildings.

"Think of magic as like electricity," said Alan. "Nick's power is like lightning in the sky. It's powerful, it can strike the ground and burn everything it touches, but you couldn't use it to turn on a light or iron a shirt. The magicians are conduits. Through them, the magic can be transformed into something smaller but often a lot more useful."

"So Gerald wasn't lying. Nick could use Jamie as a channel for his power. It would help him to have a – a pet magician."

"Yes," Alan admitted. "But Nick's too proud to come to anyone for help, even if he needed it. And he doesn't. He's not hunting for power, and it's not why we came here."

"I didn't think it was," said Mae. "I know better than that. Gerald might think so, though. And that's interesting."

Alan's eyes narrowed thoughtfully, as if seeing things from a different point of view. Then he nodded, and Mae felt a pleasant little sense of accomplishment, like she'd been working on mathematical problems with a very bright partner and had found one answer before he could.

"So let's say Nick kills them all," said Alan, and the slight warmth that had gone through Mae was followed by a chill. "Do we stop there?"

"I don't understand."

"Destroying the magicians would be a good thing to do," Alan remarked distantly. "I'd be pleased. Next time somebody came to me for help about a different Circle, Nick could kill them, too. He could start an all-out crusade against the magicians. He'd be up to his elbows in blood by the time he was done, and once he'd killed every magician in England there would be the messengers they use, and criminals, and at that point . . ." Alan touched a wall, sandstone so old it looked rusty and red, as if blood had seeped into the stone long ago. "At that point he would cut down anyone in his way."

"Do you mean – you're not scared for yourself. He'd never—"

"I'm not scared of being hurt," Alan said quietly. "I'm scared of what he'll do. He could tear himself apart or tear the world apart, and next to those two choices what happens to me doesn't matter at all."

"Hey," Mae said sharply, and reached out and touched the hand that hung by his side. "It matters."

He gave her a beautiful smile then, brilliant and surprised, which broke her heart a little because nobody should look startled that there is someone in the world who cares if they live or die.

"I can't offer up Nick to help Jamie," said Alan. "I have to draw a line for him."

"Since he found out," Mae murmured.

"Since always," Alan told her sharply. "This hasn't been the right sort of life for him, hasn't been a life where he could have the things I want for him, where he could learn—"

"How to be human?"

"Kindness," Alan said.

Mae was getting all her questions wrong today. She fell silent, and they went under the low tunnel through St Stephen's Church into the heart of the shopping centre.

"I did try to keep him from the worst of it," Alan continued. "When there was a particularly nasty kill to be made. When it was going to be torture, and death was going to be slow."

Mae couldn't quite believe they were having this conversation, strolling around the environs of the Princesshay shopping centre. Hemmed in by neon-lit shop fronts and the stones of St Stephen's, its walls worn down by twelve centuries, stood the remains of an old almshouse. They hadn't been allowed to tear it down when they built the shopping centre.

Alan stooped and studied a plaque.

"You had to do it instead," Mae said, her voice wobbling in the cool air. She wrapped her arms around herself.

"I was glad to do it," Alan said. "I can help Jamie some other way."

"*We* can help Jamie," said Mae, and Alan nodded, accepting the correction in his turn. "I'm sorry. I shouldn't have asked. I didn't understand." She took a deep breath.

"You and Nick," she went on. "You're not getting on, are you? When I called, there was that storm. Did something bad happen? Did he do something?"

Alan drew in a slow breath that answered her even before he spoke. "Mae," he said. "Do you want me to lie to you?"

He put a hand up to his face, fingers smoothing away the worried line between his brows. Soon it would be etched there, Mae thought, and no hand could erase it. Least of all his own.

"No," Mae breathed. "No, I don't want that."

Alan took a detour inside the almshouse ruins, roofless and with only part of the walls remaining. The nameless government types who hadn't allowed the almshouse to be torn down had allowed glass doors to be built in the places doors would have been inside the almshouse, doors in the shape of glass windows and filled with artificial light. Suspended in the glass were fragments of Roman pottery lined up alongside old cola cans, and Alan was looking at those rather than her when he said, "You'd believe me if I did lie to you."

"So tell me something true. Did you never want anything for yourself?"

Alan looked at her then.

"Yes," he said. "One or two things."

Mae looked down and kicked an eight-hundred-year-old wall.

She glanced up at the sound of movement and saw that Alan had circled so there was a glass door between them, lights captured in the glass casting an aquamarine glow on his face. He looked as though he was underwater, pale and otherworldly, his palm against the glass as if he was reaching out a hand to drag her down.

"I always thought those doors were kind of silly," Mae said at random, trying to make this moment not serious, make it not matter.

"Really?" Alan asked, fingers light on the glass, touching carefully, as if he had one of the artifacts in his hands. "I like them. I like the idea that the past and the present are always tangled together, making us who we are."

"Clearly the bright lights distracted me from the deep symbolism," Mae said, and smiled at him.

He smiled back at her, the same smile as when she'd told him it mattered if he was hurt, surprised and sweet.

"After we go to Celeste Drake tomorrow, after Jamie is safe," he began, and paused. "I thought Nick and I might stay here in Exeter." He traced the shape of a broken cup with musician's hands. "I was wondering what you were doing Saturday night."

It was such an ordinary thing to say, such an overwhelmingly normal way to ask someone out after a conversation about demons and sacrifice, that it struck Mae speechless.

Alan watched her behind the door of light, his eyes dark serious blue. He waited patiently for her to answer.

"I don't know. Does a rave sound like your idea of a good time?"

"It might," Alan answered, lowering his eyes. His eyelashes sparked gold in the fluorescent lights. "If you were there."

"You can't ask me this now," Mae blurted.

"Is it the wrong time, or is it that it's me asking?"

"There's a boy at school," Mae told him. "We're not going out, but I more or less promised him a chance. I don't go back on my word."

Alan stepped away from the door into the arms of the gathering shadows.

"I appreciate your honesty," he said. "I'll be honest too. It's something I try, every now and then. Not often." He smiled, and this time it was an ordinary smile, friendly and making her smile back involuntarily. "I hope that boy wastes his chance."

Mae ducked her head to hide the smile, though it was in her voice as well. "You never know, but . . ."

"No, I understand," Alan said. "What are you doing Saturday night? I'm asking as a friend. I thought we could go – just as friends, of course – back to the Goblin Market. If you're interested in visiting it again."

Mae burst out laughing at how sly he was.

"You don't play fair."

Alan drew her out of the ruins, still smiling. "You don't say."

Jamie wasn't back by the time Mae got home. She had to face the fact that he would rather spend time with someone he was afraid of than come back and talk to her.

Either that or Nick had put him in the hospital.

Since she assumed she'd get a call if it was the hospital, she went to bed in one of the guest bedrooms. She could talk to Jamie tomorrow; she wanted a night so they could both rest, and so she could hug the thought of the Goblin Market to herself.

She remembered seeing a wood hung with glittering lights, magic being sold like toys at stalls, hearing drums and chants and knowing that she would rather be there than anywhere in the world. She was going again. She almost loved Alan, just for that.

But it wasn't fair to Alan to love him for the potential of magic. She owed him more than she could ever repay: it was due to Alan that Jamie was alive at all. It wouldn't be fair to Alan to love him for that, either. The idea of building love out of gratitude or pity made her feel sick, and she imagined it would make Alan feel sick too.

Loving Alan because of his smile and his smarts and how kind he was, that would be fair, but she'd had the chance to do that already. She'd known how he felt about her. She'd been so worried about Jamie, so swept away by the spectacle of magic, she hadn't thought about it, and then when she wasn't paying attention, somehow it had become all about Nick.

Things were different now.

It wasn't fair to let Alan be second choice, either.

This wasn't about romance, though. She'd given Seb her word, and she intended to keep it. This was just about friendship.

And magic.

She heard Jamie come in and immediately run upstairs and start drawing a bath. Now that she knew he was safe, she thought she could sleep.

The shutters on her window were open, and she could see the grey spire of St Leonard's Church rising like a Gothic turret against the sky. When she shut her eyes she did not see that grey-on-black vision, the colour of scissors slicing through black paper and cutting the night in two.

Mae remembered the music and the lights and the magic, and at the centre of it all the dancers who called up demons. The girl in red who Nick had called Sin. She'd been dancing when Mae had first seen her, every movement clean and purposeful, every movement lovely. And every time she went still, the audience's breath caught and their attention fastened on her. She was powerful and beautiful, and in the midst of shining magic she belonged completely.

When she went to the Goblin Market, she might see that girl again.

Caught in a blurred warm place between sleep and wakefulness, Mae relived that moment, seeing that girl and feeling a pang of sudden visceral longing.

If I could have anything in this world, she'd thought, all I'd want is to be like her.

Sleeping with her new talisman safe around her neck, she dreamed she heard snarling and pacing outside her window, as if her garden was the stalking ground for hunting cats. She knew they could not get in, but she could not shut out the sound of their hungry cries.

6

Spirit for Your Skin

M AE WOKE TO THE SOUND OF THE DOORBELL RINGING. SHE cracked open one eye, saw the blinking red numbers that told her it was six o'clock in the morning, and planted her face back into her pillow.

The doorbell rang again. Mae wondered if they had a new milkman. One with a death wish.

The bell shrilled again, the noise echoing off the high ceilings.

"Oh my God, why is this happening to me," Mae moaned, and dragged herself half out of her warm bed and onto the chilly window seat. She almost overbalanced and fell on the floor, but clung to her sheets and the edge of the window seat and managed to spare herself that at least.

She squinted through a pane and saw the back of a tall, dark boy.

Seb.

She was going to kill him. Did he have some sort of plan for them to watch the sun rise together? Any guy who woke Mae for the sunrise was going to end up seeing stars, because he would have forced her to punch him in the face.

She couldn't let Jamie answer the door. She fished on the ground for her jeans and dragged them on while still under the covers, then actually left her bed and found shoes. As she was tying them the doorbell rang again.

"It would serve you right if my mother answered the door," Mae muttered as she ran down the stairs still finger-combing her hair. "And beat you to death with her briefcase."

Annabel was always appalled by Mae's boyfriends. The idea of her mother's face when she met Seb amused Mae enough that she answered the door smiling: It was just possible that Seb's romantic gesture was not going to backfire on him after all.

When she opened the door it took her a moment to process. The world seemed to hold still for a moment and then hop to another reality, the situation was that different from the one she'd expected.

It wasn't Seb at the door. It was Nick.

He was at her door and he was almost dressed up, for Nick. Instead of the usual T-shirt, he was wearing a shirt that actually appeared to button up and a blue jumper over it that Mae was prepared to bet Alan had bought him. His face was the same as ever, cool and betraying nothing.

Mae was suddenly very aware of the fact she was wearing a sleep shirt with RISE AND WHINE on it. And a picture of a puppy.

"Nick?" she asked, trying to fight down the unreasonable embarrassment that had started in the pit of her stomach and was clawing a hot path up her neck. She reminded herself that he was the one who'd turned up on her doorstep at oh-God-no o'clock in the morning. "What do you want?"

Nick leaned against the wall of her porch and said, "I want to talk."

"Uh," Mae said. "Don't take this the wrong way, but were you abducted and brainwashed by aliens in the night?"

Nick raised his eyebrows. "I don't want to talk about my feelings or anything," he said. "Let's take a walk. I don't like your house."

"I beg your pardon, there is nothing wrong with my house."

"It's too big," Nick told her, frowning at it. "You can't tell where people are in it, and you can't hear everything that happens. There are too many places for something to hide in and leap out at you."

Mae rubbed the sleep out of her eyes.

"Did you show up here at this time of the morning just to say 'Hi, Mae, your house is a death trap, want to take a walk?'"

"For starters," Nick said. "Coming?"

"Let me grab my jacket," Mae answered, shaking her head, and left Nick on the doorstep as she went to the coatrack and rifled through the heap of coats until she found her denim jacket. Anything to cover up the puppy.

They walked down from Mae's house and ended up taking Larkbeare Road, which led down to the river. It was chilly, early morning winds ruffling the waters and their hair. Mae tried finger-combing some more, pretty sure it was doing her no good, and Nick strolled along at her side, apparently oblivious to the cold.

"For someone who wants to talk," Mae said, "you're being awfully quiet."

Nick just looked at her.

"So what have you been up to since I saw you last?" she

inquired, and when he kept silent she rolled her eyes at him and made sure he saw it. "It's called a conversation, Nick. Let's have one. Humour me."

A particularly chilly gust of wind hit Mae in the face. She winced, and Nick half closed his eyes against the onslaught.

He said something at last, and naturally said it into the wind so she missed all but the last word, which was "vanquish".

"Sorry, what did you vanquish?" Mae asked.

"Nothing," said Nick. "Well, a few things. That's not the point. I have a Vanquish."

"Um," Mae said. "Run that by me again."

"An Aston Martin Vanquish."

"Oh a car," Mae said, enlightened.

"A classic car," Nick told her, a little sternly. "Came into the garage in London in a state, and I bought it. Alan says if I restore it without using any magic at all, I can keep it. So that's what I've been doing lately."

The list of everything Mae knew about cars wouldn't have taken up a page and would have probably contained items like, "They take you from place to place" and "Moving vehicles that are not airplanes", but she nodded and tried to look as if she understood the serious business of car restoration.

"How did you get it down to Exeter?"

Nick grinned. "Well, there I may have used magic. Slightly."

"Just a pinch," Mae suggested. "You seem to have plenty to spare."

Nick slanted her an amused glance. "You want me to flex my magic for you, baby?"

"I guess. I wouldn't want you to feel pressured to do something you didn't want to do. Leave you feeling all cheap and used."

"I'm basically okay with that," said Nick. "Let me show you my magic knife."

He took out the switchblade he'd been playing with down at the magicians' alley the day before and tossed it to Mae. She fumbled the catch but managed to grab it anyway; the engraved metal was warm from being next to Nick's skin. Close up, the markings on it were a bit rough, like sketches rather than runes. There was a jagged line snaking up the silver hilt that looked like it had been gouged in, creating a deep furrow with sharp edges that almost cut her palm.

"Did you do the carvings yourself?" Mae asked, and at Nick's small nod she said, "Impressive. So tell me, what magic does this knife do?"

Mae believed firmly that you could be tactful without telling lies. It was a smarter and better way to do things, and if people noticed what you were doing, it encouraged you to be smarter and better next time.

"It cuts things."

Mae blinked. "Amazing," she told him. "Next could you display your great magic by creating a wheel that goes round and round?"

She wasn't entirely sure of how you opened a switchblade, but she turned the knife around in her hands until she discovered a little catch. She went to touch it.

The sudden vice-like grip around her wrist made her flinch and glance up at Nick. He wasn't even looking at her; his eyes remained focused straight ahead, as if he'd simply reached out and grabbed by instinct.

Mae tried to wrench her arm away. He looked at her then.

"Don't open that," he said, sounding as indifferent as ever.

"I told you, the blade's enchanted. It'll cut through anything."

He confiscated the knife from her and flipped it open. The blade gleamed in the light, so sharp that it seemed multifaceted, catching the rays of the sun like a jewel.

"Why do you get to open it?"

"Tell me about your nine years of experience with knife work," Nick invited her. "Then you can have it right back."

"Nine years – oh, that's ridiculous, you would have been eight years old!"

"Seven," said Nick.

The word was simple and cold, like dropping a stone into deep water. Nick threw his knife up and caught it: it made a thin tearing sound, as if it was ripping the very air into pieces.

She always forgot he was more than a year younger than she was, younger than Jamie. Of course, demons lived forever. He was impossibly old as well.

He'd been human for barely sixteen years, though. If you could call him human at all.

"What—" Mae heard her voice shake and forced it steady. "So this miracle knife, could it cut a diamond?"

"To the heart," Nick said, taking a certain slow, cold delight in the words. "It can cut through bones like butter."

"And that's better than being able to change the weather."

Nick frowned. "That sort of thing comes naturally to me," he said. "The weather. Power over things like fire. Water. Blood. This was a spell, and it wasn't easy." He gave that glinting deadly blade what Mae was disturbed to realise might be a longing look, and then flicked it closed. "I have power," he said softly. "I don't have control."

"You can learn," Mae told him, equally softly. She felt like

77

she was speaking low so she wouldn't attract Fate's attention. She didn't want to think of what would happen if Nick couldn't learn control.

"You owe me, right?" Nick demanded.

Mae stared. "What?"

"I mean," Nick went on in a rough voice, "Alan and me, we helped out last time, and we're here again now. I'll help Jamie. So you owe—"

"Yes, I owe you!" Mae interrupted, stung for reasons she wasn't sure she should examine all that closely. "What do you want, Nick?"

"I want your help," he said.

For a tall guy, Nick was very good at keeping pace with her, used to measuring his steps for someone slower than he was. He obviously wasn't expecting her to stop dead, though, and when she did he took several long strides and then wheeled back around to face her. Mae had seen him circling a threat the same way, watching for a weakness, waiting for his chance to attack.

"How on earth," Mae said, too shocked to even try and be tactful, "can I possibly help you?"

Nick looked annoyed, as if she was missing something incredibly obvious instead of being understandably confused about the fact that he had gone insane and was talking nonsense. He looked out over the river, jaw set tight, and said, "I want you to teach me how to act human."

"Oh," Mae breathed, stunned and softer than the morning wind. She wasn't even sure if he heard her. She swallowed painfully, feeling as if the breath were a bit of broken glass placed on her tongue, and asked in a scraped-raw voice, "Why?"

He glanced away from the river and back at her. "For Alan."

His tone supplied the *of course*.

"He risked a lot for me," Nick continued slowly. "I owe him. I don't know why he did what he did, but I don't want him to regret it."

"It's about owing him?" asked Mae, her voice still sounding weak and almost lost to the rising wind.

Nick shrugged. "What else would it be about?"

He viewed what Alan had done for him as a debt that had to be paid and nothing more. He saw no other reason to be human.

"Why ask me? Why not go to Alan?"

"You're good at that sort of thing," Nick said. "Alan isn't, not when he's telling the truth. He grew up with me and Mum, and he never learned how to be like the other humans. He just learned to lie to them."

Mae recalled Alan talking blithely about dead bodies in the trees.

"All right," she said. "I can understand that. But I'm sure he'd like to help. Why sneak over to my house when the dawn chorus has barely got started on the tambourines? Why do you want it to be a secret?"

"Because I want to lie to him and I can't!" Nick shouted. "Because it's all going wrong and he keeps looking at me. He's afraid of what I'll do, and he's sorry he ever freed me."

So something had gone wrong between Nick and his brother, then. Something had gone badly wrong.

All Mae could think of to say was, "I'm sure he's not sorry."

"He won't be," Nick said with vicious emphasis, not as if he was hoping it was true but as if he was insisting it would be.

"Because you're going to help me. You're going to teach me ways to seem human and he'll think I did it on my own, that I'm what he wants me to be, and he'll be happy."

He stopped pacing then and stood as still as a predator that had caught sight of his prey and did not want to startle it. He reached out as if he was going to touch her – he'd wrapped her hair around his wrist, once – but he did not.

His voice crackled like a low-burning fire, sounding stranger than ever mingled with the murmurs of the river.

"If you can make Alan happy," he promised, "I'll give you anything you want."

Mae straightened a little, feeling better for being even a fraction of an inch taller.

"You don't have to bribe me, Nick," she said. "I know I owe you. I'd be glad to help."

Nick nodded and did not thank her. He simply began retracing their steps, heading back in the direction of the church. The wind seemed to change course so it could blow into their faces.

Of course, since she was walking with a guy who was tall, dark, and in control of the elements, there was probably no "seemed" about it.

"When you say awful things and people react badly to them," Mae yelled into the wind, "you might want to try saying something like you didn't mean it."

"I always mean it," Nick told her.

"Um. Okay. You might try saying that you didn't mean for them to take what you said the wrong way."

"Why?"

"Because it will make people feel better to think you just made a mistake. Because humans say idiot things all the time, and we're all allowed to take it back, and that way everyone mostly forgives everyone else and civilisation isn't destroyed," Mae said. "Because the worst thing you can possibly do is seem like you don't care."

Now they had turned and were no longer walking by the river; the wind was whistling overhead, shaking branches at them and launching surprise attacks from the tops of walls.

Nick appeared to consider this and find it reasonable. "Okay. I can pretend I care."

"Well," Mae said, "if you want to be human, it might be a good idea to try actually caring a little."

Nick gave her a long, thoughtful look, and then he smiled.

It wasn't a nice smile.

"I think you've misunderstood me," he said. "I don't want to be human."

Mae blinked.

The sound of a slam and a sudden barrage of noise made her jump violently, as if someone had started shooting a gun behind her ear, but it wasn't a gun firing. It was a dog, throwing itself against a garden gate and barking in wild, loud animal panic. Trying to get to Nick.

It was a big animal, a German shepherd, with white teeth bared and gleaming. When Nick started to walk towards it, its efforts to break through the gate redoubled. Its body slammed against the black-painted iron so hard that the bars shook with the impact.

Nick leaned against the gate. A terrible, guttural growl was coming from the animal's throat now, the noise stuttering and fracturing in the air.

"Animals can tell," Nick remarked.

He looked almost normal, with his scruffy jeans and his

shock of hair; for a few moments this morning things had felt like they had before she knew. Except that there was something so profoundly wrong with him that animals feared and hated him on sight.

"I'm not human," said Nick. "I never was, and I never will be. We don't work in the same way you do, we don't feel or think the same, and I don't want to. Why should I? What's so great about you people? You spend your whole lives in a stupid emotional mess, and then you die. You torture each other and you don't even mean to."

He glanced casually over at the dog and its belly hit the gravel, a whine breaking from its throat. Nick shut his eyes for a moment.

"When I torture someone," he said, "I mean it."

There was a long pause, filled with nothing but the sound of the wind shrieking overhead and the small, terrified noises of the animal behind the gate.

"That's a shame," Mae said at last. "I had this picture of you, you know, all dark and brooding and anguished. Longing for humanity. Listening to piano and violin music. Sometimes you'd stand on top of a tower, feeling impossibly lonely. Then you'd cry a single perfect tear."

The corner of Nick's mouth curled up. "Can't spell 'demon' without 'emo'."

"It was very romantic," Mae went on soulfully. "You've ruined a beautiful dream for me."

"Alan has some piano and violin stuff at home," Nick said. "I could listen to it. I'm pretty sure I would start thinking tormented thoughts about five minutes in."

"I don't even have the words to tell you how disillusioned I am." Mae glanced at the sky, which was changing from the pallid grey of early morning to bright blue. "I'd better get back and wake Jamie if we're driving to London today. You got him in fairly late last night."

Nick left the gate and fell back in step with her as she started walking.

"I didn't keep Jamie out that late. And he wouldn't let me drive him home. Want to bet he went running to warn those magicians about what we have planned?"

"Jamie's not a magician," Mae said, her voice coming out louder and more frantic in her own ears than she'd expected, sounding more doubtful than she liked.

"I didn't say he was," Nick returned. "But don't pretend his sympathies aren't divided."

"What if they are?"

Mae heard her own voice come out taut with fear, reflecting the sensation in her chest where it felt as if her heartstrings had been pulled tight by something sharp, like an arrow fitted against a bowstring. She knew how Nick felt about magicians.

She looked at Nick to see he was looking away from her, his jaw tight. "It doesn't matter. If they leave, good. If they don't, Celeste Drake will make them. If she doesn't, I will." He turned his eyes back to her. "Because we have an agreement, you and me. Don't we?"

Mae lifted her chin. "We do."

They were walking up the slope towards Mae's house now, passing gardens with summer roses in them, the sunlight turning warm gold against the grass. A man in a suit drinking coffee by his car and a woman in a kimono collecting the paper both gave Nick a slightly doubtful look.

"They think you're a hooligan," Mae reported. "That

woman's probably locking up her daughters as we speak. The jumper doesn't fool her for a minute."

"What I really wanted to wear was a shirt with a puppy on it," Nick drawled. "But mine's in the wash."

Mae laughed, sun warm on her hair like someone laying a hand gently on her head. She felt in control for the first time since she'd seen Gerald; better than that, she felt useful. You're good at that sort of thing, Nick had said.

"Don't worry, you still look pretty," she said. "I like your new ring. I've been wondering about it, actually."

"Aw," Nick said. "I can't have nice things?"

He touched the ring with his other hand, a strange sort of gesture coming from someone whose only unnecessary movements usually involved knives. The silver darkened under the shadow of his fingers, making the carving look tarnished for a moment. There were snakes on it, tangled with thorns.

The Obsidian Circle's master ring.

"I took it from my father after he was dead," Nick said. "To remember him by. It seemed a human sort of thing to do. But Alan didn't like it at all."

Mae cleared her throat and tried not to think about that dark room in London, with blood on her hands and bodies on the floor.

"You killed Black Arthur. It wouldn't have looked to Alan like you were taking a memento. It would have looked like you were taking a trophy."

"Oh," said Nick.

It hadn't occurred to him because he wasn't human; he didn't even have the faintest idea how to be really human, and here she was walking with him and feeling happy for no reason at all. Other than the reason that she was the stupidest person in the world.

"Who's this guy?" Nick asked suddenly.

Mae blinked. "Uh, guy? What – what guy?"

Nick was looking at her intently now. It was a little unsettling having all his attention, black gaze unwavering and swallowing up all hers in return, making the human world fall away.

"The one you're giving a chance to or feeling up behind the bike sheds or whatever. The one Alan was talking about. Who is it?"

"Well," Mae said, and felt a blush creep up her neck. "Well, Seb McFarlane."

Nick threw back his head and burst out laughing. Mae stared at him in outrage.

"What?" she demanded. "What, why are you laughing? Lots of people think he's good-looking! Lots of girls want to go out with him – he's very – just stop!"

Nick stopped. Mae shoved her hands in her pockets, fingers curled tight into her palms, and made for home.

When she was at her front gate, on her own turf, she stopped and spoke again.

"Why do you even want to know?" she asked, her voice quiet.

"I didn't mean for you to take that laughing thing the wrong way," Nick said, doing an enormously bad job of mimicking her own voice advising him.

His deep voice didn't even seem to go high, but she stopped at her gate and grinned at him anyway. He grinned back, catching his ringed hand in the looping iron pattern of her gate and leaning down towards her.

"McFarlane's good-looking," he admitted. "But if you choose him over my brother, you're crazy."

"Oh," said Mae.

The word popped out of her mouth, blank and stunned. She wanted to snatch it back out of the air and swallow it to hide the evidence. Nick was still looking at her, his hunter's eyes missing nothing. The morning light cut down his profile into stark lines, something that could have been on a coin.

Mae took a deep breath. "It's not some kind of tragically stupid love triangle. I'm not going to choose one guy out of two and settle down. It doesn't have to be either of them for me, or have to be me for either of them. The world's full of people, if you hadn't noticed. I could ask any of a dozen guys out, and any of them could ask me out. I didn't ask for your advice on my love life," she added. "And it's not necessary."

"Glad to hear it," Nick told her. "One last thing."

He leaned in closer, his hand held up to screen their faces, as if he didn't want anyone watching to even read his lips. His fingers were curled about half an inch from her cheek.

"I'm sure you're right," he said, his voice a whisper that seemed to curl in the air like smoke, to find a way into her stomach and twist there, low. "I'm sure there are a dozen guys who will ask you out if McFarlane loses his chance. I just want you to know something."

"What?" Mae asked, whispering because he was whispering, tilting her face up because he was leaning down, and for no other reason.

Nick looked down at her, his face obscuring the rest of the world, stripping everything else away until she was left with cold black eyes instead of a summer sky.

"I never will," he said.

Then he turned and walked off, leaving her standing at the garden gate. He didn't look back.

The leader of the Aventurine Circle would only agree to meet them over running water.

"So we're meeting them on the Millennium Bridge," Alan explained as he drove around more tall grey office buildings than even London should have been able to hold, until they found a five-storey car park near the Bankside and parked the car on the fourth level.

Mae was simply glad to get out of the car, after hours of driving with the boy who'd just asked her out and the boy who had just announced that he'd never ask her.

Not to mention the brother who was apparently not talking to her. Jamie avoided Mae's gaze when she tried to catch his eye, standing close to Alan, as if Alan was his only possible ally out of the whole group.

His and Nick's little knife-throwing bonding session had obviously not been a resounding success. Nick was standing to one side, looking generally uninterested in the entire world.

Mae started walking through the car park, the rubber soles of her shoes squeaking on the concrete as she stalked through oily puddles. The streets by the Tate Modern museum were narrow, the buildings varying shades of yellow and brown brick. She walked north towards the bridge and refused to let herself look back.

They drew level with her just before she reached the red brick courtyard of the museum and started up one of the two steel slopes that led to the bridge.

She allowed herself to glance across at them, wondering how Jamie was holding up. He was looking a little apprehensive, but Alan was taking care of him. He had a hand on Jamie's shoulder and he was talking in that lovely, soothing voice that meant it didn't matter what he said because every syllable was gentle as a touch, like someone stroking a frightened animal with sure, steady hands.

"This was really the first important horizontal suspension bridge to be built in the world. There was a competition for the design," Alan said. "The effect is meant to be like a ribbon of steel, or a blade of light, and" – his voice slid into a warmer note, amused and affectionate – "I'm sure you're fascinated by this lecture on architecture and engineering."

"Fascinated's a strong word," said Jamie, dimpling up at him. "Maybe a bit reassured."

Alan smiled. "I'm told many people find engineering very soothing."

"A blade," Nick repeated from his place behind them, and gave the bridge before them a slightly approving look.

"And now I am all unsoothed again, thank you," Jamie said. "Does it always have to be about pointy weapons of death, Nick?"

"You want me to start killing people with blunt instruments?" Nick asked. "Well, okay, if it makes you happy."

He was holding on to the glass-and-steel rail, his grip white-knuckled. Though it was hard to tell with Nick, Mae thought the edge to his voice was sharper than usual.

"You all right?"

"Fine," Nick bit out with enough force to make Alan turn his head.

"Is it the running water?" he asked, his voice more like the voice he'd used to talk to Nick last month, before Nick erupted from a demon's circle in a rush of magic and fury.

The tight, unhappy line of Nick's shoulders eased a fraction.

"No," he said. "I've been feeling weird for a while."

Alan slackened his pace so that he was walking beside Nick rather than Jamie. "Why didn't you tell me?"

Nick shrugged. Alan studied his face as if he had a chance of reading something from it.

"You'd call me stupid if I asked whether you wanted to go back to the car and sit this one out, right?"

"Right," said Nick, his voice a little less sharp. "Stupid."

Mae stopped eavesdropping and looked straight ahead to find that Jamie had gone on in front, apparently determined not to walk with her.

Beyond Jamie's thin, held-straight back, she saw the glittering spread of London laid out before her, glass-fronted buildings and neon lights shedding their brightness on the dark river, and the white cathedral dome of St Paul's going grey in the gathering dusk.

The thin steel bridge was empty except for the magicians.

The Aventurine Circle must have cast some sort of don't-notice-us-but-don't-come-by spell. Mae thought keeping the Millennium Bridge clear of London commuters was pretty impressive magic.

The Aventurine Circle looked pretty impressive as well.

There were seven of them standing on the bridge, two men and five women. They were all in pale clothes, standing out against the cobalt blue of the sky and the reflecting waters below.

The woman at their head wore white.

Celeste Drake herself was the least impressive figure of the group. She was the shortest, and she was not even beautiful. She was pretty, like a china doll made human, with silvery blonde curls ruffling in the wind, a slim body covered in white wool, and a pale throat with a black pearl dangling in the hollow. Mae thought that if Celeste had shown up at her mother's tennis club, she would have been welcomed with open arms and bullied into making the sandwiches.

"Hello," said Celeste, opening her white-woollen arms, and Mae realised who her sweet smile was for.

"Hi," Jamie responded, sounding awkward but pleased.

"It's a most unexpected pleasure to discover one of our kind at this little meeting," Celeste said. "You're very welcome to our territory."

"Oh, thanks," said Jamie. "Um, it's very nice. Your territory. Good shopping, and – I'm sure other good – magical stuff."

Celeste laughed and a silvery ribbon appeared as if her laugh had created it, the sound ringing out and the ribbon drifting towards Jamie, twisting in the breeze and leaping back like a puppy who wanted to play. He reached for the silvery line of magic: it touched his hand, shining on his skin for a moment, and then bobbed backwards. Jamie took a few more steps towards the Aventurine Circle, reaching out to have the magic again.

"Jamie, don't be an idiot!" Nick snarled.

Jamie blinked and stopped, the silvery tendrils clinging to his arm like a bracelet of light.

Celeste's eyelashes, little golden fans like the lashes on a doll who could be sent to sleep, snapped up. Her grey eyes were cold and still as lakes in winter.

"I don't think any of us require a lecture from a demon."

She stepped forward, and the others all stepped with her in what seemed for a moment like a procession.

Mae took a step backwards to be on Alan's right as Nick

was on his left, so they were flanking him in as much of a show of solidarity as they could make with Jamie still standing to one side, wrapped in magic and wonder.

Mae noted with disgust that even tiny china doll Celeste was taller than she was.

Alan held out his hand and said, "I'm—"

"I know who you are," Celeste told him, ignoring his outstretched hand. "You're the traitor, the boy who has managed to cut himself off not only from his own people but from all of humanity; the one who stands with the demons."

"And you agreed to meet with me anyway," said Alan. "Why is that?"

There was a tiny, smug curl to Celeste's lips. It made her look like a cat smiling. "Put it down to a curious nature. What do you have to tell me?"

"The Obsidian Circle invaded your territory last month," Alan said. "They're in Exeter now. I understand the penalties for trespassing on another Circle's territory are fairly severe. I wanted to point you in their direction."

"Oh, I see," Celeste remarked in dulcet tones. "Thank you so much. I'm delighted by the idea of being a tool in the hands of a demon."

Alan's voice stayed calm and friendly. "I just thought you might like to know."

"Well," said Celeste. "I'd like to let you know some things. I know perfectly well where Gerald Lynch and the remains of Arthur's Circle have run. I know that Arthur Dee, the maniac who gave a demon its own body and who dared to come into my city without my permission, is dead. I know that I am not the kind of woman who would start murdering my own kind, particularly when their new leader is young and promising and was only following orders when he did me a wrong. Some of us have loyalty to our own kind, Alan. Now tell me something I don't know – could you possibly have anything interesting to say to me at all?"

Some of the Aventurine Circle magicians were smirking. Mae had a sudden urge to grab Alan's hand, but she didn't want to betray even that much weakness to their watchful eyes.

"I guess I don't," Alan said quietly. "Sorry for taking up your time."

Celeste shrugged. "That's perfectly all right. It wasn't a wasted trip."

Mae really did not like the tone this woman was using. "And why's that?" she demanded.

Celeste's eyes rested on her, betraying nothing.

"Speaking of young and promising magicians," she purred, "you brought one to my city. Do you think I would abandon him to a demon, or even let him waste his power on the ruined fragments of the Obsidian Circle? That would be a crime."

The shining bracelet of light around Jamie's wrist became thick as a steel snake, closing around his arm like a metal tentacle. Celeste held out a hand and curled her fingers, and the other end of the shining line leaped into her palm. Jamie yelped as the silver leash of magic tightened and twisted, and he stumbled forward, falling over his own feet, inexorably drawn to her side.

Before Mae could even move, her brother was trapped in the midst of the Aventurine Circle.

"We're keeping the young magician," Celeste said, still smiling. "Have a good evening."

7

The Blade of Light

Y OU'RE WRONG," SAID NICK.

He was the last person Mae would have expected to speak, but his voice carried clear and deep over the whispering, rushing sound of the Thames below. The magicians seemed surprised that he had spoken too; they stirred and went still. Jamie's wide eyes swung to Nick's face.

"Oh?" Celeste inquired, her voice becoming a little higher and sharper. "And what am I wrong about? Do please feel free to enlighten me, demon."

"You're not taking him," said Nick. "He's ours."

"I really kind of am," Jamie put in. "I mean, I'm mine. Nick is being horrifying and inappropriate as usual, but I'd much rather go home with them. Not that I don't appreciate the kind offer of hospitality as expressed by kidnapping me."

Celeste looked over her shoulder at Jamie, who was still breathing hard and shocked by the way magic had turned from wonder to a weapon before his eyes.

It didn't even make sense. Gerald's spell was meant to protect him from this sort of thing.

"Everything is all right," Celeste cooed. "I don't blame you for an instant. It's made you promises, hasn't it? It's made you want to do anything it wishes. It's shown you marvels."

Jamie blinked. "If you're talking about Nick, all he's shown me is this car he's fixing up. And honestly, I wasn't that interested."

"You said you were interested," Nick commented, his voice dry.

"Well, I was being polite."

It eased the knot of panic in Mae's chest, tighter than the one around Jamie's wrist, to see that Jamie looked slightly calmer after this exchange. She wanted to run in and wrest him away from Celeste, but doing that risked getting Jamie hurt, risked getting herself hurt and doing Jamie no good at all.

She thought of her mother saying that you gave tasks to those equipped to deal with them. Annabel had been talking about delegating work in the boardroom, but Mae thought the logic still applied to a bridge by night and magicians bent on capturing your loved ones.

Nick could turn the whole bridge into a lightning rod if he liked. He was equipped, and he was dealing with this.

"Do you really think," Mae murmured, modulating her voice into a copy of Celeste's purr, "that it's a good idea to aggravate a demon like this?"

Celeste laughed. "My dear girl. What's he going to do about it?"

Nick's voice turned thick, coiled around a snarl. "I'll show you what I'm going to do!"

His voice rang out like a thunderclap. Mae braced herself for lightning.

None came. There was just the still night and the sound of the river, currents running as regularly as a clock, washing the seconds away.

"Well?" asked Celeste, dropping the word into the silence at the exact point when it became too much to bear. "I'm waiting. Show me."

Mae ripped her eyes from Jamie's scared face to whirl on Nick, but the demand on her lips died when she saw him. He was looking not at Celeste, but at his brother.

"Alan," he said, "I can't. I don't understand."

Alan pushed his shoulder slightly in front of Nick's. "I think I might," he said slowly. "Arthur never came down by this part of the river, did he? A river would have been pretty useful when dealing with demons, but he wouldn't have dared. You've made this place, Southwark – your territory – you've made it so nobody else can use magic here. Like a giant . . ." His voice changed. "Like a giant magicians' circle. Oh. That's clever."

He sounded appreciative, which Mae considered totally unacceptable when what Alan was appreciating was how brilliant he found Celeste's methods of kidnapping.

"What's clever?" she demanded.

Celeste's smile was mocking. "Buried treasure."

"Alan," Mae said between her teeth.

"The magic circle," Alan said. "The one every Circle's power is based on, the one made of stones as big as they can find. She's buried her aventurines in a circle under London. She's made the Bankside her magicians' circle. And once a demon steps into a magicians' circle, its power is gone. For as long as it remains in the circle. But she's in her own circle, so she can't command the demon, either."

"I'm the one with the power," Celeste said, soft. "So I can command you all. Leave now. And leave the young magician to me."

Alan stared at her for a long moment, his profile briefly as unreadable as Nick's. He glanced at Jamie, then bowed his head.

"Maybe we should."

"Leave?" Mae shouted. "Leave without my brother? You must be mad!"

Alan leaned in and said into her ear, "We should come back when they're not expecting us. As opposed to now, when they are looking right at us and about to blast us off the bridge."

Alan's mild, sensible voice stung as if he had touched her somewhere she was already bruised.

"Okay, you're right," she said. "You two go. I'm staying with Jamie."

"That wouldn't . . . be a good idea," Alan told her. "Mae, I understand how you feel, but they won't hurt Jamie. You, on the other hand, you're not a magician. You're like a pizza delivered to the door for their demons."

Mae looked at Jamie. He didn't even look small next to Celeste; he just looked like a boy standing among far more sophisticated adults, shivering in his thin T-shirt. He still wasn't meeting her eyes. She would have killed the whole Aventurine Circle if she'd had the power, and never cared how many dark, bloody dreams she'd have later. He was worth it all: worth more.

"I will not leave him here alone," she said. The lights of London blurred before her eyes, as if they had all been plunged underwater, but she clenched her fists and refused to let tears fall. "You guys go. I will not!"

"You don't have to," said Nick.

He'd been standing by his brother, still and silent as Alan's shadow, since he'd turned to him for understanding. He was scanning the ranks of the Aventurine Circle as he spoke.

He was almost smiling.

"None of us are going anywhere. I've got a plan."

"Nick?" Alan sounded very alarmed.

"Hey," Nick said to Celeste Drake. "You magicians have duels, right?"

"We do," Celeste replied slowly. She looked affronted that a demon was talking to her.

"You've laid claim to something that's ours. Pretty good grounds for a duel, I think." Nick tilted his head. "So let's have one."

Celeste's eyebrows soared upwards. "I believe I've already pointed out that you don't have any magic. Do you want me to fry you from the inside out until you turn into a torch blazing for this whole dark city to see?"

"Oh, don't," Nick said. "You'll get me all hot and bothered in public."

Celeste looked disgusted. Jamie laughed, and when one of the Aventurine Circle glared at him, he turned it into a cough.

"You're wrong on two counts," Nick continued. "I don't want to duel with magic. And I don't want to duel with you."

Mae remembered what Alan had said last night: One of the Circle has a special interest in using magic for fighting. Her eyes flew to the two men in the group, trying to size both of them up in the space of a second.

She felt thoroughly ashamed of herself when Nick said, "Can you resist a challenge, Helen?"

The tallest woman in the crowd was as blonde as Celeste, but there the similarities ended. Her silvery blonde locks were cropped short, her angular face was hard, not like china but like stone, and her white clothes were made of such old material that they moved with her like skin as she pushed past the other magicians and walked across the bridge to meet Nick in the middle.

She wasn't as tall or as broad as Nick was, but there was a sureness to her movements and a solid, settled look to her muscles. There was a quality about this woman that reminded Mae that Nick was a boy.

Younger than Jamie. Not as tall or as strong as he would be one day.

And he had no magic.

Helen the magician reached behind her back with both hands and unsheathed two swords, long and thin and bright as if they were rays of light cast on water.

"Do you think you'll even be a challenge, demon?"

"I'll do my best," said Nick, and drew his own sword.

It was his favourite sword, the one Alan had given him at the Goblin Market. Mae remembered it as she remembered everything about the Market night. It looked like nothing compared to Helen's swords, which caught the fluorescent lights set into the steel of the bridge, the glow of the city spread out along the river, and turned all the lights into magic. Every time she moved her swords, they painted vivid trails of gold dust against the night.

They walked around each other in a slow, tight circle, watching the way their opponent moved.

"Two swords," Nick commented. "Trying a bit too hard?"

"Maybe you're not trying hard enough," Helen said. "If all you can handle is one."

Nick circled around, and Mae caught the flash of his savage grin.

"Oh, I think all you need is one. If you use it just right."

Their swords met with a sudden ring, like the peal of a bell. Nick's sword hit the spot where Helen's blades met, crossed before her. She smiled, face framed by sharp steel, and Nick disengaged. Helen went low, snake-fast, and struck out at knee height. Her intention was so clear that for an instant Mae saw what Helen wanted as if she'd already made it happen: Nick's legs scythed out from under him, having him bleeding and helpless for her final strike.

Mae moved forward and was pulled up short by the hard bite of Alan's fingers into her arm. He pulled her back, tight against his chest, and said into her ear, "Don't move."

She didn't move. She figured he must want comfort, though she wouldn't have thought he'd seek it by grabbing someone hard enough to bruise.

It didn't matter for long. They both had to keep watching Nick.

He jumped to avoid Helen's swords and landed crouched, the aluminium deck reverberating under his feet.

Helen thrust, one sword cutting a golden wound in the night sky. Nick had to slam against the railing to avoid the blow, and then she was sweeping with the sword in her left hand to run him through where he stood.

Nick vaulted over the rail and onto the fragile cables on the side of the bridge, dancing backwards on them as if they weren't impossibly dangerous monkey bars suspended above murky waters.

Helen sliced out at him in a double stroke that could have beheaded him if she'd had more reach. He leaned backwards, away from the swords, and for a moment either he or the bridge swayed and Mae shut her eyes, convinced he was going to fall.

"Stop playing around," Helen snapped. "Let's cut to the chase."

Mae opened her eyes and saw Nick crouched like a huge cat on the end of a cable, sword washed in city lights and turned into a sweep of cool silver.

"This is the chase," said Nick. "Cutting comes later."

He grabbed the steel rail in one hand, and his arm tensed: the only sign before he threw himself over it, landing rolling on the deck and turning the roll into a stand almost too swiftly to see.

Not too swiftly for Helen. She swung, and Nick swerved. Directly into the path of her second blade, which slid between his ribs.

It was so simple and done with so little fuss that for a moment Mae forgot to feel alarmed. Then she heard the sound Alan made in the back of his throat, scraping and pained, as if he was the one who'd been stabbed. She saw the bloodstain spread slow and red across the white of Nick's shirt.

Before Helen could draw her sword out, Nick attacked her unprotected side, his sword slicing in. She dived away, her shirt torn and bloody, pulling her sword out of Nick's chest as she went.

Nick clenched his free hand into a fist and pressed it hard against the bloodstain, then swung in while Helen was still off balance. She fumbled the blade that was still dark and slick with Nick's blood, and Nick struck her wrist hard with his sword. She gave a hoarse cry and dropped it.

"Now we're even," said Nick.

"We're not even," Helen said. "I was using magic and my swords before you were ever born."

"I was killing long before you were born," Nick told her, suddenly soft, as if struck by a pleasant memory. "I'll be killing long after you're dust."

"You sure about that?" Helen said. "I'm not."

Their swords met again, once, twice, three times in a ringing flurry of silver and gold, sparks flying into the darkness. Nick pressed in, and even Mae could see that wasn't good for Helen: with their blades locked, Nick had the advantage of height and weight. He could drive her down.

Mae's leaping heart went still and cold as a stone in her chest when Helen's remaining sword flared into sudden vibrant life, humming and glowing with the white intensity of the sun.

Nick's sword, locked tight with the magician's, broke in two against it. The blade went clattering to the deck, and Nick was left standing there holding the hilt, a broken shard of steel still attached to it. It looked pathetic, especially next to Helen's shimmering weapon.

Nick tossed it up into the air, caught it by the shard, and when Helen's eyes followed the movement for an instant he moved past her guard and hit her hard in the nose with the hilt, then dropped it and punched her in the stomach. When she doubled over, he lunged away from her and across the bridge to seize the other sword, the one she'd dropped.

Helen looked up, blood streaming down her face, as he bore down on her.

She parried Nick's blow and then struck. The sword Nick held was dimmed, ordinary again, while the one she still held was ferociously bright. It seemed to leap in her hands, and Mae clenched her fists at every blow, the ring of blades meeting turning into a murderous little song. Nick's and Helen's feet were moving together, back and forth, like a dance.

Nick was bleeding too much. There was a scarlet trail leading down from the wound his fist was still clenched over, and from the end of his shirt blood was dripping, forming a dark pattern on the bridge.

"I'm sure," Nick said. Their blades flashed and rang, again and again, faster and faster, until all Mae could make out was a metallic blur and Helen's white face. "And I'm sure of something else. You should've spent your time learning to use these swords, not magic them."

The humming of Helen's sword was more like shrieking now, a thin sound with steel and rage behind it. She went in again, wilder and sloppier, going for the kill. That bright sword kept coming within inches of Nick's heart, his throat, his ribs. She scored another cut on the outside of his thigh.

Nick kept his blows steady and controlled, making every one count. Helen feinted to his wounded side, and he faltered. She dived in to exploit the moment of weakness, close to his body, and Nick struck her a blow that forced her arm up.

Her sword went flying into the air, sketching a golden arc against the night sky. Then it fell, all brightness lost, and was swallowed by the dark waters of the Thames.

Nick kicked Helen's kneecaps, sending her legs out from under her. She tumbled down to her knees before him on the bridge, and he rested his sword lightly against her neck.

"Finish it," Helen ground out, without lifting her bowed blonde head.

All Mae could see was his back, his black head bent to

survey his kill. He looked huge and menacing suddenly, now that the woman was on her knees. Now that she was helpless.

"No," Nick said at last.

Helen did look up then. "Why not?"

"I don't want to," he said calmly. "I want you to go home, magician, and practise the sword without using magic. I want you to get really good. And then I want to fight you again."

His voice changed a little on that last line, dark and anticipatory. Helen smiled.

"You've got yourself a date, demon."

Nick strode forward to where the Aventurine Circle stood, transfixed and appalled.

Celeste Drake looked as if she might be considering taking some action as a demon advanced on her with a blade in hand.

"He won his prize," Helen called back sharply over her shoulder.

Nick kept walking, swinging his sword in what seemed to be an idle manner. Celeste's eyes followed it. Her free hand glowed a little, magic building hot in the centre of her palm, and her other hand tightened on Jamie's silver chain. Jamie wasn't fighting any more, but he was standing as far away from her as he could, the line of magic held taut between them.

"My prize," Nick repeated. "You don't have any slightly more impressive prizes on offer? Yeah, I thought not."

Jamie looked indignant.

Nick said, "You are so much more trouble than you're worth," and brought his sword down viciously hard, cutting the magical tie between Jamie and Celeste Drake in two.

Jamie launched himself bodily away from the magicians and at Nick, almost knocking into him. Mae's relief at seeing that silver cord severed was cut short when she realised why Jamie, who usually kept his distance from Nick, was pressed up against him with a hand over his. Jamie was trying to staunch the bleeding.

It was hard to tell when Nick was pale, but his lips were leached of all colour, white and set in a thin line.

"Come back whenever you need to, Jamie," Celeste said gently. "Demons always turn against you in the end."

Nick turned his back without a word. Jamie went with him.

"C'mon," Alan breathed, and Mae turned in time to see him slip a gun into the waistband of his jeans.

Alan hadn't pulled her back and held her bruisingly hard for comfort. He'd positioned her deliberately, had her exactly where he wanted her, so she stood between him and the magicians. So her body blocked their view of his gun.

Jamie was on one side of Nick and Alan on the other as they went down one of the twin ramps, and Nick had relaxed enough to sag against his brother.

It occurred to Mae that Nick hadn't pushed Jamie away when he flew to him because Jamie was helping him stand up.

"Jamie, let me."

"No," Jamie told her. "I've got him."

"I want my sword," Nick said without looking over his shoulder.

"Right," said Mae, and ran back.

The Aventurine Circle were in the process of leaving the bridge, going north towards St Paul's, which was white as carved bone gleaming in the city lights. Helen was holding her side, one of the male magicians hanging solicitously around her. Celeste was still facing south, and she saw Mae coming.

Celeste's eyes narrowed as she watched Mae kneel down on the deck and reach for the broken sword.

"The demon's errand girl, are you?"

"The magician's sister," Mae corrected.

Celeste's eyelashes swept down, modest as a lady hiding behind her fan. The china doll face was restored, a perfect mask now that the incongruously intelligent eyes were hidden.

"When you're ready to be your own woman," she said, "come and find me."

She reminded Mae of a different magician suddenly. For an instant the cold bridge at night slipped away and she saw Olivia again, Nick's mother, with her midnight hair and her mad eyes, leaning close to whisper.

It's probably best to change the world yourself, she'd said.

Before she died.

When Mae focused on Celeste again, the woman had already turned, fragile shoulders hunched slightly against the cold, the lights of riverside London blurring the gold of her hair and the white wool of her dress into one iridescent shape walking away. Mae had no chance to ask her what she'd meant.

She cut her hand picking up the broken blade that was half of Nick's sword, and felt hot blood well up in the chilled hollow of her palm. She closed her fingers over blood and blade and ran to catch up with the others.

They were near the car park when she reached them. A couple of pedestrians had noticed how Nick was staggering and looked torn between worry and disapproval. Mae hoped fervently that nobody would call the police. Nick needed to get out of the city fast, and besides, she doubted her mother would react well to Mae ringing and requesting bail money.

"Got the sword," she called out.

"Good," Nick said between his teeth as they tried to manage the ramps inside the car park, oily puddles harder to avoid now. Under the flickering fluorescent lights, Nick's footprints were vivid red.

Mae tried to avoid walking in them.

"Lucky they let us go," she said, talking mostly because she thought it might soothe Jamie. "I mean – I didn't expect them to play fair."

"Having us trapped in a magicians' circle and kidnapping Jamie isn't exactly playing fair," Alan observed.

"No," Mae said. "I just meant that they kept by the rules of the duel. You didn't."

It wasn't that she disapproved exactly, but seeing the flash of the gun as Alan tucked it away had caused an uneasy shift in her stomach. You expected the bad guys to be the ones doing the double-crossing.

"It's true," said Alan, and manoeuvred his brother so Nick's back hit their car. Nick leaned against it and panted, long shuddering breaths like an animal in pain. "I was cheating. They were going after my brother. When losing isn't an option, it doesn't matter what you have to do to win."

He spoke in a distracted voice, as if he didn't really care what he was saying. Mae didn't care either, though, not really. Not when Nick looked as if he was about to collapse before their eyes.

Alan rested his bad leg against the car for a second as well, then opened the door to the back seat and pushed Nick into it. Nick went sprawling, head tipped back. There was a sheen of sweat on his throat.

Alan climbed into the car with him.

"You were going to shoot that magician?" Nick asked, his voice a thread Mae could hardly follow.

"If necessary," Alan told him, voice calm and sweet. His face told a different story, but that didn't matter. Nick's eyes were closed.

Alan reached out and pushed the sweaty hair back from Nick's brow, and Nick turned his head restlessly away. Alan withdrew his hand

"I had her number the whole time," Nick murmured. "You have so little faith."

"Well, faith's hard," said Alan, voice so soothing it was practically a melody. "Especially when you're such an idiot. You realise this shirt is ruined."

He ripped the shirt apart with efficient hands, the buttons flying behind the headrests and into the front seat.

Nick's chest was heaving, slick with sweat and blood. There was a thin line where the sword had skittered over his ribs, and then the deep, terrible wound on the right.

Mae tried not to panic.

"That's going to need stitches," Alan remarked. "Mae, my first-aid kit is in the boot of the car. Would you go grab it for me?"

He threw the keys over his shoulder at her without looking and she caught them, grateful for something, anything to do.

"Don't bother," Nick rasped.

Mae glanced at him, startled, and saw his fingers wrap around Alan's wrist, forcing Alan's hand away.

"Why mess around? All you have to do is drive me out of here and I can fix myself up."

"Oh," said Alan, his voice entirely changed, gone flat. "Of course. Stupid of me. I wasn't thinking." He paused. "Mae, would you grab the first-aid kit anyway?"

"Sure," said Mae, and went and grabbed it.

When she got back, Alan was scrambling out of the car, wincing as he jolted his leg. He flipped the box open and sorted through it, then ducked his head into the car.

"Here," he said, his whole air terribly casual. "Here's a pad. Hold it to the wound as we're travelling, would you? We don't want you bleeding out before we cross the boundaries of the circle."

Nick took it, hissing as he pulled himself into a sitting position.

"I can take the back," Mae volunteered.

"No," said Jamie. "I will. It's fine."

He climbed in beside Nick a little tentatively, as if convinced that if Nick was even slightly jostled he would die on the spot.

Mae figured the only thing she could do was get into the car so they could get out of there, so she did that as fast as possible. Alan backed out of their space and went out of the car park driving just a little over the limit.

She twisted around in her seat as they sped through the streets of Southwark, at the same time Jamie asked hesitantly, "How are you feeling?"

"Someone drove a very sharp sword between my ribs," Nick said evenly. "How do you think?"

Jamie laid a hand on Nick's arm. "Well," he said, a bit awkwardly. "Th—"

"Don't touch me," Nick snarled.

Jamie removed his hand as if scalded. "Sorry," he said, and tried to tuck himself into a corner of the car as far away from Nick as he could.

Nick leaned his head back against the headrest, teeth gritted against the pain as they went over a speed bump. He'd gone so white he would have looked like stone if not for the sweat making his black hair spike up and pooling in the hollow of his throat.

"I didn't mean for you to take that the wrong way," he said abruptly.

Mae stared at him in amazement. So, for that matter, did Jamie.

"What?"

"Demons don't touch anyone without a reason," Nick went on, his eyes shut again. "You can imagine what kind of reasons we usually have. I don't like – not anyone – I didn't mean anything by it."

"Oh," said Jamie. "Oh, that's okay! That's fine. I understand. I am filled to the brim with understanding and, and, acceptance! I'm very Zen like that."

Nick snorted.

"Thank you," Jamie said, fast, as if he wanted to get it out before any more misunderstandings appeared in their path. "You didn't have to do that. If you guys had left me, I know you would have come back later. I mean, you could have done that. I was expecting it. You didn't have to, um, get stabbed for me. So thanks."

"Stop talking like a moron," Nick drawled. "If you can."

"Thanks," Jamie repeated in a much less sincere tone.

He shut up. The harsh, laboured sound of Nick's breathing was the only noise in the car. In the front Mae sat and regarded the broken sword on the dashboard and Nick's strained white face in the rear-view mirror.

They were not quite out of London when they passed the boundary of Celeste's circle. Nick's breathing changed, became light and easy. His normal pale face in the mirror was such a contrast to the drawn reflection Mae had been studying a moment before that it appeared his cheeks had flooded with colour. When she glanced downwards she saw his wound had closed, chest whole beneath the blood and torn material.

"You look better," she said lamely.

"I feel pretty good," Nick told her, low and pleased. "I like winning. I told that magician I'd win too."

Only he hadn't said exactly that, Mae thought, staring out of the window as the wide grey expanse of the M4 opened and swallowed them up, leading them on the road back to Exeter, where Gerald and his magicians waited. They were no closer to solving the problem of Gerald than they had been the night before.

What Nick had said to Helen the magician was, I'll be killing long after you're dust.

Alan's hands were tight on the steering wheel, knuckles a shade too pale. In the mirror, Mae saw Nick cross his arms over his ripped and bloodstained shirt. She took up the pieces of the broken sword and fitted them together, as if that could possibly help, even though she knew the only way to mend it was magic.

8

In Two Worlds

THE NEXT DAY WAS A SATURDAY, AND MAE CAME AROUND TO GIVE Nick his first lesson in acting human.

Once she was there, she found she had absolutely no idea what to do.

The house the Ryves brothers were living in this time was even worse outside than their last one. It was brown, part of a solid block of houses that all looked as if they had been shaped by a giant child playing with mud. The Ryves house was at the end of the row, and someone had spray-painted in green and pink on the side.

It was nicer inside. There was a grey carpet peeling up at the corners in the hall, but next to that was a fairly big kitchen, and up the stairs was a sitting room and one bedroom. Alan and Nick must be sharing it.

Mae would've felt a bit uncomfortable doing something without Alan's knowledge in Alan's actual room, so she was grateful when Nick led her to the attic.

They had a lot of weapons and books stored up there in

boxes, and half the floor was fibreglass insulation and wooden slats, but the other half was worn floorboards. There was even a high, small window, filtering the sunlight in like a slow stream of honey.

Mae sat on the floor with her back to the wall and said, "I keep trying to think of a lesson plan for humanity. I keep trying to think of any sort of plan, but I don't have one. Nobody taught me to be human. I picked it up as I went along. I don't even know where to start."

She didn't actually expect any suggestions from Nick, standing silhouetted and silent at the window.

But he said, "I thought we could start with this," and threw a child's copybook at her feet.

Mae stared at it for a moment, wondering if it was an old one of his or Alan's, but when she turned it over she saw no name written on it, and when she thumbed through the pages she found writing that looked adult.

"It's my dad's diary," Nick said.

Mae almost dropped the book. "Black—"

"No! I mean Alan's father. Daniel," he said. "Alan gave it to me after I knew everything. He said he thought it would help me to read it, and I tried, but I can't read when I'm – disturbed."

Daniel Ryves. Olivia had talked about him, a little. She'd said that no man ever tried as hard as he had. The guy who'd saved her and Nick when she'd run to him, who had died to protect them all from magicians, who Alan had said would've wanted them to help people in trouble. St Daniel of the Shelter for Women and Slightly Demonic Children.

Mae couldn't imagine what he could have written to upset Nick.

"Well," she said. The front of the copybook was grey and

nubbly under her fingers, like worn old cardboard. "Well . . . sure."

She opened the book to the first page and read.

l am writing this for my son to read, after l am dead.

l have to accept that this is a possibility.

The life l have chosen for us is dangerous. Four years ago l would never have believed any of this was possible. Four years ago l thought l had suffered as much as any man could suffer, that l could never suffer more.

Four years ago l was a fool. Now l have seen magic written on the air in letters of fire, l have cut through enemies with an enchanted sword, and l have stared into the eyes of demons. l can't be sure l will live to explain to Alan how l could have betrayed him so completely.

l do not know how to explain it, but l want to try so that if l die he will know my last thoughts were of him: that l love him, and that l am so terribly sorry.

l am letting my child grow up in the centre of a nightmare.

lt happened like this.

His mother died, and l think l went a little mad. Marie did not die quickly or easily. Alan was still a baby when we started going to the hospital regularly. He was learning to talk while she was losing her hair.

l kept thinking she would get better, and then she was dead, and l felt like it was my fault.

l had been married before. l was very young, and so was my first wife. Olivia was beautiful and wild and almost never kind. We were not happy. We were not happy, but l was charmed, enchanted: l felt as if she could do magic.

Of course, I was right. I just didn't know it then.

I missed her when she left. Even after I married Marie, even though I loved her and we were happy, sometimes I would dream of Olivia coming back to me.

Marie died, and I felt like I had betrayed her with my dreams. I felt like I'd wished her dead.

I was half mad with guilt and grief. That's the only way I can explain what I did.

Four years ago I was sitting in front of the fire on a winter night. There was a storm shrieking outside and doors rattling through the house and a fire burning that seemed to have mocking faces hidden in its depths. Alan was sitting by the fire playing with his dinosaur cards and trying to talk to me. I couldn't think of a word to say to him. Marie had been dead less than a month.

I thought the pounding on the door was part of the storm but it continued, insistent and purposeful, and eventually I went to check.

I never even had the chance to invite her in. Olivia came out of the storm and out of my dreams, running into the room towards the fire as if it was the first warmth and light she had seen in years.

She looked so much older, she looked so wild and scared, I barely noticed the bundle that she let fall on the floor. I thought it was a bundle of possessions, perhaps a bundle of rags. I didn't know. I didn't think it mattered. Not with Olivia come back to me and so afraid. I held her hands and they were like claws. She was talking about magic and demons and darkness even as I tried to warm her, to reshape her hands into a shape that felt more human. I thought it was simply madness.

l didn't pay attention. l am ashamed to write this now, but l was – l think l was happy. My dreams had come true. She was back, and we could heal each other. l had a wife again, and hope.

If l had only known.

While l was looking into Olivia's mad eyes and dreaming, my son left his game and his place by the fire. l didn't even notice as he went towards what l had thought was a bundle of rags. l didn't notice as he turned it over and drew back the blanket, lifted it carefully in his small arms.

l only noticed when he spoke.

"Look, Daddy!"

Then, too late, l turned around. l did not know what l was seeing, but even then l felt a sudden lurch of shock and dread. l felt as if l had looked away at a crucial moment and my child had fallen into the fire and been horribly burned.

l saw my son, my Alan, my darling boy, and in his arms a creature with staring, terrible black eyes. Something that had not stirred or cried out even when Olivia threw it on the floor.

"Daddy," Alan said, glowing. "lt's a baby."

The first entry stopped there, a line drawn decisively under the last words in blue ink that had bled slightly into the paper. Mae risked a look up at Nick. He was standing against the attic wall, a little hunched in because of the slope. He hadn't moved, and his face was as still and cold as ever.

"How're you," Mae said, and swallowed. "How're you feeling?"

She realised an instant later that this was probably the wrong thing to say to Nick, but he met her eyes and answered readily enough.

"Surprised."

"Uh, surprised?"

"Yeah," Nick said roughly. "I didn't know that was how he thought about me. Makes sense, though."

It did make sense. The little paper book felt too heavy in Mae's hands as she thought of that poor man with his dead wife and his son suddenly in danger, thought of a silent child with empty eyes. She couldn't argue with Nick, couldn't even blame Daniel Ryves.

He'd had every reason to hate it.

"Don't think anything bad about him," Nick ordered. "He never let me see what he thought. I always – believed he liked me."

Nick seemed to pause, a faint clicking in his throat as he swallowed, to find the right words. Mae stared up at him helplessly and wished she knew how to read him. She thought she could fix this situation if she just knew what was going on.

"C'mon," he said to her eventually. "I'll run you home."

Mae hesitated and then saw how the sky outside had dimmed, sunlight leaching away until what had been a soft grey sky turned steely. She'd only just have time to change and grab something to eat before Alan arrived at her house to take her to the Goblin Market.

They went down the attic stairs, the old wood so worn with age that the stairs groaned softly instead of creaking under their feet.

When they reached the hall, the kitchen door was flung wide, a summer breeze flooding in. Mae only had time to think that Alan was home early and had left the back door open and to feel an unreasonable rush of panic, as if they'd been caught doing something wrong.

Then Nick broke from her side in a sudden violent spring, and the thin figure standing at the kitchen table with his back to them turned, and it wasn't Alan at all.

It was Gerald.

"Wait," Gerald called out.

Nick did not pause, but he did turn so he was circling Gerald like a predator waiting for the right moment, instead of like a predator leaping straight for his throat.

"Sorry to intrude," Gerald continued, his voice losing its note of urgency and becoming pleasant. He slid his hands into his pockets and blinked in a slow, friendly way, apparently unfazed by Nick's glare.

More than anything, Mae hated the way he taunted them by being polite. She hated that she kept almost believing in his act.

"Not at all," Nick murmured. "Make yourself at home. Sorry for being such a shocking host – I can't offer you any refreshments, and I'm probably about to stab you in the liver. What do you want?"

Gerald's calm smile didn't even flicker.

"Well, I want the Obsidian Circle ring back."

Nick raised his eyebrows. "This ring?" He touched the back of his hand to his mouth, ring pressed to his lower lip as he smiled. "But I've just decided I like it."

"I didn't come for it today," Gerald said mildly. "I came for Alan."

Light broke apart the sky, a single brilliant ray of sunlight or summer lightning. Its reflection struck off the kitchen tap and spun through the air, a stark line of pure white light turning solid as a dream made steel.

A long bright knife landed in Nick's hands and against Gerald's throat.

"You don't get it, do you?" Nick snarled. "I'm just looking for a reason to kill you. Stay away from my brother!"

Gerald stepped forward, into the knife. Mae couldn't see Nick's face, but she guessed that Gerald's move startled even him, because he took a step back.

"I didn't come here to hurt him," Gerald promised, and Nick's tense shoulders relaxed just a little. He took another step back as Gerald stepped forward.

The knife disappeared like a light going out, leaving nothing but shadows in Nick's hands. Gerald reached through the shadows and laid his hands against Nick's chest. Between his fingers and Nick's T-shirt there were sparks, as if someone had left a wire exposed and bursting into electric life in the space between them.

The flare of magic knocked Nick flat on his back on the kitchen counter, Gerald's hands still pressed against his scorched grey shirt as he leaned over Nick and said, "But I have no problem with hurting you."

Mae hadn't been scared once she recognised Gerald. She was scared now.

What scared her even more was the fact that while she was quietly panicking and wondering whether she could possibly use a kettle as a weapon against a magician, Nick didn't look scared at all. He lay there breathless and with his hair blown back, as if he'd been hit by a sudden blast of wind indoors, and said coolly, as if he was observing a fact that was only slightly interesting, "You shouldn't be able to do that."

Nick's eyes were flat and dark as lakes at night. He didn't look in the least alarmed, even as threads of fire crept over

Gerald's hands, flames licking at his wrists and wrapping around his fingers in bright lines. In fact, Mae realised, Nick's lips were curling up in a smile.

Then she followed Nick's calm gaze and understood why.

Behind Gerald stood Alan, with a gun pointed at the back of the magician's head, face flushed from the outdoors or maybe because he'd seen the open door and come running.

"Let's see if you have spells set against bullets," Alan suggested, and fired.

The crack of the gun in the quiet kitchen was terrifyingly loud. Gerald flinched, but that was all. Mae had seen this happen once before, seen bullets bounce off a prowling wolf who'd later turned back into a magician.

Alan must have seen it a hundred times.

"I guess you do," he said. "Too bad."

"After you shot down members of our Circle in our home? I always have spells set," Gerald informed him without turning. "What's your plan now, Alan?"

"Improvise," said Alan, and popped his left wrist sheath. A long blade glittered, sharp and wicked, between his fingers. Gerald spun around to deflect the knife blow, power shimmering in his palms, and magic caught Alan's knife and held it still.

Nick rose from the counter already drawing his sword.

"Can I kill him now?" he demanded.

"No," said Alan, popping his other wrist sheath. He got the point of his blade against Gerald's stomach and they stood locked for a moment, magic against blade, looking into each other's eyes.

"I came to talk to you," Gerald whispered. "Just to talk."

"Really," Alan said. "So why were you trying to burn Nick's heart in his chest?"

"He attacked me," said Gerald.

"If I'd attacked you, you wouldn't be whining about it," Nick growled. "You'd be dead."

"Besides," Gerald continued, ignoring Nick completely, his eyes on Alan. "That's not his body, is it? That's not his heart."

"That's my brother," Alan said, very soft.

The fire shining from Gerald's palms shimmered a little, light faltering as if he'd been speaking and his voice had wavered. Mae narrowed her eyes and watched him closely.

"I'll stand down if you will," said Gerald.

Alan nodded slowly, and withdrew his knife as the magic ebbed away out of Gerald's hands. He rolled up his sleeve and replaced the knife in his spring-loaded wrist sheath, not looking at it as he did so, the movements practised and smooth. He held Gerald's gaze the whole time.

"Nick, put the sword away," said Alan without a glance at Nick.

Nick hesitated, sword a silver arc of light in the dim kitchen. There was something about his pale face in the near dark that made Gerald shudder slightly and turn his eyes away.

"Now," said Alan.

Nick put his sword away and turned his back on Gerald, stalking clear across the room from him to lean against the wall, arms folded, and glare.

"Takes orders well, doesn't he?" Gerald observed. "They were made for it: they don't know how to do anything else. Do you think that'll keep you safe? All they know is obeying and betraying humans, crawling and then turning like worms. Pain and power is all they can give you. It's all they are. He'll turn against you in the end. Don't you know that? Or is the power worth so much to you that you've let this treacherous, bloodthirsty thing loose on the world and you don't even care what it will do?"

There was a blur of motion. Then the punch connected and Gerald went crashing onto the floor. He sprawled and hit his head against the washing machine.

For a moment Mae was sure it had been Nick: the movement had looked like one of Nick's, like something savage breaking its leash.

It wasn't Nick. Nick was still at the far end of the kitchen, leaning against the wall.

Alan stood over Gerald's crumpled body. He had gone white.

"Shut your mouth," he said. "That's my little brother you're talking about."

Gerald touched his mouth delicately with the back of his hand. The gesture looked just like that of an ordinary person, a ginger touch to assess the damage, but when he drew his hand away from his mouth it was healed, the splash of blood looking out of place on his unharmed mouth. It didn't look like real blood now, somehow.

It looked like he was playing a game.

"Struck a nerve, did I?" Gerald asked from the ground.

"Obviously," said Alan. "Is that what you came here to do?"

Gerald climbed to his feet slowly, not making any sudden movements, as if he wanted a wild animal to come closer to him.

"I came because I wanted to make a proposition to you," he said. "I can't do it with the demon here."

They were watching each other the same way they had before, with magic and a knife between them.

"Aren't you curious?" Gerald asked, after a long moment.

Alan's mouth twisted into a shape a shade away from a smile. "Always," he admitted. "Nick, do you maybe want to go work on your car? Just for a little while?"

"What?" Nick demanded. "No."

He shifted his stance, braced against the wall as if Alan would've had a chance if he tried to push him physically out of the room.

"It won't do any harm to hear what he has to say."

"It'll do you some harm if he fries the meat off your bones," Nick countered. "I'm not leaving you alone with him."

"I won't be alone," said Alan. "If Mae agrees to stay with me."

He turned his eyes to Mae, and she started. She was almost shocked at being addressed, as if she'd been watching a play and suddenly one of the actors had spoken to her.

"I have to confess I probably won't be much help," she said. "My big plan to save Nick before you arrived was to toss a kettle at the magician's head."

Alan grinned. "You willing to defend me with a kettle?"

"Putting your faith in my awesome kettle-wielding skills doesn't strike me as your brightest idea ever."

"I think I could do a lot worse," said Alan, and looked back at his brother. "Nick. He's determined to talk to me, and I'd like to know what he has to say. You'll be within earshot."

"And what," Nick retorted, "I'm supposed to come running when you start screaming?"

"Come running when I start shooting," said Alan.

Nick's mouth turned up at one corner, though whether that was at his brother or at the thought of shooting, Mae didn't know.

"Nick," Alan said. "Go."

He looked at Alan and reached behind him, fingers curling

around the hilt of his sword. The gesture might have been Nick seeking reassurance, Mae thought, like a child clutching at a favourite toy.

Or he might have been thinking of using it.

"I don't like what you've done to me," Nick told his brother, his voice ugly, and moved fast.

He went for the door and stalked out, slamming it shut behind him. The crash of the door was the only sound in the kitchen for a moment.

Then Mae moved past the counter to stand shoulder to shoulder with Alan as they faced the magician.

Gerald, clearly unimpressed by the awesome threat they presented, took a seat at the head of the kitchen table and stretched his long legs easily out before him.

"You seem to expect things from him that he can't possibly give you," he observed. "That's almost cruel."

"Yes," said Alan. "I know."

Mae sat down, leaning her elbow against the table and her chin against her fist and training her gaze on Gerald. She'd noticed that her mother's clients often found a direct unblinking stare very disconcerting.

Gerald looked back at her, eyes bright blue and tranquil.

"Do you love him?"

"Who?" Mae demanded, then closed her eyes and cursed herself as she realised that Gerald had of course been talking to Alan.

When she opened them, Gerald looked a little amused. Alan seemed not to have noticed.

"Alan," said Gerald, "do you love him?"

"It's none of your business," Alan replied. "But as a matter of fact, I do."

Gerald tilted his head, giving Alan what seemed to be a genuinely sympathetic look. "That must be terribly difficult."

"Don't you love your family?" Alan asked mildly.

Gerald actually flinched. "No, I don't," he said. "But that's not important."

"Oh," said Alan, soft, making it clear he knew he'd scored a point.

"What's important is your demon," Gerald told him, his eyes narrowing. "And what he'll do."

He clicked his fingers, and light came streaming in from unexpected places, under the back door when there was no daylight left outside, filtering like steam from the kettle.

"He never does anything like this," Gerald murmured, "does he? His magic's not for anything beautiful or kind. Do you know that storm he created in Durham killed two people?"

Alan was leaning against Mae's chair, because it always took him a moment to stand up, and with a magician in the room they might not have a moment. She felt the single tremor run all along his body.

"Alan didn't kill them," Mae snapped. "And how many innocent people have you killed?"

Gerald nodded and smiled in her direction. Magic light touched his face softly, the rays gentle and playful as if they were the fingers of someone who loved him.

"People die so I can have my magic. People die so you can have your brother," Gerald said. "We're the same, Alan Ryves."

"Are we?" Alan murmured.

When the light glanced off Gerald's eyes, they turned a brilliant, dazzling blue. "I think so," he murmured back. "We're both willing to sell our souls for a price. And neither of us is stupid."

"Who would you consider stupid?" Alan asked.

Gerald answered, "Arthur." His mouth twisted. "My former ever-so-fearless leader. The one who put a demon in a child and then managed to lose it. He was stupid enough to unleash a demon on this world and never care about the consequences, but you're not. Don't tell me you haven't had doubts."

"Don't waste your time telling me how I feel," said Alan. "Get to the point."

"I am not Black Arthur. I'm the one who has to deal with the mess he made. And I need you to help me."

"To deal with Nick?" Mae demanded.

"I told you I'm not stupid," Gerald said. "I can see Nick is trying. He owes you, doesn't he? I can see he's well-disposed towards you, and you." He glanced at Mae. "And Jamie," he said, his voice changing a little on the name. "That doesn't change the fact that he calls down storms whenever he gets angry, and the death of half a world would not disturb him. How can you justify setting him free?"

"I can't justify it," Alan answered.

Gerald smiled. "You did it because you loved him, and you wanted to save him from Arthur. I can understand that. He couldn't, though. If you told him how you felt, he wouldn't even know what you meant. He's not human."

"I know that," Alan said between his teeth.

"He's a danger to all of us."

"I know that."

"He killed a couple of people by mistake. It's only a matter of time before something worse happens, and it will be your fault."

"I know that!" Alan shouted at him.

Gerald leaned back, loose and easy, still smiling.

"Then please," he said, "let me help. I have a plan to save us all. Including Nick."

Alan moved then, his warm weight against Mae's side gone. He took the chair in between Mae and Gerald, his shoulder blocking Mae's view of half of Gerald's face. She could make out only one eye and the end of a smile.

"I'm listening," said Alan.

"I could do it," Gerald said. "I could call up another demon and bind Nick's powers. I could make him as human as he can be, and you can keep your brother. Only he'd never agree to having his power stolen from him, would he? So I need your help. He'll trust you. I need you to lead him somewhere deserted and trap him in a summoning circle for me."

"Oh, you need Alan to betray Nick and then you'll steal Nick's powers and kill them both," said Mae. "Great idea. Hey, can I come? I'll bring a picnic lunch if you promise not to let blood get on the sandwiches."

"She makes a good point," Alan observed, speaking more slowly than Mae would've liked. "How could I trust you?"

"How could I trust you?" Gerald asked. "You can get your demon to kill me anytime you want. I'm trusting you because we both have a lot to gain by making this bargain."

"I'd have a lot to lose, as well."

"Would you?" asked Gerald. "Nothing that you won't lose anyway, if you fail to keep the demon in check. Which you know you will."

He leaned forward a little so he was totally obscured from Mae's view.

"I know what you're afraid of, Alan," Gerald told him quietly.

"But how many people have to die before you risk him hating you?"

Mae made up her mind and got to her feet.

"All right," she said. "You can leave now."

She could see Gerald's face clearly now, lifted to hers and vaguely startled. She reached out, grabbed his hand, and hauled him to his feet. When his fingers curled automatically around hers, all the magic lights went out.

"I'd say you outstayed your welcome, but you never actually got a welcome, did you?"

She used her grip on Gerald's hand to tow him away from the table. She felt perfectly prepared to get behind him and shove his horrible magic self every step of the way to the front door, but then Gerald decided it was too much trouble or that he'd said all he wanted to say. He pulled his hand away and made for the door.

He stopped on the threshold and said, "Alan."

Alan was still sitting down in the middle of that shadowy kitchen, head bowed over the table. "Mae's right. You should go."

There was a pause. Mae looked defiantly at Gerald, Alan looked away, and Gerald looked like he was trying to find a way to make the winning move.

"In two worlds, he is the most dangerous thing alive," Gerald said at last. "And you made him. I'll be in touch."

The kitchen door swung closed, and a moment later Mae heard the sound of the front door closing too, imagined a brief flare of magical light as Gerald went humming down the road, congratulating himself on a job well done, and left them here in the dark.

"Alan," said Mae, kneeling on the floor by his chair and thus getting a look at his shadowed face. "Don't listen to him. He's lying to you."

"He's not lying," Alan said. "Nick killed those people."

"Sorry," said Nick from the door, his voice toneless. "Am I interrupting something?"

He flipped the switch, and the kitchen filled with ordinary, non-magical light. Mae thought of Gerald saying that Nick would never think to use his magic for something beautiful or kind, and then reminded herself fiercely that Gerald was an idiot. Nick would think using his magic that way was crazy, and he'd be right. There was a perfectly good light switch.

Nick leaned against the door frame, arms folded.

"Heard the magician leave," he observed. "He had me down in five minutes. He shouldn't have been able to do that. He had ten times more power today than he did outside the graveyard."

Alan leaned back in his chair. His expression was suddenly thoughtful, now that Nick could see it: Nick hadn't seen what he'd looked like before, hunched over in the dark.

"Looks like Gerald really has invented a different kind of mark," he said. "I wonder how much stronger he is now."

"I wonder how we're going to deal with it," Nick said sharply.

"I don't know yet," said Alan. "But I will."

Nick nodded, seeming to accept that this was settled and Alan would be learning all the secrets of the murderous magicians' Circle anytime now. Mae steeled herself for the inevitable questions about what Gerald had wanted, and what Alan had said to him in return, and why that had left Alan and Mae talking about murder in the dark.

Nick said, "You're going to be late for the Goblin Market."

"He's right, we should really go," said Alan.

Mae had wanted to do her hair, put on some kind of outfit,

worry about what she looked like, as if the Goblin Market was some weird mix of a job interview and a boy she liked. Now there was no time and she didn't care. She didn't care about magicians and the bargains they offered, either. For a shining second all she could see were lanterns strung from bough to bough and magic for sale.

"I'm going to work," said Nick. "Got the evening shift."

He turned away, and Alan turned in his chair towards him in a sudden, violent movement. "Nick."

Nick glanced over his shoulder.

"In two worlds," said Alan quietly, "there is nothing I love half as much as you."

There was an expression on Nick's face now. He went still, his fingers white around the edge of the door.

He didn't look at Alan, who was leaning back in his chair, watching him. He held the door, as if he would bolt if he wasn't hanging on to something, and stared at the floor.

Gerald's voice echoed in Mae's ears as if he was still there. If you told him how you felt, he wouldn't even know what you meant.

Every line of Nick's body was tense with the desire to leave, and for a moment Mae was sure he would, that he'd just turn without a word and go.

"Sometimes," Nick said, still looking at the floor, his voice rough and shocking in the silence. "Sometimes I want to be human for you."

"But usually not," said Alan. It wasn't even a question.

"No," Nick said. "Usually not."

He turned away, closing the door behind him.

9

Come Buy

MAE HADN'T REALLY THOUGHT ABOUT THE FACT THAT THE Goblin Market was held in a different place every month. It made sense to her that a secret gathering would be held in a different place every month, but still the image of people dancing in a wood filled with fairy lights had stayed with her. She'd thought it would be more or less the same.

On the hour-long drive to Cornwall, Alan explained that they were holding this Goblin Market on the sea-bound cliffs of Tintagel Castle.

"Is this a castle like Cranmore Castle was a castle?" Mae asked, referring to the green hill, once a fort and nothing like a castle, that had been near the woods of the last Market.

"No – it's a castle like a proper castle," Alan said. "Mostly."

"Oh, mostly?"

"Well, a lot of the castle has fallen into the sea," said Alan. "But it's very impressive apart from that."

Mae laughed, and Alan laughed with her, teeth flashing white in the dark. He looked happy, recovered from the emotion that had made his face drawn and desperate in the shadowed kitchen. It didn't take much to make Alan happy; he was used to living on crumbs.

It made her feel terribly sorry for him, but she couldn't really understand it. She was pretty comfortable with wanting a lot from life.

"So if a storm comes, we could all be blown out to sea with what's left of the castle," she said lightly, and then stopped and cursed her own stupidity as they both thought of storms.

"It's the first weekend in June," Alan said after a moment, his smile dimmed but his voice still trying to be light. "I don't expect storms."

Mae looked away from the loss of Alan's smile to the open night road, the tarmac briefly white in the car's headlights and then fading to black in the side mirrors.

"Gerald said there was a storm in Durham," she said. "Wasn't that where – where your family lived?"

Alan's family: his aunt – the sister of Alan's long-dead mother – and her children. The aunt Alan had written to in secret. The family Nick had not known existed, because he'd thought Olivia was Alan's mother, because he'd thought that he and Alan were really brothers.

He had taken the revelation that they were not actually related extremely badly.

"Yeah," Alan said, rough and short as his brother for once.

"And the storm that was going on in the background when I called you," said Mae carefully. "That was due to—"

"It was my fault."

When she glanced at Alan, she saw his jaw was tight.

"I shouldn't have gone there."

He looked over at Mae suddenly, just a glance, soft and

gentle as if he'd reached out and touched her, or as if he wanted to.

"We should have come back to Exeter with you guys."

"I'm glad you're here now," said Mae, which was true. "So this place is meant to be where King Arthur was conceived," she said to change the subject, since if she knew anything about Alan, she knew it would make him happy to go on about history and legends. "That's really nobody's business but the queen's."

"Think the king might've been slightly interested as well," said Alan. Mae made a dismissive gesture, and Alan laughed.

"Also, there's the problem that probably none of it happened. At least, not here."

"Well, maybe and maybe not," said Alan, and looked immediately enthusiastic. "During excavations in 1998 a stone was discovered on site with the word 'Artognou' on it, which could mean 'descendant of Arthur'. It's interesting how people want to believe; words have so many different meanings."

"It'd be more interesting if it was one of the druidesses," Mae said.

Alan had read Malory, and Mae had read Marion Zimmer Bradley. They were able to talk about King Arthur until they turned right for Boscastle and Alan paused in his mini-lecture on seventh-century Britain to check the signpost. When he chose what Mae hoped was the right narrow country road lost in pitch blackness, she clenched her fists and tried to be patient as Alan parked his car somewhere high up in the hills that definitely wasn't a car park. She climbed out and they walked together, crossing a bridge to Tintagel Island and going farther uphill with every step, until they came to an open gate.

"This gate's meant to be locked, isn't it?"

"Sure," Alan said, with an unexpectedly wicked smile. "Meant to be."

He gestured in a courtly manner, and Mae rolled her eyes at him and went through the gate first.

Then she gazed up at the mountain beyond the gates, slate balanced in a haphazard, tilting pile as if a giant child had stacked stones into something that was meant to be a tower. Except it wasn't a tower; it was just a towering heap. One that they would have to climb.

Mae looked up and up at the jagged grey crest of the mountain, like a black crown inscribed on the twilight sky.

She opened her mouth to say she wasn't really very athletic, but then remembered Alan's lame leg and shut it. She began to climb the wooden steps that wound up to the cliffs.

She'd danced at clubs and raves until five in the morning, even if she did walk through relay races in PE. She should have been able to climb steps. Only dancing was euphoric, made her feel dizzy and delighted, keenly conscious of where to put her feet but not truly aware of their weight.

Her feet felt like dumb-bells she was lifting with every step now, and there were hot lancing pains in the backs of her thighs. Behind her she could hear Alan. He was not panting as much as she was, but every second step he drew in a tightly controlled breath, snatching back a moan just before it escaped into the air.

Alan didn't like being asked if he was all right.

"I've been giving some thought to the importance of Arthurian legends and historical sites," Mae announced to the night wind. "And I've come to the conclusion: sod them."

Alan laughed a little, shaky and hurting. Mae was very sure

that he hadn't told Nick they were holding the Goblin Market on top of a mountain this month.

They were only halfway up the mountain. She should really suggest to Alan that they turn back and go home, that this wasn't worth it. Only Alan wouldn't go, and besides that . . . guiltily, horribly, in spite of the fact that Alan was in pain every step, Mae wanted to go to the Market more than anything.

They followed the steps in a steep curve around the mountain, dirt on worn wood crunching under Mae's shoes, the wind turning her hair into whips that cut across her face.

She was just staring at her feet, dragging up one after another, when she came to a door in the dark.

It was curved like a chapel door, but the wood in front of her was rough and unpolished, ghost grey in the moonlight. She put her hand to it, and it felt cool and smooth as pearl, worn down by years of sea breezes.

The door swung open and revealed a fairy-tale castle.

It looked like someone had been planting stars. The castle was in shreds, flagstone floors tiny islands in a sea of stones and wild grass, but clusters of lights were nestled on the castle floor and the earth of the cliffs alike, lanterns strung from the crumbling battlements.

There were so many lights they cast a shimmering haze over everything, bathing the ruins in a pale glow. Mae walked, hardly aware that she was walking, through Tintagel Castle over stones washed in brightness.

There were stalls nestled around the castle the way the lights were, not in rows but in odd spots, as if the stalls had grown there or alighted on random places like birds. There was one stall with ringing chimes that was set halfway up a ruined wall, so the customers had to climb sliding pieces of slate to get to it. There were more stalls set in the grassy hollows among the stones and nestled into the corners of the walls. One woman had actually turned a ruined wall into her stall, brightly coloured jars arranged on the jagged, protruding shards of stone.

All through the fragments of a lost castle lit by magic moved the people of the Goblin Market. There was a man hanging up knives alongside wind chimes, which made dangerous and beautiful music as they rang together in the sea breeze. There was a boy who looked about twelve stirring something in a cauldron with a rich-smelling cloud hanging over it, and bark cups ranged along his stall.

There was a toddler who had just walked into Mae's knee.

"Whoa," said Mae, who had nothing against toddlers but didn't know any personally and wasn't that interested in the whole sticky children business.

The toddler, who had golden curls and wide blue eyes and looked like he had recently been eating grass, charged into her knee again, as if sheer willpower could remove this obstacle from his path. He looked mildly bewildered when he bounced off.

"That's Toby," said Alan's voice behind her, making her jump. She'd almost forgotten he was there. "He's the baby of the Davies family. And he's a pest."

Alan supported this statement by saying every word in a delighted, caressing voice that made even Mae turn to him and Toby laugh. He wasn't looking at Mae but at the child, a smile making his narrow face shine like the ruined castle.

"He's always escaping from his crib and making his sister worry herself sick. Aren't you, you little fiend?"

Toby beamed with the wide, somewhat crazy grin kids get, and lifted his arms to be picked up. Alan did so at once, the baby cradled carefully in the crook of one elbow, his head bowed down over the smaller head.

"You really like children, huh," Mae said, mystified but charmed as well. There was no denying that Alan with a kid was about as adorable as a basket of kittens wearing tiny kitten bonnets, and it also meant that she wasn't going to have to mind Toby.

It occurred to her that this might be why women went for men who were good with kids: it meant they wouldn't have to be.

"Hmm? Oh, they're all right," said Alan, obviously besotted.

The baby squirmed, and Alan knelt with some difficulty so he could let him down and still keep him safe in the circle of one arm. Toby made a grab for something shining up Alan's sleeve: Alan produced the knife for him and flipped it, making sure the hilt caught the fairy lights and keeping the blade always trapped between his deft fingers, away from the child's small reaching hands.

"There, Toby," he said. He flipped the knife again and smiled, and Toby laughed, either for the knife or the smile. "I remember Nick at this age," Alan continued, his voice gentle as his free hand stroked the child's hair.

Mae looked down at Toby's small, bright face. The lights of the Goblin Market danced in his fuzzy curls and seemed to create light, gold irradiating his hair like a hazy halo. It was hard to think of Nick as anything like this.

"Was he cute?" she asked doubtfully.

She thought Alan might be offended, but he laughed. "No, I suppose he wasn't. But he was mine."

Toby made a spirited lunge for the knife, and Alan blocked him.

"No, I won't let you hurt yourself," he informed him, pocketing the knife and turning the child around in his arms so they were facing each other. Toby regarded him solemnly for a moment, and then reached up to curl a fat fist around one of the lenses of Alan's glasses. "Speaking of belonging to people, I suppose I should return you to the people you belong to. That'll be fun."

He gathered the child back up and rose as he did so, using a ruined wall to help him stand. His eyes travelled to Mae.

"Do you want to go see the dancing?" he asked, with a small smile, a little wicked, that was for her and not the child. "I'll catch up."

"Well," said Mae, because it seemed tactless to say that she wanted to run to wherever the dancing was more than anything in the world.

Alan's wicked smile became a wicked mind-reading smile. "Have fun," he told her, and limped away with Toby in his arms still negotiating over the possession of his glasses. Mae smiled after his retreating back.

Then she turned and walked through the beautiful ruins, reaching a part of the castle that was paved over for tourists, stone smooth and modern as a brick road. Even that was iced over by the goblin lanterns. Light turned a brick road into something like a path cast by the moon, leading the way to magic.

She knew which way she was going. She could hear the singing over the sound of the sea.

Mae followed the music and reached a place where the ruins were cut almost in two by a crevasse with a river rushing through it to crash into the sea and foam against the rocks below.

Across the crevasse was a bridge made of ropes, spangled with lights and tied to the crumbling ruins at either end. It looked like glittering gossamer. It looked like it could snap at any moment.

There were four couples dancing on the bright threads suspended over the rocks.

Mae saw the girl right away.

She was unmistakably the leader again, with a red crown of flowers in her hair. She'd been like a vivid forest creature in the woods, and now she was like something born from the sea foam.

She was wearing white that reflected the moonlight, material that the night wind sent clinging and fluttering down her body, so thin you could almost see her skin dark and soft beneath it. Her hair was threaded with silver ribbons, and her skirt was slashed into silver ribbons as well, trailing over and wrapping around her legs as she danced. Her feet landed light as air, perfectly balanced in the strange web above the waters.

The ropes trembled whenever a foot touched them, shivering over the abyss. The boys were all in black, shadows following the brightly coloured girls, none of them as arresting as Nick had been when he danced. The girls in red and yellow and blue looked like shadows as well, next to the girl in white.

Lanterns were swaying over Mae's head. She looked up and saw the thin, steely flash of the wire supporting them, and then down, all the way down the cliffs that the light laid bare. They were jagged and cruel-looking, stone sharp as knives and going on for miles, and Mae's stomach sank even as a thrill chased up her spine.

By lantern light the sea below looked a strange, clear turquoise. Mae wondered if that was more magic.

There were people singing on the other side of the abyss, their voices high and rising as the girl in white was thrown up easily as a white flower into the night sky and came tumbling down like an acrobat, feet curving onto the exact same strand of rope she'd been standing on before.

The audience murmured, voices warm as the sound of the waves was cold. The girl paused, hanging there, being still in beauty as much a part of the dance as hurtling through the air. Her dark hair streamed out with her silver ribbons, like a flag of shadows and light.

Then she lowered the arms held in a triumphal arch over her head and dismissed her audience by simply turning away, walking along a tightrope more lightly than Mae could have walked along a street. She leaped from the rope to the edge of the cliff and stood facing Mae, her dark eyes suddenly wide.

"Oh," said Sin of the Market, red lips curving back from her white teeth. "It's you."

Her look and smile were brilliant: Mae glanced backwards to see who they were for and saw nothing but ruins and the sea by night.

"Yes," she responded, disbelieving, a little breathless. "It's me."

Sin's attention was like a spotlight. She smiled, and the whole world became brighter and more intense, seemed to hold the possibility of becoming another world entirely.

She said, "I was hoping you would come back."

10

Sin on the Market

THEY STOOD AT THE EDGE OF THE CLIFF LOOKING AT EACH OTHER for some time. Mae still could not quite manage to believe the surprised pleasure in Sin's eyes.

"I liked your style," Sin told her. "Most of the tourist girls don't think much of dancers, and as for dancing themselves . . ." She snorted, scarlet mouth curling scornfully.

"I can't dance like you," said Mae, feeling shy for the first time in her life, like a new girl in school humbly lingering at the fringes of a group and wishing desperately to belong.

"You can be taught," Sin said confidently. With an arch look back over her shoulder at the assembled watchers, she pushed back her hair and ribbons, letting them spill into the wind. "I'm a good teacher," she continued, the practical words sounding strange and incongruous in her husky voice. "Are you dancing tonight?"

"I wasn't planning on it," Mae said slowly, and then she smiled at Sin. "But maybe I will."

"I would suggest you decide quickly," said a voice behind

Mae, and she turned around so fast she almost toppled off the cliff.

There, where she would have sworn nobody had been an instant before, was Merris Cromwell, her black dress flaring like raven's wings as she walked towards them. The leader of the Goblin Market stood with fairy lights playing on her talisman brooch and on the white streaks in her black hair, making them glint like Sin's silver ribbons.

Her dramatic appearance was a little spoiled by her voice, which was slightly rasping and distinctly sour.

"I remember you," she told Mae.

Mae swallowed, keenly aware of the last time she'd seen Merris, at the House of Mezentius, which Merris wanted to keep secret from the Goblin Market people at all costs.

Mae smiled a small, careful smile. "It's nice of you to remember," she said. "We only met once, but I was really grateful that you let me dance. I was hoping I could do it again."

Merris tilted her head, regarding Mae with what seemed to be a fraction less distaste and more interest. Mae's message was obviously received loud and clear.

"I suppose it would do no harm," she conceded eventually. "You do seem to have the right attitude. Who will you be dancing with, child?"

"Me," said Sin, the single word warm and certain.

Mae looked into her laughing eyes.

"Um," she said. "I thought that it had to be a girl and a guy."

"Not necessarily," Sin told her, that husky voice seeming about to tip into a laugh at every word. "It usually works best that way, but I think we could manage to tempt a demon or two together. Don't you?"

The whole Market was humming and shining with magic,

its leader had welcomed her, and now Sin of the Market reached out and offered Mae both her hands.

Mae let herself relax at last, almost at home amid all the wonder. She took up Sin's challenge and touched the tips of the other girl's fingers, which were outlined by fairy lights.

"I'm not totally convinced," she said, grinning at Sin's startled look. "But I'm willing to give it a try. Let's see what you've got."

Sin threw back her head and laughed. She seemed more real suddenly; less like an ideal and more like someone Mae wanted as a friend.

"Try to keep up with me, tourist," she said with the laugh still lingering in her voice. She swayed away from the cliff edge, already dancing, and called back over her shoulder, "If you can."

Mae followed her to a place in Tintagel where there was no stone and only a grassy dip in the ground, like a forest grove – if forests were made of ruins instead of trees. There were dancers in the clearing already cutting circles in the ground with ceremonial knives, drawing the lines of communication and intersection between the worlds.

Mae had always had a knack for graphs and maps. She remembered these symbols.

"Hey, Sin," she said.

Sin turned. "Yes?"

"Let me cut the circles."

Sin's eyebrows were the expressive kind, ones that could indicate surprise when the rest of her face was still. Just now the delicate black arches looked about to take flight off her face.

"Pretty confident, aren't we?"

"Usually," said Mae, and Sin reached around to the back of her dress and produced a long knife, which she tossed at Mae. Mae crushed down her instinct to duck away from the huge sharp thing hurtling towards her, and caught it easily enough by the handle.

She knelt down on the ground, the dew on the grass soaking the knees of her jeans, and her blade parted the earth easily, forming shapes and angles. It was like doing maths equations or reading music, foreign at first glance but making so much sense in the end, and beginning to come naturally.

Once she was done with her own circle of summoning she did Sin's, the second circle just touching hers.

Only then did she look up and see Sin's intent eyes as she returned to Mae, holding a bright, fire-like fruit.

"I'm impressed."

"Thanks," said Mae, and offered Sin her knife back.

Sin took it in one hand and then, fingers moving deftly, she cut the fever fruit in her other hand into gleaming, tempting slices. The golden juice spilled into her palm, then slid slowly down the inside of her wrist, shining in the faint fairy lights against the tracery of veins.

Mae remembered, with a sudden visceral pang of yearning, how the fruit had tasted. All other food had tasted like ashes in her mouth for days afterwards.

"It's all right," Sin whispered. She held the fruit up to Mae's lips and said, "Taste."

Mae leaned forward, mouth brushing Sin's fingers, and the fruit burst on her tongue, cool and sweet as a promise of love or adventure.

"And now you're feeling much better, am I right?" Sin asked, withdrawing with a wink and popping a piece of fruit into her own mouth.

"Can I have some more?" asked Mae, and was startled: that hoarse voice did not sound like hers.

"No," said Sin. "You ate too much last time. You were all messed up."

Mae remembered standing with Nick in the shadow of trees, her whole body straining into his.

Sin shook her head as if she could read minds. "Nick always needed more than the rest of us," she said softly. "Guess now we know why."

Because he wasn't human, and he had never cared about Mae.

Sin tucked her knife into the sheath that must have been hidden under the frail white dress, which looked as if it concealed nothing but Sin's body, and that not terribly well. She smiled as if the weight of a knife against her back pleased her.

"So let's see if you can really impress me," she said as the drums began. "Let's dance."

The music seemed to be coming out of nowhere until Mae saw the ruined wall. Drummers were hidden there like an orchestra concealed in a pit; other people were playing the guitar and the flute, all the instruments coming together in a strange blend of harmonies. There were three people in front, and they were all singing different songs. One was about Tintagel, and one about the Goblin Market – the chorus was "Come buy!" – and the last was singing a stream of nonsense words Mae didn't even understand.

"Taw, Cenio, Tamar," sang the woman's voice, climbing high, as Sin took Mae's hands in hers.

Mae expected them to be soft, but the long fingers were calloused and strong. She led Mae into the summoning circles, touching but separate, their hands joined over the place where their circles met.

Mae felt the difference as soon as she entered the circle; the ground beneath her feet changed somehow, as if the lines she had cut in the earth were charged with electricity and she had to balance along a humming live wire. The singing was louder now. Mae wasn't able to make out any of the words. It had all become a delirious rush of noise that mingled with the sound of the sea.

Sin winked at her again and let go of her hands.

"I call on the shadow in the forest who lures travellers to die far from home," she said, her voice chiming with all the other sounds, imploring and sweet, as if she was begging her lover back to bed. "I call on the dream that turns people from real love and warm skin. I call on she who drinks blood and rises from the ashes. I call on Liannan!"

As Sin spoke, she began to dance, and the lines within the circles began to move, blurring like the spokes on bicycle wheels, and Mae had to move with them. The blurred lines shone beneath her, and she felt as if she had gone dancing on the web of ropes after all, dancing balanced above a dark abyss, just a stumble away from cold, screaming destruction.

Hair lifting in the night wind, Mae grinned.

Sin was spinning in the corner of her eye, a blur of white silk and white fire, better than Mae could ever be, but that was all right. Nick had been better too. Seeing someone do something so well was not only beautiful to watch, it was exhilarating and inspiring. It was a challenge.

The lines between the demon world and the human spun so fast that they seemed to disappear, turned into a shimmering haze like a veil between the worlds. A veil that could be torn. The circle seemed almost to tip into the cold abyss below, like a trapdoor turning beneath Mae's feet. The singing sounded almost like a distress cry, tense hush had fallen on the audience, and Mae could hear her own and Sin's harsh breathing forming a rhythm together.

Mae put her hands up over her head the way Sin had on the cliff edge, added a hip sway just for fun, and danced.

The dance came to a natural conclusion, like a fight or a piece of music, the drums slowing as the pulses in her own body slowed. She stood panting and thinking that she'd loved doing it, that she loved the whole Market, and she knew no way to keep any of this.

She'd almost forgotten the reason for the entire dangerous and overwhelming dance when she saw the demon emerging from the point where their circles touched and blazed fire.

The demon woman rose wrapped in magic, like a dark goddess wrapped in a shimmering cloud.

Then magic slid away as if it was really a wrap, pooling and glowing around the demon's – Liannan's – feet. She looked like she was standing in a cloud bank.

Mae had never seen a demon who appeared as a woman before.

She didn't look much like the demon Mae and Nick had summoned last time. Mae had seen Anzu twice, and both times he had been a dark presence, golden beauty under a shadow of rage and wings and claws.

Liannan was soft and shining and lovely, her red hair drifting around her as if it was a second cloud, dyed fiery shades by a sunset nobody else could see. Her eyes gleamed, crystal-coloured but full of secrets, like glass balls waiting to tell Mae's fortune.

The talisman around Mae's neck hummed and stung like a bee trapped under her shirt. That was when Mae noticed that Liannan's skin was white not in the way human skin was white, but in the way paper or china was white, too smooth and too blank. The shine of her eyes and the crimson glow of her hair suddenly seemed like the bright flowers poisonous plants grew to lure their prey.

"It's the beautiful dancer again," said Liannan. "And you brought a little friend."

Mae felt disoriented for a moment after she spoke, and then realised why: Mae was used to hearing people use tones when they spoke, use real voices. But Liannan wasn't talking to Mae, not really. The magic was. The lines of communication in the circle were simply letting Mae know what the demon meant.

All demons were silent, except one.

"I'm not that little," Mae snapped, and then realised she possibly shouldn't be talking back to a demon.

Liannan's eyes swung to her. She smiled slightly, her mouth a vivid red slash in her white face, like blood on snow.

"If you're not happy with your body," she said, tracing the outline of Mae's shape in the night air, "I'll take it off your hands."

Her fingers made a sound like Nick's sword did when he swung it, and after an instant in which Mae could not quite process what she was seeing, she recognised why: Liannan's fingers were icicles, catching the fairy lights and reflecting them back in a dozen brilliant colours, sharp as blades.

"Think I'll hold on to it for a while," she said, a little breathless. Unexpectedly Liannan was reminding her not of Anzu but of Nick: holding his gaze sometimes felt like this, as if you could hold time while your heart ran a race. "Thanks."

Liannan smiled. "Pity."

She lowered her bright sharp hand to her side.

"Liannan," said Sin, her voice snapping the demon's head

around as if it was a whip around her neck, "I have some questions for you."

Mae was startled by the change in Sin's tone, and then she met Sin's dark eyes through the shining cloud of Liannan's hair. Sin's eyes bored into hers, her gaze heavy with a significant and deliberate weight, and then she gave a tiny shake to her head, and Mae understood.

Sin was deliberately distracting Liannan. She was protecting Mae.

It made Mae wonder how many of her dance partners Sin had seen taken by demons.

"Ask," Liannan commanded.

It dawned on Mae, with a dawning that felt more like an eclipse, something dark and terrible blotting out all she knew, that she was linked to Liannan by the lines of the summoning circle as if the lines were puppet strings.

She'd been aware of Anzu's rage, but that had been obvious as a battering ram or a storm, and directed at Nick. Liannan's thoughts were insidious, like a cold draught seeping in under the door of Mae's soul.

If Mae could analyse them the same way she could analyse problems, if she could work her out, perhaps she could work Nick out and help him to act human.

Liannan looked over her shoulder at Mae, eyes narrowed into chips of ice, and Mae knew suddenly that the demon could feel a little of what Mae was feeling. Liannan's glance was sharp and cold as a frost-bound twig raking Mae's face, searching, and the dark rush of Liannan's thoughts rolled through Mae's heart like alien and strange thunderclouds in a familiar sky.

The move forward of the petitioners outside the circle attracted the demon's attention as well as Mae's. It was a man and a woman, both looking terrified and somehow closed-off at the same time, as if they had shut down half their minds so they could cope with the spectacle of magic and demons.

"Jenny Taylor's daughter ran away from home three years ago. She wants to know if she is alive," Sin said. "Is she?"

"Your information is incorrect," Liannan answered.

For a moment Mae thought that was all she was going to say. Then Liannan's eyes slid from the woman's face to the man's.

"Your daughter never left you," she said. "Your husband buried her out under the apple trees you planted when she was born."

The woman's eyes met Liannan's then. She looked like a victim caught in a riptide, stunned and cold.

Liannan laughed. "Think it over," she said. "And when you decide you want revenge, call on my name. I'll creep inside him and make him so very, very sorry . . ."

The man by the woman's side turned and ran. The Market's knife seller leaped at him as he went by and brought him down in a wailing, struggling heap to the ground.

Merris Cromwell strode out of the night and drew that poor woman away. Mae squinted and tried to make out their dim grey shapes, fading into the night, and saw the woman's hands cupped over Merris's, and then Merris sliding her hand into her pocket.

She was paying Merris for that news, for her daughter under the apple trees.

Mae let one breath come out ragged and hurt, then turned her face away. This was a business.

Sin was looking at Liannan already.

"Enjoyed that?" she asked. The words had a bite to them.

Liannan swayed closer to Sin. "Oh, I did. And that's your

149

second question, Cynthia Davies, daughter of Stella. Hope you didn't have any more."

Sin's mouth went tight and straight, like a line drawn abruptly under a last sentence so more unwise words could not come spilling out.

"I didn't."

Liannan looked at her, demon's eyes lit in strange ways by the stars and the pale lights shimmering off the sea.

"Four thousand years ago there were girls dancing in Mohenjo-daro under torchlight, as beautiful as you are now," she whispered. "I remember Grecian girls who danced the Ierakio for their goddess at festivals, who moved just the way you move for me. I saw them fall. You'll fall too."

Sin raised an eyebrow. "Not today."

"Oh," said Liannan, "I can wait."

She turned whip-fast towards Mae, hair trailing her like a comet's tail as she moved and then settling, glorious, around her white shoulders.

"What about you?"

Mae folded her arms. "What about me?"

"You want something," Liannan said. "I can tell."

"I could use some information," Mae admitted slowly.

"Oh, you want so much more than that."

"Your prices are too high," said Mae. "You're like a loan shark. Only desperate people go to you for help. And I'm not desperate – I can help myself, given the right tools. I don't want anything but information from you."

Liannan tilted back her head and laughed so Mae could see her rows on rows of pointed teeth, small and white as sharpened pearls.

"You were born for the Market, weren't you?" she asked.

"The dance gets you two questions, and the beautiful dancer used them up. So tell me, haggler for the truth, what else do you have to give?"

"What else do you want?" Mae returned. "Besides the obvious."

Liannan tilted her head, considering.

"I want a kiss."

Mae blinked at her. "A – a kiss?"

Liannan stood watching her, silent, as if she felt an echo deserved no reply. She was still smiling a little, razor-sharp teeth indenting her lower lip. Mae was suddenly very aware of the demon's mouth, red and lush with the promise of ripe fruit. She thought again of poisonous plants.

"A kiss?" Sin echoed from behind Liannan, easy and beguiling. "I have a certain amount of expertise on the subject."

"No," Mae said quickly. She appreciated the gesture, but she didn't want to be rescued from anything she could handle herself. "You can have your kiss. I'll do it."

She reached out, her hand trembling, magic lights and darkness flickering around her fingers.

Liannan laughed, and Mae felt it like a knife running along her spine.

"I'll keep you both in mind for later. But I don't believe I mentioned who I wanted the kiss from."

"Ah," said Mae, feeling both saved and at the same time, terribly embarrassed. "Right."

Liannan turned away from them.

"I've always wanted to do this," she remarked. "Summon one of you. Make you see what it's like. I call on the one the Goblin Market calls a traitor. I call on the liar, the demon lover, the murderer. I call on Alan Ryves!"

Alan stepped out of the shadows of ruins and into the moonlight, limping across the night-grey grass to the circles where magic fires were blazing. There was a sudden hiss rising all around the Market, like a nest of snakes waking and uncoiling, ready to strike.

The demon smiled and beckoned Alan on.

"I do hope you won't think I was being too harsh," Liannan murmured.

"No," said Alan. "It was just the truth."

"It always is," Liannan told him. "And people always hate hearing it."

She was standing at the very edge of the place where the circles joined, magic glowing palely at her feet. Alan stopped about an inch away from her, still standing on shadowed grass.

"Come," Liannan coaxed. "This little girl promised me a kiss, and you know what happens to her if she can't keep her promise."

The threat was clear and the thought – possession – like a blow to the stomach, but even though Mae felt sick and winded, she didn't feel afraid. Alan wouldn't let it happen. Not in a thousand years.

She opened her mouth, trying to think of some way to phrase, Sorry, I know saucy demon action wasn't what you had in mind for tonight, but Alan looked at her and smiled with his ridiculous amount of charm.

"It's all right, Mae," he said. "It's all right, Liannan," he added in the same warm voice. "I don't mind."

"And what if the Market folk stone you to death?" Liannan asked. "Will you mind then?"

"I probably will mind that, yes," said Alan, as calm as she was.

Liannan shrugged, a loose, sinuous movement. "Men have

died for less than a kiss from me before now. What do you desire, Alan Ryves?"

They were watching each other. Mae was surprised at how disturbed she felt by the sight of them, both so clearly fascinated.

"Safe passage."

"Nobody's ever safe," Liannan said. "But you will come to no harm from me tonight. Now take it off."

Alan put one hand up to his shirt collar and flicked open a couple of buttons, then drew out his talisman, crystals catching magic light in a brief moment of beauty. He reached into the circle and placed his talisman in Mae's outstretched hand, the knotted leather the talisman hung from coiled neatly under it, Alan's only protection gone.

He closed her fingers over the talisman with his own. Its warning glow was hidden from sight.

Alan stepped into the demon's place where the circles overlapped and two worlds collided, where Liannan stood waiting for him.

He stood looking down at her. He wasn't trembling as Mae had been. He looked across his breakfast table at a demon every morning, Mae thought. It made a strange kind of sense that he wasn't afraid.

Liannan reached out and ran her icicle fingers down Alan's cheek, light but still drawing blood at the first touch. A bead of blood welled up and then ran down his face to follow her hand, tracing down Alan's throat to the exposed hollow where his talisman should have rested.

"I have a memory of you," Liannan said slowly.

"Yes?" Alan asked. "Well, have another."

Alan reached out and touched the demon creature, beautiful hands gentle on her jaw, tilting her head up a little. He kissed her,

153

light as a shiver in a sudden cold breeze, and then not so lightly.

Liannan's red hair curled around Alan's shoulders like bloody tendrils, seeking, trying to wrap around him and bring him closer even as she sighed and melted against the hard line of his body. The air was electric and crackling with magic, the whispers of the demon world too close. Alan curled his fingers around the demon's neck and pulled her closer.

Then he let her go. They stood in the electric air with eyes locked instead of mouths.

"What price would I have to pay," Liannan whispered, "for you to let me out?"

"If I loved you," Alan said, "I'd do it for free."

"And what does it take to make you love someone?"

Alan smiled then, a small, rueful smile. "I don't know," he said. "Nobody's ever tried."

Liannan's hunger reached out with cold tendrils and went all the way through Mae, as if the demon had touched her and pierced her skin, as if it was Mae's blood on the ice of Liannan's hands.

"So here's my question," Mae said in a calm, clear voice. "Gerald of the Obsidian Circle has invented a new mark for magicians. Tell me about it."

That didn't just get Liannan's attention. The crowd that had been staring, hostile, at Alan and the demon shifted suddenly. A ripple of unease went through them as they absorbed the words "Obsidian Circle", and remembered who the real enemies were.

That was just a bonus. What Mae really wanted she got as well. Liannan turned away from Alan and fixed her eyes on Mae.

"You want answers about the mark?"

"That's what I said."

Liannan smiled at Mae. It was the kind of smile that said, All the better to eat you with. "Then you'll find the answer on the body of a boy you know quite well."

Mae stared for a moment, outraged. "That's not an answer!"

"Oh, it's an answer," Liannan said. "And it's true. Nothing else is required. How useful the answer is to you is your problem. After all, what I took was not all that useful to me."

"I think I'm slightly insulted," said Alan, sounding amused.

Liannan laughed. "I was right about you," she said to Mae.

"What about me?"

Liannan reached out with both hands, as if she wanted to touch Mae's face, icicles coming right at Mae's eyes. She felt a rush of sheer horror – Liannan could stab them right out in less than a second, blotting out sight in pain and blood – and flinched back.

"I knew you couldn't be useful," the demon told her. "But I thought you might be entertaining."

She slid those ice-coloured eyes from Mae to Alan, and then surveyed the whole Goblin Market at her leisure, like an adult surveying children and their array of silly toys.

"We have no more need of your services, Liannan," said Sin. "And no need of the mischief you cause, ever."

The balefire Liannan was enveloped in started to shrink, magic diminishing at Sin's dismissal. Mae felt Liannan's hatred pressing down on her chest, heavy and deadly.

Liannan just smiled, beautiful and serene. She put her bloodstained icy knives to her mouth and blew Alan a kiss from their razor-sharp tips. Alan mimed catching it, mouth quirking, and he had to be aware of how this looked to the Market people. Liannan certainly was, going down in flames with that smile on her face.

The circles were dim and still. Alan's hair turned from gold to blood as the lights went out.

"Are you dancers or what?" Sin asked the bright girls and boys in black clustered around them. She clapped her hands and they ran to their own circles, and the tourists trailed after them, eager for a new show. A few other tourists wandered away to the stalls, and that meant a few Market people had to leave to serve their customers.

Mae let out a held breath in a deep and thankful sigh. She wanted to call it back when Sin followed up her words by coming at Alan like a bolt of lightning in her white dress.

"How dare you come here?"

"Cynthia," said Alan, his voice far sharper than when he was talking to demons, and Mae remembered what she'd somehow forgotten, since Alan seemed to get on so well with most people: that these two did not like each other.

"Traitor," Sin said distinctly, in such a white-hot rage that she had to enunciate every word, condemn him with all the clarity she possessed. "Never come back. You are not welcome."

She spat into his face. Alan just stood there, pale and still. Sin cast him one more burning look and then ran as if she could not bear to be close to Alan for a second longer. Mae started furiously after her.

Alan's hand flew out and grasped her wrist, his fingers clamping down hard.

"Don't, Mae," he said quietly. "Her mother was a dancer who slipped up and got possessed last year. She has every right to hate the demons. And me."

"Oh," said Mae.

"Oh," Alan echoed, sounding tired. He let go of her wrist. "You should go after her," he said. "She could probably use a friend. Don't worry about me. Sin's their future leader and she's banished me, so nobody else will try anything. I'll go and wait for you in the car."

Mae looked around at the Goblin Market people, who were still glancing at Alan with eyes glittering under the fairy lights. She stepped in close to him and felt shielded suddenly from wind she had barely noticed before; she always forgot unassuming Alan was so tall. She reached up and clasped her hands around his warm neck, tying together the two ends of the cord on which his talisman hung. She felt his breath stutter against her cheek as her fingers slid along the back of his neck.

She had honestly meant it to be a simple gesture of comfort.

"I'm on your side," she whispered, and drew back.

"I know," said Alan, and walked away so she wouldn't be leaving him in a crowd of enemies. She watched him go, disappearing in plain sight, not making for any ruins or shadows, just fading unobtrusively into the night as he walked with his head down.

She went to find Sin, following in the direction she'd run.

Five minutes later she was stumbling blind down a hill, convinced she'd got turned around at some point and was about to plunge off a cliff, when she lost her footing and fell into what seemed in the moonlight – which was not very much light at all – to be a grassy shelf in the hills where there were wagons.

Mae had never seen real wagons before, not wagons, with high wheels and wooden trim painted red. There was a painted sign on the front of one wagon, with chimes hanging in front of it in the shapes of ballerinas and knives and masks. Mae felt as if a wizened fortune-teller was about to pop her greying head out of the billowing red curtains and demand whether she wanted to dream of her true love tonight.

Sin's shining head emerged from the curtains instead, hair

free of her ribbons and tumbling dark against the vivid material.

"Mae," she said, and smiled. "Great. Come on in."

"I can't," Mae said. "I came here – I came here with Alan Ryves."

Sin's face, lit by sparkling eyes and cherry lips, seemed to shut down, tucking laughter and colour away. It made her look quite different.

"My brother had a third-tier demon's mark," Mae continued. "Alan took the mark to save him. My brother's alive because of Alan. If people are taking sides, I'm on Alan's side every time. I owe him that. So now ask me again to come in. Or don't."

Sin's brown hands grasped at the curtains.

"For your brother," she said eventually. "I can understand that." She grinned again, all bright resolve. "Come in."

Mae grinned back. "Okay."

Inside the Davieses' wagon was small as expected, and bright in the way Mae would have expected the place where Sin lived to be. She climbed in the door and imagined how someone taller would have banged their head doing it, thankful for once that she was ridiculously short. There wasn't much in the wagon: a tiny red-covered table with a crystal ball on it, a pile of schoolbooks, a fox's skull. Three beds took up most of the space, jammed up against each other but with an attempt made to distinguish them: one was a crib rather than a bed and had a blue blanket with teddy bears on it, one was red with black fans stitched on the coverlet, moving gently as if they were being plied by invisible ladies, and one was black with skulls and crossbones.

"My baby sister Lydie loves pirates," Sin said. "Don't ask me why. Bedtime stories are about walking the plank all the time. Toby gets nightmares."

Toby. *He's always escaping from his crib and making his sister worry herself sick.*

"I think I met your baby brother earlier tonight," said Mae.

There was a tightness suddenly to Sin's smooth brow. "Was he with Trish? She's meant to look after the kids on Market nights, but he's always getting away."

"Alan took him back to Trish," Mae told her, using Alan's name deliberately.

Sin made a face. "You're not going out with him, are you?" she asked, going over to the copper basin on her chest of drawers. There were rose petals floating in the water inside. "Because leaving aside the traitor issue, you could still do so much better."

Mae sat down on the bed with the red duvet and watched as Sin twisted her dark hair up in a knot and splashed her face with the rose-petal water.

"There's nothing wrong with Alan," Mae said to her back.

"Well," said Sin, laughing in a slightly brittle way as she reached for a towel, as if she was trying to make the whole conversation and her own heart lighter by sheer force of will. "He's not exactly the kind of guy who makes a girl's heart start racing. I'd be surprised if he could urge anyone's heart past a gentle jog."

She laughed again, and Mae reminded herself that Sin was walking a bright, fragile bridge over the cold horror of what had happened to her mother.

Sin glanced over her shoulder at Mae, and Mae blinked. Without her make-up, especially the vivid lipstick, Sin looked quite different. She was still beautiful if you looked at her properly, but it was suddenly possible to overlook her. Her whole demeanour had changed, as if the make-up was a mask that carried a role with it.

"Maybe Alan's a chameleon," said Mae. "Like you."

Sin's arched eyebrows arched further, like swallow's wings in a painting.

"Oh, you've noticed that, have you?"

"I'm quick like that."

"I can see," said Sin, and spun away from her dresser, ribbons flaring.

She grabbed at the red shawl covering the table and whipped it off with easy grace, the crystal ball on the table not even moving. She flourished the shawl, and it described a red arc and landed on her hair as she leaped onto the bed beside Mae.

"Tell your fortune?"

"You're a gypsy fortune-teller?" Mae asked.

"No," said Sin. "But my exotic beauty does make people think so." She smiled a flashing smile, strong brown legs hooked over Mae's jeaned lap, as if her beauty was a joke. "Because, you know, dark-skinned girl telling fortunes, what else could I be?"

Sin's mouth twisted, and Mae searched for something to say that definitely wouldn't be racist.

The way Sin's grin turned wicked indicated that she knew exactly what Mae was thinking.

"My dad's family was from the Caribbean originally. My mother was Welsh, and she told fortunes. So," Sin said, "let me read the secret of your heart's desire."

"No secret," said Mae, twitching the shawl aside so it fell. "I want . . ."

To be like you, she would have said before today, but now Sin was a person and not an ideal to aspire to. She had all these problems Mae did not know if she could have dealt with; she had a life that had shaped her into something very different from Mae.

She didn't want to be Sin, but there was still something about her that drew Mae close, something about the whole Goblin Market. She felt like a moth diving for a succession of jetting flames. She didn't think she'd be burned if she learned how to dance around them.

"I want to belong here," she said finally.

Sin unhooked her legs from over Mae's, leaping to her feet, and went over to her chest of drawers. She took the crown of red flowers she'd pulled from her hair and drew two blossoms from it.

"I thought you'd say that." She crossed the floor and looked down at Mae, dark eyes steady and serious for once. She took one of Mae's hands and laid the blossoms in it. "Cross your palm with scarlet," she said, and smiled. "I'll let you know where the next Market is being held. And if anyone questions you, show them these."

"Two flowers means an invitation?"

"Two flowers is an invitation to the Market. One flower's an invitation to something else." Sin smiled. "Three flowers, I tell people it means an invitation, and it means I want them killed on sight."

Mae nodded slowly. "Thanks."

Sin shrugged. "I love the Market. If you come ready to love the Market too, then I'm your friend."

"Then you're my friend," said Mae, and rose. "I have to go and meet Alan now. He's my friend too."

"Fine," Sin said. "I was going to shoo you out anyway. I have a guy coming over."

"Oh, really," said Mae, and it was suddenly like talking to Rachel and Erica at school, laughing over lunch about who fancied who. "Someone special?"

At least somebody was getting a little fun from the effects of the fever fruit.

Sin elbowed her. "Oh, he's something else. Come back to the Market next month, and I'll tell you all about it."

Mae backed away, already missing the Market. Alan was waiting, though.

She put her hand on the door and looked back at Sin, who was sitting on the bed doing her make-up fresh. The new lipstick she was applying, smoothly and expertly without a mirror, was a rich, dark red. This was red for something besides attracting a glance. This was a red to linger over.

"I can't wait to come back," Mae told her.

Sin smiled at her, slow and deliberate, becoming yet another person.

"I'll save you a dance."

The only way Mae knew back to the car was to go through the Goblin Market again. She had promised herself she would not delay, but it was hard walking through all the shadows and the spotlights, hard not to obey the cries of "Come buy!"

She did not stop at any stall. She might have looked around just a little.

There was a stall full of different-coloured and labelled lamps. One looked like an old-fashioned lantern, black iron bisecting the light into four steady beams, and had the words BEACON LAMP written on its label. Another was rose pink and tiny, like a rosebud that glowed; it was labelled LIGHT OF LOVE.

"Gives off just enough light to see love by," the stall owner called out to Mae. "If you can see love in this light, you know it's true!"

Mae laughed and walked on, promising herself she would

stop at that stall next time. She couldn't allow herself to stop now.

Then she stopped.

There in the busy throng of people buying and selling, dancing and laughing, she saw Sin's little brother Toby.

Gerald was here, in the very heart of the Market, holding the child in his arms.

She strode over to him, her heart pounding too hard in her chest. "Do you want me to tell everyone who you really are?" she demanded as she drew closer. "Then I could have the pleasure of watching you being torn limb from limb."

He whirled and started as he recognised her. He didn't draw back from her as she stepped in, though.

"You do seem to turn up a lot, don't you?" Gerald said.

"I could say the same about you."

They stood together in one of the spaces of shadow in the Market, just another young tourist couple. Gerald could freeze her right now, hold her trapped in the air like a dragonfly in amber, and maybe nobody would notice.

Mae reached out over the tiny distance that separated them.

"Give me that child," she said, and tried to make it sound commanding.

She snagged her fingers on the front of Toby's little shirt, curling around the material, and then slid an arm around the child, even though that meant having her arm trapped against Gerald's chest.

He did not let go of Toby. Mae looked down at his arm and saw a shadowy mark on the inside of his wrist, but before she could make out the mark Gerald smiled, and his sleeve slithered down past his wrist as if it was alive.

He spoke, and she felt the vibration of his low voice starting in his chest, then soft in her ear. "He was wandering around alone and I picked him up. I don't wish any harm on a child. And I don't wish any harm on you. You're Jamie's sister."

"How very reassuring," Mae bit out. "I know who the child belongs to. Give him to me."

"If I do," Gerald said, "you won't go making any rash announcements to the Market?"

"He is a baby!" Mae hissed. "Not a bargaining chip."

Gerald was silent. Mae looked away from his face, thoughtful and pitiless in the half-light, and into Toby's. Toby seemed happy enough caught between them, big eyes staring back at Mae, mouth forming a loose and wondering O.

"Okay," Gerald said finally, and pushed Toby into her arms.

He was unexpectedly heavy, and she had to shift him awkwardly around to get him at any sort of reasonable angle. Gerald backed away.

"I have somewhere to be, anyway," he said, uncomfortable as she'd never seen him before, as if displaying mercy was an unforgivable breach of good manners and all he could do was get away and pretend it had never happened.

Then he was gone. She was fairly sure he'd used magic to do it: nobody really disappeared like that, swallowed up by the air as if it was dark water.

Nobody else seemed to have noticed.

"Necklace, lovely lady?" asked an Asian guy with a grin like a skull and twinkling dark eyes. "Necklace for the pretty baby?"

He looped a necklace over Toby's head with swift, clever hands, clicking his fingers as he did so.

"Are those bones?"

"Finest bones, lady," said the man with a hint of reproach. "Rat for brains, bird for song, fox for cunning and – just between

164

you and me – a little human bone to bind the spell."

"You're just like a fairy godmother of death," Mae snapped. "Do you know where I can find Trish? She's meant to be looking after Toby."

"Oh," the man said, his face changing. "Sorry, lady, didn't know you were one of the Market people. I'm pied, you see."

"You're pie?"

He smiled. "Not Market, then. I'm a pied piper. We make the music for the Market, but we're not Market people ourselves: we use magic. I can start a tune and make children, animals, or pretty young things follow me anywhere."

Mae grabbed the two blossoms from her pocket and waved them under his nose. "That must be a useful skill. Where's Trish?"

The piper grinned. "Didn't mean anything by it," he said. "Honestly, you're not my type. And I haven't seen Trish."

Toby blew a bubble of saliva into Mae's ear. "Great."

The pied piper smiled mockingly at her pain and moved on.

Mae came to a decision. Sin was busy with a guy, but surely she could go and knock on the door and Sin could tell her what to do with the kid. Sin didn't seem the type to be easily embarrassed, and Alan had been waiting long enough.

She marched back in the direction from which she'd come, walking a good deal more carefully with Toby in her arms. Even so, she almost stumbled four times going downhill, and clutched at the baby too tight in panic. He made small crowing sounds whenever she did that. Either she was being mocked by a two-year-old or he was going to grow up to be a fan of danger sports.

Mae put one foot in front of the other, walking blind and burdened, and reached the shadowy gathering of wagons just in time to see Gerald knock on the door of Sin's red wagon and be let in.

11

Caveat Emptor

MAE BURST INTO A BREAKNECK RUN FOR THE WAGON EVEN AS the door swung shut, the curtain billowing gently in the night air.

She had a hand on the door and a warning on her lips before it occurred to her that they were two girls alone, and once Gerald's cover was blown he would have no reason to play nice.

And she was holding a baby. Sin wouldn't thank her for carrying her little brother directly into the line of fire.

Okay, Mae thought. Back to the Market, alert them all there's a magician in the wagon with the heir apparent, save Sin, and most important, get someone else to hold the baby.

Before she went, she wanted to check that Sin was all right.

She shifted Toby into the crook of her elbow and reached out with her free hand to twitch the curtain aside just a fraction.

There were lit candles floating in the bowl of rose petals and water.

Sin was standing by her bed, wrapped in red silk with black

flowers and thorns stencilled on it. The silk looked fragile enough to tear at a movement, and there was plenty of potential for movement in the curves beneath.

For now she was still, dark red lips curved and dark eyes thoughtful.

All Mae could see of Gerald was his back and a sliver of his face as he tilted his head to look at Sin. His eye was lit by a gold gleam from the candles. "You said you wanted to talk."

He took a step towards her, and she flowed towards him like a red silk river until she was pressed up against him, hand at the nape of his neck where his sandy hair curled. Gerald's hand hesitated, wavering in midair, and then settled on her hip.

Sin laughed, her eyelids lowered as if she was sleepy, as if she'd just risen from bed and wanted to crawl right back in.

"Sure," she murmured, throaty, and slid the red silk robe off both brown shoulders at once.

Then she grasped ivory handles and drew out long knives with the sleek sound of tearing silk. Before Gerald could take a step back, the blades were kissing behind his neck.

Sin said, "Let's talk."

Mae felt her lips curve into a grin. There was no need for a rescue mission after all. Apparently Sin had the situation under control.

That was when she felt the hand touch her shoulder.

She refused to let herself scream, clamping her jaw shut and whirling to face whatever was behind her. Her hand was suddenly cradling Toby's head, her first strange impulse to shield it.

Behind her was Merris Cromwell, standing over her looking surprised and displeased, as if she'd caught Mae trespassing in her garden.

"There's a magician in there," Mae said, low.

"Cynthia has already notified me and lured the magician away from the Market," Merris replied in her normal voice. "Why you feel torturing a magician might be appropriate entertainment for a toddler, I cannot imagine."

"I did not know—"

"Well, now you do," Merris said. "Could you perhaps remove the child from the vicinity before—"

The door to the wagon banged open, Gerald stumbling as Sin pushed him out and then followed close behind him, her knives at his back. She was striding easily until she saw Mae.

"What's Toby doing here?"

Gerald's eyes flashed to Mae's face and then to the child in her arms. He had obviously absorbed something from the sudden tightness of Sin's tone. He looked thoughtful.

"He was wandering," said Mae. "I thought I should bring him back to you. Sorry to interrupt."

"Yeah," Sin said, kicking Gerald in the back of his knees so they buckled and he went down hard onto them in the dirt. "It's a very special night."

"Sin," Gerald asked, "do you know who you are serving?" He jerked his head towards where Merris Cromwell stood with her face like a carving in stone. "Do you know who she is, the cold mistress of Mezentius House? Do you know what that means?"

Mae couldn't help but remember the scream of that woman in Merris's institute, being tortured by a demon that was living inside her husband and destroying him from the inside out. Merris made the relatives of the possessed people pay to have them restrained, and pay extra to stay with them and watch them die slowly.

Judging from what Mae had seen of Mezentius House, she made them pay a lot.

Sin grabbed a fistful of Gerald's sandy hair and held her long knives clasped in one fist, both blades sharp against Gerald's throat.

"I lived a month last summer in that house," she said, soft. "My mother died there. I know who I serve."

Gerald looked in Merris's direction, ignoring the knives that shifted dangerously as he moved.

"I'd like to offer you an opportunity," he said. "Send them all away, and we can talk. I have some things to say that you might find interesting."

"If he continues to talk like a door-to-door salesman," Merris said to Sin, "cut his throat."

Sin smiled. "With pleasure."

Merris's voice had been deep and measured, completely without emotion as far as Mae could see, but Sin's glance upwards was at once fond and pleased, as if she had just been praised by an adored teacher.

"You trust her," Gerald said. "That's nice. Be nicer if she trusted you, of course."

"Shut your mouth," Sin snapped.

Gerald did no such thing. "Did she tell you when the pain started, Sin?" he asked, voice soft and impossible to stop as the wind blowing in from the sea. "Did she tell you what the doctors said? Do you know how sick she is?"

It might not have worked, if Sin hadn't been looking at Merris.

Mae, watching Sin and Gerald, did not see Merris's face, but she saw the change that swept over Sin's.

Gerald struck.

He seized the moment of indecision and broke backwards, rising to his feet and into Sin's body. He knocked her off her feet and whirled on her, magic streaming from his palms in two bursts of light.

She made a small, choked sound and hit the ground hard.

"Well," said Gerald, wheeling on Merris, his hands still blazing with power. "I imagine you'll be willing to talk now."

Mae was holding Toby so hard he was whimpering softly in her ear. She looked desperately at Merris.

Merris was smiling.

Gerald collapsed on the ground with a knife in his back.

"You always say you want to talk," Alan said, walking out of the shadows of the hills with a new throwing knife already in hand. "And then you attack people. It doesn't make me feel very chatty."

From the night-dark grass, Gerald let out a low groan and then twisted, raising himself up on one hand. He pulled out the knife and let it drop, bloody, to the ground.

"I might point out that she was the one who pulled her weapons on me," he said.

Alan stopped by Sin where she lay in a tangle of torn silk gone grey in the moonlight, mouth pulled tight in agony but trying to sit up. He offered her his free hand; she glared up at him and shook her head. Alan shrugged and limped forward to Gerald.

"You invaded our Market for purposes of your own," Alan told Gerald. "You did not ask permission. You trespassed, and you thought you could do so without fear of retribution because you're stronger than we are."

"I am stronger than you are," said Gerald. "I took down your precious brother, didn't I? You have no idea what I can do to you."

He rose slowly to his feet, slivers of magic glinting through his fingers as if he was running gold coins through his hands and they were catching the light. There was a snick as Alan popped his left wrist sheath and suddenly had knives in both hands, and one of them lifted to Gerald's throat.

Gerald laughed. "And a knife won't stop me."

Mae didn't see Sin move. The first thing she saw was Sin standing pressed up against Gerald's back and lacing her knives with Alan's, until it looked like Gerald was wearing a sharp-edged and gleaming collar that caught moonlight and drove him to his knees, held him afraid to move.

The first thing she heard was Sin saying in Gerald's ear, "How many knives will? Because we have a selection."

Alan looked into Sin's eyes and gave a small nod.

"Deal with one of us and the other one cuts your throat," he said. He looked like a young priest, serious and well-meaning, and then he flicked his wrist casually and Gerald's head was pushed back against Sin's knives. "If you want to strike, be very sure you're fast enough. Or maybe you can tell us what the hell you meant about Merris."

"What have you done to her?" Sin demanded.

"I didn't do a thing," Gerald said. "It's just one of those things that happen . . . that come creeping into your body like an intruder, like a mindless demon. Bone cancer. Too advanced for any of your small magics. I guess you could try having Alan's demon cure it: his magic's about as subtle as a battering ram, and the disease is bound up with every bone, threaded throughout every part of her body. At least when he shattered her into a thousand pieces, it would be quick."

"No demon is going to lay a hand on her!"

"Then she'll die slowly," said Gerald. "You ready to lose her? Ready to lead the Market?"

171

When Sin spoke, it was not to Gerald.

"Is it true?"

"Yes," Merris said distantly.

Mae couldn't look at Merris. It was almost too much to look at Sin.

"Why," said Sin, and her voice trembled, "why did you not tell me?"

The knives in her hands trembled too, and Alan's voice lashed out in a command. "Hold fast!"

"Don't you dare give me orders, you filthy traitor," Sin snarled, her dark eyes narrowing. Her knives did not tremble again.

There was something rising in Gerald, like the wind rising as it came in from the sea and sent chills rushing down Mae's neck.

Toby began to cry, a long, thin, despairing sound. Mae rocked him and pleaded with him quietly, desperately afraid that he was going to distract Sin at exactly the wrong moment.

There were flashes of magic running through all of Gerald's skin now, not just his hands: like veins of gold in rock, like the sun's rays painted faint across the sky.

"Listen to me, Merris," said Gerald, turning his face to her as magic's shining fingers stroked up his jaw. "You don't have to die. I can save you."

"Can you?" asked Merris, her voice very calm. "And what would you want in return?"

There were sparks of golden magic bursting from Gerald's lips. The words kept spilling out too.

"A truce. The Market isn't getting anywhere fighting magicians. Don't pretend that the good fight is what you care about either. The Goblin Market is a business, and I have no quarrel with that. Stop selling talismans to tourists, stop taking off their marks, and I'll make it worth your while: there could be magic in your Market that you don't dream of now. All I want is to remove a nuisance from my life."

"And all I want is to remove some of your important appendages," Sin panted. "Is that wrong?"

She and Alan were both breathing hard, their knives taking on some of Gerald's luminescence and apparently trying to bend backwards in their hands. Gerald made a single gesture, palm up, and for a moment the very air around him was flooded with gold. The knives flew out of their hands. Sin and Alan were both knocked onto their backs.

The child in Mae's arms screamed. Merris Cromwell moved forward to meet Gerald.

"Think it over," Gerald told her, smiling. "You know where to find me."

Sin was on her feet already, dancer-swift. She paused as she passed Alan and then gave him her hand. He took it, gritted his teeth, and hauled himself up with her help. Mae saw his shoulders set and his refusal to flinch.

They fell on Gerald like wolves, bringing him down at Merris's feet. Gerald struck out with a fistful of magic, and Alan made a hoarse sound. Sin put a knee in Gerald's stomach and leaned down hard, her knife pointed at his throat. Her robe was red ribbons attached to her neck and wrist, streaming out like blood-coloured banners. Beneath was a white shift, streaked with blood and dirt, rising and falling fast as she panted out, "I'm tired of you," and brought the knife down for what Mae recognised as a killing blow.

Gerald threw magic at her chest, and Sin fell back with a scorched smell in the air. Mae started forward.

"Mae, no," Sin yelled. "Toby—"

Mae halted her charge and hung on to the howling child hard to stop herself from just putting him down and running in anyhow.

Gerald was on his feet again. So was Alan, a knife in hand and then in Gerald's shoulder.

"He's mine, Ryves," Sin grated, staggering up.

Alan's eyes narrowed. "I'm willing to share."

"I didn't want to have to do this," Gerald told them quietly.

The cold note in his voice had Mae turning from him even as he lifted his hand. She started running away with her back to him, shielding the baby.

Something hit Mae from behind. She went tumbling to the ground, trying to guard Toby, and found Sin on top of her with her hair come loose and streaming around Mae's face.

"Shh, sweetheart, my darling, it's okay," said Sin, and Toby unclenched his fat, clinging fists from Mae's shirt and turned between them, bawling and snotty, to grab at Sin. Sin detached herself from Mae, sitting on the ground with her arms around her brother.

Better her than me, Mae thought, and clambered to her feet to see what was happening.

Alan had another knife in hand, driving in towards Gerald's gut. Gerald sent a bolt of magic from his fingertips to Alan's bad leg, and Alan gave a low scream and hit the ground.

Sin swore, shoved Toby at Mae – oh, not again – and ran back to them. Mae followed her even as Toby's wailing started up again in her ear.

Merris Cromwell had a large ceremonial knife in her hand. Mae slackened her pace a fraction, relieved, and then saw Merris step back, lowering the knife.

Gerald said one last thing to Merris that Mae could not catch, and turned and ran.

Alan seized up one of his throwing knives from where it lay on the grass.

Merris shouted, "Don't kill him!"

Alan threw and missed. Gerald disappeared over the crest of the hill. Sin came flying back to where Alan stood, seized him by the arm, and shouted up into his face, "Why didn't you get him?"

"Merris said not to kill him," Alan snapped. "Throwing knives only have so much range, and guns don't work, so—"

"So why didn't you run after him?" Sin demanded, every inch the princess of the Goblin Market.

Alan's voice in response was a low snarl. "And how do you suggest I do that?"

Mae's step slowed. She didn't want to be there. She didn't want to see Alan's face as it looked right now, white and somehow wiped clean, caught in a moment of pure, furious despair.

"I—" Sin said, and stopped. She let her hand fall from Alan's arm.

"Don't worry, Cynthia," said Alan, looking down at her. "I take it as a compliment, really. It's the first time you've ever forgotten for a moment about my leg."

He didn't sound as if he was taking it as a compliment. He sounded tired and bitter.

Mae reached them, and she smiled at Alan a little desperately. He transferred his attention to her entirely, smiling back, and Sin turned away and snatched Toby out of Mae's arms as she went.

The absence of the baby was an enormous relief. Mae's face must have made that very clear, because Alan actually looked amused.

"Don't tell me," he said. "This is just how you pictured the night going."

With Gerald gone, the alliance against the magician was lost. Sin was at Merris's side, Toby cradled to her chest. Merris and Sin were staring at Alan, both of them dark and dignified for a moment, looking alike even though they looked nothing alike. In the space between them and Alan, the grass was stained with blood.

"There's nothing else I can do?" Alan asked.

Merris said, "You've done enough."

They drove back from Cornwall with the sun rising slowly in a cloud-pale dawn sky, the roads grey and empty before them. Mae was so tired she kept finding herself napping with her face against the window of the car door, and she had no idea how Alan was managing to drive.

In between the bursts of power napping, she tried to stay awake and keep Alan company. She was too tired to be at all tactful.

"So how come you and Sin hate each other?" she asked as Alan turned the car left at Alphington Junction.

Alan gave a soft, startled laugh, hands light on the wheel. He didn't look tired, but the lines at the corners of his eyes were deeper than they should have been. "We don't hate each other," he said. "We're just too different. If the Goblin Market was one of the American high schools you see in the movies, she'd be the head cheerleader and I'd be the captain of the chess club."

"Good at chess, are you?" Mae asked.

"Not bad," said Alan. "You play?"

"Oh, every now and then."

"We should have a game sometime," said Alan, his voice so

mild the dark thought occurred to Mae that sometime soon she might get beaten at chess, something that hadn't happened since she was eight years old.

"We should," she agreed. "Seemed a bit worse than the eternal rivalry of the chess club and the cheerleaders, though."

"Well," said Alan, "dancers don't like seeing people even stumble. I get it, I do: Stella – Sin's mother – I saw her fall. I've seen a lot of dancers fall. I know why Cynthia reacts the way she does to me. She can't help it. But I can't help it either. When a girl shudders every time I walk by, it doesn't make me particularly well disposed towards her." Alan shrugged, eyes still on the road. "Some people are just destined never to get on. I don't hate her. I just don't like her. It's not a big deal."

"I don't imagine Sin gets that a lot," Mae commented.

"What?"

"Boys not liking her," said Mae. "She's kind of amazing. And beautiful."

She spoke almost absently, forehead pressed against the glass as she tried hard not to sleep. There was morning mist obscuring the fields on either side of the road, so dense and white it looked like there were mutant sheep lurking on all sides.

It was possible she was overtired.

"You're just as beautiful as she is," said Alan. That was a flat-out lie, like so much of what Alan said. Like so much of what Alan said, it sounded true. "And you read," he added.

"Uh, hot," said Mae, feeling quite a bit more awake.

"Well," said Alan, faint colour in his cheeks, "I think so."

She wasn't the only one in the car feeling tense. There was a slight defensive posture to his shoulders now, as if admitting any sort of honest emotion, even something as simple as liking girls who read, was bound to get him hurt.

Mae remembered Nick, obviously desperate to leave the moment Alan told him how he felt. She could see how lying might make Alan feel more comfortable.

She made the decision to defuse this conversation, since they were stuck in the car together for the next three-quarters of an hour. She did not want to be forced to leap out into the morning and face the mutant sheep if things got awkward.

"I'd rather be amazing than beautiful."

"I think you are," Alan began, a warm flush spreading along the tops of his cheekbones, and Mae was struck and saddened all at once by how different he was now than he had been with Liannan.

She had to wonder whether it was just that he had a crush on her, or if he was simply more comfortable with demons.

"You wait," she told him. "You have no idea of how awesome I can be. Next time someone else is holding the baby."

Alan laughed. "You did look a little . . ." He waved one hand expressively above the steering wheel. "As if someone had given you a sack of potatoes that might explode."

"'What a way with words you have, Alan Ryves,' our heroine said with deep bitterness. You had the easy job: all you had to do was throw knives and menace a magician."

"I like to think of myself as throwing knives with deadly precision," Alan told her, a laugh still caught in his voice. "And I was hardly menacing him."

"C'mon, you and Sin totally had him for a minute there. Two minutes, even."

"I wish we had," Alan said, serious again. "He could have killed us both anytime he liked. He didn't. He wanted to say his piece, and he said it, and then he left. What we did was irrelevant. Well – we might have annoyed him a bit."

"I imagine so," Mae said dryly. "Since you stabbed him twice."

"Yeah," said Alan in a soft voice, eyes on the misty road ahead. "That made me think he may have come in good faith."

"So when he asked Merris to let him kill a lot of people, he really meant it?"

"Well, yes," Alan said calmly. "And when he asked me to help strip Nick's powers. He might mean to keep his end of the bargain."

Mae stared. "That's a pretty big chance to take!"

"I know."

There was no sound for a while but the car jolting along the road towards morning. There seemed to be very little Mae could say, aside from the one thing she was afraid to voice.

She wasn't a coward. She said it anyway.

"Alan. You're not actually considering it, are you?"

Alan said nothing. He said nothing for so long that Mae stopped waiting for him to speak.

She leaned her head back against the car window, vision blurring between the brightness lent to the world by fever fruit and her own exhaustion. There was a cold place somewhere under her ribs, but she told herself Alan was tired too. He didn't mean it.

Alan's voice was so low and measured, almost musical, that it was like a lullaby. Then what he was actually saying began to seep through the mist enveloping her mind.

"Even if it all worked out, if Nick obeys all the stupid human rules I want him to follow, someday I'll die. And he won't. He could keep the body alive forever or do without one. And he could get lonely and invite his demon friends in out of the cold. He could lose every word he ever learned. He's lived a thousand different lives and forgotten them. He could forget this one. There are so many ways for something to go wrong that in the end one of them will. A lot of people will die. And it will be my fault."

Mae was awake now. Chill morning air was filtering in from the outside even through the closed car window, slipping slivers of cold down her neck.

"I was the one who put my brother ahead of the whole world," Alan said softly. His voice was still beautiful, even though it was so bleak. "I had no right to make that decision. I wasn't acting in some sort of thoughtless desperation. I thought. I chose. Two innocent people are dead already, and I had absolutely no right!"

"You had your reasons."

Mae remembered the magicians of the Obsidian Circle and that terrible man, Arthur, gathered around the circle where Nick had stood trapped and snarling, like witches around a cauldron with a child in it. Someone Alan loved had been in danger. Mae had done something similar with the magician she'd killed for Jamie. She'd wanted to kill someone for him, she'd planned it, and she'd seized the chance when she had it, and then she had discovered she could not move on. Decisions like that cast long shadows; darkened your whole future, as far as you could see.

She knew how it lingered in memory, the blood on your hands.

"No reason could be good enough," said Alan, his voice breaking on the words.

They drove through the mist in silence.

When they pulled up outside Alan and Nick's house, Mae thought for a moment that somebody had left a light on.

Mae hadn't brought her house key, and Jamie was in no mood to let her in if she threw pebbles at his window. What Annabel would say if Mae rang the doorbell at half past five in the morning didn't bear thinking about, so Alan had volunteered his bed.

"I will be taking the sofa," Mae said mid-yawn. Alan reached over and undid her seat belt, and she batted at him feebly, yawning again. "I am prepared to fight you for it."

That was when Alan leaned forward, squinting through the windshield. Mae's eyes followed his line of vision, and they both noticed the light.

Nobody had accidentally left the lights on, Mae realised after a moment of staring. The lamp set in the window was shining with a peculiar brightness, sending out brilliant yellow rays like searchlights. Its glow was cut into four sections by black iron.

"That's a—" Alan began.

"Beacon lamp," Mae finished.

"Lights the path back you have to follow," Alan said, as if he was quoting. "Calls your wanderer home." He shook his head, mouth curving a little, and then swung out of the car, hand on the door helping him do it smoothly. "Nick had a few objections to me going to the Goblin Market," he said as he came around to her side.

Mae foiled his chivalrous intentions by opening her door herself and leaping out. Alan shrugged, smiled at her, and went to the door, sorting his keys and still talking, very casual, head bent over the keys as if he thought he could possibly hide how pleased he was.

"He shouldn't be wasting a beacon lamp like that, though," he said, opening the door to let her in. "I'll have a word with him about it. They're expensive. It was silly."

"Sure it was," said Mae, and Alan shot her a look over his glasses, warm and a little embarrassed.

The light from the beacon lamp was coming from the sitting room now, filtering through a door left ajar into the little hall. Alan pushed open the door gently, and once it was fully open Mae understood why.

Nick was asleep on the sofa, one elbow pillowing his head, long legs hooked over one of the sofa arms. That couldn't have been comfortable.

Alan limped into the room.

"Hey," he said quietly. "Hey, wake up. We're home."

Nick's eyes snapped open and he said, "I'm awake, I'm up," in a clear voice, then turned his face into his arm a little, eyelashes sweeping his cheeks and casting shadows on his pale face.

"No, you're not," Alan told his brother, voice pitched low and sweet with no intention of waking him. He reached out and brushed black locks carefully back from Nick's brow, a gesture Nick would in no way have allowed when awake.

Even in sleep it made Nick shift uneasily, the grey T-shirt twisted around his torso climbing, baring the sharp angle of his hips and the flat of his stomach where a black leather band was fastened, the hilt of a knife pressed against his skin.

"Does he, uh, generally sleep armed?" Mae asked, and then saw Nick stir and shut her mouth. She put a foot over the threshold, testing, and his head came up a little. She withdrew.

Alan glanced back at her. "We both do."

Mae didn't want to wake Nick, so she stayed quiet. Alan stood there looking down at Nick, fingers poised a fraction of an inch from his sleeping face.

Nick did not make any of the usual noises of someone

sleeping, no snores or sighs, not a murmur. He did not even sleep like a human being.

Alan made a small, worn sound that was not quite a sigh and limped away to put out the beacon lamp.

Mae went to the kitchen to get herself a glass of water. She hadn't realised how thirsty she was until she poured the water down her throat, feeling it splash cold and lovely onto her parched tongue. She leaned against the counter and hung on to her glass, fingers sliding in the condensation.

"Hey."

She twisted her head around to see Alan at the kitchen door. He still looked a little pleased about Nick's beacon lamp, faint warmth lingering in his eyes and his smile.

"Hey."

"So I don't mind taking Nick's bed," said Mae. "Then we can both get some sleep."

"Yeah, well, about that," Alan said, rubbing his eyes. "Sunday means time and a half, so I kind of have to be at work by seven. Nick's bed or my bed: ladies' choice. I'm going to make some coffee."

He went and turned on the kettle, getting down his cup and some instant coffee. Annabel had a coffee grinder at home that was the only thing in the kitchen she and Mae knew how to use. Annabel wouldn't allow instant coffee in the house.

"So," Mae said slowly as the kettle puffed hot bursts of mist at them, "you're going to do a day's work on no sleep, and Nick was worried that someone was going to hurt you. You had to climb up a stupid mountain with your bad leg. And you knew how the Goblin Market would react when they saw you. Why on earth did you want to go?"

Alan stirred his coffee and bit back a laugh.

"Isn't it obvious?" he asked. "I thought it would please you."

"Um," said Mae, turning her water glass around in her hands. "So you took me somewhere that you really didn't want to go and you knew you wouldn't enjoy, and you had a terrible time. You know, that's a lot of guys' definition of a date."

There was a window across from the sink and the countertops covered with a stick-on sheet that gave the glass a frosted look. The sticker was peeling away from one edge, but the dawn light still came through fuzzy, touching Alan's curly hair with blurry gold fingers.

A corner of Alan's mouth came up.

"My definition of a date includes the girl agreeing to go on one with me," he said. "Don't worry about it, Mae."

He moved past the counter, cup angled so there was no chance of spilling it on her, and Mae thought about Sin laughing and saying that Alan wasn't exactly the type to make a girl's heart start racing, about how pleased Alan had been by something as simple as a light in the window calling him home. He looked so tired, and the happiness was already slipping off his face as if it did not belong there.

"Aside from that small detail," Mae told him slowly, "I think it was a pretty good date. You definitely deserve a kiss on the doorstep. Or, you know. Wherever."

She said the words on an impulse born of fever fruit and sympathy, and then she was panicking. It wasn't that she had any objection to kissing Alan, but she wanted to be fair. She didn't know if this was fair.

She did know that she liked the way happiness flooded back into his face, eyes on hers suddenly, warm and private, as if he was about to lean over to her and whisper the best secret he knew in her ear.

"Just one," she told him. "There's that other guy. I said I'd give him a chance. But I'd like to – to see."

"I understand," Alan said, soft. He still looked so happy.

Mae put her glass down, though it seemed to want to cling to her suddenly sweaty hands. The kitchen was full of shadows, but Alan was close enough to see clearly. She tipped her face up to his.

He put his hands on either side of her, holding on to the counter and holding her bracketed between his arms, apparently so he could survey her at his leisure. He was all lit up.

"Ah," Mae said, hesitating. She reached out and curled her fingers around the blue shirt Alan had unbuttoned, knuckles resting against the warmth of the T-shirt and chest beneath, and smiled. "Are you waiting for anything in particular?"

"Oh," Alan said softly, in a response to her "Ah". He moved in a little closer to her, being surprisingly tall again. There was just a fraction of space between them now. "No," he continued, sliding off his glasses and pushing them away down the counter.

He looked different without them, younger, the slow flush rising in his cheeks very plain. He bent his head down, the warmth of his mouth and body touching hers even though he wasn't touching her, not quite.

He lifted a hand to her face, not even touching that, fingers playing about a centimetre from her jaw.

"I like to take my time," he murmured, words a whisper in the tiny space between them. "I want to get it just right."

Then he kissed her, slow and thorough, his mouth capturing hers and his body suddenly pressed all along hers, and she grasped at his shirt collar and a moment later his hair, fingers closing around the curls. His mouth moved against hers, soft and catching every broken breath she let out. She felt the shape of his small, warm smile pressed against hers, the edge of his teeth light on her lower lip, and his tongue sliding inside her mouth.

Mae found herself making a little choked sound and pulling his head down to hers, trying to bring him closer. Suddenly she was flat on her back on the kitchen counter, one leg wrapped around Alan's good leg, one of Alan's hands cradling the back of her head as he kept kissing her, exploratory, his lips lingering over hers even as his breath came harsh in her ears.

She was pulling his shirt off his shoulders when he drew back, mouth a bitten-red line and eyes bright, and pushed himself off from the counter to lean against the kitchen wall about a foot away.

"Just one, you said," he reminded her.

Mae sat up. "Um," she said, and laughed. "Wow."

Alan laughed with her, cheeks stained pink, and moved around her to snag his glasses and his cup of coffee. When he slid them back on he looked more like the usual Alan, even though his hair was still mussed and his mouth still red.

"Thanks. Well. Nerdy guys try harder, you see," he explained. "The other guys, they're so busy with sports and actually getting more girls, but nerdy guys have time to think about it."

"And to learn how to throw knives with deadly precision."

"And that, obviously," Alan said, nodding. He rubbed the back of his neck, glancing down to the floor and back up at her. "You should go and get some rest. I'm going to try and wake Nick with coffee, tell him about what happened with Gerald."

"Okay," said Mae.

She made no move to get off the kitchen counter while Alan went to the kitchen door, opened it, and then hesitated on the threshold. "Mae."

"Yes?"

He smiled at her, gradual and pleased. "You're pretty wow yourself."

He left, closing the door behind him. Mae took a minute to admire the kitchen ceiling and get her breath back before she went up to bed.

12

Lying with Demons

M AE WOKE TO THE SOUND OF STEEL ON STONE. SHE HIT THE bedclothes heaped over her head and sat up, fighting her way out of the sheets, to find Nick sitting at the window, sharpening his sword. He raised an eyebrow at her no doubt dishevelled appearance.

"Who's been sleeping in my bed?"

"I didn't know which bed belonged to who," Mae snapped. The sheets smelled of steel and cotton, but that hadn't told her much. They both smelled like that. She looked across the floor and saw her jeans, too far out of reach for her to scoop up and wriggle into. "Do you mind?" she asked. "I'm not wearing any trousers."

"No," Nick said thoughtfully. "I don't mind at all."

Mae rolled her eyes at him. "And what were you doing here, Nicholas? Decided to watch me sleep?"

"Yes," said Nick, and bowed his head over his sword again. He had tissues, oil, and sandpaper laid out on the windowsill in front of him, and a little stone block he was passing his sword up and down, very carefully. "I came to gaze on your sleeping face. Only you had the blanket over your head, so I just had to gaze at a lump I thought was your sleeping face, and that turned out to be your shoulder. Which just wasn't as special."

"Your life is hard."

Sunshine was pouring in through the window, turning his sword and his ring into brilliant lines of light. Mae wondered what time it was.

Nick threw the battered old copybook at her, barely pausing as he sharpened his sword, as if it was a throwaway gesture.

"I thought," he said. "Since you were here. That we could maybe have another lesson."

Mae clenched her fingers on the sheets and found herself looking at the book as if it was a snake. She turned away to the curve of Nick's back over his sword, and swallowed.

"Funny thing. I can't seem to teach anyone to be human while I'm not wearing any trousers."

"Is that so?"

Mae made a regal gesture, dismissing him from her presence. Nick threw his sword up into the air and then stood to catch it.

"Fine," he said. "I need to go and wet the sandpaper anyway."

Nick left the room and Mae lunged for her jeans, stepping into them and pulling them up over her underwear, which had polka dots. She did up the button of her jeans and felt a lot better.

Normally she wouldn't have been all that bothered, but today she felt the urge to be in full armour. She wasn't feeling entirely comfortable with herself.

She had kissed Alan. Alan had kissed her. She'd really liked it. She'd given Seb her word, and now she was leading Alan on.

That fever fruit stuff was lethal.

It would've been reassuring to be sure that she could attribute what she'd done entirely to the fever fruit, but she'd been able to handle it better this time. She hadn't been stumbling around trying to make out with Gerald – God forbid! – or anything. Maybe the fever fruit had made her a little more reckless, a little more inclined to give in to desires she already had.

She was in such a mess.

Mae put her face in her hands and then pulled herself together. So she was confused and conflicted and all kinds of embarrassed. She had a demon to teach.

And these were pretty basic human emotions.

"You decent?" Nick asked from behind the door.

"Yeah."

"Pity," he said, coming back inside with the wet piece of sandpaper, which he was smoothing gently up the blade of his sword. Mae had no idea why he was doing it, but he was absorbed enough that she wasn't sure he would have noticed any indecency right away.

He went for his bed, sitting on the end and resting his sword against one knee.

"Do you get embarrassed?"

"Do you mean am I worried about people seeing me with my jeans off?" Nick asked. "Sure. Sometimes people are overcome. They fall down. They hit their heads. It's worrying."

"I actually knew you were shameless already," Mae informed him. "I asked you about being embarrassed. Do you ever think about something you've done or said, and want to curl up and hide?"

Nick considered.

"No."

"Humans do," said Mae, sitting down on the bed herself. "You should try to avoid embarrassing us, or we might kick your ass."

Nick laughed. "That's a concern."

He lay back on the twisted sheets, one arm curled under his head, free hand resting against his chest.

"Hey," Mae said. "You should hold my hand."

She reached out and touched his hand, and he flinched violently away.

"Why?" he demanded. "You were in the car. I told Jamie—"

"You told him why demons don't touch humans," Mae said. "You want to act human, though. Humans touch other humans. Comfort, love, duty, or fear, we do it for a thousand different reasons. If you give a damn about a human, if you want to even pretend to give a damn, then sometimes you have to touch them."

Nick rolled like a cat and suddenly Mae was flat on her back against the pillows, with his face an inch away and his hands pinning her down.

"What difference does it make?" he said into her ear. "I've touched you before."

Mae punched his chest and turned her face away, trying not to register that the corner of his mouth brushed hers as she did so.

"You touched me for a reason," she said in a strained voice, concentrating on the wall and not Nick's warmth and weight. "Sometimes you have to touch someone for no good reason except to let them know you're there."

The weight and warmth was gone suddenly, and Mae lay on the bed unmoving for a moment before she sat up and saw

Nick lying where he'd been before. He was glaring up at the ceiling.

"I don't like it," he said through his teeth. "It doesn't feel natural. I touch people to hurt them. I don't want to – and I don't want to get—"

"Aw, Nick," Mae said. "I promise not to hurt you. Since you're so delicate."

Nick slanted an amused glance at her. "Stop harassing me to get in on my hand-holding action. I feel pressured. And used."

Mae huffed a little laugh, but her heart wasn't really in it. She looked around at the bedroom – at Alan's bookshelves, the kit Nick had laid out to sharpen his sword, and the dark grey carpet that looked like a giant wire scrubbing brush – and wondered what the hell she was doing there. It was clear she couldn't help.

"I—" said Nick, his voice halting. "I don't mind it as much when – when people touch me. Some people."

Mae looked down, and Nick, who had looked more relaxed when he'd been stabbed, slowly lifted his hand from his chest and laid it on the tumbled sheets between them, fingers half-curled into his palm. He was still regarding the ceiling with a fixed glare.

"Because you trust them not to hurt you?" Mae asked tentatively.

"No," Nick said, his voice harsh. "Because I'd let them hurt me."

Her fingertips brushed his, and she resisted the sudden nervous urge to snatch her hand back as if she'd just received an electric shock. Instead she swallowed and laced her fingers with his. Her hand was stupidly small in his, and he had calluses from the sword.

She was far too aware of such an unimportant thing, of so little of his skin against hers.

"So why're we doing this?" Nick continued. "What human emotion am I meant to be expressing here?"

"Affection," Mae said. "Platonic affection."

"Oh, really."

"Actually, I'm faking it," Mae told him. "I hope it's good for you. Your first time should be perfect."

The ends of Nick's hair caught against the rough cotton bedclothes, and Mae's free hand tingled with the desire to reach out and brush it back, maybe play with it a little.

It was a stupid impulse. Nick wouldn't appreciate it. He'd made that very clear.

She sat with her legs drawn up to her chest and her socked feet tucked up in the ridge of sheets between them, and tried to ignore the way he was lying back on the bed, graceful and lazy and laid out for her.

His ring was warm with their body heat against her palm.

"Be gentle with me," he murmured.

"Yeah, we'll see."

She'd been kissing his brother last night. This was pathetic. Mae was not going to allow herself to pine.

"So," said Nick. "Are you going to read the book?"

Mae took a deep breath and looked at the book. She was holding hands with a demon, but she didn't want to touch that book.

She did, all the same. She drew it onto her lap gingerly, as if it might explode if not handled with great care, and started to flip the yellowed pages to reach the point where she had stopped before.

Please, she thought to a dead man. Please stop hating him.

She did not let her voice tremble as she read out.

There should have been a point where l said, "This is madness," and took any steps necessary to save Alan. There must have been a moment where it was possible to go back.

The first time the magicians came, we escaped through sheer luck. Perhaps they underestimated me. After all, l was just a human who knew nothing about magic. How could l possibly defend myself against them?

The magicians think we're stupid.

Olivia was crying and shouting spells beside me. Alan was in the back, scared and trying not to show it, clinging to that thing and murmuring a little song.

l ran two of them down with my car. l reversed over one of their bodies to make sure he wouldn't be able to follow us, to make the colour of magic and the rising storm go away. It was the first time l had ever harmed another human being in my life.

It wasn't the last.

l felt like l had to keep Olivia safe. l couldn't abandon her, not in the state she was in. l could not have left anyone in so much pain, let alone someone l loved.

l had to learn so much so fast. l had to spend so much time running, and learning, and trying to help Olivia in the worst conditions imaginable. l could not take her to anyone who might give her real help, because of course they would think that her talk of magic was more madness: they would try to cure her of her memories as well as her delusions. l could not even take her to the Goblin Market, because they would have known her immediately for what she was. A magician. A killer.

l sacrificed my son because it seemed like the right thing to do at the time.

l did not think much about the creature then. l knew

there was something wrong, but I was not sure how much of what Olivia said was truth and how much was madness, and when she talked about her child, she was at her worst. Those stories were the worst. I did not want to believe them.

I was tired all the time. I was distantly grateful that the horrible thing never cried or made a fuss. I didn't like looking at it, but I told myself that was because it was Arthur's child, born of a man who was evil and God knew what suffering on Olivia's part, the child of a man I hated and a woman I loved.

I let Alan fuss over it, since that seemed to make him happy. God help me, when Olivia tried to hurt it I told him to take care of it. I made it his especial charge. I made him responsible.

God forgive me.

It was more than a year later that I realised what I had done. We were fighting a demon possessing a dead body. Olivia was throwing spells and I was hitting it with a poker. I had to beat an already dead thing into pieces, and as I looked at its blank, rotting face, I knew.

I thought, My son is upstairs putting a demon to bed.

Olivia had told me what it was a thousand times. Neither of us had the slightest idea how to save what might once have been Olivia's child. There was no child left, and no hope. There was one of a race of murderous, evil things in my home, and I was filled with senseless, unreasoning terror. As if that had not been the case for a year. As if I had not already betrayed my son by refusing to recognise the danger I had put him in.

As soon as the dead thing stopped moving, I left its messy remains on the rug and ran upstairs. Alan was still in the creature's room, bending over the cradle and singing a song his mother used to sing to him. And in the cradle there was that monster, beyond the reach of human words and feelings.

I should have taken Alan then. I should have taken Alan and driven away from Olivia and the nightmare in the cradle, turned my back on it all and saved my son.

I couldn't bear to leave Olivia. I told myself I would be careful, I would watch it, there might be some way to exorcise it, that Alan was too young to understand and he would be terribly distressed. I told myself that demons were cunning and the creature knew it was helpless and Alan was caring for it. There would be no profit for the demon in harming my son.

Only, of course, demons hurt humans for sport.

There are times when the true horror of the life I have condemned us to settles on me, like stones pressing down on my chest, and I think that soon I will be mad too. There was one day, when Alan was almost seven and came home straight from school as he always does. When Alan is at school I have to keep the creature with me in case Olivia tries to hurt it again.

It is part of his daily routine, as soon as he comes in the door, to give it a kiss and say, "Hi, Nick. Did you miss me?"

As if it could.

That done, he takes out his schoolwork and shows it to me, gold stars and teacher's praise, the little offerings he brings in his effort to make my day brighter.

Sometimes I wish he wasn't so good. It just makes everything else look so much more twisted, so much worse.

That day I noticed something new, though: that the creature's eyes tracked his movements when he was in the room. They don't track mine or Olivia's unless we make a move that is directly related to it. It seems as indifferent to humans as if they were particularly mobile chairs. But it was watching Alan.

My blood ran heavy and cold through my veins, as if terror could turn me to stone, and I tried not to think of what bloody game or dark purpose the demon might intend for my son.

That night I went upstairs with an enchanted knife in my hand and stood over the cradle. Drowning hadn't worked, but this knife had the strongest spells the Goblin Market knew laid on it.

The night-light was on, casting a pattern of cheerful rabbits on the opposite wall. It lay sleeping in a pool of light, but even sleeping it doesn't look like a child.

Not quite.

I stood there sweating, the hilt of the knife turning slick in my grasp. Then from the door I heard Alan say, "Dad?"

I turned and saw him looking at me, and the knife, and the demon. My little boy's face went so pale it seemed translucent. He looked like the tired old ghost of a child long dead.

"Nick," he said, coming into the room, almost stumbling in his sleepy haste. "Nick, wake up."

It doesn't wake like normal children, grumbling or yawning or rubbing sleep from its eyes with small fists. It is simply alert in a moment, black eyes watchful and cold. Alan lifted it out of the cradle with an effort — the body is three years old and big for its age. The demon tried to squirm away. It does not seem to like being touched, but Alan clung to it, staring up at me with huge, terrified eyes.

I said his name.

"Come on, Nick," Alan said, his voice breaking even as he tried to sound calm, as if the demon needed comfort. "I had a nightmare. I need you to come and sleep in my bed."

Alan has it trained to hold his hand and follow him when crossing roads. When he held its hand then, his knuckles were white.

As soon as he left the room I heard him break into a run, dragging the creature with him.

I went to put the knife away. I hid it and came back. Alan had dragged his wardrobe in front of the door. He'd barricaded himself in with the demon.

In the morning I had Olivia spell her way in, silently. I did not wake them as I came in over what remained of the wardrobe.

When I drew the blanket back, Alan was sleeping with one arm curled around the monster. In his other hand was an enchanted knife.

I'd never dreamed he knew where I kept the weapons, let alone that he'd stolen one. And now he was clinging to the demon and the knife, not even to defend against the magicians but to protect that thing from — because he was scared of—

I can't write it. My little Alan, my baby boy.

What would Marie think, if she saw what had become of him?

"Come downstairs," I said. "I'll get breakfast."

We have never spoken of that night. He pretends it never happened, hugs me without hesitation, still brings home good marks and trophies like offerings, acts like he has never doubted or feared me for a moment.

It scares me sometimes, how well he can pretend.

Mae stopped reading, breathing as if she'd been running a race. Her throat felt too small, as if it was closing up in an attempt to stop the words coming through.

"Another human reason to hold hands," Nick said, his voice distant. "Crossing the street. See? This isn't my first time."

Mae's voice came out stifled. "My mistake."

Nick's eyes did follow Alan. It was one of the first things Mae had noticed when she was getting to know him as more than just a devastatingly good-looking jerk. She'd seen and thought he was as scared for his brother as Mae was for hers.

"Why are you holding on so tight?" Nick inquired. "To comfort me?"

Mae looked down at their linked hands. She could barely feel her own hand, she realised slowly. She was holding on to his so hard her fingers had gone white and numb.

"I guess so," she said softly.

Nick's voice was freezing cold. "It doesn't work. I can't imagine why you think it might."

"Okay."

"Can I stop touching you now?" Nick snapped. "I don't like it. This whole idea was stupid!"

Mae pulled her hand sharply away and into her lap, where she held it with her other hand, trying to massage warmth and movement back into her fingers. Nick rolled off the bed and caught his sword up from the floor, stalking over to the window and starting to put away his sharpening kit.

She thought of Alan, seven years old and barring his bedroom door because he was terrified of what his own father might do.

"Alan's fine," she said. "He's all right now."

"Sure," said Nick, staring out the window and rolling his shoulders as if he was planning to punch someone. "Why wouldn't he be? Dad's dead. Mum's dead. Every human he ever thought of as family is either dead or wants nothing to do with him. Whatever game I want to play with him, whatever purpose I have for him, I can go right ahead. The monster has him all to itself."

Mae took a deep breath. "Don't talk about yourself in the third person. It makes you sound like a serial killer. And Alan has me and Jamie too."

Nick sheathed his sword and turned away from the window. Sunlight did nothing to soften his face at all. It just lit up the restless, dangerous glitter of his eyes.

"Yeah," he said, suddenly predatory and intent. "Alan seemed happy this morning. You two have a nice night, did you?"

Nicholas Ryves, ladies and gentlemen, Mae thought. The only person in the world who could make a matchmaking scheme sound like a death threat.

"Sure," she said, her voice chilly.

He'd made it extremely clear he wasn't interested, but this was just rubbing it in.

"How nice?" Nick demanded.

"None of your business!"

"Oh?" he said, and smirked. "That nice. No wonder he was in such a good mood."

"There were—" Mae said, and stumbled on her words. She glared at a random corner of the room rather than keep looking at Nick. "A lot happened at the Goblin Market, you know. He had plenty of things to think about."

"Did he kiss you?"

Her gaze snapped up from the corner to Nick's face, an outraged reply burning on but not leaving her lips.

"Yes," she answered slowly, instead of telling him exactly how inappropriate his question was. He had no reaction to the news that she could see. "It wasn't that big a deal," she went on, putting one verbal foot carefully in front of the other. "We're not going out or anything. I mean, for God's sake, he also seemed to have a good enough time kissing Liannan last night."

That got a reaction.

Nick lunged across the room at her, and she jumped off the bed and stood with one hand raised, knowing that there was no way on earth she could stop his vicious rush.

He stopped himself, body straining as if he'd hit an invisible barrier. "What?" he bit out, with the force of a blow behind the word.

"Liannan," Mae repeated, trying to make her voice so light it couldn't disturb the fragile equilibrium Nick seemed to have reached.

"Kissed Alan," Nick said flatly.

It occurred to Mae now to wonder exactly what Liannan was to Nick. She knew that Liannan knew him. Anzu the demon had spoken about some kind of alliance, the three demons together, and Alan had said once that Liannan acted like Nick was her boyfriend.

Perhaps he missed her. She was his own kind.

"Nick," Mae said. "Are you jealous?"

He broke and ran, slamming the door, and Mae charged after him. He was so much faster than she was, she heard him knocking into or possibly leaping over the stair rail before she was at the bedroom door. She ran after him anyway, knowing by the crashing where he was headed, and she was in the kitchen by the time he strode into the garden and lifted a hand.

Dark clouds raced from the corners of the sky to cover

the sun, jagged stitches of lightning bright against the shadowed heavens. There was no thunder, only silence, until Nick spoke.

"Liannan!" he shouted. "Come and face me!"

Lines broke the ground in every direction from the spot where Nick stood, as if he was at the centre of an earthquake. The demon's circle formed around him violently, dust rising so Mae almost lost sight of him.

Nick's entire backyard was a demon's circle, and flames were licking and leaping from every line. She didn't dare go outside.

The balefire was burning high, making the whole circle glow, shimmering against the garden fence and turning the air above it smoky and hazy. If any of the neighbours looked out of their windows, questions were going to be asked and the fire brigade was going to be called.

At the other edge of the demon's circle, under the gnarled yew tree, there were two shapes forming.

That wasn't right.

Liannan and Anzu rose together out of the flickering balefire, not touching but with their bodies curved towards each other. Liannan was as beautiful as she had been last night but much less soft, skin the stark white of alabaster and hair flying, a being of stone and scarlet.

Anzu's wings were ragged and black, like the wings of a moth in the night. The bright red of Liannan's hair showed through his tattered wings, as if he was already enveloped in her fire and burning away.

Nick stood in the whirlwind of fire and wings, the still, dark centre of the demon's circle. They drew in towards him at once.

He stood waiting for them, his shoulders held stiff. Mae recognised his stance. He was ready to fight.

Liannan got to him first, her long arms reaching out. The gesture looked sinister, like a mermaid reaching up to pull a man into dark, drowning waters.

She twined ice-pale arms around Nick's neck and kissed him. She took her time doing it, her body clinging to and wrapped around Nick's at the same time, like seaweed, like ropes. Nick stood still.

The kiss looked like Liannan was laying claim.

After a long moment, the demon pulled away and took Nick's hands in hers, cutting them and hardly seeming to notice as blood welled from the cuts. She was looking up at him, her eyes huge and tranquil, shining like deep, cold pools.

"I knew you'd call for us," she murmured.

After a beat Nick said, "I don't remember calling for him."

Anzu's wings snapped restlessly. His whole body seemed caught in constant turbulent motion, mouth curling and fingers closing on nothing, in movements that reminded Mae of a bird's talons. She didn't know why until she realised that the dark points his nails ended in actually were a bird's talons, obscene on the ends of his long, beautiful hands.

He would have been model-beautiful in a golden and angular way if it had not been that your eye could not settle on him long enough to appreciate any one feature. His beauty gave Mae vertigo.

He said, "I thought I'd come to collect."

Nick tipped his head back. "Yeah?" he asked, casual. "And what do you want?"

Anzu moved in like a bright moth to a dark flame. Liannan detached herself from Nick slightly, one icicle-sharp hand lingering on his wrist and drawing blood. They circled him for a moment, watching and waiting, utterly silent. Three demons together.

"What do we want?" Anzu breathed, mouth curving, cruel as a scimitar or a hunting bird's beak.

He leaned against Nick, talon-tipped hand flat against Nick's chest. Nick did not back down or look away, and Anzu's pale eyes shone, like crystal caves filling with sunlight and refracting it into a thousand shards of brightness.

The dark veil of his wing hid them both from Mae's sight for a moment, the edges of the feathers shadowy, blurred in the rising magic. Then the wing drew away like a curtain as Anzu moved back. Whatever he had whispered or done in that hidden moment, Mae could not tell. Nick's face betrayed nothing.

Anzu's voice had more than an edge of anger to it now. "Only what we're owed!"

"And what's that?" Nick asked, his voice still level.

Anzu's eyes lowered, as if he was suddenly sleepy or had just had an extremely pleasant thought. He looked like a fairy-tale prince waiting for a princess's kiss to wake him up.

Through barely parted lips, he whispered a single hungry word. "Bodies."

Liannan closed in now, as if they were taking it in turns to trap him. She kissed Nick again, this time light against his jaw, rows of sharp teeth glinting close to his skin.

"We kept our part of the bargain, didn't we, Hnikarr?" she asked. "You went into that baby and we guarded you. We came every time you called us at the Goblin Market. We came for you. Didn't we?"

"You did," said Nick.

"Good," Liannan murmured, as if she was a teacher incredibly pleased that her student had given her the right answer. She leaned her face into the curve of Nick's throat, not touching but close, her profile looking a little less like something carved on a coin. "I'll always come for you," she whispered. "Even though you have no soul to share with me."

Nick said nothing.

"You owe us," Liannan reminded him sweetly. "You remember how cold it is. You won't leave us out in the cold."

She kissed him again, on the line of his jaw, more a nip than a kiss. Her lips left a frosty mark with pink rising underneath, as if her mouth was so cold it burned.

Nick turned his face away.

"You could choose them, if you liked." She reached up and tried to turn his face towards her, icicles iridescent in his black hair, bloody lines scored along his cheek. "Choose me any body you want."

"It's not like you can keep them long," Nick said, still looking away, his jaw tight. "The bodies die. Someone will notice if I spread death everywhere I go."

Mae sat down heavily on the back doorstep and hugged her knees to her chest, chilled and alone, the only human there.

"Let them notice," Liannan murmured. "Wear death like a garment. It looks good on you." She smiled. "Always did."

"I agree with Hnikarr. We want someone with no family," whispered Anzu. The scarlet feather patterns in his golden hair seemed to melt and spread like blood, dyeing his hair almost red. "Someone with no friends. Someone who won't ever be missed by anyone at all."

He arched his neck, putting himself on display, and the

balefire circled his head and made his face shine as it changed.

The bones shifted, his face went thinner and paler, his eyes turned blue. His hair was really red now.

Nick made a low sound in the back of his throat.

Anzu looked like Alan and not like Alan, the planes and angles of his face a little too sharp, the red hair the heavy dark colour of arterial blood. He looked like a cruel, beautiful version of Alan, and he smiled a smile that wasn't Alan's at all.

"I want this body," said Anzu.

Nick snarled, "No."

"Drop it," Liannan told Anzu sharply.

That didn't have the desired effect at all. Nick wheeled on her.

"And you," he snarled. "What were you doing last night at the Goblin Market? What were you doing with my brother?"

Liannan looked at Nick and then, after a long pause, she laughed. She shook out her hair, and it flared up like a gust of flame. Her hair stayed suspended in midair, ignoring petty human concerns like gravity. The ends shimmered with what really seemed to be fire, sparking along the strands, burning but never burning out.

"He didn't tell you?" she asked, and smiled, displaying a sharp row of teeth.

"I suggest you tell me," said Nick. "Now."

"By your brother," Liannan continued, her voice soft, "who do you mean?"

"You know who I mean!"

Liannan moved away, almost dancing, hair a burning banner. "Even the bodies aren't related, are they? Different parents. Not a single drop of blood shared. And you are not this body. You are not human. So how is he your brother? In what possible sense is he your brother?"

Nick strode over lines glowing with magic as if they weren't there. He grasped the demon's burning hair in his hands, handled it like a whip, and wrapped it tight around her long neck.

He leaned down to whisper in her ear. Loose strands of her hair rose where there was no wind and opened up bloody stripes on his cheek, but he did not relax his strangling grip. He did not seem to notice.

"In what sense?" he repeated, his voice colder than hers. "In the sense that he's mine!"

"I have had enough!" Anzu shouted. "Stop trying to talk him around, Liannan. Accept the fact that he's a traitor."

"It's all right if Nick wants to have a pet," said Liannan. "It's not unheard of, you know."

"Have a pet?" Anzu echoed. "He is a pet! He could do anything in the world, he could rule the humans, he could slaughter every one of the magicians who feed us on crumbs, he could help his own kind! And instead, what does he do?"

Nick didn't spare Anzu even a glance. He was still looking at Liannan.

"Just tell me what you did," he said.

Nick's hands were tangled up in Liannan's hair. He made no move to untangle them, to defend himself, when Anzu swooped on him and caught Nick's face in his hands.

"You care so much about humans, traitor?" Anzu crooned at him, saying the word "traitor" as if it was an endearment. "I'll have them all. And that precious brother of yours, I'll have him first. I'll eat his heart. I'll make you watch. I swear."

Nick glanced at Anzu and smiled.

"I'm not worried about you. Liannan's the one who eats men's hearts. You're the one they write songs about," Nick continued, turning back to her, turning her hair around his wrist. "Nightmare lover."

Liannan smiled. "You remember."

Nick's voice went dark. "What did you do to Alan?"

"Why don't you ask him? Surely you don't trust me more than your own brother?"

Nick stared at her, then threw her hair from him as if he was throwing away a weapon he might be tempted to use, and vanished.

There was just the shimmering garden then, and the two demons in it.

Liannan turned and prowled towards the doorstep, smiling as if now she got to play a game.

"Hello, pretty thing," she said to Mae. "I remember you. Talk to me."

"No, thanks," said Mae. "I don't have any questions just now."

"Liar," Liannan said, laughing. "Humans always have questions."

She was slinking towards Mae, but Mae didn't get up, just sat there hugging her knees on the step. Liannan was not deterred for a moment. She dropped until she was at eye level with Mae and then came forward, moving not like a human on her hands and knees but with the fluid grace of an animal on four legs, swift and predatory.

Anzu did not come forward, but he turned his head in her direction, hair shining like newly discovered treasure.

Mae raised her eyebrows at him. "You're not my type."

Anzu gave her a long look like a parody of a normal

flirtatious look, lashes fluttering over hungry eyes, sinister under the sweetness.

"I'll be seeing you, sweetheart," he said. "I'll be your type then."

Mae flashed him a brief, cold smile, her mother's, which said better than a frown that she was neither amused nor impressed. "I'll be waiting."

"I'll be thinking of you," Anzu told her. "Your soul in the palm of my hand. About to be crushed."

He kissed the palm of his hand, then blew her the kiss. It floated to her, shining, a demon's mark made of light, and blew apart like the seeds on a dandelion clock when it hit the edge of the circle.

Anzu disappeared the same way, turning into motes of light in the air that hung for a moment and fell like bright dust.

"Just you and me," Liannan said, crawling to the edge of the circle, body moving in S shapes like a snake. "Can't leave until Hnikarr comes back and releases me, you know. He called me by name. Keep me company, and I'll give you some answers. For free."

She was wearing a necklace, Mae saw, shimmering and dangling in the shadow cast by the front of her white dress. There seemed to be a charm hanging from the silver chain, but the charm kept changing shape, from a silver rendering of a demon's mark, to a world in a jewelled cage, and then to one of Nick's quillon daggers.

"So if I asked you about Gerald," Mae began.

Liannan laughed and rolled over onto her back, the silver chain streaking like lightning across her white skin.

"Not useful questions, my darling girl," she said. "But those questions that humans ask, as valuable as tears in the ocean.

Will we be happy, is it too late? Does he love me?"

"How human can a demon be?"

Liannan's eyes narrowed to bright slits like fissures in ice. She licked a pink tongue across her razor-sharp teeth.

There was silence in the garden except for the hiss of the balefire, magic brimming against the garden fence, and the urge running all through Mae's body to lean forward just a little when Liannan whispered, to hear the words slide soft into the space between them.

"Being human," Liannan murmured. "And what is that? Being attached beyond all reason, being too easily hurt."

"Yes."

Liannan laughed and bowed her head, the ends of her hair blowing against Mae's cheek. The strands tingled against her skin in a kiss that seemed balanced between frost and fire.

"I know a demon like that."

"Do you?" Mae breathed.

Liannan showed her sharp teeth. "It isn't Nick. It's Anzu." She paused to savour Mae's reaction.

"Of us all, Hnikarr was the least human," she continued softly. "I never in a hundred centuries saw him show the smallest sign he had warmth in him. He is not like you. He is something entirely different. Would it make you feel better about wanting him if I said he was not like the rest of us, was the one shining example of our kind, that he could be trained to beg and heel and love? If he is nothing but a demon and you still want him, what does that make you?"

Liannan's nose was almost brushing Mae's, she was so close, and there were uncontrollable shudders running down Mae's back. Her hair might be burning, but Liannan's skin was ice.

"If Anzu is the most human, and Nick is the least," Mae asked, "what does that make you?"

It was only when Liannan's hands closed on her wrists that Mae realised that, caught in Liannan's eyes and her answers, she had come too close to the circle.

She hadn't made this circle. She wasn't safe inside it.

Mae's talisman burst into pain against her chest, in a warning that came too late.

Liannan's fingers clamped down like burning-cold manacles, their freezing strength biting down to Mae's bones. She was still smiling.

"I'm the best," she whispered.

She dragged Mae into her arms and the demon's burning circle.

"Oh no, you don't," Nick snarled, appearing behind Liannan and grabbing her hair again.

Her hair turned into red mist, diffusing in the air like blood in water and slipping through his hands. It was suddenly clear that earlier, Nick could not have held her for a moment, had she not wanted to be held.

Nick's other hand was fastened around Alan's wrist, but he lost that too when Alan pulled violently free and fell on his knees at Mae's side.

"You left Mae here with a demon?"

"Two, actually," Liannan murmured, her voice curling around the words like a smug cat. "Another second and I would've had her."

"It's okay, Alan," said Mae. She was still shaking, caught in constant uncontrollable tremors, from the chill of Liannan's embrace. His hands on her, warm and supportive under her elbows, felt too good after Liannan's. She had the impulse to collapse into his arms and weep, so she shrugged him off. "I'm fine," she insisted. "It was my fault. I got too close."

"Nick called her up," Alan said. "He shouldn't have left you alone with her."

"Alan, Alan," said Liannan. "Aren't you pleased to see me? You aren't being as sweet as you were last night."

Alan cut a swift look over to her, standing wreathed in ivy-clinging ribbons of fire and apart from them all.

"Don't talk to him," Nick snapped.

"I can handle myself," Alan told him. "Liannan, you just tried to possess and thus slowly murder someone who means a great deal to me."

Liannan raised an eyebrow. "Does that mean we can't be friends?"

"It means I'm going to be less sweet."

She reached out a hand to Alan, fire crawling in lovely patterns up her arm, as if she was wrapped in lace made of light. Nick put his arm out to stop her reach, but Alan was already looking at her hand and shaking his head, laughing a little.

Liannan laughed back. "I think we understand each other, don't we?"

"Understand this," Nick began, and Liannan turned on him in a circle of sparks.

"I won't touch him," she said. "I want to be on your side. I'll take your terms. Set aside one human, two humans, as your playthings, I do not care. I'll leave them alone. I will protect them from the others, even, and if you do not think they need more protection than you can give, you do not know Anzu. And you know him."

"Yeah," Nick said. "I know him."

"You know me, too," Liannan said, no kissing or drawing close now. She sounded businesslike. "I will be on your side, but you need to make it worth my while. I want a body."

"No."

"I do not want to be against you, Hnikarr," Liannan told him softly. "Don't do this."

Nick turned his face away, in Alan's direction without actually looking at Alan. "What else can I do?"

"Make me an offer," Liannan commanded. "Or I'll make you sorry."

"Liannan," said Nick. "I dismiss you."

The balefire began to ebb at once, receding from the outer rim of the circle to the heart where all the lines crossed. Liannan stood at that heart as if she was trapped, a dragonfly in burning amber, her eyes narrowed.

"Nick," she said, making the name an insult, "you disappoint me."

He did not answer. He waited until she was gone, until there was no trace of magic or demons in the garden but the broken earth and a shimmer that might have been heat haze lingering in the air.

Then he lifted his head. His eyes were like torn black holes in a white mask.

"Sometimes," he said to Alan, "I think you must be the stupidest person in the world."

"I'm not the one whose temper tantrums involve summoning up demons and endangering our friends," Alan snapped.

"You kissed her," said Nick, advancing on him. Alan fell back from Mae's side, more to move the conflict away from her than retreating, Mae thought. "You could have been marked. You could have been killed."

"That was my fault too," Mae put in.

"A lot of things seem to be your fault," Nick said, shooting her a furious look. "Why can't you stay out of trouble?"

Mae wanted to ask why Nick couldn't stop being a jerk, but she considered the fact that he'd pulled a demon off her five minutes ago and shut her mouth.

"Leave her alone," said Alan. "I knew what I was doing."

Nick pushed his brother up against the side of the house, Alan stumbling before he hit the stucco wall. "No, you don't! You think – you think demons can be handled, but we can't. We are not creatures that can be controlled. Anzu and Liannan are both coming for you! I know them. They won't stop. They never do."

"Let go of me," Alan ordered.

"No," said Nick, eyes boring into Alan's. "You have to stay away from demons. Promise me."

"That would be a little tricky, wouldn't it?" Alan asked softly. His eyes slid down to Nick's hand grasping his arm, and away again. "You sound like the people from the Goblin Market. They think demons are nothing more than weapons that can turn on you. They say that when I freed you I made a terrible mistake."

"Well," Nick said, his voice rough, scratching in his throat. "Maybe you did."

"Oh," said Alan, as if he had been punched.

Nick broke away from him in a burst of a violent movement, like a wild horse. Alan did not reach out to him. He just stood there leaning against the wall. He looked a little ill.

"They'll wonder where I've gone at the bookshop," he said at last. "I have to go."

Nick nodded without looking at him.

Alan drew a hand through his curly hair, making it stick out in every direction. He offered Mae one of the least convincing smiles she had ever seen from him before he walked away, his lame leg dragging more with every step.

Mae didn't like to think about how tired he must be. Too tired to deal with any of this.

"You shouldn't have said that," she told Nick's back.

He looked over his shoulder at her, the movement too fast, as if any voice at that moment sounded like a threat to him.

"Why not?" he asked. "It's true. Alan keeps wanting me to talk to him about the past, but he doesn't get it. I don't know any stories about history or anything he would like. I know that Liannan once had a human lover who was a sultan with magicians at his beck and call, and he gave her a slave girl to possess every day so long as she would come and tell him a story about demons every night. She came to him for a thousand nights, and then on the thousand and first he overstepped his boundaries and she had his body too. I don't want to tell him that."

"Because you're different now," Mae ventured, and Nick looked at her as if she was crazy.

"Because I'm not different," he said. "When I remember how it was, with Anzu and Liannan . . . I remember we were allies. I made a bargain. I am a traitor. And if I think about the past too long, I want to give them bodies. Why should I care what some human feels about it?"

Nick pronounced the word "feels" as if it was in a foreign language.

"Okay," Mae said, and took a shaky breath. "Don't tell Alan that, either."

Nick couldn't tell Alan any of this. He didn't know Gerald

had offered Alan a way to control his demon brother, a way to take back his freedom.

Only Mae knew that.

"Why not?" asked Nick. "Because it would hurt him?" His mouth twisted. "Demons don't have pity."

Mae knew some other things. She remembered Nick trapped in a circle at the magicians' house, Nick bleeding in the back of a car. He'd stepped into a circle and onto a sword for her brother.

Her wrists were still burning with cold and she felt a little sick, but there was nobody else here. She walked across the grass to Nick's side and curled her fingers around his.

"They don't talk, either, do they?" she said. "You manage that all right. You're just learning."

Nick's shoulder beside hers was tense and his hand unmoving in her grasp, certainly not holding her back. But he didn't move away.

"Oh, and I'm such a great student."

"No, you kind of suck," Mae said. "But luckily, I'm your teacher, and I am awesome on so many levels."

She was looking intently at the garden fence rather than Nick. His ring was cool against her fingertips, his shoulder relaxing slightly by hers.

"I want to help," she said quietly. "It's obvious something's gone wrong between you and Alan. Can you tell me what happened in Durham?"

She felt Nick move and moved with him almost without thinking, stepping into his personal space as he stepped into hers. She had to tilt back her head to look into his eyes, and his breath was warm on her face; she had the sudden wild conviction he was about to reach out for comfort.

"Can you tell me something first?" Nick asked her. "Why are you still here?"

His voice was very soft, so soft that at first Mae was simply confused. Then she pulled her hand sharply away from his.

He leaned in closer.

"This is none of your business," he said in a savage whisper. "I'm tired of listening to you. I'm tired of looking at you. Go home."

"Go to hell," Mae said.

Maybe she should have insisted on keeping him company and offering him comfort no matter what he said, but she wasn't the ministering angel type, and she didn't appreciate being talked to like that.

She went home. She walked all the way back and was basically clinging to the banister as she made her way up the stairs, putting hand before hand and foot before foot as if she was climbing some steep and terrible mountain. Jamie emerged from the shadows of the landing above, passing the stairs with a set look that said he was determined to ignore her, and then he saw something on her face that stopped him.

"You haven't been home for two days," he said, his voice strange and stilted, making it clear he was still angry. "Been having fun?"

"Not really," Mae said, dragging the words out. "It's all a bit
. . ."

Talking broke the equilibrium she'd had going, the steady march to her bedroom and oblivion. She ended up collapsing on the stairs with her elbows on her knees, and for a moment she was sure Jamie would pass on regardless.

She should have known better. He came down the stairs at

once and was kneeling on the step below her, brown eyes warm and unguarded.

"Mae," he said. "Mae, what is it?"

Mae didn't know. She found herself humiliatingly close to tears. She wanted to spill out the whole story: Alan actually considering Gerald's bargain, Daniel Ryves standing over a cradle with a knife, Liannan whispering about demons and what Mae wanted. She didn't know how to fix any of it, or even how to fix herself and Jamie, make certain that things were as they always had been, him and her against the world.

Jamie took her hand in his and held on, looking slightly horrified and so concerned.

"I love you," Mae said, stumbling over the words, trying ferociously hard not to actually cry. "I know you're mad at me, but I need – I need things to be okay."

"Things aren't okay," Jamie said, and then he leaned in and eased himself up, tucking her cheek against his thin shoulder, and said in her ear, "You have the worst taste in men in the world. But I love you, too."

It was that simple, and she felt stricken at the thought of how awful it must be for Alan, never to have this warm human contact, the certainty of someone saying it back. Mae closed her eyes and held on to Jamie's soft T-shirt with clenched fists, and did not let go for a long time.

That night the demons whispered outside her window in Jamie's voice, small and beseeching, asking for help. But she knew Jamie was safe in bed, and she put her head under the covers when the low, terrible sobbing began.

13

Bargains at the Gallows

MAE'S MONDAY MORNING WAS SLIGHTLY BRIGHTENED WHEN Jamie came downstairs wearing the purple LOCK UP YOUR SONS T-shirt she'd given him, which he usually only wore to bed.

"Nice," she said as Jamie fished around for the purple knit cap in the cupboard where they kept their hats. Nobody really knew where the purple knit cap had come from. It was a purple mystery. "Do you want me to put some eyeliner on you?"

"No, Mae. We've had this discussion."

Jamie spoke lightly, as if everything between them was fine, but if that were true, Jamie wouldn't be dressing this way. Mae had told him Seb was going to be polite to him from now on. Jamie was clearly determined to be defiant in purple.

"Hang on a second," said Mae, and she dashed upstairs and changed out of her black HEATHCLIFF HAD IT COMING shirt and into a matching purple LOCK UP YOUR SONS shirt.

Unlike Jamie, Mae wore hers quite often.

Today it was a uniform, something that said *I am on the same side as you and willing to fight with you.* Jamie smiled, crooked and pleased, when he saw it, and Mae knew her sartorial peace offering had been accepted.

They walked to school, talking about how much they were longing for the summer holidays.

"Oh, I am planning things," said Jamie. "Great, great things. I could join a band."

"You gave up the guitar after two lessons."

"Well," he said, "I could be a backup dancer."

"Backup dancers have to wear belly shirts and glitter," said Mae. "So obviously, I support this plan."

"The answer to glitter is the same as the answer to eyeliner," Jamie told her. "In fact, put all forms of make-up into the big box of no."

"You'll never make it as a backup dancer with that kind of attitude."

"Well," said Jamie, "maybe I'll learn a new skill."

They were drawing level with the school when Jamie did something very unexpected: he smiled.

It was a particular smile, warm and slow as sunrise, that he used when he saw Mae, Annabel, boys he had usually disastrous crushes on, and friends he no longer had at all.

"Hi," Jamie said, happy and a little shy. "Um – what are you doing here?"

Mae turned to see Nick leaning against the door frame, schoolbag slung over one shoulder.

"Going to school," he said. "This building. Right here."

"Yes," said Jamie. "But why do you go to school at all when you're a . . ." His eyes slid around the playground. "When you're a spy?" he offered eventually.

Nick stared at Jamie for a moment, blank black eyes

possibly trying to convey that Jamie was a strange human being who bothered him.

"I wonder the same thing myself," he said. "Alan insists, though."

"Oh," said Jamie. "Well. But this is great!"

"Great's a strong word," Nick drawled.

He peered through the glass into the darkened hallway of the school. Someone very misguided had painted the hall turquoise once.

Mae couldn't blame Nick for a certain lack of enthusiasm.

"See, I had this thought," said Jamie.

"Congratulations."

"I thought," Jamie said, narrowing his eyes slightly, "that maybe sometime . . . I mean, you have trouble reading, don't you?"

Nick straightened up from slouching against the door frame, which made Mae realise how relaxed he had been before, how relaxed he'd allowed himself to be, since it was just the three of them.

"What's your point, Jamie?"

Jamie frowned, face screwed up, as if he was trying very hard to think of the exact right thing to say. "The thing is," he said, "Alan's really smart, isn't he?"

A certain tension eased out of Nick's shoulders. "Yeah."

"Well, so stuff is really easy for him – because he's so smart," said Jamie, who was quick about feelings even if he did say ridiculous things about spies. "So he probably skips over about half the steps a normal not-so-smart person would need for learning something. And when it's something that doesn't come naturally to, uh, spies, it must be even harder. But I'm not particularly smart."

"You amaze me."

"So we could go over some stuff together," Jamie persevered. "We'll be in the same class. It will just be homework. Everyone has to do homework. Maybe sometimes I could read the assigned books to you. Auditory learning helps a lot of people with reading problems. And it would help me remember as well!"

Jamie looked up to see how this sales pitch was going, and frowned some more.

"And if I help you with schoolwork," he continued in a small, reluctant voice, "it would be great if you could help me with . . . self-defence."

"You want to learn how to use knives?" Nick asked. He might have dwelled on the word "knives" an instant too long.

Jamie flinched. "Absolutely," he said. "Instruments of brutal death? I'm very keen."

"I see that," said Nick. There were other people streaming through the gate now, the gloomily murmuring Monday morning crowd about to form where they were standing. Nick glanced over at them, always hyperalert around strangers, body held ready to attack.

He looked back at Jamie.

"Okay."

"Okay?" Jamie blinked and then smiled again, gradual and sweet. "Okay."

He kept smiling, an obvious hopeful invitation for Nick to smile back at him and seal the bargain. Nick stared at him, face blank as a stone, for a long moment. Then he let one corner of his mouth curl up and looked away from Jamie, as if to indicate that that was as much as Jamie was getting.

Jamie beamed.

Mae and Nick had not exchanged a word yet. He didn't deserve even a hello, considering the way he'd acted yesterday, but he hadn't shot down Jamie's offering of gratitude for Friday. She relented.

"I didn't do so badly in my classes last year," she said. "If you little ones need help, feel free to come to me."

Nick rolled his eyes. Jamie gave her an impish grin. Things seemed all right among all of them for a moment.

The usual morning crowd was not behaving as usual, Mae noticed. Normally everyone massed against the front doors, but today they were scattered around the playground, standing in separate but equally far-flung knots of friends. Every one of them seemed impelled, by some mysterious warning impulse, to keep their distance from the demon.

Mae's train of thought was cut off by an arm sliding around her shoulders.

"Hey," said Seb in her ear, squeezing her shoulders briefly and then letting go. "Hey, Jamie."

Jamie peeled away from Mae's side and went to Nick's. Nick's eyes tracked the movement as if he was not quite certain how to deal with it either, and then apparently he made up his mind. He shifted slightly in front of Jamie, protective.

Unfortunately, he was used to doing that with a weapon in his hand, and he hit Jamie in the chest with his schoolbag.

"Ow!" Jamie exclaimed. "What do you have in there? Um. Wait, never mind. I retract the question. I never need to know."

"Spy stuff," Nick murmured.

Beside her, Seb had gone rather still. "Ryves," he said. "Didn't know you were back in town."

Nick stared at him without speaking. Clearly, his air

suggested, here he was, and he didn't find it necessary to bother actually talking.

"Friend of yours?" Seb asked Mae. There was something odd in his voice. She'd seen Seb and Nick hanging around together when Nick had lived here before. She would have assumed they were friendly enough.

Evidently not.

"Yeah," Jamie snapped, bristling like an angry cat.

"That reminds me," said Nick. "You're not bothering Jamie any more."

He put it as a statement of fact, something that could not possibly be called into question. He sounded a little bored doing so.

"You don't actually get to give me orders, Ryves," Seb informed him. "But I wasn't planning on it."

"Good," Nick said softly.

Seb was actively glaring at Nick now, Mae saw. Nick wasn't glaring back, but he was holding himself in a way that was even more potentially threatening than usual.

"Reunions are so touching," Mae said, her voice breaking the tense silence. "Had a good weekend, Seb?"

She had thought for some reason that Nick and Seb looked more alike than they really did, possibly because they both fitted the paradigm of tall, dark, and handsome – if you liked the tall and dark thing.

Seb had a bit of a reputation in school. He got into fights and had a bad home life and he walked around the place looking angry half the time, and that was enough to qualify him as dangerous.

Next to Nick, he didn't look dangerous. He looked like a spaniel placed beside a Rottweiler. He wasn't as tall, or as broad across the shoulders, and Mae had seen what Nick could do even without magic. Nick could tear Seb to pieces.

Seb wasn't a magician or a demon or anything who deserved that. Mae felt a sudden rush of protectiveness.

"My weekend was okay," Seb said, glancing back at her and smiling. There was a sweetness tucked like a secret in the lines of his mouth, a potential for warmth that Nick simply did not have.

Mae curled her hand around Seb's arm. He didn't flinch back from her touch or go tense. He looked startled but pleased, and there was the sound of a key opening the doors of the school behind them.

"Come on, Nick," said Jamie, his voice abruptly hard, and Mae realised how her gesture must have looked to him. He refused to look at her when she tried to catch his eye, concentrating on Nick.

Jamie looked terribly relieved to have someone to be walking away with. Mae didn't know how this had gone so wrong.

She hadn't realised how much Jamie disliked Seb. She also hadn't noticed when Jamie had started liking Nick, even though now she thought about it, they were well past due for his next hopeless crush.

Nick looked at Mae before he followed Jamie down the school hall, eyes unreadable as ever. He leaned down and said something to Jamie as they went. Jamie's laugh drifted back to the door where Mae and Seb were still standing.

Mae said, as lightly as she could, "That went well."

"It wasn't anything you did," Seb told her, scowling into the shadows of the hall. "He came prepared to be mad. Wearing all that purple."

"You could tell?"

"Um, yeah," said Seb, as if it was obvious. "He never dresses that way normally."

Seb saw that as well as the way Jamie was hiding something. He was observant in a way she wouldn't have expected of someone as rough and careless as he sometimes seemed to be, but there was the artist thing to consider.

They had better all be careful.

She liked that Seb didn't know anything about the magic. She didn't want to upset Jamie, but she didn't want to give this up either, something normal, a boy who really liked her and a place in the normal world, a space where she had some control.

"You have to keep trying," she said, and Seb nodded, as if that went without saying. She smiled at him, and they went into school together. She didn't hold his hand, but she walked a little close.

"Where were you this weekend?" he asked. "I looked for you in all the usual places."

Mae smiled at him because he'd looked for her, and thought of sword fights on the Millennium Bridge, the Goblin Market on the cliffs of Cornwall, and demons in the garden.

"I was in some unusual places."

That day at lunch Tim and Seb joined Mae at her usual lunch table, Tim settling by Erica's side and sliding his arm around her waist.

"Hey," Erica said. She was always torn between her boyfriend and her friends, wanting everyone to be happy and nobody to be left out. She looked relieved when she saw Seb hovering by the table, and gave Mae a meaningful smile.

Mae raised her eyebrows at Erica and nodded at Seb to sit down.

Glancing up from her lunch, she saw Jamie at the door. He must have forgotten to pack a lunch today. He was standing in the cafeteria looking a bit lost, as if he was there so seldom that he'd forgotten where they put the food. Mae raised a hand to signal him over to their table.

Jamie didn't see her, since Nick had just appeared at his side. Nick walked on and then looked back and jerked his head, in an impatient and peremptory way that indicated Jamie should follow him.

Jamie hadn't had someone to sit with in the cafeteria for almost two years.

"Look, isn't that Nick Ryves?" said Rachel. "I thought he moved. Or went to prison."

"Rachel, he did not go to prison," Mae said, glaring.

"He could've gone to prison," Rachel told her. "Hazel told me she saw knives in his schoolbag once."

"I find that extremely unlikely," said Mae, with a laugh she hoped everyone else found convincing.

"I don't," Erica offered in her soft voice. "He does kind of look like a serial killer."

"A hot serial killer, though," said Rachel.

"Uh, I have no opinion on that," Tim said, coughing. "Seemed an okay guy. Not chatty, though," he added thoughtfully. He darted a look over at Seb for approval, obviously having received the Jamie memo, and said, "Maybe we should ask him and your brother to sit with us?"

Mae looked over at Jamie, who had certainly spotted her by now and had deliberately turned his back on their table, shoulders hunched up in two sharp, defensive points, as if he was trying to grow spikes like a hedgehog.

"Jamie wouldn't be crazy about the company," she said. "He'll come around."

"He shouldn't be hanging out with Nick Ryves," said Seb, speaking for the first time. He had one arm looped around his knee, and he was scowling at the apple on the table before him. "He's dangerous."

"Hey," Mae said in her most authoritative voice. She saw Rachel and Erica both sit up and take notice. "Nick's a friend of mine. And Jamie's."

She picked up her sandwich and, in the sudden silence, began to eat. Across the room Jamie and Nick were eating too. To her enormous lack of surprise, Jamie was doing most of the talking, but at one point, when Jamie made a vehement gesture and knocked his apple right off the table, Nick caught it before it hit the ground.

Jamie would get over being mad at her and get over his crush, Mae knew. But she fell silent anyway, leaning against Seb, who seemed a little quiet himself, and let the conversation wash over her without making it flow her way.

When she went up to buy a Coke, Nick cornered her against the vending machine.

Trapped between the humming red box and his body, Mae couldn't actually tip her head back far enough to see his face without thumping it against the vending machine. She settled for raising an eyebrow at what she could see, which was basically Nick's shoulder, the faded black-to-grey material of his shirt stretched tight over muscle and drooping out of shape at the collar, showing the bare lines of collarbone and throat.

Mae closed her hand tight on the damp metal of her Coke can.

"About yesterday," Nick said, and stopped.

"Forget it," Mae told him.

Nick braced himself against the vending machine with one hand over her head.

"All right." He pulled away, her Coke can gleaming in his hand. "Alan's going to a lecture tonight. Come by and read to me."

Mae pushed off the machine and snatched her can back as she walked past him.

"I'll think about it," she said over her shoulder. "If I don't get a better offer."

The better offer she wasn't really expecting came from Alan, and it wasn't an offer at all.

Seb gave her a lift home from school in his surprisingly nice car, which was tan-coloured and sleek and which, she had to point out, Seb was actually too young to drive.

"What are you talking about?" Seb asked, all innocence. "I'm eighteen. It says so on over half the IDs I own."

Mae snorted.

"I wouldn't dream of doing anything illegal," he assured her, with the smile that had made her notice him.

They were hardly past the school gates when they drove by Jamie, bobbing happily along to the sounds of his iPod as he walked. Mae grinned just seeing him, and she was gratified that Seb slowed the car without her asking.

"Hey, Jamie," said Seb. "Want a lift?"

"Hey, Seb," Jamie responded without missing a beat. "Drop dead."

"Right," said Seb, and pulled back from the side of the road, knuckles white on the wheel.

"It takes more than a day," Mae told him.

"Not for Nick Ryves," Seb remarked, his voice grim and his eyes on the side mirror, where Mae could see Jamie climbing into Nick's car and making his instant lunge for the car radio. She grinned to herself and hoped Nick would be able to put up with the country music.

"I told you, we know him."

"I know him," said Seb. "He hung around behind the bike sheds with us for, like, a month, and I knew from day one there was something really wrong there. And don't tell me he and Crawf— Jamie were anything like friends back then. Jamie was scared stiff of him!"

"We went away to a rave in London," said Mae, reusing the lie she'd made up for Annabel. "We met up with Nick and his brother there. All of us got to be friends."

"Alan," Seb said, his voice different.

"You know him, too?"

"Not really," Seb said slowly. "I just used to go into the bookshop and look at the art books. The big coffee-table things, you know, thousands of pictures, but I couldn't aff— didn't want to actually own them. And there was this redheaded guy, and a couple of times a new book would come in and he'd have it behind the counter and then come over and put it on the shelves somewhere I could see it, when I was in the art section. I didn't work out what was going on until it happened a few times."

Considering Mae'd already seen that Seb was pretty quick to work stuff out, she doubted Alan had meant him to work it out at all. She wondered how many small, unnoticed kindnesses Alan went around doing for strangers, because he was naturally kind or because he wanted to be, because he felt he had to pay the world back for keeping a demon in it and knew he could never pay enough.

"Heard some nasty things about him later," Seb went on, his hand steady on the gear stick. "Not sure about them."

Mae's phone rang. She slid her hand into her pocket and grabbed it, and almost laughed when the little green screen read ALAN. She pressed the answer button and held the phone up to her ear.

"Mae?" said Alan. "I hate to ask you this. But I need a favour."

Mae found her heart beating too hard, the normality and calm with Seb in his car sliding away already, like a pretty picture superimposed on reality being pulled off to show what lay beneath.

"Yeah," she said. "Of course. What is it?"

"It's dangerous," Alan told her, serious and not trying to persuade her, his voice hardly beautiful at all.

"Learn to listen when girls have already said yes," Mae told him. "Where are you?"

He hesitated. "If you're coming, I need you to promise me you won't tell Nick about this."

Mae hesitated in her turn, but she wanted to know. "I promise."

"Come and meet me at Manstree Vineyard," Alan said, and hung up.

Mae hung up less precipitately, closing her phone and resting it thoughtfully for a moment against her lips. Then she turned and looked at Seb, who looked back at her, his always curious face even more curious than usual.

"Could you drop me off somewhere?"

She met Alan in Manstree Field, since the vineyard was closed after five. Seb dropped her off with a worried look and a repeated offer to come with her wherever she was going. Mae hoped he didn't think she was sneaking off to random vineyards to buy drugs.

She was familiar with the vineyard. She'd been sent on several summer grape-picking expeditions, where she always ended up burning her nose bright pink to match her hair. It had always been a fun day trip, standing in rows of cool, lush green, smelling freshly turned earth and grapes as she and her friends shouted back and forth to one another.

It looked just the same today, sunshine bright on the high green lines stretching up along the slopes. In the other direction were fields, dipping down and curving up until they were met by the dark border of Haldon Forest, like joined-up handwriting with a black line drawn under it. Sitting in the grass of Manstree Field was Alan, with his head bowed over a book, his hair catching russet and gold lights in the sun.

He looked up as she approached, shielding his eyes with a hand.

"What are you reading?"

"He Knew He Was Right," said Alan. "Anthony Trollope."

"Oh, right," Mae said. "I'm not usually keen on stuff written by dead white guys more than a hundred years ago. All those guys with codpieces and ladies on the fainting couch. I don't really see the point."

"The point is classic works of timeless genius," Alan told her. "Keep talking like that and you'll have to fetch the smelling salts, because I may swoon."

Mae settled on the grass in front of him, sitting lotus-style, and Alan's eyes flickered down as he read her T-shirt and grinned.

"Yeah, I still don't care about the dead guys," said Mae.

"They had their say back then. Time for my say now."

Alan shut the book and said, "I want you to dance up a demon for me."

He said nothing else for a moment, reaching for his worn bag and sliding the book inside. He took out protective amulets, stones with strange, curving traceries on them, little wooden statues of women, glittering necklaces of jewels strung together with symbols Mae didn't recognise, and an enchanted knife she did recognise.

All of this magical paraphernalia lay spread out on the grass, in the sunlight. It was a day for picnics, and instead Alan wanted her to call up a demon.

"If you dance for a demon alone, sometimes they come," Alan said. "But without a partner, without the fever fruit, you haven't paid for anything. They can ask for anything they want in exchange for an answer. The price is guaranteed to be high. And you could die just trying. You've only danced for them twice. If you slip up, or even if you don't, the demon might ask for something you can't afford to lose. You could get possessed. You could be dead within an hour."

Mae looked at him, his dark blue eyes serious and his mouth a straight line. She nodded slowly and reached out for the knife Alan had got at the Goblin Market in May.

Alan grabbed her wrist before she reached it, pinning her hand to the ground. The grass was cool under her open palm, and his fingers pressed down like a vice.

"You shouldn't do this because you think you owe me," he whispered. "You shouldn't do this at all. I shouldn't ask you."

It occurred to Mae that Alan was so unused to the truth that his voice went harsh when he spoke it, as if he was speaking a strange tongue. It made him sound a little like Nick.

She gave the demon's brother a level look.

"But you are asking me."

Alan smiled. It was a terrible smile. "Yes."

"Because there's nobody else you can ask," Mae said. "Because Nick can't know. Which demon am I calling?"

Alan's shoulders went tight at that, the way she'd turned it into a done deal, his fingers biting into her wrist. "Liannan."

"Well, okay then," said Mae. "It's been more than twenty-four hours since I saw that shark-toothed little smile. I was starting to miss her."

She reached out for the knife again, pushing at Alan's hold so he had to really hurt her or let her go. He let her go and snatched up the knife instead.

"I'll cut it. I've been going to the Market since I was four years old. I had my hand on Nick's to guide him when he cut his first circle, and I'm not going to make any mistakes."

"Oh, and I am?" Mae demanded, outraged.

"Mae," said Alan, his voice low. "You're going to risk your life for no other reason than because I asked you. Let me do this one thing."

He kept looking at her with terrifying determination, and she supposed it wasn't worth fighting about. She made a sweeping gesture that gave him permission, and lay back in the summer-warm grass as Alan sank his knife into the earth and made all the symbols, trapped within one circle.

She closed her eyes against the summer sky and smelled the broken earth, crushed grass, the cool leaf and grape smell the breeze was drifting over to her from the vineyard, and the cotton and steel smell of Alan close by.

Eventually he said, "I'm done."

Mae sat up, feeling a little dizzy. There was the circle laid out before her, there was no Market and no Nick and no Sin and no magic. She had to do this herself.

"I have a speaking charm in my bag," Alan told her.

"No," Mae said. "I can speak for myself."

Alan swallowed and nodded. He was rising slowly to his feet as she scrambled up and walked into the circle. She could feel his eyes on her back, watching, but he couldn't help her now. Nobody could touch her.

Mae closed her eyes and remembered the lines of the circle, then put what she knew into action. She lifted her arms and danced, demanding entry into the demon world, making her steps as fast and as confident as she could. She refused to think about what would happen if she faltered.

The sun was hot on her hair, a light breeze lifting strands and playing on the skin of her neck. She thought about that instead, about summer in the vineyard, Nick's hand in hers with the silver ring growing warm between their palms, Alan's mouth on hers in the dark, quiet kitchen. She couldn't dance the way Sin danced, like poetry in motion, so she made the dance different, made it negotiation in motion.

Mae held out her thought of the world like a glittering bauble, held it up mockingly just out of Liannan's reach, and she smiled with her face lifted to the sun.

It was more of a smirk, really. She was thinking, You know you want this.

"I call on the nightmare lover," she said, and twisted through summer air turning cold. The circle seemed to be tipping somewhere else, to a place she didn't want to go, and her hair was streaming suddenly in an icy wind. "I call on she who waits for dancers to fall. I call on she who had me and lost me yesterday. Come and get me, Liannan! If you can."

The circle flipped as if she was standing in a snow globe, and she found herself enveloped in chaos. Summer had been torn away and she was in darkness, hearing screams that sounded tortured or triumphant, horrible low laughter, and never any words. She felt cold fingers touching her hands, pulling on her clothes; she looked down and saw nothing. She shuddered uncontrollably and then looked up and saw Liannan leaping for her like a tigress, all glowing eyes and teeth.

"Mae!" Alan shouted, far away. "Don't move!"

She locked her muscles to stop herself from running. She hadn't trespassed in this circle, she belonged here, and she was wearing her talisman. Liannan couldn't touch her.

There was no partner to share this with, nobody to help bear the burden of linking the worlds, nobody to comfort her in the presence of demons. Liannan's breath was a cold blast in her face, like some freezing alternative to a furnace. The cord of her talisman had turned into a line of ice as well, the cold of it burning so all she wanted to do was scream and tear it off.

Mae didn't like it when someone tried to scare her. She held still as needle-sharp invisible fingers ran down her body, still as her own talisman burned her, still as a clammy sheen of sweat gathered on her skin and she began to shake. Liannan was a fraction of an inch away, her breath cold in Mae's mouth.

"Can you call demons, little one?" she asked, her voice low and almost musical. Her presence flooded through Mae's mind like disease. "Of course you can. All humans can. Whether the demons will come when you call, oh, that's another thing."

Mae took a deep breath. "And yet here you are."

Liannan's crystal-coloured eyes were dulled in the darkness, pools full of shadows with no light to reflect. She smiled.

"Here we are," she said. With a flicker as if Mae had blinked, though she hadn't, they were standing in Manstree Field and lights were playing brilliantly in Liannan's eyes. "Now," the demon continued, still smiling, "what do you want?"

"It wasn't her who wanted to speak to you," said Alan, his voice close now and hoarse, as if he'd been shouting. "It was me."

Mae wondered what he had seen when she saw the demon world, but she didn't even dare look at him. She wouldn't risk taking her eyes off Liannan.

The demon laughed, stretching her arms over her head as if she was enjoying the sunshine. Her hands looked almost like a normal girl's hands today, the ice formed into the shape of human hands and faintly flushed with pink, as if someone had mixed a few drops of blood in water before it was frozen. She even had nails, though they glittered like steel.

"Why, Alan," she said, giving him a lingering look. "All you ever have to do is take off your talisman and say my name, and I will come slipping sweet into your dreams."

"I share a room with my brother," Alan said pleasantly. "That'd be a little awkward."

Liannan lifted one shoulder in a shrug. She seemed to be dressed in a waterfall, water tinted just green enough to veil her body rather than reveal it. Even her hair was wet, rivulets of water running through the dark red curls like ribbons. Her shoulder rose right out of her liquid wrap, white and wet.

"Instead you get your little girlfriend to risk her life so that you could see me," Liannan said, and Mae did look at Alan then, and saw the red stain on his cheeks, as if he'd been slapped in the face. Liannan laughed. "It happens all the time," she said, as if she was soothing him. "A man who was hanged in this field once promised to love a woman forever, and the next year handed her body over so he could have me. He lived to be sorry for his bargain. They usually live long enough to be sorry."

A man who was hanged, Mae thought. She'd known why the field was called Manstree Field, of course, and the vineyard was called after the field, but it had never really hit home until now. People had hung from a gibbet here, their bodies swaying like fruit from trees. They were all standing in the shadow of a gallows.

"Come to make a bargain with me?" Liannan inquired.

Alan hesitated. "Yes."

Liannan seemed almost tender, as if she was speaking to a child or someone she loved very much. Mae could feel her cold, clawing hunger. "Think you're going to be sorry for it?"

"Oh yes," Alan breathed.

Liannan turned away from both of them, her watery train a circle that foamed and gleamed about her feet. The sunlight hit her full on and made her dazzling, like the sun breaking the ocean into a thousand sparkling points of light.

"At least it sounds interesting. Ask me, then."

"Something else first," said Alan. "Let Mae go."

"What?" Mae demanded.

"I need to be alone with Liannan," Alan said. "And I can't – I can't think the way I need to while you're in danger. I want Mae free to step out of the circle with no consequences."

"You can have that," Liannan told him. "At a price."

"I'll pay it."

The demon began to look amused. "I haven't told you what it is yet."

"I know."

"And what do you have, Alan Ryves, that makes you believe I will give you an answer and let a human free of my circle?"

Alan looked at her the way he looked at demons, steadfast and calm, as if they had just walked into his bookshop and asked for a recommendation. As if they were people.

"I have a winning card to play," he said. "I think."

"Better hope you're right," Liannan murmured. "Or you go home to your brother tonight wearing black eyes and a smile. All right, Mae, you can leave."

Mae stared into her cold eyes. They reflected the summer vineyard of Mae's childhood like carnival mirrors, twisting everything.

"And if I don't leave?"

Liannan laughed. "I'd be delighted if you stayed. It won't let Alan out of his bargain. A bargain's a very personal thing between two people, you know. Maybe the most personal thing there is."

Mae narrowed her eyes. "Maybe for you."

She could feel Liannan's dark presence receding like chains being unlocked and slipping away from her. She could feel the whole demon world slipping away. The sense of pressure, as if she was leaning against a door and trying to keep it shut, was suddenly and blissfully gone.

She hadn't wanted Alan to buy her freedom, but it would be stupid not to take it.

She stepped out of the circle, the sun warm on her arms and the back of her neck, her muscles unlocking from tension and terror and turning liquid, the heat of a normal summer day as shockingly sweet as having hot water poured all over her aching body.

Alan caught her as she stumbled, both her hands landing on his arms. She got only a glimpse of his eyes, wide and a little frantic, black pupil swallowing up the blue, and then he was kissing her. He held on to her a little too tightly, making her remember with a jolt that he was strong, and he kissed her almost desperately, as if they were standing at a harbour somewhere about to be parted. As if he was saying goodbye.

"Hey," Mae said, after a breathless, warm moment. She stopped clinging and pushed him backwards; it didn't really work. "Stop that."

"No, sorry, I know," Alan told her, eyes still mostly black. "There's this other guy. It isn't fair."

"Right." Mae took a deep breath, and then another. For a moment she was sure Alan was going to kiss her again and not sure what she would do about it when he did; then he tipped his head forward and laid his forehead against hers, quite gently.

"I thought you were dead for a second there," Alan told her, soft. "And it was my fault."

Liannan's voice came as a surprise, cold in a world that had gone warm and small.

"You're boring me. Either get to the point or ask me to join in."

Alan took Mae's hands in his, palms up and fingers linked as if they were about to dance, and then he dropped them instead.

"Mae," he said, "would you please go to the car?"

"Oh, you have got to be joking," Mae exclaimed. "I'm not a child. I'm not scared of danger. I was the one who called her here!"

"And you were the one I asked to call her," Alan said. "Because I trusted you to leave me, so I could ask what I need to ask. In private. Please."

"I want to help you!"

"And you did," Alan told her. "But I'm not helpless just because I can't do magic. Just because I couldn't call a demon myself. You helped me and I'm grateful, but I have to do this on my own. Can you trust me enough for that?"

His eyes were on her, worried and terribly focused. As if she was going to tell the guy who'd insisted on saving her brother that she didn't trust him. As if she was going to make anyone feel helpless for being without magic.

Mae felt her mouth curve in a smile, half rueful and half just surrender. "I can trust you enough for anything. Doesn't mean I like it."

She backed up a few steps away from the demon's circle and Alan both, into the tall grass and closer to the trim rows of vivid green vines. Alan threw her his car keys, and they described a neat little silver arc against the sky before she caught them in one open hand.

She walked away and left him with the demon.

14

The Lesson of Fear

S HE LAY FLAT IN THE BACK SEAT OF THE CAR FOR HOURS, STARING up at the worn grey roof and trying not to think about Alan's hands holding her too tight and the kiss that had tasted like a goodbye.

If Liannan killed Alan, she was the one who was going to have to carry the news back to Nick.

It would be all her fault.

She shut her eyes and tried to concentrate on the music, while Alan's death played out against her eyelids.

"Mae, are you asleep?" Alan asked, at which point Mae opened her eyes, scrambled up on her knees, and punched him in the chest.

"No, I was lying back contemplating the fact of your death and listening to some truly embarrassing music!"

She pulled out the earbuds and turned off her iPod, shoving it into her pocket to hide the evidence. Alan looked hideously tired, grey shadows under his eyes, as if someone had rubbed their dusty thumbs over the tender places directly below his lashes, but he smiled.

"What were you listening to?"

"I don't wish to discuss it at this time," she said loftily.

What she did want to do was give Alan a hug, hold on hard to make sure he was real and alive after all the horrors she had been imagining, but he looked like he might break or fall down if she touched him.

She climbed into the passenger seat instead, and Alan got into the car, moving carefully, as if he was old. He turned the ignition, and Mae reached out as the car came humming to life and touched him, very gently, on the shoulder.

"What did you ask her, Alan?"

Alan did not look at her. He looked over the steering wheel. The sky was ashen, all the blue bled out of it as grey evening set in, and Alan's face had a tinge of the same colour.

"I asked her whether I could trust Gerald to keep his part of the bargain," he said hoarsely. "And she says that I can."

Mae felt as if someone had pulled her stomach out from under her.

"The bargain where you betray your brother and rip his powers away from him? That bargain?"

"Mae," he said.

"Aren't demons meant to be – aren't they meant to be magic? They are their power; you'd be cutting him in half. Less than half. You'd trap him in a box and start sawing, is that it?"

Mae was almost surprised to find herself raging. She'd been so relieved to see him, such a short time ago. It was ridiculous to be so relieved you felt dizzy and so angry you felt dizzy in such swift succession. She looked down at her knees rather than at the fields of home passing her by, or Alan's face.

"And you'd lie to trap him."

"I lie all the time," Alan said quietly.

She looked over at him, and his hands were steady on the wheel, as if he wasn't bothered about any of this, as if he didn't even care.

"What happened between you and Nick in Durham?" she demanded. "When the storm came and those two people died. Sometimes it seems like you hate him now. Is that it? Do you want to take revenge for something? What did he do?"

Alan stopped the car in the middle of the road with a screech of tyres, and Mae, not wearing her seat belt, jolted forward in her seat. She bit her tongue hard, and her mouth filled with the taste of blood, hot and bitter.

"I don't want to talk about it!"

"Well," Mae said, slamming open the car door and jumping out, banging her shoulder against the frame of the door as she went, clumsy with anger. "I don't want to stay in this car."

She held the door in one clenched fist as she ducked her head, glaring into Alan's startled face.

"I wouldn't have risked calling demons for you if I knew you were planning to betray your brother," she told him. "I thought you were better than that."

She slammed the door and stormed forward, walking in the ditch, and did not quite realise that she'd expected Alan to stop the car and argue with her until she heard him rev the engine and watched his tail lights disappear into the grey evening.

❧❧❧

It was only about two miles' walk home. Mae put her head down and walked through the warm evening, trying to concentrate on walking and not let herself think.

That was going tremendously well. She was so lost in thought that when her phone rang she almost walked into a tree.

"Sorry," she mumbled automatically. It did not accept her apology, on account of being a tree.

She glared at it anyway, and then transferred her glare to her phone. Someone whose number she didn't recognise was calling her.

"What is it?"

"Get a better offer?"

"Huh, what, crazy person on the line," Mae said, before it sank in that this was unmistakably Nick's voice, deep and a little scratchy as usual, sounding as if he'd just taken about five shots of whisky an instant before she picked up.

"If you're not coming over, I'm going to get Jamie and start him on some hand-to-hand blade work."

"Oh good, crazy person I actually do know and who wants to cut up my brother," said Mae. She didn't want to see Nick, not so soon after Alan had let her know that his awful plan was actually happening.

She remembered feeling as if Nick was going to raze the city. She didn't know what he had done in Durham.

She wasn't about to let Jamie get hit with surprise knives.

"I'm coming over," she said, her voice sounding soft and a little worn. She couldn't believe how tired she was, but it wasn't much farther to get to Nick's house. She could make it.

"I'll work on my car until you get here, then," said Nick, who had no idea that his brother was planning to hand him over to a magician. That there was no way for him to become human enough.

"Try not to die of excitement before I get there," Mae told him, brittle and bright as her mother was before a board meeting, when she knew she had a problem to fix and had no idea how to do it. Mae knew she had to be twice as confident and convincing, put up a facade so brilliant nobody could see past it, in order to buy enough time so that somehow she could figure out what to do.

She got off to a bad start when she walked in the door and found Alan on the sofa. It took her a moment of sheer frozen panic, knowing she couldn't meet his eyes or talk to him right now without Nick knowing something was wrong, to realise that he was asleep.

"Yeah," Nick said from the door. "He was meant to be going to his boring talk on whatever, but he came in and collapsed on the sofa. That bookshop manager thinks she can run him into the ground. Don't wake him."

His voice sounded taut. When Mae looked over her shoulder at him, he looked too tightly wound all over. It was the way he sometimes got when they were all living together in London, when his answers to questions would become shorter and snarlier until Jamie was looking really alarmed. Nick would eventually jump out of his chair without another word to anyone and go into the garden to practise the sword for about four hours.

Mae wondered if he knew something, but when she looked at him, he just looked irritably back at her and said, "Are you ready to read yet?"

"Oh," she said. "Oh, sure."

She followed Nick up the rickety attic stairs to the little

room that the setting sun was turning into warm gold and red and shadows, and sat down on the floor with the copybook. The wood was so old, even the splinters seemed to have given up and gone soft, feeling almost fuzzy under Mae's clenched fist as she opened the book and began to read.

I tried to leave again today. Yesterday was Saturday, the day when Alan's football team plays. We have been living in this town for a month, and Alan has been playing almost as long. He loves it. Watching him play is one of the things that make me happiest.

Sometimes I wish I could watch him at school. I wish I could see him enjoying himself more often.

A brilliant student, an athlete, the sweetest boy in school. You must be so proud, his teachers say, and I am proud of him. I am ashamed of myself.

Sometimes all his promise seems like a reproach to me. What is going to happen to my son in this world?

Even at his games we are not quite free. Alan insists that I bring the demon with me to watch him play football.

We got the whole row of seats to ourselves. Alan insisted that it start preschool this year too. It turns my stomach to think of its presence in a room full of real children. They can't possibly be comfortable around it.

Nobody has been hurt. Nobody is ever hurt. If I just knew what the demon was planning, if it is planning anything at all, then I could bear this better. As things are, dread keeps me awake for hours, keeps me listening for the sound of a demon stirring in my home.

Demons have influence over the minds of humans, Olivia

says. Sometimes I think my son is simply the demon's puppet. That I have to kill the demon to set him free.

The other football team was bigger, older, and a little rough. Parents around me were muttering and concerned, but I'm used to my son being in far more danger than could be posed to him by other children. I only noticed when Alan went down hard and was lost in a pile of seething bodies; when I heard him cry out.

I leaped to my feet then. And I felt a cold presence at my elbow. The creature was on its feet too, black eyes scanning the field.

All the hair stood up on the back of my neck. I felt as if Olivia's voice was whispering in my ear, laughing, at her most mad. Demons crave strong emotions. They love tasting things like fear, like pain.

When Alan came off the field laughing, proud of his trophy and his loose tooth, he put an arm around it and tried to show it the trophy.

The demon turned around and touched Alan's mouth. Its hand came away stained.

Demons want blood.

Alan laughed and hugged it closer. "Don't worry," he said. "I'm okay. It doesn't hurt."

That was yesterday. Today in the early morning I carried Alan downstairs, as if we had to move. I murmured to him that it was all right, that I had everything taken care of, that I had Nick.

I was driving as fast as I could. I was almost out of town when Alan woke up properly. I saw him yawn and stretch, rub his eyes and almost knock off his glasses. Then his eyes travelled from my head to Olivia's.

"Where's Nick?"

This time I was not going to be stopped by seeing fear on his face. This time I wasn't thinking about slaying a monster. I was simply taking the coward's way out. I was running away. Let the magicians have it. Let someone else deal with it.

I met Alan's eyes in the mirror head-on, so desperate that I was almost calm.

Reflected in the glass, my son's eyes narrowed.

Then he threw himself out of the speeding car. I stopped with a screech of brakes, far too late

Alan had already picked himself up off the road and was running fast, becoming a speck in the distance. My Alan, the athlete. If I'd leaped from the car and chased him, I doubt I would have caught him.

"Poor thing," Olivia remarked as we drove back. "Alan," she said after a moment, as if she had trouble recalling his name. "He seems like a nice child."

I don't know what else I expected. Alan doesn't think of her as his mother. It would break my heart if he did.

She's not fit to be anybody's mother.

It's not her fault. But the way she is now breaks my heart too.

Alan was not back in the house as I had expected. He was at the top of our road instead, he and the demon. There were blood and tears streaming down Alan's face, making a grisly mask for my child as he shook and held the demon in his arms. It looked the same as it always does.

Alan looked at me, defiant. "He was coming to look for me," he said, based on no evidence at all. Then he returned to whispering comfort in the demon's ear.

"All right, Alan," I said loudly, trying to drown out that soft sound. "You win."

He looked at me for a moment and then resumed his years-long one-way conversation with the demon: telling it that everything was fine now, that it was safe, that above all else it was loved.

I sat with the car door open, hearing the small sounds of the engine cooling, and looking straight ahead. The wind blew the long locks of Olivia's hair across to the open door, obscuring my view like streamers of shadow, like the bars of a prison window between me and the world.

Perhaps Alan is not enchanted. Perhaps he is simply his father's son, loving the most where there is no happiness and no hope of return to be found.

Mae stopped reading.

She had no idea what to say to Nick.

He was just standing there, braced against the window frame, his head bowed. The sun was no more than a red sliver against the horizon, like the edge of a knife smeared with strawberry jam. Everything she'd read was screaming through her head, like a storm made out of words. Demons want blood. Demons have influence over the minds of humans. Let the magicians have it.

"Alan, the athlete," Nick ground out, which Mae had not been thinking at all.

"Oh," she said.

"Do you know how it happened?" he asked.

"No," said Mae, her stomach sinking. She'd never asked about Alan's limp. She'd pretended it wasn't there, thinking maybe he'd been hurt in some awful fight, maybe he'd been born with it. Pretending seemed like the most polite thing to do, and after a while the politeness became real. It wasn't like she didn't notice it, but she was used to it, the limp as much a part of Alan as his careful smiles.

She wasn't sure she wanted to know.

"It was my fault," Nick said stonily, and Mae barely had time to gasp before he went on. "I took off my talisman, the night Dad died. Alan gave me his. They were throwing fire, and he got caught. He lost his father and his leg and it was all because of me."

Mae bit her lip. Alan, the athlete. The football player, the kid his frantic father couldn't catch. She thought about Alan's face when he asked Sin how he was supposed to run.

"Couldn't you . . ." she began, hesitating, thinking of Gerald saying that Nick couldn't heal Merris. "Are you able to fix his leg? Can you do that?"

He looked up, eyes slices of shadow in his cold face, and Mae felt a thrill of fear run down her spine as she realised that she'd said exactly the wrong thing.

"Yes," Nick said, his voice a whisper, chilling as the sounds that run through an empty house at night when you wake scared from nightmares. "That had occurred to me, actually. But Alan won't let me."

That last made her almost laugh. It seemed so absurd to hear him say something like that, something as simple and childish as that.

"How can he stop you?" she blurted.

Mae saw his fingers clench hard on the windowsill, white and terribly strong.

"You're right," he snarled. "Nobody can stop me. I can do anything, anytime, and not a soul in this world would be able to stop me."

Her nerves, pulled tight and strumming to every sound he made, almost broke when his voice changed. Then she realised that his big shoulders had hunched in, just a little, and the roughness of his voice was not only anger.

"But he doesn't want me to," Nick said. "And I don't – I don't know why."

"Because he wants you to act like a human," Mae offered. "He doesn't want you to do magic."

She needed to give him some kind of answer; she'd promised him help, and she didn't know if that was right, but it made Nick glance her way.

"It's like how he makes you go to school," she continued, stumbling over her words.

"And kills himself in that stupid bookshop to do it," Nick muttered to the floor. Then he looked up. There was a strange glint in his eye. "What about you?"

"Beg pardon?" said Mae.

He turned away from the window and looked at her full on. He looked suddenly and terrifyingly interested, like a cat absorbed in his game with a mouse.

"What about you?" he repeated. "What do you want? I could give you anything." His voice lowered to a snarling purr, all his promises turning into threats. "I could take you anywhere in the world. You could be beautiful or powerful or rich beyond your imagination. There has to be something that you want!"

"I want lots of things."

Nick's mouth curled. "But you're scared to take them."

"I'm not scared," Mae said. "I want lots of things, but I want to get them for myself."

His gaze dropped to the floor and for a moment Mae thought she might have said the wrong thing again. When he spoke, though, his voice had returned to normal, flat and calm, and she thought that might mean what she'd said had made sense to him.

"All right." He looked up abruptly. "Pity."

"Uh, pity about what?"

"No," Nick said impatiently. "Pity. You told me about embarrassment last time. Tell me about pity. What's it like?"

"Oh, well," said Mae, and put down the copybook and linked her arms around her knees, thinking hard. "Pity's – when you hear that something bad has happened to someone, or see them hurt or upset, and even if you don't like them, it doesn't matter, you just feel bad because they feel so bad. You want to help."

Nick slid, his back to the wall, down to the old wooden floor. He drew up one knee and left the other leg stretched out, fixed Mae with expressionless eyes, and shook his head.

"Sympathy."

"Like pity," Mae said, "but warmer."

She remembered Liannan saying that in a hundred years she had never seen the smallest sign Nick had warmth in him. She wasn't surprised when Nick shook his head again.

"Fear," he suggested, his voice rippling slightly over the word as if he liked it. Mae was fairly sure, though, that what he liked was inspiring it; he liked the way it looked from the outside.

She thought about the moment when Alan, who at the time had been little more than a stranger, had told her that the strange black markings on Jamie meant he was going to die.

"The cold feeling that something terrible is coming," she said slowly. "Like being a kid in the dark, and feeling paralysed even though you know you have to act, because you're sure that if you even move, the most terrible thing you can think of will happen."

Nick looked at her for a while and then, eventually, he nodded.

"I think," he said, "I'm getting the hang of fear."

He did not look afraid. Mae didn't want to ask him what had taught him the lesson of fear that he had not learned for centuries trapped out in the dark. She didn't want to hear what his fear was – being betrayed by his brother, being taken by the magicians again – because if she learned that, she would betray Alan. She would tell Nick that the one thing he feared was about to come true.

"I want to go home," she said.

Nick nodded and stood up, jerking his head towards the door. He was going to give her a lift home, then. Mae could only be grateful for it. Her whole brain felt tired, like a caged animal that had been trying to break out for too long. She kept trying to think of ways for them all to escape from this mess, and she could find no way, and there was nobody to help her.

Before they left, Nick went into the sitting room and knelt down by the sofa, shaking Alan. Mae stood at the door and watched Alan twitch and blink awake, stretching and then biting his lip when he stretched his bad leg too far. His face looked white, crumpled and a little soft with sleep, reminding Mae of old tissue paper. He blinked blue eyes gone wide and unfocused.

"You can't sleep here all night, you idiot," Nick said roughly. "Your leg will be a mess in the morning. Get up and go to bed."

"Where're my . . . ?" Alan began, vague but questing.

Nick took Alan's glasses out of his own pocket and held them out. Alan accepted them but seemed unsure what to do with them, fingers curling around them and falling to his chest as his eyes slid shut again.

"Get up," Nick ordered, and hauled him upright on the sofa by main force. "Go to bed. Now. Look at you. You haven't been lifting boxes again, have you?" he asked with a sudden extra edge to his voice.

"No," Alan said fondly, and he reached out sleepily to ruffle Nick's hair.

Mae had made the same gesture towards Jamie a thousand times, but never once had Jamie pulled back like that, knocking Alan's hand away in his haste. Alan did not even look surprised, only a little more worn, and he smiled at Nick tiredly and then at Mae as he passed her, apparently too sleepy even to find her presence odd, and limped up the stairs to bed.

On the way home Mae and Nick did not speak. Mae curled up away from him, her cheek against the cool wet window, her eyes on the night that had drawn in black and starless around them.

She kept thinking of what Gerald had said to Alan: I need you to lead him somewhere deserted and trap him in a demon's circle for me.

Mae did not want to tell Alan's secret. All her anger against him seemed drained out of her, thinking of that running boy grown up crippled and fatherless with nobody in the world to reach out to.

More than that, though, she realised that she didn't dare tell Nick his only nightmare in the world was about to become reality. He was not human. He was beyond pity and yet not beyond rage, and she was completely terrified of what he would do if she took away the only reason he had to act human.

15

Lady Errant

MAE WOKE FROM UNEASY, DEMON-HAUNTED SLEEP TO THE sound of a crash. She rolled out of bed and ran out onto the landing, and then stopped dead at the sight of Jamie panting and leaning against the stair rail.

Nick was sitting on the top step. He was breathing hard too, chest rising and falling fast under a thin grey T-shirt. He leaned his wrists against his knees and looked over at Mae.

That made Jamie look too. He smiled at her, which showed they were all right except when Jamie was offended by Seb's actual presence, and made Mae grin back.

"Mae, he made me go out for a run," Jamie called out. "Tell him I don't run!"

"Jamie and I are lilies of the field. We toil not, neither do we jog," Mae informed Nick.

She came over and slipped her arm around Jamie's waist. He leaned heavily on her, sweaty cheek against hers, and made a piteous whimpering noise.

"Turns out he does run," Nick drawled. "Given an incentive. And he wouldn't be so out of breath if he hadn't kept shrieking."

"That was not a shriek," Jamie said with dignity. "It was a husky masculine cry of terror."

"Maybe you should start with something a little more soothing," said Mae, patting Jamie's back.

"Yes, soothing," Jamie said gratefully. "Less knives. More Yogilates!"

The doorbell rang. Mae went to change into jeans, as Jamie was apparently now a wreck of a man and couldn't answer the door. She peeked out of the window and saw who it was before she came down the stairs and let Seb in.

"I thought maybe you could use a lift to school," Seb said, car keys in hand. He almost dropped them at the sight of Nick and Jamie. "Hey," he said warily. "What's going on?"

"Nick is spotting me during my new exercise regimen," Jamie announced, giving Seb the evil eye. "I wish to be more toned. And attractive. To men."

Seb went a slow, horrified red.

Nick laughed, and Mae bit back a smile so he wouldn't feel they were ganging up on him.

She was glad to see him. When she'd looked out of the window, she'd known it was him and not Nick this time, and not just because Nick was already on her stairs. The memory of both of them was fresh with her, the way they stood, their exact heights. Seb looked totally different from Nick. He looked normal and lovely and like he couldn't break her heart, and besides that, she hated walking to school.

"C'mon, let's go," she told him.

She opened the door to a beautiful summer morning, drenched in light.

Behind her, Nick said, "Might see you later."

*

Today Nick said his first word: "chair".

I have not written in this journal for some time. I didn't like the thought of leaving Alan this record of misery.

Today is different from all other days. Nick said his first word today, his voice harsh, croaking like a raven rather than a child.

But he understood what he was saying. He said more than one word. Alan pointed to me and he said, "Dad."

That stunned me more than the miracle, more than the demon with words in its mouth.

If I thought of him as anyone's child, I thought of him as Arthur's. But of course Nick has not seen Arthur for four years, of course Alan has been by his side all this time whispering words to him, telling him how the world is.

Alan has been sure that Nick is his brother, and that makes me his father.

The demon's father.

I don't feel like his father, but I cannot call him "it" any more. I cannot forget the rush of happiness that came over me when I heard him talking and felt for the first time that there could be hope.

If he talks, if he can be that close to human, then I might have a real purpose at last.

I picked Nick up for the first time today. He's getting far too heavy for Alan to carry. And Alan looked so happy when I did it.

I had to put him down after a few moments. Not because he was heavy, but because I could not bear to have those

eyes and that still mask of a child's face so close to mine. I do not know how Alan can bear it.

Alan's so young. He didn't know enough about babies to know what one should look like, and he's used to Nick by now. Perhaps Nick looks human to him.

This evening before bedtime I saw Nick sitting by Alan as he usually does, an upside-down book held in his lap.

"Shall I read to you, Nick?" I asked, and I took the creature up again and put him in my lap. He tried to wriggle away as he always does with Alan, but I held him firmly, and he stopped struggling after a moment. Resting against my chest, he felt small and warm, like a real child. I concentrated on the story, kept my voice steady and even, and as I read, "The king of all wild things said . . ." Nick's head dropped into the crook of my elbow and he was asleep.

I was not quite sure what to do next, and then I saw my son. He'd dropped his book and was standing looking at me and his brother. The look of hope and fear on his face made me want to throw the demon away, reach out and hold him close.

Instead I drew my fingers through Nick's thick black hair. It wasn't much, and it wasn't so bad. Nick stirred but did not wake, and Alan smiled, tremulous but so happy.

"Come here, my darling," I said, then reached out with my free hand and drew him to me. He came willingly, nestling into me as he has not since he was very small. "This is just the beginning," I told him. "We have to think very carefully about what to do next."

If a demon can be taught to be human, then I will have done something terribly important with my life.

I think that I started writing this as a way to keep my son, who has barred doors against me and always looks for another face first, who has not been all mine since he was four years old. I wanted him to have this after my death, because I had failed him in life so completely.

Now I have an idea of what I can do for him.

I held my son close and began to whisper plans, keeping the demon safe and warm in the circle of my arm.

Mae shut the book.

Nick had come into her music room after school, hurled the copybook at her feet, and moved to the window, fixing her with an expectant look. She'd promised to help him, so she had opened the book and hoped that Daniel Ryves wouldn't try to murder or leave Nick this time.

She hadn't thought it might help.

Nick wasn't at the window like a guard standing braced for an attack any more. He was sitting on the window seat with a look of serious attention on his face. A lock of hair had fallen into his eyes, a slash of curving black that made Mae's fingers lift to touch it, even though he was across the room.

"He used to carry me when we were moving," he said. "Dad. So I wouldn't – wouldn't wake up."

It came out cool, just a statement of fact. Nick looked away afterwards, though, the angle of his jaw tight, and Mae thought it might be time to change the subject.

"What do you know about marks?" she asked.

Nick started and stared at her, eyes suddenly wide.

"What do you mean?"

Mae raised her eyebrows. "I was thinking about this mark that's giving Gerald all his power, about the magician's sigils and the three different demon's marks."

"There's only one demon's mark," Nick interrupted.

He was looking at her again and leaning back against the window glass, arms crossed over his chest. Mae would've thought that Nick might look less out of place in the music room, which she and Jamie had messed around in and danced through and used as their playroom for years, but he didn't. His eyes glittered a little too coldly in the lights of the chandelier, his clothes were worn and dark in the bright white room, and whichever way she looked at him, he was either a boy who didn't fit into her home or a demon who didn't fit into her world.

She wanted to reach out and brush back that lock of hair, all the same.

"No, you know, first there's the first-tier mark, the doorway, and then there's the second-tier mark, the triangle, and then the third-tier mark, the eye. That's what I mean."

"They're all part of one mark," Nick told her. "Just one. The magicians don't let us into this world with enough power to make our mark, so we have to work up to possession by stages. But I could do it. That's why Anzu and Liannan are so angry with me. I could put the full mark on anyone I wanted, and let a demon slide in."

"So demons have only one mark," Mae said. "But now magicians have two. It seems a bit much for Gerald to have invented a whole new one. I think it makes more sense for him to have modified one of the existing marks. What does the magician's sigil do?"

"Lets you drain power from your Circle's circle of stones."

"And the demon's mark lets you possess someone."

"Doesn't just do that," Nick said. "Anzu marked Alan and Jamie, didn't he? Couldn't possess them both."

It had never occurred to Mae before that of course Anzu, the Obsidian Circle's pet demon, would have been the one to mark Jamie. She made a face at the thought.

"So what was his plan?"

"Possess one," said Nick. "Save the other for later. The full demon's mark, it forms a channel between humans and demons, so you can possess them, or just control them. That way you can have slaves as well as bodies to possess once the one you're possessing breaks down. Anzu and me, we once had bodies in this desert kingdom. We had an agreement: we marked an army of slaves for the king so long as we got bodies for seven years."

"Really," Mae said. "Slaves. What happened next?"

"He didn't keep his part of the bargain," said Nick. "So we called up a storm and buried the kingdom under the sand. It's probably still there now. We buried it deep."

"I meant what happened to the slaves," Mae clarified. She thought she did a good job of keeping her voice even.

"Oh, they died too," Nick said. He sounded as indifferent as ever, but he kept his eyes on her and watched for her response. She thought he might be feeling a bit wary.

"You could have let them go."

"No," Nick answered. "What I mark is mine. It's the same way for magicians. A magician takes a sigil to show he belongs to his Circle. When we're going through magicians, the magicians' blood can ransom a mark. A mark can be transferred. But there's no way to make a mark cost nothing. A mark always costs someone everything."

"So if Gerald had invented a mark to make humans obey him . . ." Mae said.

"Wouldn't give him any more power, would it?" Nick asked. "Most humans don't have magic."

Mae nodded. It was the magician's sigil Gerald had modified, then, it had to be. But exactly how he'd changed it, there was no way to know. Until they knew, how could they fight him?

Gerald had been able to knock Nick flat, and he was after Jamie. She didn't know what to do.

"Do you think you can beat Gerald?" she asked quietly.

Nick's face did not change, but the chandeliers above them rang out like wind chimes with the breeze picking up.

"I know I can," he said. Mae looked into his eyes and tried to find something reassuring there, something she could rely on, but they were full of sliding shadows. "Don't," Nick added abruptly. "Don't be scared about Jamie. They can't have him. He's my friend."

Mae took a deep breath, feeling lighter in the chest area. She did believe that, even though it hadn't occurred to her when Nick offered to be friends. She wondered why she hadn't realised that Nick meant it, as he meant everything he said. Jamie was under his protection forever. Jamie was safe, if Nick could make him so.

"I know that," she told him, and smiled.

"When you talked about demons' marks, I thought you knew something else," Nick said, and looked away.

She didn't even realise she'd risen until she was halfway across the floor, and by then she wasn't stopping until she reached the window seat. He had to tilt his head backwards against the glass to look up at her.

"Nick, what do you mean?"

"I don't want to possess anyone," Nick said softly, eyes shining like ink. "So I didn't think I'd want to mark a human. But the marks don't just mean possession. They mean being mine. They mean I can watch, and guard, and none of the others can touch, and I could—"

"Control someone," Mae said. "Make them your slave."

Nick blinked slowly, eyelashes sweeping the top of his cheekbones. "That too."

He was devastatingly beautiful, Mae thought, and "devastating" was the word: she could see storms and cities burning in his eyes.

"I didn't think I'd want to mark a human," he said. "But I do."

"Alan," Mae whispered.

"Yes," Nick whispered back. "And you."

Mae went still, torn between the impulse that said the demon's eye was on her, that she should run, and the impulse to move closer. Nick had never said anything to indicate she mattered to him before.

"Oh," she said.

"And Jamie," Nick continued.

"Oh," she said, in a very different way. "Well. Thanks for my part in the compliment. Naturally I'd love to be watched and controlled, but I think I may be washing my hair that day."

Nick grinned. "Yeah, all right."

He looked more relaxed, Mae noticed. He was pleased about that book, she thought, pleased by the idea of the past and his father reading to him, his brother happy.

"I think we can get by without that," she said. "Even if I, as the bombshell of the group, have to take one for the team and go and seduce Gerald's secrets out of him."

"That's ridiculous," Nick told her. "I'm clearly the bombshell of the group."

Mae laughed and held out her hand.

"What?" Nick demanded warily. "I'm not sure I'm ready for more hand-holding."

"What?" Mae echoed back at him. "Another lesson for you, Nick: when you want to make a human happy, do something they enjoy with them. Besides, I'm having a moment of probably soon-to-be-destroyed optimism about the future. Don't worry. It probably won't last."

She ran to put in a CD she liked that was a little bit rock and a little bit blues, and then she went over and grasped Nick's hands in hers, pulling him to his feet.

Her confidence was checked by the way he just looked down at her, as if waiting for the human to explain her strange customs. She opened her hands and his slipped out of hers, down by his sides.

Mae's skin was prickling with sudden shame. She wanted to run away so he would stop looking at her, slam as many doors as she could between herself and his eyes, and she wanted to somehow carry this off so he thought nothing was wrong.

"Come on," she said, her voice going too high to be really light. "You know how to dance, don't you?"

He reached for her waist and then slid his big hands down along her body, fingers curling around her belt. His ring was a cold shock on the strip of skin between her shirt and her jeans.

"Yeah," Nick said, his voice curling in the air like smoke from a raging fire, filling her lungs and making it hard to breathe. "I know how to dance."

Mae looked up at him and saw nothing she could read: lowered eyelids and the line of his mouth. She put her hands up anyway, catching at his shoulders and the rhythm. Her hands curved around the fragile barrier of his T-shirt, grasping the worn cotton as if it was all that was holding her up. Her knuckles pressed tight against the swell of his shoulders, feeling his muscles shift as he moved with her.

She dipped down with him a little, his hips touching hers, stepped back and then up against him again. Her breath hitched every time he stepped in to her, a warm scrape in the back of her throat, and she wished desperately that she could stop it, but she couldn't. He must be hearing it, every time.

When they neared a wall, she almost blundered backwards into it, not expecting it, barely aware of things like walls, for God's sake. He palmed her hip, the hollow of his hand pressing down against her hipbone, and turned her easily, swinging her against him.

Mae's death grip on his shirt went loose, fingers curling up of what seemed to be their own volition to touch his neck, and that was a mistake. Nick started slightly, his cut-short hair prickling under her fingertips, and then she completely lost her mind, because she suddenly had both hands in his hair and was pulling his head down to catch the part of his lips, his tiny indrawn breath.

His mouth brushed hers for an instant, and then strong hands grabbed her shoulders and pushed her back at arm's length, hard.

"No," said Nick.

Just that, short and brutal. He let her go and walked back to the window.

Mae's first impulse was to die of shame, but she realised after a hot, stomach-clenching moment that this was probably impractical.

"Right, sorry," she said, forcing her voice to sound entirely unmoved. She'd just been carried away by the music. It was no big thing. "I get it."

She paused and knew for a sinking moment that Nick wasn't going to respond, and she could think of absolutely nothing to say, and the best she could hope for was that he would just leave in total silence so she could work on her dying-of-shame plan. Then Jamie, her beautiful, beautiful, timely brother, opened the door and looked rather surprised.

"Nick!" he said, smiling. "What are you doing here?"

"Looking for you," Mae lied promptly. "Where have you been?"

"Oh, I think we know where he's been," Nick said in a dark voice from the window.

Mae hadn't even thought about where he'd been until that moment, when she looked into his sunny, open face and saw magicians written on it, as if Gerald had already set his mark there.

"I suppose you wouldn't believe I was signing us both up for Yogilates."

Nick's silence was answer enough.

"Would you like me to read you a couple of chapters?" Jamie offered, brightening further at the thought of homework rather than knives. "We can't practice self-defence now – what a shame! Because it's too dark."

"Knife work at night is something you're going to have to learn," said Nick. "You have to train your eye to catch the glint of metal in the dark."

There was a horrified pause.

"Seriously," Jamie said. "I think Yogilates is my calling."

Nick laughed and moved towards Jamie in a few quick

strides. His glance over his shoulder at Mae said he was leaving this situation and they would never speak of it again.

"Okay, you can read one chapter. And you can stop talking about Yogilates."

"Oh, but" – Jamie's eyes flickered to Mae – "I could come down here with the book," he suggested. "I could do a dramatic reading!"

"I'm good for dramatic reading just now," Mae told him, and waggled her fingers in clear dismissal. Nick shepherded Jamie out of the door.

Mae went over to her armchair and tried very hard not to relive the last few minutes of the dance.

She clutched her hair in her hands, remembered grasping Nick's soft hair in handfuls, and let go, nails biting into her palms instead.

She didn't know what was wrong with her. She'd made passes and been shut down before. That happened when you had a tendency to take a chance rather than wait for guys to make their move. It didn't matter, not at all.

It had just been a stupid thing to do. That was what had her tied in knots. She wasn't usually stupid.

Nick had already made it very clear he wasn't interested.

So she'd leap at Seb next time she felt leaping urges, Mae told herself firmly, and went downstairs to make herself some coffee. She had gone through half a pot and had Dorothy Parker's Here Lies propped up on the table in front of her when she heard Annabel's heels going off like gunshots in the hall.

"Hello," her mother said, going for the fridge. Mae waved her coffee cup in greeting and watched as Annabel drew out a packet of lettuce leaves that had turned brown and dispirited. "Oh dear," she said. "Thai food all right by you?"

"I'll be honest: I wasn't going to eat salad either way."

Annabel nodded with just a hint of pain. She and Mae had gone back and forth on this a thousand times, and Mae had made it extremely clear that she cared more about eating cheese sandwiches today than being skinny when she was forty. "Is James home? I'll ask him what he wants."

"Yeah. Um, he has a friend from school with him. They're studying."

Mae realised what an enormous tactical error that had been when she saw her mother's face light up.

"A friend?" she asked. "Jamie?"

"Yeah," said Mae, getting up very quickly and almost spilling her coffee in the process. "Look, maybe you shouldn't—"

"A girl or a boy?" Annabel asked, and went for the stairs.

She was much too fast for a woman in six-inch heels, Mae thought, and dashed after her.

"A boy," she called after Annabel's swiftly ascending back, stricken with horror at the very idea of her mother opening Jamie's bedroom door expecting a studious young lady, possibly in a blouse and spectacles, and finding Nick Ryves.

"He must stay for dinner," Annabel said with determination, doing a wickedly fast turn on the landing and heading for the second set of stairs. "I'm so glad that James is getting on better at school. I couldn't think what to do. He said he didn't want to move schools."

"I didn't know you wanted him to change schools!" Mae shouted after her. Annabel was outside Jamie's door now, and Mae wasn't going to reach her in time. Disaster was inevitable. "How do you move so fast?"

"All my shoes are designer," Annabel informed her. "Quality always tells," she added as she opened the door.

"'There are few people whom I really love, and still fewer of whom I think well,'" Jamie read out, doing what Mae thought was supposed to be an upper-class Victorian lady's voice. He sounded as if someone was choking him to death with bonnet ribbons.

He was sitting on the window seat, feet up on a chair.

Nick was sitting on Jamie's bed. Only the lamp in Jamie's room was on, a yellow pool of light stopping short at Nick's feet, throwing tiny yellow shards of light into the dark hollows of his eyes. He was turning his magic knife over and over in his hands, the rough carvings glinting in the light.

"Mavis and I were wondering if your friend wanted to stay for dinner," Annabel said in a voice that lacked all conviction, but also belonged to a woman so dismayed she had no idea what else to offer.

Nick lifted an eyebrow. "Mavis?"

"Shut up," Mae told him.

"All right," said Nick. "Mavis."

Annabel was going to do damage to her manicure, hanging on to the doorknob like that. Jamie got up from the window seat and went and stood between Nick and Annabel, hovering a little uncertainly but with clear protective intent.

"Sure, Mum," he said. "Everyone likes food. Um, so where's the menu?"

Annabel kept sneaking peeks at Nick over Jamie's shoulder, as if to verify the full horror of the situation. Nick did not look especially surprised that someone's mother was clearly appalled by him.

"Yes," Annabel said, her voice distant because she was obviously trying to place herself in an alternate universe, one where her son did not entertain knife-wielding delinquents in his bedroom. "I'll go and find it. The menu. So we can choose what to eat."

She turned away and, very carefully, closed the door behind her. Then she began to descend the stairs. Despite the high-quality designer shoes, she was tottering a little.

"You two must get these tastes from your father," she said as Mae drew level with her. "I was never in the least drawn to the dangerous type. Even in college!"

"Dad dated dangerous guys in college?" Mae asked. "I had no idea."

"You know what I meant!"

"Also," said Mae, "I think you have a firm grip on the wrong end of the stick. Nick and Jamie are just friends."

"Oh, please," said Annabel. "Boys like this Nick aren't just friends with anyone."

They reached the bottom of the stairs, and Annabel went to the hall table, sliding out the drawer where they kept the menus.

"I think the Thai menu's stuck up on the fridge," Mae said. "And Nick's my friend too."

Her mother gave her a shocked look and went to the fridge, sliding the Thai menu out from under the ladybird-shaped magnets that Jamie had bought once in an attempt to make their kitchen look more cheerful.

Nick and Jamie came downstairs while she was looking at the noodles list.

"So I'm leaving," Nick announced.

"No, you should stay. Mum, tell him," said Jamie, and Annabel made a non-committal gesture that could have meant anything between Certainly and Get off my property before I call the police.

"You guys don't have any food in the house, you're ordering in, it's a pain to have to order for me, too," Nick said. "I'm leaving." He paused and added slowly, as if remembering something Alan had taught him long ago, "Thanks for having me."

"You're quite welcome," Annabel said automatically.

"We've got plenty of food in the house," said Mae. "It's just none of us can cook and our housekeeper leaves early Mondays and Tuesdays. We order take away half of the days in the week. You wouldn't be a pain. Stay."

"Oh," Jamie offered in a bright voice. "I could cook some—"

"No!" Mae, Annabel, and Nick all exclaimed as one.

Annabel gave Nick a slightly startled look. He was too busy giving Jamie a forbidding look to notice.

"Look, I am getting better," Jamie argued.

"I saw you put rice in a toaster once," said Mae. "I was there when you made that tin of beans explode."

"It was faulty," Jamie protested, his eyes shifty. "I am sure of this."

Nick took a short breath, as if coming to a decision, and took the three steps down to their kitchen in one bound. Annabel craned her neck in order to look up at him in alarm, and Nick looked back down at her, eyes narrowing into dark slits. He reached out, hands strong on the wasp waist of her business skirt, and pushed her onto a stool as if she was a child.

"Are you people helpless?" he asked. "Sit down. I'll make you something to eat."

Jamie came over and sat at the kitchen counter on a stool beside hers.

"Nick cooks quite well, Mum," he assured her.

Nick started to look in the fridge and take out things like peppers and onions, and Mae drifted over to the kitchen counter so they were all sitting in a row observing Nick perform the mysterious ritual of preparing food.

"I cook better than you," Nick corrected absently. "I think monkeys can probably be taught to cook better than you."

"I'd like to have a monkey that cooked for me," said Jamie. "I would pay him in bananas. His name would be Alphonse."

"I agree, that would be awesome," Mae said. "People would come for dinner just to see the monkey chef."

"You're raving," Nick said, defrosting chicken in the microwave. Mae was a bit impressed with how he seemed to look at the appliance and instantly comprehend its mysteries, when she'd been heating up ready-made meals for years by a method of pressing random buttons and hoping. "I know that's the only way Jamie communicates with people, but I expected better of you, Mavis."

"We're cutting out the whole Mavis thing right now, Nick," Mae said warningly.

"How many bananas would be good payment for a monkey?" Jamie wanted to know. "I would want to pay Alphonse a fair wage."

Jamie kept talking, the way he did, and Mae batted back ideas about the monkey chef. Nick threw in an occasional withering remark that did not wither Jamie in the slightest. Annabel propped her chin in her hand and watched Nick, looking suddenly thoughtful, and then surprised everyone by saying that if they were studying, Nick was welcome to stay the night.

Things got awkward again when they were sitting down to dinner. Nick's face was impassive, of course, but his shoulders were set a little combatively. He was obviously used to eating in a kitchen at a slightly shaky table, and not in a dining room with low lights gleaming on a mahogany table so polished it looked like their plates were suspended on the surface of a dark lake.

Mae should not have grabbed some plates when Annabel said they had a guest and were going to eat in the dining room, but she'd thought it seemed like a good sign.

Now here they were, and Nick might as well have been wearing a T-shirt that said NOT SUITED TO POLITE COMPANY. It wasn't a huge surprise that he was no good at making conversation.

"So you're in class with James," Annabel remarked, bright and brittle as cut glass. "Are there any particular subjects that are your favourites? I know James enjoys science."

"No," said Nick.

"In science you are allowed to blow things up," Jamie said wistfully. "Sometimes."

He seemed a little squashed by how badly things were going. Mae wished she could think of some way to make things go better, but really she knew the best-case scenario was just to get through this. There was not a single thing that Nick and Annabel could possibly have in common.

"And what are your interests and hobbies, Nicholas?" Annabel asked faintly, sounding like a cross between a television interviewer and a hostage.

Nick considered this for a minute, and then said, "I like swords."

Annabel leaned over her plate and asked, her voice changing, "You fence?"

"Not exactly," Nick drawled. "I'm more freestyle."

"I used to take fencing classes in school," Annabel told him, eyes bright. "I won some trophies. I wasn't bad, if I do say so myself. I was in a fencing club for my first couple of years in college, but Roger was a tennis fanatic, and I couldn't keep up both sports. I've always rather regretted it."

"I knew a fencing master once," Nick told her. "He did proper tournaments and things. My dad used to bring me to see him at the— every month for a while, when I was a kid."

"I thought everything in the trophy case was for tennis," Mae said, startled.

"Well," her mother said, and smiled the smile she shared with Jamie, which was crooked and less dignified than Annabel usually liked to be. "Your father certainly didn't win any fencing trophies. He was a bit hopeless at it, to tell you the truth."

Nick was leaning back in his chair by this point, one hand behind his head and tugging at his hair in thought. He seemed to have forgotten he didn't feel like he belonged here.

"I have a couple of swords about as light as fencing foils in my car," he said eventually. "If you'd like to show me what you can do."

He glanced at Mae, and she remembered telling him that if he wanted to make a human happy, he should do something they would enjoy.

"Oh, well," said Annabel, a little flustered, in a clear prelude to refusal, and then she put down her napkin by her empty plate. "Why not?"

That was how they all ended up in the night-time garden, where the lights turned on in response to movement in certain places and thus kept flickering on and off at crucial moments. Mae huddled beside Jamie on the garden steps because the night air was cool, and unlike Nick, who had just taken off his shirt

275

and thrown it to the ground, she wasn't exercising.

"Foul!" yelled Jamie, who seemed extremely happy not to be the one facing a blade. "Distracting technique! Put your shirt back on right now."

"Yeah," Mae said, nudging him. "Maybe it's distracting for you. I kind of hope Mum doesn't feel the same."

"Oh, please," Jamie scoffed. "That whole tall, dark, and whatever thing isn't even my style. He couldn't distract me if he tried."

Annabel had looked somewhat shocked when Nick pulled his shirt over his head, but her face smoothed out into its usual calm expression after a second. She was weighing the sword in her hand.

Nick looked down at her, his bare shoulders white in the darkness, his own sword dangling carelessly from his fingers.

"Okay, maybe he's distracted me for a minute or two," Jamie admitted. "Here and there. Now and then."

"Am I too distracting?" Nick asked their mother, sounding amused. "By the way, you should probably remove those stupid shoes."

"Unlike you, young man, I do not intend to take anything off at all," Annabel retorted, and thrust.

Nick parried and the match was on, their swords ringing out like Christmas bells, the sounds of blades meeting almost musical. The flickering garden lights were green-tinted, so the brightness that flooded the scene on and off was like underwater light, making shadows flow strangely. The carefully pruned bushes, black and vivid green and then black again, formed new and weird shapes behind Nick and Mae's mother. Their swords looked like bright ribbons.

"Stab him, Mum!" Jamie encouraged, laughing, and Mae

laughed too. Annabel wasn't bad at all; Mae had learned that much from watching Nick practise the sword in a garden for hours and hours, day after day. He was responding to her rather than just blocking her, making her his partner in a game.

Of course, it was a game. It wasn't a challenge for Nick, handling his sword lightly and dancing away from engaging with her. It wasn't a matter of life or death for either of them, not for her mother chasing him, laughing and breathless. Not for the demon who nobody could have expected to enjoy something like this, playing with someone clearly not in his league, having a game in a summer garden.

"Your form is terribly undisciplined," Annabel told him, and lunged again, higher this time.

Nick ducked and came up laughing. "But it does work," he pointed out softly, and fell back as she went for him one more time.

The garden lights went out and the night was clear all the same, as if the black sky was a stage curtain held pinned up by the brilliant points of stars.

Nick stood against it, sword flashing and tracing silver patterns against the dark.

For a moment he seemed like an ink-and-paper drawing of a villain, with pitiless black holes where eyes should have been. Then he laughed again and his face changed: he did not look human, but he did look young. He looked like someone who could be hurt.

Alan might think he was going to betray Nick, but Mae wasn't going to let it happen.

Mae looked at Nick and thought, *I'm going to save you*.

16

Hunted

THE NEXT MORNING MAE WENT TO WAKE JAMIE, WHO HAD clearly overslept, and the moment she walked into the darkened room her feet were pulled out from under her. She landed flat on her back with a knife pressed against her throat.

"Ah," she said involuntarily, pain shuddering through her body at the impact, and bit her lip to make the sound come out gently, because the edge of the knife felt far too sharp against her skin.

Nick's eyes flicked open.

"Oh," he muttered. "It's you."

The pressure of that magical knife, sharp enough to cut diamonds to the heart, eased but did not quite lift. It was close enough to her skin to chill it, like a cold whisper.

Mae's consciousness began to expand from its state of narrowed-down focus on the knife. She became aware of morning light filtering in around the heavy curtains, the shapes of Jamie's bed and wardrobe, and the fact that Nick was lying on top of her with hardly any clothes on.

"Uh," she said. She put up her hands to ward him off, to push him and his stupid knife away, but her palms met warm skin, and she hesitated and just touched him. "Right," she said, a lock of his hair in her face and his heartbeat under her hand. "Where are your clothes?"

Nick stared down at her for a moment, eyes darker than anything in the shadowy room, and then rolled off her. Mae was left breathless, mostly because he'd leaned all his weight on her for a moment.

"Now I know what the Wicked Witch of the East must have felt like," she said accusingly. "You weigh as much as a house."

"Mae?" asked a voice almost drunk with sleep, slurring from beneath the covers, and then a hump on the bed resolved itself into Jamie.

"You'll never guess what just happened," Mae said, levering herself into a sitting position and glaring at Nick.

"I bet I will." Jamie turned on his bedside lamp, which revealed that his always-spiky hair had turned into a chaotic blond jungle that tiny explorers could enter, never to be seen again. His eyes were haunted. "I got up in the night to go to the bathroom."

"I get edgy in strange places," Nick said.

"In your sleep?"

"You'd thank me if we were attacked by magicians in the night."

"I wouldn't thank you if Mum had come in to wake me!" Jamie said.

Nick shrugged, as if conceding this was a fair point but not caring much, stood up, and began to slide into his jeans. Mae and Jamie both went a bit quiet.

279

Things could have been a lot more distracting, Mae thought, if Nick went commando. Small mercies.

"Is there breakfast?" Nick asked. "I mean, cereal or toast or something?"

"Of course there's cereal, we are not savages!" said Jamie.

"The three of you live in this big stupid house and none of you even know how to feed yourselves, I don't know how you are all still alive. I couldn't count on cereal."

Nick leaned against the wall and looked expectant of breakfast. Jamie began to struggle out of his nest of bedclothes, and Mae got to her feet. Her eye was caught by Nick's talisman – net, bones, and crystal in a glittering circle against his skin – and then by something else.

She stepped in to Nick and took his talisman, quite gently, into the hollow of her hand.

Where his talisman had been there was a silvery scar raised on his chest, the criss-crossing threads and points of crystal etched on his skin.

"Does that hurt?" Mae asked him.

"Yeah."

"So why wear it?"

"Because that's what Alan wants," Nick snarled at her. He pulled the talisman out of her hand so it fell down to cover the mark, and turned away.

"I wasn't distracted," Mae said. "I was just, uh, thinking about something else."

She had been thinking about something else all day. It was all well and good to decide she was going to save someone, but she didn't have the first idea how to go about doing so. Everything she could think of ended up sounding like the modern equivalent of a single knight saddling up his horse and going on a quest to rescue a princess – very brave and showy and all, but unlikely to actually work.

If Mae had been a fairy-tale knight, she would've brought an army.

"What were you thinking about?"

She glanced from the passenger seat to Seb and his gorgeous profile at the wheel, feeling a flash of guilt. Gorgeous profiles should not be ignored like this.

She gave him her best smile. "Armies."

"Uh, joining one?" Seb asked. "Not the career path I would've expected you to choose, but okay."

"Leading one," said Mae.

"That does sound more like you," he admitted, and smiled at her sidelong.

Seb had been pretty fantastic so far this week, Mae thought, all things considered. He'd tried to be friendly to Jamie, had offered her lifts home and to school and to demon-infested vineyards, and he hadn't presumed or been pushy about the chance she'd offered him. He'd never once gone in for a kiss.

He didn't even look annoyed about her ignoring him all the way through the drive home from school.

Months ago now, Mae'd met a guy down at a pub on the high street who talked about somewhere people could go for solutions to weird problems, a guy who had led her straight to Nick and Alan. There were certain people out there, mingling unseen with the crowds who knew nothing. Those people had answers, and they might be willing to help.

Even if she didn't find them, she could use a break from

worrying. She could use anything that would take her mind off Nick.

"Do you want to do something tonight?"

Seb blinked. "Well," he said. "Well, what do you want to do?"

Mae's phone went off, and she fished it out of her pocket and read a text message off the screen that said: WHERE ARE YOU?

It was from Nick.

She was going to save him, but she wasn't going to be at his beck and call. She didn't have to spend all her time teaching him to act human when she'd like to have some time to act human herself. She didn't need to see him alone today when he'd said no to her yesterday.

"Oh," Mae said, turning off her phone. "It's Friday night. I thought we could go dancing."

Timepiece was the club everyone went to, but it had a ground floor where it would be quiet enough to talk, and Mae liked it okay, largely because of the indie music they played on Fridays. Seb didn't have any other ideas, so they met up at the top of Little Castle Street and made their way down.

"Your shirt's funny," Seb told her abruptly as they went in through the bar, which was all fiery red lights and charcoal grey booths.

Mae plucked at her clinging grey shirt, which read USED TO BE SNOW WHITE, BUT I DRIFTED.

"It's a quote from Mae West," she said. She reached out and touched his arm, and Seb flinched and jerked back.

"Who's Mae West?" he asked.

"Seb," she said in a level voice, "are you all right?"

Seb hesitated, then nodded. "I'm just a bit—" he said in a

282

harsh voice, and cleared his throat. "I have to go to the bathroom!"

"Uh," Mae said. "Okay."

Seb looked at her with wild eyes and added, "That's just the way it has to be."

He fled before she could demand an explanation for his bizarre behaviour, and she stared around, wondering if someone had unleashed airborne crazy in the bar.

Then she saw the dancing. People didn't usually dance on the ground floor of Timepiece, saving it for the upper levels where the dance music played, but in a corner of the room there were people shaking what their mama gave them in a way their mamas probably wouldn't approve of. And there was someone whistling, so softly Mae could hardly hear it, and yet the sound slipped down the back of her neck, ran along her skin like a whisper. She found her feet moving, tapping out a rhythm.

She went across the room to the dancers, stopped just before she reached them, and said, "Hello, piper."

The pied piper was lounging back in his chair, knee up against a table. His dark eyes glinted red as he glanced up at her, and he grinned the same grin as he had when he tried to sell her bones at the Goblin Market.

"The girl who isn't a Goblin Market girl," he said, and stopped whistling. The dancers faltered, their movements going jerky and self-conscious. "I didn't catch your name."

"Guess you need to be quicker," Mae drawled.

He unfolded himself from the chair, his skinny body all angles but somehow graceful in motion. "I'm pretty quick."

"I'm not seeing it."

"I'm Matthias," he said, grinning again. He started to hum,

and Mae felt it reverberating in her bones; the dancers were suddenly all moving smoothly again.

"I'm Mae," she told him, and he took her hands in his.

His hands felt like bone. They were smooth and hard as stone from playing a hundred different musical instruments.

His humming seemed to be shaping the air, guiding her like hands on her hips: she knew exactly how he wanted her to move, exactly how the dance should go.

Mae concentrated on moving wrong. She stayed out of step with the piper's rhythm.

"What are you doing?" she asked warily, looking around at the undulating dancers.

"Nothing you should worry about. I told you, you're not my type. I like them tall, old enough to be experienced, and with beautiful voices." Matthias sneered down at her, framing her throat briefly in one hand. "You sing off-key," he said into her ear. "I can tell."

Mae was distracted enough for a moment to slip into the piper's rhythm, moving like all the others, in waves to his shore.

She kicked him deliberately in the ankle with her combat boot.

"You're feeding off this, aren't you? Somehow, the sounds, the way people respond to them – it's giving you magic."

The grey and scarlet of the club blurred a little before her eyes, she was concentrating so hard on not dancing to the piper's tune. The colours wreathing Matthias's thin face seemed like the colours of a hell that was burning itself up from the inside out.

"Better to drink energy than feed people to demons,

wouldn't you say?" Matthias asked. "But learning this comes at a price. My parents haven't spoken in years. They write me little notes, though. They say they're proud."

Mae stared at him. "You stole their voices?"

Matthias laughed. "Someone's got to pay the piper, my dear. And I don't fancy the magicians taking what was so dearly bought. Do you know what's going on with the Goblin Market?"

"No idea," said Mae honestly. "Did you know the Obsidian Circle has invented a new mark?"

Matthias stilled, and the dancers with him. "What does it do?"

"Multiplies their leader's power by ten."

The piper whistled, a thin sound that went through Mae's head like a fire alarm. "And what can we do about that?"

"Might be time to make new allies," Mae said softly, over the sound of the renewed humming. She let herself fall into step with the others, let herself be caught up by the music and held up against Matthias so she could whisper, "Nick Ryves has a lot of power."

The piper's humming picked up, more like a continuous whistle than a hum. He whirled Mae in his arms, and she saw the other dancers whirling with her as if they were choreographed, even their hair flaring out at the same moment.

He paused long enough to say, "Caught between the devil and the deep blue sea."

Mae had only meant to surrender for a moment, but now she didn't know how to escape the beat, the steps all in time with hers. She shut her eyes, red light filtering in between her lashes and spreading scarlet tendrils across the darkness behind her eyelids. She thought of the stories of people dancing in red-hot shoes, dancing until they died.

The piper's voice was music in her ear. "I'd rather burn than drown."

The magical sounds stopped. Matthias stood before her for another moment, grinning his skull-like grin.

"Is there a plan, then?"

"There will be," said Mae.

"When there is," Matthias told her, "I'll be interested to hear it." He stepped back, out of crimson light and into the shadows. "If it's good enough, I might even pipe all your bad dreams away."

He was gone before Mae could ask him how he knew about the dreams, the only sign of him a low humming that travelled further and further away into the shadows. The dancers who had surrounded her started, one by one, to follow after that sound.

Mae took a deep breath. Her bones ached, and she felt suddenly exhausted. Her throat was so dry it burned.

When Seb returned they got glasses of water and went outside, where the management had turned on the heaters, red ribbons of pretend fire casting a glow on the knots of people and giving scarlet haloes to the gravestones scattered across the ground. Mae chose one that read SACRED TO THE MEMORY OF OUR BELOVED DAUGHTER and sat on it, tucking her booted feet up underneath her.

Seb stood looking awkwardly down at her. Mae had to wonder if his much-talked-about choosiness was actually painful shyness. Maybe she was supposed to be the girl who petted him soothingly and murmured, "There, there, Sebastian, I know you're an animal!"

"Mae West was a movie star in the thirties," Mae said

instead. "She wrote plays and tons of her own lines, and she was a forty-year-old sex symbol, and she had a boyfriend who was thirty years younger than she was."

Seb looked appalled. "She had a boyfriend who was ten?"

"Um, no," Mae said, and laughed. "I think she got the boyfriend when she was in her sixties. Anyway, she was awesome! Salvador Dalí made a sofa shaped to look like her mouth."

"A really tiny sofa?" Seb asked.

Mae glanced up at him and saw him grinning to himself, and realised he'd been quietly making fun of her the whole time.

She was no good at being a ministering angel anyway, and no matter how tired she felt, she wanted a dance. She put her glass down, jumped up from the gravestone, and grabbed his hand.

"You're good enough at flirting when you're a yard away from me. Let's see how you do on a dance floor."

Mae led him inside and up towards the balcony bar, which was usually the best bet if you wanted a bit of space to move around in.

"This is going okay, isn't it?" Seb asked at the top of the stairs.

"We'll see," Mae said, amused. Then they reached the balcony bar and she felt her smile snatched away, as easily as if it was a stolen purse.

Nick was standing against the wall, half-lit by shimmering scarlet lights and half in shadow. He pushed himself off the wall and headed straight for them.

"Where have you been?" he demanded, and Mae found herself suddenly enraged.

"Where have I been?" she echoed, and dropped Seb's hand

as she clenched hers into a fist. "What are you even doing here? Why are you everywhere? Why can't I escape you for one night?"

Nick looked down at her, face still, and the urge to hit him was as overwhelming as it was ridiculous.

"Jamie's upset," he said.

It was no answer at all, but it made Mae's questions not matter. She stopped paying attention to either of them as she scanned the room for her brother.

He wasn't hard to spot.

He was the only one in the balcony bar who was dancing. People were staring at him because he was leaping around the place far too energetically, doing spins and staggering mid-turn, flailing his arms. He was so thin, and his hair was sticking up in so many directions. He looked like a stick figure having a fit.

"Has Jamie been drinking?"

"Not that much," Nick said.

"Not that much for you," Mae asked dangerously, "or not that much for someone half your size who has been known to sing a song and fall over after a sherry at Christmas?"

"He said it would make him feel better!" Nick snapped. "How was I supposed to know it wouldn't?"

Mae opened her mouth to respond, when Seb's voice cut through the music, turning her head because it was so deliberately quiet and controlled.

"Maybe we should go and get Jamie now? You two can argue later."

"Don't be an idiot!" she said sharply, and Seb looked surprised. Mae took a deep breath. "If I take him away now, he'll be completely humiliated in the morning."

She turned on her heel and headed for the dance floor.

The soles of her boots were sticking to the floor a little, so she was aware of a peeling sensation with every step. It slowed her down a fraction, long enough so that by the time she reached Jamie, she'd remembered to put on a smile.

"Hey," she said, loud above the seriously ill-advised funk music, and Jamie spun around.

He stood there staring at her, looking bewildered and a little wary, and she caught his hands in hers and stepped in to him. His eyes widened.

"Hey there," she said again, and began to play the game. "So where did you learn to dance?"

Jamie laughed and hiccupped in the middle of the laugh, then started to dance with her.

"I learned to dance on a battlefield," he told her. "I was the only soldier who knew how to avoid the minefields with style."

Mae laughed and Jamie spun her, and when he faltered she spun back to him by herself, sliding her arms around his neck and smiling at him until he smiled back. The smile lit up his flushed face, and suddenly it was just the two of them playing the game, under chandeliers in an empty house or under scarlet lights in a dance club. It didn't matter.

Jamie put his foot forward and Mae drew hers back, legs moving in sync, back and forth, him and her united against the world.

"How about you, where did you learn to dance?" Jamie remembered to yell at her, breathless.

"I was in a Spanish convent when the sound of the maracas by my window made me jump out to join the dancers," Mae said. "Landed in the sisters' cabbage patch already running. Never looked back."

She twisted when Jamie did and caught his elbow in her palm

when he stumbled. Now a couple of people were joining them on the dance floor with the advent of a new song. This wasn't a spectacle any more, just a dance, and they were good at dancing.

Over Jamie's shoulder she saw Nick and Seb watching, leaning against the balcony rail. Nick was slouching, lazy and graceful and utterly indifferent, but Seb was smiling in their direction. His whole face was lit up in a very particular way. Mae sent him a wink.

Then she turned back to Jamie, waltzing again. He was leaning on her a little too much, his eyes big and his smile the faltering, crooked one that was never as convincing as he liked to believe.

Mae sighed and pressed her forehead briefly against his. So the crush was a bigger deal than she'd hoped.

The second song slowed, and she lifted her arms up, hands linked with Jamie's, in a small gesture of victory.

"Hey," she said, forehead still against his. "You ready to go home now?"

Jamie gave a little sigh. "Yeah."

She led him off the dance floor. He brightened like a small, happy candle when he saw Nick.

The sherry had made him tell Annabel and their aunt Edith he loved them both, and he'd become intensely sad when they did not say it back, Mae recalled with a deep sense of foreboding.

"Hi, Nick!" he said. "Mae and I were dancing. Did you see? Look, here's Mae!"

"I did see," said Nick. "Hi, Mae."

Jamie wobbled, and Nick straightened up from his slouch against the rail, even though her brother kept his balance on his own. Despite the intensely dry tone in which he spoke, Mae thought this might qualify as Nick's version of being indulgent.

"You said not to have another drink," Jamie told him. "And do you know what I think? I think you were right."

"You amaze me," Nick said. "Come on, you're going home."

"We're going home together," Mae informed him, shooting Seb an apologetic look and sliding an arm around Jamie's shoulders to show she wasn't changing her mind. Jamie leaned against her with a small, contented sound.

"I'll drive both of you," Seb offered at once.

Mae nodded at him with gratitude.

"No," Jamie said sternly. "I'm never getting into your horrible car. I promised myself that, because – it's horrible, and you're horrible. So take that!"

Nick snorted. Seb walked on the other side of Jamie as Mae led him gently towards the stairs, even though this made Jamie's already meandering progress go farther off course as he tried not to even brush against Seb. Nick circled them slightly as they went, like a wolf who'd decided to take up a career of sheepdog without much natural aptitude for it.

"Seriously," Seb said to Mae. "You wait outside with him, I'll get the car."

"Nick is driving us," Jamie informed him. "Nick has a car. Nick has two cars. Ha!"

Jamie chose that moment to almost fall down the stairs. Mae took his whole weight and grabbed the banister. Seb reached out but Jamie shied away, and Nick gave Jamie a push in the chest that was clearly intended to right him, but that nearly had him toppling over backwards.

Balance eventually restored to them all, Jamie gave Nick an approving look.

"You are my friend," he told him.

"Yeah, I am," said Nick.

"But these stairs," Jamie said sadly. "They are not my friends."

Mae was pretty glad they'd decided to take Nick's car by the time they were out of the club. He was parked at the other end of the street five minutes away, and even so Jamie had to pause and be sick once.

Luckily, they were near a bin. Mae stood beside it and stroked Jamie's hair, and after a moment he straightened up, wiping his mouth with the back of his hand.

"Does he need water?" asked Seb. "I could go and get him some."

"No, he doesn't need water," Jamie snapped. "And he speaks and everything!"

"Frequently," Nick murmured.

Apparently Nick could not even speak in Seb's presence without annoying him, because for no reason at all Seb shot him a look that might not have qualified as a death glare, but it certainly counted as a punch-in-the-face glare. Then he looked at Jamie.

"I don't understand why you always have to be like this!"

"Really?" Jamie said. He straightened up and shook off Mae's arm. "Try this on for size, Sebastian McFarlane: because you ruined my life. Because I was fine, I got shoved a bit in the lunch line and that was all. I had friends, I was kissing Mark Skinner behind the arts building every other day, and then you came to school and you never let up and nobody would speak to me and you made me miserable for two years, and I can't forgive you just because you're trying to play nice now. Just because you have the hots for my sister!"

Seb blinked, then focused, eyes narrowed. "You were kissing Mark Skinner?"

Jamie looked outraged that anyone in the world could so comprehensively miss a point.

"He was going through a phase," he said at last. "Oh my God, don't hassle him as well. Nick! You have to protect Mark!"

"You're going to have to point out which one he is to me at school," Nick drawled. "Get in the car."

He pushed Jamie into the back seat, and Mae climbed in after him. She leaned over Jamie and started to wind the window on his side down so he could be sick if he had to be.

She was a bit surprised when Seb climbed into the passenger seat. Nick shrugged, as if he was writing off this whole night to mass human insanity, and started the car.

"Look," said Seb. "You were always laughing, so I never thought . . . Look, I'm sorry."

The car passed under a streetlight that made the window a sudden square of glowing orange. Mae saw Jamie properly for a moment, his head tipped to one side, earring gleaming for a second like a tiny star. He looked tired.

"I know you had your reasons," he said. "I just don't think any of them were good ones."

He sounded bleak and terribly young, and Mae was always on his side before she was on anyone else's. She put her arm around him and he snuggled into her side, and she was only a little concerned he might be sick on her awesome Mae West shirt.

She had been so stupid, not watching Jamie and not realising that he was so irritable and unhappy because he liked someone who would never like him back.

She glared at the back of Nick's head and said, furious and irrational, "You could have danced with him at the club."

"I could have," Nick said. "There were kids from school

there. He gets hassled enough. Anyway, I don't really dance for pleasure much."

"Uh – so you, uh, usually dance professionally, or what?" Seb asked.

"Yeah," said Nick. "The ballet is my passion."

They carried on sniping in the front seat, and Mae turned back to Jamie.

"You doing okay?" she murmured.

"Yes," Jamie said, a bit too earnestly. "I love you, Mae. Your hair is the colour of flamingos! And I love Nick as well." He gazed soulfully in Nick's direction. "Sometimes when you are not being psychotic, you are quite funny. And you!" He regarded Seb for a long moment. "No, I still don't like you," he decided. "Maybe I need another drink."

"I don't think so," Nick said.

He turned the car into their driveway, wheels crunching on the gravel, and Jamie tipped over into Mae's side, head fitting neatly into the curve of her shoulder.

"Come on," Mae said to him, and shoved him as gently as she could out of the car. "We're going to be sneaking around the back now so Annabel doesn't see us," she informed Nick and Seb. "Seb, I'm sorry for being the worst date in the history of the universe, but if it's any consolation, now that Jamie has yelled at you, he's probably going to stop being mad."

Seb smiled at her, warm and pleased.

Mae and Jamie ducked under the hanging ivy that almost obscured the back gate. Jamie paused to bat at it like a kitten with a toy, but she dragged him onward and up the patio steps, through the sliding door into their house. Which was completely dark, as all the windows had been, Mae realised, when they drove through the gate.

Sneaking around had been totally pointless. Annabel was not even home.

Mae let out a deep breath, feeling her mouth twist as she did so. It didn't matter. She was glad that they could get away with as much as they did.

"Don't be sad, Mae," Jamie said. "This will be good training for when we are ninjas."

Mae flipped on the light switch and turned on the tap to get Jamie a pint glass of water. She held it to his lips and watched him drink it down.

"Ninjas often get distracted by plants, do they?" Mae smirked.

Jamie gave her a betrayed look. "Entertained, are we? Go ahead, laugh at my pain. I see how it is. I am your enterpainment."

She guided him up the stairs with a hand on his back and went into his bedroom with him, because she didn't want to leave him alone when he was still so drunk. Jamie almost tripped over the pillow Nick had left on the floor, but she righted him and dumped him on his bed.

Jamie settled himself, lying on his front on his tangled blue bedsheets, his glass of water held before him in both hands. Mae sat cross-legged on the floor in front of him.

"I know why you got drunk," she said, soft. "I know why you're so unhappy."

She was ready to tell him that Nick was a demon, that he was a monster, that he wasn't worth a moment of the pain Jamie was feeling.

Jamie leaned his face into his arm and said, muffled against his skin, "You must think I'm such a fool."

"No," she said, and reached for him. Her fingers closed

around his thin arm, and he was shaking a little. "Oh, Jamie. I understand."

"It's just he's so . . ." Jamie began, and he stopped. "It isn't that he's nice to me. It's that – he just – he always fights for the people who are his, and he tries so hard."

"I know," she said, her voice sinking. She didn't want it to sink, she wanted to be strong and able to carry herself and Jamie through this, through anything.

The low lights refracted in her vision, spilling blurred yellow lines across the dimness. Jamie's fair hair, which never looked lighter than it did in shadow, became a wavering silver crown held between his arms.

"If I could just make him understand."

"Jamie," Mae said, "I don't know if you can. I've been trying to help him understand, and he's so different from us, he's—"

"Not from me," Jamie told her. The way he sounded, lonely and small, broke her heart.

"Yes," she said, and her voice went scratchy. "Yes, he is. I understand why you love him, Jamie, but there's just no hope. He's just not human."

She stared when Jamie lifted his head and blinked at her, a corner of his mouth lifting in a faint version of his usual crooked smile. "Um," he said. "Mae. Do you think it's Nick?"

The incredulous way he pronounced Nick's name told her she'd been wrong.

"Who – who is it?" she asked, sounding stupid and not even caring. If it was Alan – and come to think of it, Alan was much more Jamie's type – then it was still bad. Alan would be kind, but he wouldn't be interested. He'd still be pursuing Mae, and Jamie would have to watch that.

Jamie hesitated.

Then he laid his head back in his arms again and said, tired and already sunk low, already hopelessly fallen, "Gerald."

"Jamie!" Mae exclaimed. It was almost a cry.

Jamie sat up. "You don't know him."

"I don't want to!" She found her gaze locked with her brother's.

"You don't understand."

"Why, because I'm not a magician?" Mae demanded. "You never told me! Why did you never tell me?"

"I was scared of how you'd react!" said Jamie. "I was scared that you'd hate me. You were always saying you were psychic, or there was something out there. I thought that you might hate it. That I had magic. And you didn't."

He turned his face away, arms sliding around his knees, making himself as small as he could be.

"Gerald says they all end up hating us," he said. "Because they want the magic or they fear it, or both."

Mae thought of Jessica Walker sitting straight-backed and hungry-mouthed in their mother's parlour, asking if she had ever hated her brother. As if any jealousy, any craving for a different, shining world or for a power that made her special, would have been enough to make her do that.

She got to her feet and went to the door, opening it and staring at the dark hall beyond, not letting herself look back.

"Then Gerald's a fool," she told him. "And so are you."

Mae crawled under the bedclothes and pulled the covers over her head. She was trying so hard not to think about Jamie that she had a dull, throbbing headache, and the pain would not quite let her sleep.

Instead she tossed and turned in the uncomfortably hot

cocoon of blankets, and finally half fell and half forced herself into an uneasy doze, only to be woken by a tap on her window.

She rose, carpet soft under her bare feet, and saw a pale face in the night, harsh lines blurred behind the glass. Nick looked at her and smiled, and she put her hand out. The metal latch of the window was easy to undo; the click echoed in her head as if it was much louder than it was.

The night air was cool on her hot face. Nick was kneeling on the window ledge, and he reached out and touched the side of her neck. His hands were cool too, and sure. The touch was just what she wanted.

She retreated to sit on her bed and Nick sat with her, the rumpled covers sinking under their combined weight. She reached out and slid her arm around his neck, and he wasn't angry or distant; he held her back.

His arm was around her, hard muscle against the small of her back, and she hid her face in the strong curve of his shoulder. The worn material of his T-shirt was soft under her cheek, and she could smell him, clean skin and hair, cotton, and the sharp smell of steel. She felt her heart catch in her chest and then, as if to make up for faltering, it started to race.

Nick stroked her hair with those cool, sure fingers, and murmured to her that everything was all right. His hand lingered for a moment at the fine, short hair at the nape of her neck, and she shivered. She was pressed up close against his chest and knew he felt the long, slow tremor run through her body. He went still.

Mae lifted her head from his shoulder, cupped his face in her free hand, and kissed him. He kissed her back without hesitation, warm and careful and thorough, tongue curling in her mouth. She let herself fall backwards against the pillows. She tugged him down.

The sheets were tangling around her bare legs, and his jeans were rough against them. He let her have control of the kiss, his lips moving lazy and sweet against hers, his fingers still stroking her neck: the nape, the sides, then resting his knuckles against the hollow of her throat. He kept murmuring to her, low, caressing words. Everything was so warm.

All along her body she felt chills following in the wake of his hands. He lifted her shirt and stroked along her spine, lifted the cord of her talisman and moved his mouth from hers to kiss her jaw, her chin, and the side of her neck where the talisman lay. He whispered to her that she should take it off.

She whispered back that she would. Then she glanced down at him and saw him smile.

That slow, malicious smile wasn't Nick's.

Mae felt the tug of the talisman lifting under her hands, catching at her hair, and for an instant felt a flash of burning pain where the talisman still rested against her skin.

She shoved him back and saw that under his hooded lids, his lowered lashes, his eyes were not black. They were cold and colourless as ice.

Mae screamed and woke herself up.

There was a moment when she felt profound relief and nothing else. Then she realised that she was lying on top of the covers and the window was open. A bleakly cold wind was rushing through it into her room, and the talisman against her chest was burning hot. She grabbed at it and looked down at what she held in her palm: saw what had been crystals, feathers, and bone transformed into a charred and twisted ruin.

Mae clenched the talisman in her fist and scrabbled with her other hand on her bedside table. When her fingers brushed over what she wanted, she grabbed her phone and pressed a couple of keys, then waited with desperate impatience until the ring was cut off by a voice.

"What?"

"Nick," she said breathlessly, and she hated the begging sound of her voice, but she begged anyway. "Nick, it's an emergency, please—"

There was a disturbance in the air around her; she recognised that moment just before you turn around when you realise there is someone else in the room. She also knew there could not possibly be anyone else in the room.

She turned around, and Nick was standing at the foot of her bed.

"What?" he said again, his voice curt and crackling and not some dream whisper that was only in her head, and yet he looked so much the same that she found herself struck speechless and hugging her knees to her chest like a child.

"Close the window," she ordered at last, and felt better just because she was giving an order. Nick raised an eyebrow and shut the window.

The room was still icy and smelled of smoke, but at least the howl of the wind was trapped outside. Mae kept hugging her legs. She didn't feel any warmer.

Nick looked down at her. "So there's an emergency in your bedroom," he said slowly. "Well, I can't say it's the worst line I've ever heard."

Mae snorted and felt steadier, steady enough to get out, "It was Anzu."

Nick tensed. "Sure?"

"Yes, I'm sure!" Mae exclaimed. "He was here, and he almost got my talisman off, and it's all burned, and he had eyes like—"

She choked the words off because she couldn't bear hearing herself sound like this, this helpless scared thing. She was furious at how easy she'd made it for that demon, how willing she'd been to open that damn window for no good reason.

Nick looked down at her, his eyes opaque as the night outside her window, with no way to know what was hidden in the darkness.

"What do you want me to do?"

Mae had the sudden, terribly vivid memory of Nick putting his arms around her in the demon dream. The thought of him being affectionate was so bizarre, so unlikely: she couldn't imagine how Anzu had come up with it. She couldn't think why it had worked.

Her hands were shaking. She recalled the exact sensation of leaning her cheek against Nick's shoulder – and here Nick was, real, and the idea of asking him for comfort was absolutely unthinkable. He would not even understand why she might ask, and she would be humiliated.

"What do I – there was a demon in my bed," she cried, and then registered what she'd just said and shut her eyes in horror. "Nick. I was terrified."

She opened her eyes in time to see him turn away from her in a movement that looked almost violent.

"I can – I can see that," he snapped. "I don't know why you called me. What do you expect me to do? I don't understand what you want!"

Mae didn't understand herself. She'd just dived for the phone without thinking. She'd wanted help and she'd called him. He was right to ask her what the hell she thought she was doing.

She looked away, past him to her dressing table cluttered with CDs and the debris of discarded make-up, and thought about her room filled with broken glass and cold air, about the demons outside her window every night.

And then she realised she knew what she was doing.

Mae lifted her chin and said, "Let me explain it to you."

Nick looked at her for another unreadable moment, and then nodded and sat down – not on her bed but in her chair, ignoring the fact that it was draped with clothes and piled with books. Mae wished she was dressed; she thought she could sound much more authoritative if she wasn't wearing a floppy purple nightshirt.

"I'm the weak link, aren't I?" she said. "Gerald wants Jamie's ties to the human world broken, and that's me. Gerald wants to attack you and Alan, and – and Alan would care if I was possessed. Possibly he thinks you would mind if I was too."

"Possibly," said Nick.

"It doesn't matter," Mae lied. "We need to – we need to think this through. I'm the one with no magic and no idea about this world. I'm the one they targeted, and I'm the one they'll keep targeting. What we need is a plan. What we need" – she uncurled and leaned over, bracing herself on one hand, towards Nick – "what we need is to make marking me impossible."

She was prepared for an argument, but not for the sudden fury in Nick's face. "No."

"You said you wanted to do it," Mae reminded him. "So do it. You can mark me, and then no other demon will be able to touch me. I'll be safe."

Nick made a sound, halfway between a laugh and a snarl. He rose to his feet in one too-fluid, too-easy motion, and Mae felt the tremble of unease in her stomach that she always felt when he moved like that. He paced the room, three steps from the window to the chair and back, and then he put one knee up on the bed.

His lip curled from his teeth in a silent snarl. "Do you know what having a demon mark means?"

"It's not like you'd possess me—"

"But I could," he said, lingering on every word, as if he delighted in saying each one. "Anytime, I could. I could do a lot more than that. I put a third-tier mark on you and I could reach inside your mind anytime. I could make you think anything I wanted." He leaned down, voice going even softer and more disturbing. "I could make you do anything I wanted," he whispered. "And you think that you'd be safe?"

"Safer than if it was Anzu, yes," Mae said sharply, and shoved him hard.

Or that was the intention. He caught her wrists in strong hands, and when she hissed between her teeth, his grip did not ease. He was trying to hurt her.

He was trying to scare her.

"Do you know what getting a mark is like?" he demanded. "You know that demons use emotions to break your control." He bared his teeth, too close to her face. "To take control. Do you want me to tell you what it feels like?"

He leaned in even closer, her wrists trapped against his chest, and he hissed in her ear. His voice sounded less human than it ever had, clotted nightmare sounds that did not strike the ear like human speech but somehow formed into words. It made her insides coil up with dread.

"I'll hurt you," he said, breath hot against her skin. "I'll scare you. And I'll really like it."

The last time he'd been this close, he'd smiled a terrible smile and there had been burning pain. She'd screamed then. Panic twisted inside her, and she wanted to scream now.

That hadn't really been Nick, though. This was.

"And you're warning me," she pointed out, unable to stop her voice shaking but trying to pretend it didn't matter. "You're trying to protect me. I appreciate that; that's why I trust you to do this. I've thought it through and I want you to mark me, I'm telling you to mark me, because that is the best way to keep me safe."

"You're right," Nick said in that growling, nightmare voice. His cheek brushed hers, and she turned her face a little into the touch, feeling scared and dizzy and a little crazed. The corner of his mouth touched hers. "I am warning you."

"And I'm telling you," said Mae, and this was bargaining, she knew how to do this. Nick wasn't going to win this fight. "I'm helping you with being human. I haven't told Alan. This is how you help me."

Nick's mouth was suddenly in a thin straight line, his big shoulders bunched, and she saw his fingers curl as if they wanted to be around the hilt of his sword. He looked overcome with rage.

For a moment she didn't understand what she had said, and then she realised and opened her mouth to tell him that wasn't what she'd meant: that if he didn't do it, she would tell Alan.

"I wouldn't—" Mae began, and then voice and breath were both jolted out of her.

Nick dealt her a clean, swift blow, shoved her right off the bed and into the wall. He held her there with his arm hard against her throat, cutting off half her air supply. She was trapped between the wall and his body; he'd moved after her without giving her a second's chance to escape, and she struggled suddenly, wild and hopeless.

Her back was flat against the wall, her breath rising in a trapped whine from her throat. He had her wrists in a brutal grip and her legs trapped between his, his free hand at her hip. She could feel the cold metal of his ring biting into the flesh, through the material of her nightshirt. She couldn't get away.

His eyes gleamed like ink in the low light, filling her vision.

"I tried to tell you," he said, low in his throat. "You can't trust me. And you are not safe."

He bent his head down and put his mouth to her collarbone, and she screamed.

It felt like he'd bitten her, but he hadn't. There were no teeth, just his mouth on her skin and wrenching, savage pain spreading from that point of contact. It felt like he was burning her somehow, branding her, and she howled at him that she'd changed her mind and she wanted to stop, tried with all her strength to twist away and was completely unable to move an inch.

The pain was blinding: she couldn't see, it pulsed through her in waves, and each wave shuddered through her whole body, each wave was worse than the last. And the pain still wasn't as bad as the wild animal panic. She knew now why animals chewed off their legs to get out of traps. She would have done anything to escape.

And it wasn't all pain. It wasn't all fear. And she was helpless against that, too.

It stopped before she blacked out, but only just. It stopped, and he did not move for a moment, just rested with his mouth warm on her skin. Her breath was sobbing in her throat, and her throat was raw.

Nick stepped away from her and released her wrists, and even that movement seemed violent and alarming. He stood by the window, across the room from her, and all she could see was his unmoved and perfect profile.

"I'm – sorry," he said. "That's the way it is. That's what I am. I don't know how to make it any different."

Mae was covered in cold sweat, feeling it slide all over her skin as she trembled. Now that she could move away from the wall, she felt that she wouldn't be able to, that her own legs would not be able to support her.

"I asked you to do it," she said, her voice hoarse. "I chose to do it. That makes a difference."

Nick laughed. It was a terrible sound.

"Enough of one?" he asked, and she was silent.

He shook his head after a moment, then looked at her again, and she could see him come to a decision: he'd done what he could, done what she'd asked for.

He wasn't going to offer her comfort, and she wasn't sure she wanted it. She wasn't sure she'd let him come near her.

She wasn't sure she wouldn't.

She did not get the opportunity to find out, because he nodded, then disappeared like smoke.

Mae walked a few unsteady steps and collapsed on her bed, her shaking hand going up and finding the spot on her collarbone where his mouth had been, where his mark was now. She could feel something there, a difference in the quality of her skin, as if it was newly healed from a wound or the lingering scar from a burn.

She couldn't look in the mirror, didn't want to see either the mark or her own face. She wondered what in God's name she had done.

17

Playing and Losing

THE NEXT MORNING MAE WAS STILL NOT SURE WHAT SHE HAD done, but she was sure she couldn't change it. She settled on being intensely thankful it was Saturday and went down to the kitchen for a pot of coffee. One cup wasn't going to cut it.

She met Jamie on the stairs, looking pale and woebegone, and she clutched the neck of her robe closed instead of reaching for him.

He reached for her instead, his hand cupping her elbow.

"You're right, I'm an idiot," he said against her cheek.

"I'm always right," Mae told him, instead of telling him that the idiocy seemed to be genetic. She gave him a kiss, lips barely brushing the edge of his jaw, and said, "How are you feeling?"

"So, so bad," Jamie confessed, and then the doorbell rang.

Mae opened the door and found Seb on the doorstep.

"So, so much worse," Jamie said, his voice floating down from the top of the stairs.

"Hey," said Mae, ignoring her drunkard brother and hoping that Seb liked the just-rolled-out-of-bed look, since she was more concerned with finding coffee than a hairbrush.

"Hey," said Seb. "How's Jamie doing?"

"How are you doing, Jamie?" Mae asked in pointed tones, which subtly indicated that Seb was being very polite and Jamie had better acknowledge that or face sisterly retribution.

"Oh God, Mae," Jamie said in a hollow voice, descending the stairs. "I will never drink again. I'm only seeing in black and white. My arms feel all floppy, like flightless wings. I caught a glimpse of myself in the mirror and I looked like a very sad penguin."

Seb made a sound that was almost a laugh.

"You know what," Jamie said to him. "I'm having a bad day. So if you don't mind, I was thinking that today I would pretend you don't exist."

"There is no use even trying to have a civil conversation with you!" Seb said, his voice rising.

Jamie winced. "You're very loud for someone who doesn't exist."

Mae gave him a look. "You're very rude to guests in our home, Jamie. I suggest you try being nicer, and as you may recall, I'm always right."

The bargain was pretty much laid on the table. Give Seb a chance, and Mae would forget about Jamie doubting her. Jamie's mouth quirked appreciatively, and he shrugged.

"I'll do a deal with you, McFarlane," he said. "You can exist. And you can even have coffee. But if you raise your voice or make any sudden movements, I shall die. And that'll show you."

Seb shrugged in return, hiding how pleased he was pretty badly. "Fair enough."

Mae turned away and towards coffee, hiding a smile. She'd been pretty sure her bargain would work. She'd told Seb as much last night: Jamie just wasn't very good at being angry. He lost his grip on it somehow.

That definitely wasn't genetic.

"You again?" Seb asked, his voice suddenly harsh.

Mae spun on the kitchen steps, hand going involuntarily up to the neck of her robe again, as if she was some shamed Victorian maiden. Nick was on the step, not looking at her or even bothering to acknowledge Seb's existence.

"You ready?" he asked Jamie.

"Ready?" Jamie echoed. "Yes, yes, I am ready. I am ready to drink a lot of liquids and lie on the sofa moaning faintly all day long. That is what I am ready for. I cannot engage in physical activity of any sort or my head will fall right off. Is that what you want, Nick? Because if so, I find that hurtful."

"You'll feel better when you start running."

Nick looked wound too tight. Mae wondered why he had even come here, and then it occurred to her that it was just possible he wanted Jamie – that he was disturbed by what had happened last night, and in search of company and comfort. Demons weren't supposed to need those things, but Nick had been wrapped in watchful love for fifteen years, been the audience to what Daniel Ryves had described as Alan's "years-long one-way conversation" until he had finally started talking back.

Now there was something badly wrong between him and his brother, and he'd chosen Jamie, with the same warmth and the same ridiculous sense of humour and capacity to talk for hours, and he was coming to get him.

Or possibly torturing Jamie cheered Nick up.

"But we were going to bring my old guitar over to Alan so we could see him play it and stuff," Jamie said with deep cunning. "We need the car for that."

"Didn't bring the car," Nick told him.

"You should go and fetch it," Jamie urged. "I'll wait here. I won't move. Why would I move? My head might fall off."

"Seb and I can bring the guitar over later," Mae offered.

"Good," said Nick abruptly, and reached out for Jamie's arm. Jamie was too busy giving Mae a betrayed look to be vigilant, so Nick grabbed him without much difficulty and pulled him out of the door.

Nick had his hand on the door, no doubt to slam it, when Annabel came downstairs.

Mae was aware that her mother owned pyjamas. She'd seen them neatly folded in her wardrobe, but Annabel never emerged from her room unless she was fully dressed and fully made up.

Today was no exception. Annabel was in crisp tennis whites, swinging her racket, with her hair in a shimmering ponytail that made the very idea of wisps seem like a horrible dream.

"Mum, help me," Jamie said beseechingly. "I don't want to go for a run."

"Good morning, Mavis, James," Annabel carolled out. "Lovely to see you again, Nick."

Nick inclined his head and almost smiled. Annabel looked at Seb, a faint curl of her lips indicating vast polite distaste.

"One of Mavis's young men, I presume."

Seb looked overwhelmed by the unfairness of the world.

Annabel visibly dismissed the painful thought of Seb's existence from her mind. "Enjoy your run, boys."

"Mum!" Jamie wailed.

"Exercise is good for you," she said serenely. She sailed past Mae on her search for coffee, and Nick shut the door.

Seb was left standing in the hall. "I think," he said, "I kind of hate Nick Ryves."

"Coffee?" Mae asked.

Mae amused herself by watching her mother's dismay until she felt mean about tormenting Seb, so she finished her coffee and ran upstairs to get dressed and get the guitar. She did it in less than five minutes, but Seb's pale face when she returned suggested that the moment Mae'd gone up, her mother had whipped out the thumbscrews.

"Sorry about her," said Mae, going out with Seb into the sunshine, which was a warm yellow splash on their high walls. "She's kind of like a high-powered modern White Witch. It's always office hours, and never casual Friday."

She thought of Annabel going up the stairs quick as a cat in her teetering high heels and grinned slightly. Seb caught her smile and reflected it back to her.

"It's fine," he said. "She's just worried about you. She thinks I'm like all the other boys you've dated."

"But you know you're something special," Mae teased.

Seb's smile twisted a little, rueful and something else besides. "I know I'm different."

Mae thought of Nick wielding a sword by night and Alan throwing knives on the cliffs with Goblin Market music behind him. Seb had no idea how different some of the boys she knew were.

Not that she was dating either of them.

Mae felt disloyal having had that thought, itchy and

uncomfortable about it in a way that started at the tingling spot just below her collarbone. She reached up and touched it lightly, fingers slipping under the high-necked blouse she'd dug up from the bottom of her wardrobe.

She drew her hand away and grabbed Seb's, a lifeline into a world where choices were easier. He took a breath as if he was startled, and she laced their fingers together, deciding to ignore his hesitance for now.

"So what do you want to do?" she asked.

Seb's hand was warm in hers. The sun made the pale gravel in her driveway a blinding white path full of promise.

"We should drop off the guitar to Ryves's place," Seb suggested, and the dazzle in Mae's eyes seemed to dim slightly.

She wanted to yell at Seb. Didn't he know that she had to be away from Nick for a while, because apparently whenever she saw him her brain turned off and she did stupid and insane things? And she couldn't be stupid and insane when she had to save him.

She didn't yell at Seb. There was a mark burning on her skin that felt as if a channel had been opened between her and the demon who had marked her, as if there was something connecting them that was almost like a dry river bed, burning and aching for a rush of magic or the thrill of contact.

She didn't say anything. She wanted to see Nick badly.

Mae had shoved that thought into a box in her mind and slammed the lid on it by the time they were there. Seb seemed relaxed, happy, and at ease with her once they were in the car. The trapped heat made the car luxurious and not oppressive, warmth from the car door seeping through Mae's thin blouse and an air conditioner blowing light on her knees. She was glad she'd chosen a skirt for once, glad the next week of school would be the last, and glad Seb was there. He was living proof that she could be normal and not seduced by magic, that she could have both worlds.

The garden gate on the side of Alan and Nick's house was open. When Seb and Mae walked in, they saw that Nick had wheeled a car out of the garage and was cleaning it.

It was silvery in a way that looked more like steel and shaped in a way that made Mae think of the cars her father's friends bought instead of or just before leaving their wives, but it was old and missing a door. Clearly this was Nick's one true love, the Aston Martin Vanquish. Nick was washing it, shirt off and a bucket of water beside him. Jamie was sitting cross-legged in the grass with a paperback folded open on his lap, looking less ashen and dishevelled than earlier, and Alan was fiddling with an ancient rusty barbecue.

"Are you going to tell him or will I?" Jamie asked Nick.

"Tell me what?" Alan's voice was wary.

Jamie smiled as if he was oblivious to the tension in the air. "Yesterday there was an English test," he said proudly. "And Nick got a B minus."

"Yeah?" said Alan, stilling and then smiling a beautiful, slow-blossoming smile. Jamie beamed. Nick looked indifferent, but it was less convincing than usual. "Well done."

Mae hung back, not really wanting to interrupt and spoil the moment, but of course Seb had no idea and walked right into the garden. Jamie noticed him, and the glow of his pleasure faded a little, then brightened when he noticed the guitar in Seb's hand.

"Hey."

"Hey, Jamie," Seb said in return, and gave Alan a brief,

slightly embarrassed nod. "Hi – we came over to drop off the guitar. I'm Seb McFarlane. I'm Mae's, ah . . ."

"Gentleman caller," Mae filled in.

"Hi," said Alan, straightening up. The sun was so hot that even Alan had abandoned his usual button-up shirts and was wearing a T-shirt, which made it obvious his shoulders and arms were strong and muscled in a way that did not exactly suggest a mild-mannered bookshop employee. "What's with the guitar?"

He smiled at Mae and Seb both, in his usual friendly way, but he didn't give Mae a special look or smile like he usually did. Mae wondered if that meant things were going to be awkward between them.

"Well, I took guitar lessons once," Jamie explained, "but then after, um, you know, two lessons, I sort of lost interest and wandered off." He frowned slightly. "I don't think I have the soul of a musician. But I have this guitar! And Nick said you played the guitar. So I thought I could bring it over here and you would play it. Having a musical accompaniment to barbecue is important to me."

Once Jamie had finished his spiel on how he was clearly not giving Alan a present, he blinked hopefully at him. Alan's mouth curved into a smile.

"I guess I can play you a few songs," he said, and limped up to Seb, taking the guitar. "You two want to stay around for barbecue and its important musical accompaniment?"

"Well," Mae said, and stopped.

Nick had not even looked at her, had not looked up from washing the car. She was painfully aware of him, though. Every move he made was echoed by a twinge in her mark, as if it was a second heart beating only for him.

She should probably go.

"Sure," Seb said, and sat down on the grass by Jamie. "Thanks."

That was that, then. Mae went and sat with Seb and Jamie. She wanted to use them as her talismans, as if being near them meant she was guarded from all magic.

Alan went to fetch Jamie a glass of water. He'd apparently been keeping Jamie hydrated for a while.

"My reading voice needs care," Jamie said. "It has nothing to do with my clever consumption of eleven thousand drinks last night."

"I want water too," said Nick. "I'm hot."

"Here's some water," Alan told him, coming from the kitchen carrying Jamie's glass. He took a sponge out of Nick's bucket and squeezing it so the water flooded into Nick's hair and down his back.

The water slid from the nape of his neck, where the black locks lay like inky scrawls against the white skin, and down the curved arch of his spine, droplets chasing one another down the smooth expanse of his back. Nick made a small sound of satisfaction, then resumed washing the car, sponge moving in steady strokes, ring catching the light so brightly it hurt Mae's eyes.

It hurt the same way when Nick glanced over his bare shoulder at her, and then away.

Alan just laughed at Nick and went back to fiddling with the barbecue.

Mae collapsed back on the hot grass, tired of herself and the situations she kept throwing herself into. Seb got out his sketchbook, and Jamie started to read again as Alan began cooking lunch.

Jamie's voice, talking about dancing and reading and love in a more decorous time, became a gentle rhythm to the warm air and the deep blue sky. Mae had almost fallen asleep when he cut off, sounding surprised.

"Is that a picture of me?"

"Yeah," Seb said, guarded.

"It's really good," Jamie told him, as easy as if he'd never hated him. Jamie was ridiculously generous with his feelings, all offences pardoned with no trace of resentment left, all loves absolute.

Now he thought he loved Gerald. Mae had no idea how to deal with that.

"Yeah?" Seb said the same word in a very different tone, this one startled and pleased.

"Next do Nick," Jamie suggested. "He's barely wearing any clothes. That's artistic."

"Don't volunteer my body without running it by me first," Nick drawled.

"I don't want to draw Nick," Seb snapped.

"But I guess I'll do it for art," Nick continued calmly. "I'm told I have the body of a god."

"A Greek god, or one of those gods with the horse heads or elephant's legs coming out of their chests?" Alan asked. "Next time someone tells you that, ask them to specify."

The smell of meat and smoke drifted to Mae and made her sit up, rising from the crushed grass. "All right, I'm awake. Feed me."

Seb got up and started to hand around plates, though Mae noticed that Nick had to get his own. He abandoned the car and came to sit on the grass as far away from Seb as he could manage, hair drying tufty and falling damp into his eyes.

Jamie looked mildly ill at the sight of food but also anxious not to insult Alan's cooking, so he pushed it sneakily towards Nick whenever Alan happened to glance away.

Alan turned his head just in time to see Nick eating calmly off Jamie's plate.

"Oh no, Nick," Jamie said in tones of supremely unconvincing shock. "How could you? When my back was turned for one moment. And my food was so delicious."

Alan reached out to smack Nick in the side of the head and Nick ducked, still eating. Mae was looking at them, glad that they seemed easy together for once, and she saw their faces change.

It was strange. For a moment they looked alike, eyes narrowed and lower lips drawn in, appreciative.

Then Alan smiled ruefully to himself and turned his head, Nick got to his feet, and Mae looked across to see what they'd been looking at.

Through the garden gates came Sin, like a reminder they could never really escape the magical world, a vision of beauty and danger that made Mae recall why she didn't really want to.

She looked more normal than Mae had ever seen her, but she still moved like a dancer in jeans and a scarlet string top, a bright red bandanna caught in her flying hair. She was all vivid colour, and for a moment Mae was just dazzled by how spectacular she was.

At the next moment she registered that Sin's mouth was set in a straight red line.

"Sin?" Nick asked, and he definitely sounded pleased.

"Alan?" said Sin.

"Uh, no," Nick told her.

Sin raked him with a dismissive dark glance and then looked away, her jaw tightening. "Alan?" she repeated. "I've been sent to deliver a message to you from Merris of the Market. Alone."

Alan rose to his feet, lurching a little as he did so, and Sin looked away as if she'd seen something obscene, but she followed him into the kitchen.

And it occurred to Mae that Sin was exactly the right person to help her.

She stood and went for the kitchen door, where she halted and watched.

Alan and Sin were arguing in hushed, tense whispers, Sin's back against the kitchen counter as if she felt the need to have her back to something in case a fight began. Alan was holding on to the counter, with his fingers gone white.

"Are you going to deliver the message, or did you just come here to accuse me of lying to Merris?"

"You did lie to Merris!"

"I lie to everyone," Alan said softly. "It's nothing personal."

Sin looked furious and helpless for a moment, lips parted, and then nothing but furious again.

"Merris says she'll do it. First of July. Huntingdon Market Square. There will be nobody there to stop you doing what needs doing. And I don't even know what that means," Sin went on, her voice suddenly sharp. "All I know is that you and Merris are making a bargain with the magicians, and I hate it more than I can say."

"Well," said Alan, "you're not the leader yet."

"We haven't sold any talismans," Sin said, her voice a little unsteady. "We haven't given any advice. People are dying at the hands of demons, and we are doing nothing to stop it. I follow Merris's orders, but if I didn't? I'd carve your treacherous heart out of your chest."

Alan's voice didn't change. It remained quiet and reasonable. "You'd try."

Sin made a disgusted noise. "I think we're done here."

She pushed off the kitchen counter, and Alan grabbed her wrist. She stared up at him in outrage, every inch the princess of the Market assaulted by a commoner.

Alan said, "Stay."

"What?" Sin exclaimed, sounding equal parts stunned and amused. "Because you enjoy my company so much?"

"Ah, no," Alan said. "You and Nick were pretty friendly before all this, weren't you?"

Sin put her hand behind her back, fingers curled over a slight bulge beneath her shirt where Mae was prepared to bet she kept her knife.

"What are you trying to say?"

"Go out and be nice to him. He doesn't often like people. I don't want him hurt."

Sin's mouth fell open. "Hurt? The demon? Oh my God, you're crazy. You're actually crazy."

"I'll pay you," said Alan.

"I'm listening," said Sin.

"Six-thousand-year-old Sumerian translation. It's a full ritual, too, so the going rate will be higher."

Sin's eyes widened, but she was a Market girl. Mae wasn't surprised to see that her face and voice betrayed nothing more. "Done," she said briskly, and then a thought seemed to occur to her. She smiled, the curve of her lips cynical and not happy. "So you want me to play nice with the demon, do you?" Her stance shifted, ever so subtly. Suddenly the curves of her body were on offer, as was the curve of her red mouth when she said, low, "And you, traitor? How do you want me to treat you?"

Alan laughed. Sin looked outraged.

"Really, Cynthia." He gave her a look over his glasses. "Your usual barely concealed contempt will be fine."

"It's Sin," Sin snarled.

"Want to do another deal?" Alan asked. "Watch me walk across a room without flinching, and I'll call you whatever you like."

Sin bit her lip. "Get me that translation. I want to be paid in advance."

Alan nodded and made his way across the kitchen. Sin leaned against the counter with her back deliberately to him, so she wouldn't have to see him walk.

That meant she saw Mae standing at the door. She gave her a slight smile and pushed herself up so she was sitting on the counter, one slim leg kicking out at a cabinet. "Hear anything interesting?"

"I think so," Mae said slowly. "Merris is incapacitating the Market and allying with the magicians."

Sin looked angry for a moment, then sighed and let her tense shoulders relax. Mae crossed the room to Sin and leaned against the counter, close enough that Sin's bare shoulder was pressed warm against Mae's blouse.

"Gerald of the Obsidian Circle wants Alan to trap Nick on Market night and strip him of his powers," Mae said. "One blow and he gets rid of the greatest threat they have. Nobody can stand up to him then. Merris isn't even trying to stand up to him now. How long do you think the

Market will survive?"

"The other choice is that Merris dies," Sin said, her voice a thread.

Mae closed her eyes. "I know. I'm really sorry. But you told me you loved the Market."

"What can I do?" Sin demanded.

Mae could hear Alan's step outside the door and only had time to say, "Something," before he came in. He looked mildly startled to see her but approached Sin anyway, handing her a folded piece of paper and a tablet wrapped in cloth. Sin opened the paper and scanned it with an expert's eye.

"All I have to do is pretend to like your demon?"

"Putting on a show is kind of your speciality, isn't it?"

"I thought it was yours," Sin said, level. "You had us all fooled."

"True. I know all the acts people put on," Alan told her absently, fetching a plastic bottle of lemonade out of the fridge as he spoke. "So you'd better make your act good."

He left, swinging the bottle in his hand. Sin looked very annoyed as she swung her little black bag off her shoulder and onto the counter and stuffed the tablet and the translation inside. Mae felt a little ill watching an ancient artifact being handled like Monday's homework, but she stopped herself from snatching it away.

Instead she said, "Can we talk?"

Sin looked up, her eyes narrowed. "Later," she promised, low and thrilling, the voice she used at the Market. "Right now I have a show to put on."

She left her bag on the counter and walked out into the sunlight. Even her hair seemed to be moving differently, swinging jauntily around her slim shoulders. She headed straight for Nick.

Mae watched from the door and felt the mark burn hot under her blouse.

"Now I have the boring part of the afternoon done with," Sin said, without even sparing Alan a glance, "I thought I might stick around. See if there's anything exciting going on."

Nick leaned back on his elbows, looking more relaxed as well as slightly predatory.

"What did you have in mind?"

Sin offered him her hand and he took it, thumb moving deliberately over the inside of her wrist, and let her pull him to his feet. She did not wait a moment before she stepped in and kissed him on his curling mouth.

"Surprise me," she suggested.

Then she sat down gracefully beside Jamie and gave him a smile. Jamie gave her a look of wholehearted admiration.

"You should draw her," he advised Seb, having clearly decided Seb had a use after all.

"If you like," Sin allowed, brushing her hair back. It was glinting brown and red in the sunlight, enough glowing tones to show it was dark instead of black.

Seb looked pleased to show off his artistic skills, shifting his notebook to one knee and starting to sketch, lead whispering against the smooth paper. Mae noticed that he didn't seem all that impressed by Sin, which was kind of nice after the way Alan's and Nick's eyes had followed her entrance.

While Seb was drawing, Sin wandered over and sat on Nick's Vanquish, pulling Mae over to put her hair in tiny pink braids. Nick regarded them both with amusement.

"You said I was never even allowed to touch the car,"

Jamie grumbled.

"Well, get that good-looking and I'll let you do anything you want," Nick told him. "Also, stop moaning or I'll remember that today I want to start you on sword practice."

"Sword practice?" Sin echoed. "I wouldn't mind seeing that."

"Nick fences," Mae informed Seb. "The little white outfit and the metal beehive helmet? He wears those."

Seb looked deeply amused.

"Do you know Nick from ballet?" he asked Sin.

"Er," Sin said. "What?"

Mae wasn't any good at putting on a show, but she knew how to smooth over a situation when she had to.

"I've seen Sin dance," she put in tactfully. "She's fantastic."

"Yeah, plus I look fabulous in tights," Sin said, catching on. "Not as good as Nick, though."

"Naturally," Nick drawled. "I'll go and get the swords."

"Cut it out, Nick," Alan snapped from the depths of his deck chair and his book, and when Nick's back stiffened, Alan directed a meaningful glance towards Seb. "Now's not the time."

Alan's tone was perhaps a little bit too sharp. Nick's eyes narrowed.

"Has it ever occurred to you," he said softly, "that I get very tired of playing nice?"

There was something dark in the air between them now. Mae glanced at Seb warily, and found him looking a little pale.

"Yes, actually, it has," Alan returned. "What are you going to do about it?"

"This."

Nick wheeled on Alan, who dropped his book and suddenly had his gun out. Nick's magical knife flashed in the summer sun:

a thin blinding line of light that dazzled Mae one moment and grazed Alan's arm the next. The gun fell out of Alan's hand and to the grass with a thump; three drops of blood fell on its gleaming surface.

Nick moved into Alan's space as Alan stood, knife coming around in a shining circle, and then he froze. Alan held the dagger from up his sleeve against Nick's throat, forcing Nick's head back until Nick gradually lowered his knife. Alan smiled a small, tender smile.

"Oh, baby brother," he said. "Too slow."

He tucked the dagger back into his sleeve, neat and precise, and Nick stepped away from him.

"See?" Nick said, touching the graze along his throat, ring flashing in the sun the same way his knife had. "We don't have to play nice."

The look Nick shot Seb was a challenge, daring him to make something of the sudden appearance of weapons at a barbecue.

"You want someone to play with, I'll play," Sin said, finishing Mae's braids. Mae pushed off the side of the car and saw Sin reach behind her back again, fingers closing around the hilt of her knife.

"I can't wait to see you two dance," Mae said brightly.

Sin let go of her knife with a sigh. "We could do that."

Nick threw the old guitar into Alan's hands, then went over and tipped Sin backwards in his arms so the ends of her hair brushed the grass, and as she started to laugh, Alan started to sing.

Mae had known he had a beautiful voice, but she had not heard it low and sweet on a summer afternoon, wrapped up in the sound of long-still guitar strings turning into living music under his hands.

Only the thinnest glittering sliver of sunlight could be seen between Nick's hips and Sin's. The burning of Mae's mark was actually making her feel sick.

She slid her arm around Seb's waist and shut her eyes, face pressed into his shoulder.

"Come into the kitchen a moment," she whispered.

He came with her slowly, the grass slithering warm around her bare ankles, her fingers linked with his. When he closed the door behind them, she stepped up close to him in the cool, shadowy kitchen and kissed him on the mouth. He stood there, and she stepped back, watching him, suddenly uncertain.

"Do you not—" she began.

"No," Seb said. "Yes. I'm sorry. Come here."

He curled a hand around her shoulder, careful, as if he was scared to touch her. His eyes looked darker than usual, the green lights drowned, and for a moment she felt like she was looking up at someone completely different.

She could hear Jamie singing off-key, the exuberant noise mingled with the sweet, pure sound of Alan's voice. Her bare feet were sticking to the cork tile. Seb's face was very close to hers.

He tilted her face up just so, his fingers trembling against her jaw.

"Your eyes are . . ." Seb said, stumbling over the words, his breath faltering and warm against her cheek. "They're just – beautiful." He leaned in closer. "I've wanted to tell you that for years."

He shut his eyes, leaned in, and kissed her like he meant it, soft and a little hesitant but focused. She'd had kisses before that felt like questions. This kiss felt like Seb was begging her for something, and she tried to give it to him.

"Whoops, sorry, can I just get some ice from the freezer?" Jamie asked, and Seb and Mae parted.

"I think I left my sketchbook in the grass," Seb said hastily, and exited.

"Thanks very much," said Mae.

"I said I was sorry," Jamie said from the freezer, not at all repentantly. "So, that girl from the Market, she seems to like Nick," he said with enthusiasm. "I think he needs cheering up. Well, maybe. With Nick it's kind of difficult to tell."

Mae smiled and nodded and pressed her palm protectively over the demon's mark. Her mark wanted her to do what Nick wanted, whatever that was, to be close to him. This was the way demons possessed you. They made you want to give in.

If there had ever been a possibility of her being with Nick – and of course there hadn't been, Nick had made that perfectly clear – it was gone now. She could never be sure if she wanted to be with him or if the mark was drawing her to him. She could never let herself be controlled like that.

When Mae and Jamie came out, everyone appeared to have taken advantage of their absence in order to pick fights.

"If you can sing like that, why did you never sing for the Market?" Sin demanded.

Alan was keeping his place in the book with a finger. "For the dancers?" he asked coolly. "I'll pass."

"I just don't like you, that's all," Seb snapped. Seb and Nick were standing near the car. Mae hoped that Seb hadn't tried to touch it.

"I don't think so," said Nick. "I think you're so jealous of me you can't stand it."

Mae acted fast.

"Seb doesn't need to be jealous of anyone," she said, twining her fingers with his and pulling him backwards with her and towards Alan. "Hey, how about another song?"

Alan obeyed, plucking out a low, gradual song, the kind you didn't dance to. Mae lay back in the grass and let the sun wash over her face and travel warm down her body, putting in comments as everyone talked, long pauses drifting in between the conversations.

At one point she levered herself up on her elbows and saw Nick sitting on the ground beside Alan's chair, long legs stretched out and laughing at something Alan was saying. Alan reached out and did not ruffle his hair, but traced the air above it without touching him. That seemed to be an acceptable compromise.

Alan looked happy. He loved Nick, Mae was certain of that, and so surely, surely he wouldn't betray him.

The sun was low in the sky, light flowing over the clouds like melted butter, when Sin rose and brushed the grass off her jeans. "I'd better get going," she said. "I can't leave Trish with the kids all day."

"Come back anytime," Nick said lazily, head against the arm of Alan's chair.

"Oh, I might just," said Sin, sparkling at him. She raised an eyebrow at Alan. "Good?"

"Great," Alan said, his mouth curving.

Sin shrugged and walked towards the kitchen door to fetch her bag. Mae jumped up and mumbled something about ice as she ran to follow Sin.

When she opened the door, she saw Sin with her bag open, hesitating at the kitchen counter. Mae saw the tablet and the paper inside, Sin's fingers a fraction of an inch away from them.

Sin shook her head and closed the bag again.

"Thinking of leaving them?" Mae asked from the door.

Sin jumped. "I'm not going to. I have kids to feed."

"It matters that you thought about it," said Mae.

"Why? He won't know."

"I will," Mae told her. "And you will. What do you think of Alan and Nick now?"

"As how?"

"As an alternative to being ruled by magicians," Mae said. "You told me you loved the Market, and we could be friends because I loved the Market too. Are you going to let the Market be ruined?"

"Do you have a plan to stop it?"

"Yeah," Mae said. "Actually, I do. Alan's going to lure Nick to what Nick will think is a Market night, and he'll trap him in a magicians' circle and strip away his powers. How do you think Nick will react to that?"

Sin sucked her breath in through her teeth. "Kill him."

Mae had only been thinking that Nick would never forgive him. That he might kill Alan had not occurred to her, but Sin's flat certainty made her go cold.

"We can't let that happen."

Sin hesitated. "What's your plan?"

"Are there people in the Market who would follow you without stopping to consult with Merris?"

Sin looked as if not consulting Merris was a foreign concept to her.

"You could start with Matthias the piper," Mae suggested, and Sin looked suddenly thoughtful. "I'll warn Nick. Then, instead of being trapped, he'll work with the Market people. We can all deal with the magicians together."

"Kill them, you mean."

Mae took a deep breath and thought of the magician she'd killed for Jamie, thought of the bloody knife she'd washed and kept in a drawer she never opened. Then she thought of why she'd done it, and whether the nightmares were worth it.

"Yes," she said steadily. "That's what I mean."

Nick and Jamie would both be safe, and Alan and Merris would not be able to make choices that would ruin them.

Sin gave a tiny nod. "I just wanted to be sure you knew that."

She tapped her fingers against the top of the kitchen counter, and then fished her phone out of her jeans pocket and tossed it at Mae. Mae caught it neatly.

"Put your number in it," Sin said. "I'll ask some people. And I'll let you know if we have a plan."

Mae remembered Jessica the messenger, and that she had known how Mae danced at the Goblin Market. A tourist could have talked. Or there might be a spy at the Market. "Be careful who you talk to." Sin nodded as if that went without saying.

Sin's phone was plain and cheap. Mae thought of her own phone, which slid open and was tiny, shiny, and covered in stickers with slogans and castles and cupcakes on them. Sin loved Merris. She had no mother.

She was risking so much more than Mae was.

"Thank you," Mae said.

She keyed in her number and then threw the phone back to Sin, who caught it and smiled, one of those beautiful showpiece smiles, as if she was throwing Mae a red flower.

"Don't thank me," she said. "Just keep your part of the bargain."

329

When Mae went back into the garden, she found Jamie curled up like a cat in the grass.

"I think I would like to go to sleep," he said.

"Come on," Seb said, sliding his sketchbook into his pocket and offering Jamie a hand up. "I'll take you home."

They drove home in companionable silence, the engine humming and the sun shining through the windows. The air had turned amber and slow as honey, and Seb was humming as he drove. Jamie was lying down in the back seat, his breath slow and regular, and Mae half shut her eyes against the sunlight, her lashes cutting up the world into shadows and gold.

Seb pulled up outside their house, wheels crunching on the gravel, and he reached out and touched her hand.

"Mae," he said, and she looked down at his tanned arms with the shirtsleeves rolled up and went still. "I wish every day could be like today."

"Hold off on the making out until I'm out of the car," Jamie said hastily, diving for the car door.

They did not kiss. Mae sat staring at him.

Word on the street is that Gerald's invented a whole different kind of mark, Jessica the messenger had said. Thorned snakes, eating their own tails.

You'll find the answer on the body of a boy you know quite well, Liannan had said, and laughed.

Now she knew why Seb always wore long sleeves.

The mark that meant the wearer was a magician, and one of Gerald's, was burnt black against the pale flesh inside Seb's elbow.

18

The Girl's Guide to Battle

SEB GAVE HER ONE HORRIFIED LOOK AND THEN SHOVED HER OUT of the car. Mae rolled into her driveway and sprang to her feet too late to catch Seb. All she got was a spray of gravel in the face.

She turned and ran into the house, up the stairs, and into the music room.

"Jamie!" she said, and he winced and looked up from the sofa with guilty eyes. "Did you know Seb was a magician?"

"Yeah."

"And you didn't tell me. Why?"

Mae could hear how hard her voice sounded, how unforgiving, and she could see how distressed Jamie looked, but she was so sick of being stupid, and he'd as good as lied to her.

Again.

"Same reason I didn't tell you about me."

"Well, I don't understand that, either!" Mae said hotly. "You told me right away when you figured out you were gay. I thought we told each other everything."

"It's not the same!" Jamie almost shouted. "Being gay doesn't hurt anybody. This does!" He took a deep breath as she stared at him, then swallowed and went on shakily, "I remember how scared I was you'd find out about me. I'd do something and I'd just freeze. I was so terrified. I thought there was nobody but me in all the world who could do magic, and I knew it could hurt someone if I wanted it to. I never, never wanted to hurt anyone. Then when I was fourteen Seb came to our school, and I knew. We can sense magic off each other, because magic to us is like air, it's like meeting someone who breathes air when everyone else around you breathes water. I was so happy. And he was just awful to me, from day one. I hated him. He was such a jerk. Then there were all these other magicians, and it seemed like they all wanted to kill me, so that was actually a step down from Seb. After that there was Gerald, and he showed me that I could do amazing things. He said that I was really good and it's the only thing I've ever been good at, and even Seb joined them and started hassling me about – about doing magic, being a magician, dropping the helpless act. Gerald said that if normal people found out, they'd hate us."

"I don't hate you," Mae said. "I love you."

"I know you do," Jamie told her, eyes pleading. "But you didn't love Seb. And I remembered how scared I used to be that you'd find out. I couldn't tell you. I had no right."

Mae let out a short, sharp breath and went to the sofa where Jamie sat. She'd thought she was being so clever, watching Seb in case he suspected something. He'd known everything from the start.

So much for having a normal boyfriend.

⤚⤚⤚⤚

"Did you know Seb was a magician?" Mae asked Nick Monday at lunchtime.

Nick looked up. "No," he said in a level voice. "And he can't be much good, or I would have."

"He's not," Jamie muttered. "I'm a lot better."

He didn't sound proud. He sounded as if it worried him.

Seb wasn't at school. It was kind of worrying Mae.

He'd lied to her and maybe even laughed at her behind her back, but she'd heard him on the phone with his "foster parents", obviously the Obsidian Circle, begging not to be sent away. She kept remembering Jamie's pinched white face, talking about being a magician.

Jamie had her. Seb didn't have anybody.

The way he'd sounded on the phone, maybe he felt like he had no other choice. Except that was stupid. There was always another choice.

If he'd told the Obsidian Circle that he had let slip what he was, he could be in trouble.

Seb wasn't in school the next day, either.

She'd noticed him hiding his arms weeks ago. He'd been part of the Obsidian Circle for weeks and come to school every day. Mae was pretty sure he wanted to keep looking normal, to hang out with his friends.

He'd stayed with her out by the bike sheds.

Nick would probably be quite pleased if something terrible was happening to Seb. Jamie hated him. There was nobody who knew what was happening to Seb, and who might possibly care, but her.

Seb had mentioned his new foster family lived on Lennox Street. Mae could just pass by the house.

~~~~~

The magicians had been living only a few streets away from her and Jamie all this time.

Mae found Seb's car parked in the driveway of a house next to a nursing home; the lawn looked smooth as icing, red tulips waving their heavy, waxy heads from a bright, trim bed. The house was white, three storeys with an oriel window on the top floor at the centre, flowers in the window, like a set piece in marzipan. A toy house, built to look cheerful and perfect, an idea of home dreamed up by someone who'd never had a home.

There was no sign of movement in any of the windows.

So that was that, Mae told herself. She'd come by. She couldn't see Seb. She wasn't going to risk investigating any farther.

That was when a black limousine sailed down the road, and Mae ducked behind the hedge just in time to see it stop in front of the house. Two women emerged from it.

Jessica the messenger, knives swinging in her ears. And Celeste Drake.

They disappeared inside the front door, and Mae headed for the garden gate. There was a rose trellis that scratched her as she went in, a white petal falling onto her shoulder. She brushed it off and was grateful there seemed to be no spells impeding her way; no guard dogs or, since these were magicians, guard zombies.

The back door was actually open, as if to let warm summer air filter into the kitchen, which had wooden countertops and a rosy red-tiled floor. Mae entered it cautiously, ready to bolt at any moment.

She heard Gerald's voice raised in anger.

"We are doing perfectly well without your help."

"Are you indeed?" said Celeste. "You live here under the demon's eye, and I see you haven't even managed to recruit the really interesting young magician."

"I hear you had a bit of a run-in with the demon and the interesting young magician yourself," Gerald remarked, returning to his usual mild tones. "Jamie doesn't much fancy the Aventurine Circle. And neither do I."

"I think you may both change your mind," Celeste said. "And Jamie will be welcomed with open arms. But you and yours, Gerald? When you come crawling to us for help, the terms I offer then will not be nearly as attractive as they are now."

"I'll take that chance."

"I'll take everything you've got," Celeste murmured.

"And I'll show you out," said a woman's voice. Mae was pretty sure it was Gerald's second, Laura.

Mae froze, listening for a step, ready to flee.

Seb had obviously been standing very close to the door. She heard nothing until she saw him walk right into the hall and they stood face-to-face, staring at each other.

Then Seb lunged. He came right at her and Mae backed into a door, and when he kept coming, she ran down the cellar steps.

Seb only followed her, of course, and then she was trapped in the cellar of the magicians' house, Seb blocking her way out and a huge circle of stones in front of her shimmering with cold light.

"Mae," Seb said. "What are you doing here? You have to get out!"

He was perfectly fine. He didn't look like anyone had even said a harsh word to him.

On the other hand, he also hadn't immediately started yelling for Gerald.

"What is this place?"

"This is the real obsidian circle," Seb said. "All our demon's circles are reflections of it. All our power comes from it. So believe me when I say you can't be here. You have to go."

"All your power," Mae repeated. "So what if someone takes more than their share?"

"You can't," said Seb. "That's not how the circle works. You all get an equal share, and your natural abilities do the rest."

"Natural abilities?" Mae echoed. "I hear you don't have much. Not a great magician, are you, Seb? But you are a magician."

Even in the dim light of the cellar, filtering in from the top of the stairs, she saw Seb go dull red.

"Yeah," he said. "I am. I'm sorry. But I don't want to see you get hurt. Mae, please. They'll kill you if they find you down here."

He advanced on her and she flung up one hand, defensive. He grabbed her wrist and ran, dragging her behind him up the stairs and back into the hall.

"Seb?" Gerald's voice said, sharp. "What are you doing?"

Mae and Seb stared at each other. Mae saw her own complete panic reflected on Seb's face.

Then he hurled her bodily through an open door.

"Stay there," Seb ordered her in a low voice. He went out, shutting the door softly behind him, and left Mae alone in what was clearly his bedroom.

The room was plain but big, with wood floors and a little cream-coloured rug. Lying on a mahogany desk was the sketchbook Seb always carried, its green cover curling at the edges.

Where I am now is okay, Seb had told her.

He was living in a nice house and paying his rent by killing people.

Mae went over to the desk and picked up his sketchbook. There was always a chance there might be drawings of Gerald's mark in it, details that could give her some clue how to deal with him.

She opened the book to a picture of Jamie laughing. It made her shaking fingers still for a moment. Seb's pencil had been wielded carefully: light in a way that made Jamie's spiky hair look soft; dark and clean to mark the line of his jaw, his hands that looked even in a picture as if they were in motion, and the crooked slope up of his mouth as he began to smile.

Mae started to feel angry all over again. The picture was so good. If Seb could create something like this, why did he have to be what he was?

Everything he'd ever said to her had been a lie.

She turned a page of the sketchbook with her hands shaking again.

Jamie was sitting at his desk this time, balancing a pencil on top of a schoolbook. He looked serious and intent, face turned away from Seb, earring winking above the collar of his shirt.

Mae turned another page. This time Jamie was leaning backwards in his chair, talking to someone else. The person's hair was dark and the features knife-edge clean, so she assumed it was Nick. When she turned another page, Jamie was walking with someone else, smaller than he was and softly curved, presumably herself, but all the people with him were ghosts. Only Jamie stood out, luminous and laughing and living on the page.

The door opened with a slow creak, the very hinges moaning Seb's reluctance. Mae looked up and saw him standing there, looking tall and dark and humble, and she wanted to hit him very badly.

So she did. She strode over to him and whacked him on the chest with his sketchbook.

"Even if you weren't a lying murderer," she said, "I think this means we're breaking up."

"No," Seb said, almost automatically, as if that was the noise that came out when you hit him. "No, look, Mae, you've got it wrong."

He grabbed her by her elbows and jerked her towards him, landing a kiss on her mouth like a blow. He held her as if she was a giant doll, an awkward puppet he was trying desperately to learn how to manipulate. The taste of him she got between her tightly closed lips was bitter, already hopeless.

She opened her equally tightly shut eyes when he pulled back.

"As if that's even important," she said, her mouth twisting. "When you're—"

"I'm not a murderer!" Seb snarled.

"No?" Mae asked. "Where d'you think that mark's leading you, then? Should I ask again next week?"

"Look," he said. "This isn't – this isn't the way you're thinking it is. You're confused. That demon's been lying to you."

Mae laughed in his face. "You idiot! You don't know anything, do you? Demons can't lie."

Seb opened his mouth to speak, then checked himself, and visibly faltered even on silence.

Mae got in his face, his clear green eyes filling her vision. "In April they marked Jamie."

"Jamie?" Seb echoed, the name different on his lips.

"Yeah," said Mae, and mimicked the way he'd said it, knowing it was cruel and not caring. "Jamie. And the demon and the traitor saved him. And me. I killed a magician. Did the Circle ever tell you about that?"

Seb just stared.

Mae smiled. "I'd tell you his name. But I never actually knew what it was."

"Mae, I like you," Seb said with sudden explosive urgency. "That was why – I thought I could—"

Mae sneered. "I think we both know why you picked me. And we both know who you really like."

"No," Seb said. "No. This isn't you, Mae."

"Maybe you don't know me," said Mae, and she stepped away from him, throwing the sketchbook at his feet. "After all, you don't know much. You think this Circle is an escape for you? You think this is leading anywhere good?"

"There was nowhere else to go," Seb said softly.

Mae took a deep breath. "Well, now there is," she said. "Let's go. Both of us. We can work something out."

Seb stared at her some more.

"I know you lied to me in about a hundred different ways," Mae told him. "No two people in the history of the world have ever been as broken up as we are. But that doesn't matter. What matters is that you get out of here."

Jamie. Nick. Now Seb. She was developing an unsettling habit of wanting to save boys.

"Seb!" Laura called out. "Get back in here."

Seb gave her an agonised look. "Stay there," he repeated, and left the room.

Mae sat on the bed and tried to make a plan. She didn't think for a minute that Seb running around the house like a scared rabbit was going unnoticed. Someone was going to come in that door, very soon. She had to know what to do.

The door opened gradually, and Jessica Walker stood on the threshold.

"My, my," she said. "What have we here?"

Mae gave her a bright smile. "Hi there," she said. "I was just thinking about that internship you offered me."

Five minutes later she was leaving the house of the Obsidian Circle escorted by a rival magician. Seb went pale when he saw her and Gerald looked furious, but they could all see Mae's ears. Hanging from them were knives shining in circles.

Celeste kept her gloved fingers curled at the small of Mae's back where her T-shirt did not quite meet her jeans; velvet prickled against Mae's bare skin.

"I trust you'll remember we helped you, and let your brother know we regret the little unpleasantness last time," she said into Mae's ear before she climbed into the limousine. "My offer still stands."

When you're ready to be your own woman, come and find me.

"I'll remember," Mae said, and looked at Jessica. "Do you want these back?"

Jessica smiled brilliantly. "No. They look good on you."

Mae had not known where else to go, so she found herself in the attic again, shadows slipping long fingers through the window and across the floor towards her as she read. The demon watching her was directly under the window, already lost in the spilling darkness.

Mae raised her voice and tried to make a dead man's words come clear.

"Isn't it time that I started learning how to use weapons?" Alan said to me today.

He's nine years old. Last time the magicians came I almost lost an eye, and he had to hit a man with an umbrella stand.

If he hadn't, then it would be just him, Nick, and Olivia. They would be helpless.

It is time, but the sight of him holding a gun with the same serious thought as he holds his pencil when he does

crosswords makes my stomach turn over. I should be enough
to keep them all safe.

Alan won't let Nick touch his new gun. "It's not a toy," he
said, gentle and worried.

"I know," Nick answered, not taking his eyes off it. "Toys
are stupid."

When I asked Nick what he wanted for his birthday, he
said a knife. I told him that knives were not really
appropriate birthday gifts. He stood silent, staring at me. I
don't think he understands the word "appropriate" yet, and
I couldn't think of how to explain it.

"When you're a little older," I said.

"How much older?" he asked.

"When you're seven."

He doesn't seem to have any kind of powers. Sometimes I
think that he has them and sees no need to use them, has no
desire to protect our family. Most of the time I tell myself that
it's the talisman Alan makes him wear. It hurts him. When I
saw that it was leaving a mark on his skin, I told him he could
take it off, but Alan, merciless and patient as a mother
spooning medicine into a crying child's mouth, said no.

Not that Nick ever cries.

He does like watching me fix things. When the drains or the
pipes are giving me trouble, when the car won't start, I get to
work and then I feel the hair stand up on the back of my neck, I
feel a cold, crawling premonition of danger, and I turn to see
black eyes fixed on me.

Last time we had to move I asked for an old house, a bit of a
fixer-upper. I think it's good for him to learn simple human things.

Alan stares at us as if we're performing arcane rituals and
goes off to teach himself Aramaic.

341

"Just you and me, Nicky," I said to him once, and a corner of his mouth went up, little hands in his jeans pockets.

He said, "Guess so."

When we go out to the DIY shop and leave Alan at home he reaches up and automatically catches my hand when we cross the road. He pulls away as soon as we reach the other side of the street. It's just a moment, small fingers curled against my palm. At the shop sometimes I pick him up to show him the wrenches and screwdrivers.

"My boy likes to work with his hands," I said last time, without even thinking.

There are moments like that.

Then there are moments like at the Goblin Market last month. We were terrified someone was going to notice Nick's eyes. Alan was holding his hand so hard that it left bruises in the shape of his fingertips on Nick's skin.

Nobody noticed. Nobody would expect a demon child. People thought he was a little strange, like they've heard Olivia is, but they smiled when they saw Alan holding his hand.

"Taking good care of your little brother?" Phyllis asked.

Alan smiled the shy smile that makes everyone smile back at him. "I'm trying."

She gave them both some sweets, and when Alan nudged him, Nick even remembered to say thank you.

Then we passed the dancers, and Nick stood transfixed. There was a demon in one of the circles, in the shape of a woman. She stood wreathed in fire with lips like blood, wearing winding flames as a dress, scorching orange tendrils sliding against her white skin.

She was staring back at Nick.

"Come on, Nicky." I seized his other hand and dragged

342

him away. He had to trot to keep up with me and Alan, and he looked over his shoulder and almost stumbled.

Nick, who rarely volunteers anything and even more rarely indicates his feelings on any subject, said, "She's pretty."

I looked back as well. The demon woman stood staring after him, after our Nick. Tendrils of fire wrapped like chains around her hands, and her fingers were icicles sharp as knives.

Just before I started writing this, I was putting Nick to bed. Alan was out at the shooting range with Merris Cromwell and her dancers, and Nick was standing at the window until bedtime. I thought he might be feeling a little forlorn, so I read him two stories instead of one and he seemed sleepy by the end, eyelids falling and face scrunched up against the pillow. Almost a child, and almost mine.

I did not even think about it when I said, "Do you love me?" in the same automatic, instinctive way I used to say it to Alan when he was small. Alan used to smile, wide and bright, as if he'd won something because he got to answer the question. He used to throw his arms up in the air and say, "Yes!" and then Marie or I would have to sweep him up and kiss him.

Nick turned his face away from me slightly.

"No," he said in his cold, hollow little voice.

Then he went to sleep.

Mae looked up and saw Nick, who did not look like anyone who might ever conceivably have been called Nicky.

"That's how it goes," he said, expressionless. "We never make humans happy. They always think we might."

He turned his face away and added in a soft voice, not gentle but like a rising fire, "I don't think we can."

"Did you know about Seb?" Mae asked. "Not the magician thing, the other thing. About Jamie. Is that why you laughed, when I told you I was seeing him?"

Nick's eyes flickered over to her. "Yeah," he said after a minute.

"Why didn't you tell me?"

"Alan said to me once that as I couldn't tell lies, I shouldn't tell secrets," Nick said. "I thought you'd figure it out."

She should have figured it out. Seb had been far too accepting of her set terms, far too eager to enter into a relationship where he was tested and never touched. Every time they had touched, he'd freaked out, terrified he would not meet her expectations.

"How did you know?"

"I'm a demon," Nick answered matter-of-factly. "That kind of thing, we spent years watching at human windows and learning. I know what humans want."

You're so jealous of me you can't stand it, Nick had said to Seb.

Because Nick got to spend time with Jamie, because Jamie liked him.

Mae had been so confident that Seb liked her. She felt such a fool.

"Great," Mae said softly.

"You want me to kill him?"

It was very strange to hear someone say that and know he meant it.

"Don't," Mae bit out.

"He was alone with you and Jamie with that mark on him," Nick said, a thread running through his voice like strangling wire. "He can't be very powerful or I'd have sensed magic on him, but that mark makes it not matter. He could've killed either of you, anytime."

"He didn't. I don't think he ever wanted to hurt us."

"Really," Nick said. "You know who never get a chance to change their minds about that? Dead men."

"Don't do it!" Mae repeated, and turned her face away. She heard Nick get up and cross the room towards her, stopping a few inches away from the spot on the floor where she sat.

"But you're – you feel bad," he said with his shadow on her.

Mae looked up into his face. "I know," she said. "I came here because you make me feel better."

"What?" Nick snapped. "How?"

He was glaring at her suddenly, as if she'd made him angry. Mae did not reach out for him, no matter what the mark catching at her wanted.

"I like that you don't lie," she said eventually. "I like that you want to protect us even though I don't want you to kill him. You try really hard, and you don't give up. I like all that, so I like having you around. You make me feel better, when you're not making me feel worse, which happens too. I don't know how to explain it in any way that makes more sense."

"Is that comfort?" Nick asked slowly.

Mae took a deep breath. "Yes. Something like that."

It made sense. She'd agreed to teach him about feelings, so it made perfect sense that she had to strip-mine her own heart to give him an instruction manual.

"Your dad," she said. "Daniel, I mean. You shouldn't feel bad because you didn't say it back. He liked going to the DIY shop with you. You made him feel better, even if you sometimes made him feel worse. That's what's important."

"Clearly, that's why he asked," Nick said dryly. "I want to know something about – what he asked me. About that."

"I can't define love," said Mae, feeling a sudden burst of

panic she didn't even know how to explain to herself. She wanted to leave suddenly, just go running down the attic stairs and never look back. "Don't ask me that. I don't know how to. I don't want to—"

Nick looked at her full-on for a moment, too close and too unsettling, his eyes like the night outside her windows trying to crawl in. "I have to know," he said. "And everything I can find out says something different. Some people say it lasts forever. Does it?"

"Love," Mae said.

Nick nodded slowly, not breaking their gaze.

She didn't want to lie to him, and she couldn't help remembering. Her father had been no Daniel Ryves. He hadn't been Black Arthur, either. He'd been the warm one, who made time to play with the kids, who pushed her and Jamie to play sports neither of them were interested in but that meant they were with him. He'd been the one who wanted kids. He'd loved them.

At some point he'd become disillusioned with his family; he'd realised that they weren't the way he wanted his family to be and were not fixable, and he gave up. He told Annabel it wasn't working, as if they had been a failed experiment. The starter family. So he knew not to make the same mistakes again.

The memory of how he'd left could still hurt Mae. But he couldn't, not any more.

"No," Mae said, dragging the words out reluctantly. "No. Sometimes love doesn't last. If you just keep on being yourself and you aren't the person someone else wants you to be, the person they want to love, sometimes they stop. And if – if someone doesn't love you back, sometimes you stop loving them. Everything else stays, all the pain and the mess. But love gets lost."

Nick shut his eyes and said, "I see."

Mae was aware she'd just drawn a picture clear as any of Seb's had been, of Nick failing to be human, unable to love Alan back, of what Nick feared coming true.

She wanted to tell him she wasn't going to let it happen, but she needed to be sure her plan would work.

It was then it hit her.

"Hey," she said. "I went to the magicians' house today. I saw their circle of stones."

"You did what?" Nick roared.

"Celeste Drake was there," Mae said, ignoring him, breathless with the rush of the equation finally giving up its answers, the plan falling into place. "She wanted to recruit the whole Obsidian Circle. That's how weak she thinks they are. She thought she could have them for the asking. Gerald's Circle have to be panicking, they can't trust him, and yet the only time we've seen him using a ton of power is when he's alone!"

"Oh," Nick said, and grinned.

Mae grinned back. "You see what I'm getting at?"

"Sure," Nick said. "If a man's desperate and he's not using a weapon, he doesn't have it."

"The circle gives all the magicians equal shares of power, but the mark Gerald's invented means you can drain power from the other magicians in your Circle when you need it," Mae continued, her voice gathering force as she gained conviction and the gleam in Nick's eyes grew more pronounced. "Which is very useful when you're alone, but no good if the whole Circle is there."

"The whole Circle would be a bit of a problem to face down, though," Nick said thoughtfully. "I was sort of thinking about picking them off one by one. Guess that plan's out."

Mae's plan was perfectly in place. Nick and the Goblin Market together could take the Circle down.

"We'll have to work something else out," she said, and beamed at him.

"Don't go to that house again," Nick said abruptly. He crouched down so he was almost at her eye level, and reached out for her mark. Then he checked himself and touched her face instead. He ended up with his fingers curled against her cheek and looking uncertain what to do next.

The attic room seemed to shrink, the slanted shadows of the roof rafters closing in on them so they were somewhere small and dark, alone together.

Nick smiled, easy and flirtatious in a way she'd seen him be once but not since she knew the truth about him, since she'd spent hours in his attic explaining human feelings to him, or sat on a bed holding his hand. He seemed to recognise the same dissonance she felt. The smile turned in on itself and disappeared, as if he'd gone for an escape hatch and found out it was a trap door.

He was crouched watching her, and she couldn't tell whether he looked more as if he was hunting her or more as if he was trying to work out her alien ways.

"Why?" Mae asked. "You worried about me?"

Nick frowned at her.

"Concerned," Mae explained in a low voice, and when he kept frowning she asked, "Do you want to keep me safe?"

He nodded slowly.

"Why?"

Mae wished she could take the question back as soon as she spoke. It was pathetic and obvious, and she was just left staring at him and feeling horrified at herself.

"Well, it's like you said," Nick said, his voice scraping in his throat in a way that sounded angry but which Mae suspected meant he was feeling awkward. "Sometimes I feel better around you. I kind of like your face."

Mae swallowed down breath like a desperate gulp of medicine and refused to let herself press her face into his palm. He was touching her very lightly, the tips of his sword-calloused fingers barely grazing her skin, and she was almost certain that if she moved he would shy away.

"I'm not sure why," Nick went on, as if, unlike a human boy, he was reassured and encouraged by her silence. "I know a lot of girls hotter than you."

Mae felt her eyes go wide.

"While I know nobody as charming as you," she said, and Nick grinned.

"Don't be upset about Seb," he told her, and dropped his hand to his side. "I said it from the start. If you'd chosen him over my brother, you'd be crazy."

Mae stared up at him. Her face felt cold where he was no longer touching her, and her mark burned.

Nick stood up and moved away from her. "If you choose anyone over Alan," he continued, "you're crazy."

Seb was back in school the next day.

He didn't speak to or even look at Mae. She thought he was scared of her now that she knew every secret he had.

He did spend a lot of time at lunch leaning against the bike shed with his mates and glaring over at Jamie.

Everyone was outside because the sun was beating down so hard it had made the cafeteria stifling, and now there were girls lying out on the gravel with their shirts tied up to tan their stomachs, and her little brother's earring was glittering, beaming out bright shards of colour.

"Oh look, moody stares of death from across the playground," Jamie said. "How I've missed those. Like getting your daily hate injection."

"Jamie," Mae said, and paused. "Do you know anything about Seb besides the magician stuff?"

"Uh." Jamie frowned. "How d'you mean? We don't exactly chat. He's pretty bad at maths."

"Not what I meant."

"He draws stuff?" Jamie volunteered. "And, um." His face changed. "There's just one more fact about Seb that I know and you don't."

"And what's that?"

"Well, I think . . ." he began, and he was now so unmistakably staring over Mae's shoulder that she turned around and saw Seb and Nick circling each other, gravel scattering under their feet and kids scattering away.

"Stay away," Nick growled.

Seb was facing Nick down, and his eyes were fever-bright, his head thrown back. He looked like he didn't care if he got hurt.

Since Mae knew Nick didn't care if Seb got hurt either, that struck her as dangerous.

"Oh, what," Seb said. "Want time alone with your new boyfriend?"

Nick laughed, a low, genuinely amused laugh that rolled like a panther in the sun. "Impugning my masculinity, McFarlane? Oh no, whatever will I do?"

He stopped circling and turned contemptuously away. Mae, advancing with Jamie in her wake, thanked God.

"I know what you did," Seb murmured. "I know what you

did in Durham to those people. To those children. And I know you did the same thing to Mae."

Nick whirled around and punched Seb in the face so hard that Seb spun and fell sprawled on the gravel.

At Mae's shoulder, Jamie spoke. "So the thing I was going to tell you is, I think Seb and Nick might be about to get into a fight."

Seb threw himself at Nick and Nick hesitated, visibly checking himself from reaching for a weapon, so that Seb managed to tackle him down and get in one good blow before Nick rolled him, straddled him, and started punching.

Mae said, "Good call."

Storm clouds were flying across the sky like the gravel as the boys rolled, and Mae was tensed for disaster even before she saw one of Seb's gang pull something that gleamed in the dimming light.

Jamie ran forward, pushing past Mae, and the knife flew out of the guy's hand and landed, skidding out of anyone's reach. The guy's eyes went to Jamie, shocked. Even Seb's gang was backing away now.

"Whoops, butterfingers," Jamie said. "Don't throw those things around. I hear they're dangerous!"

At Jamie's voice Nick looked around and snapped, "Let me handle this," which was when Seb grabbed him by his shirt collar and head-butted him in the face.

"Do you know what he did to your sister?" Seb panted in Jamie's direction. "He put a mark on her. A third-tier mark. He could control her mind – he could make her his slave—"

Jamie looked at Mae in sudden horror.

"It's not like that," Mae said into his ear. "I asked him to do it. The magicians kept coming at me, your precious Gerald kept attacking me at night. He didn't want to do it."

Nick snarled wordlessly, blood trickling from the side of his mouth, and then he laughed as Seb went for him again and Nick went crashing backwards. Gloom and clouds were churning together into a stormy brew in the sky. Some of the younger kids were really scared. The demon's laughter was echoing coldly through the playground, Jamie was standing there trembling and looking ready to do more magic, and Mae had no idea what power Seb could command with Gerald's mark on him.

Someone had to stop this fight.

She ran away from the boys and towards the school building, to the side of the front doors, where she drove her elbow into the glass of the fire alarm and heard it ringing a loud, harsh distress cry throughout the school.

Seb looked up at the sound, disentangled himself from Nick, and ran out through the gates and down the road, as if he was being chased.

Mae did not think they would be seeing him at school again.

"Don't worry about it, Jamie," Nick said, rubbing his knuckles against the centre of his forehead as if he could iron away a headache. "It's actually not the first time I've been expelled."

The day was mostly over anyway, and Mae felt no guilt whatsoever about skipping class. Besides which, Jamie was apparently irresistibly compelled to stay by Nick's side and agonise about Nick's expulsion.

They had ended up walking down to Rougemont Gardens, taking the side entrance by the ruined gatehouse past the plaque about three hanged witches. The sandstone ruins looked rusty under the grey sky, as if some giant child had left his tin castle out in the rain, and the trees planted along the boundaries of the gardens looked spiky and menacing.

"But this wasn't your fault!" Jamie said energetically. "This was a miscarriage of justice! Justice has totally missed the carriage! It's all Seb's fault."

"He wasn't lying," said Nick. "About the demon's mark."

Jamie looked at Mae, distressed and confused and so sorry, all at once. "She told me why you did it," he said, stumbling over the words. "I don't believe Gerald would – but some of his magicians, or another Circle . . . you put the mark on her to protect her. I understand that."

Mae grabbed his hand and squeezed it, and Jamie squeezed back, his mouth trying for a smile and collapsing like a badly put-up tent.

When Nick spoke his voice was distant. Mae did not think he was looking forward to going back and telling Alan he'd been expelled.

Giving Alan another reason to think he could never be human, another reason to betray him.

"Don't you understand?" he said. "Demons can crawl into people's minds and make them do what they want through the marks. Anything they want."

Nick did not look at her. Mae touched the mark beneath her shirt.

"We do it because we can," Nick went on. "Because what we want is more important than someone else's life."

"Oh, but you're not like that," Jamie told him anxiously, and offered him a real smile.

Nick did not take it. "Yes, I am."

"Maybe you used to be," Jamie argued. "But it doesn't – it's not the same. It was in another life, almost."

"No," said Nick.

He stopped abruptly and then headed in a different

direction, towards the war memorial sculpture in the middle of the gardens. Nick slung himself down at the foot of the plinth, long legs stretched down the two steps, and Jamie sat down cross-legged on one of the surrounding stone slabs.

Mae stayed standing. She'd always liked the top of the memorial best, the iron woman straining desperately towards the dome of the sky.

"Alan's family lives up in Durham," Nick said, staring down at his hands. "He has an aunt and an uncle there, he's got cousins, and I went up there before and scared his aunt pretty badly. But Alan wanted to go back. He thought that he could – that they could get used to me. He thought it was time to stop lying and have a family. So we moved to Durham and got a flat, and we turned up on Natasha Walsh's doorstep. She said that she never wanted to see either of us again."

"Poor Alan," said Jamie, his eyes huge. "I'm so sorry."

Nick's mouth twisted. "Yeah," he said. "Anyone who wasn't a monster would be sorry, wouldn't they? D'you want to know how I felt when I heard her say that? When I saw the look on his face?"

He laughed, and the sound cut through the air. Jamie flinched.

Nick spat out the words: "I was so glad. I didn't want anyone else to have their mark on him. I don't want anyone to have a claim on him but me."

He reached into his pocket and took out his magic knife, drawing his fingers over the markings that meant it could cut anything in the world, and flipped it over his fingers. Mae could actually hear the low whine as it sliced through the air, like a hungry animal.

"But he was so unhappy," Nick said. "And I wanted . . . I wanted to give him something. So I broke into his aunt's house."

Jamie made a small, horrified sound.

Nick continued, his voice level. "I came creeping in through the window at night, and I put my mark on them. All of them. Even the children. And I made them love him. I thought someone should. I got them to come back and say they were so sorry. Alan was – he was really glad. It took him a few days to work it out."

Nick fell silent. Mae looked at the ground, at the laces of Jamie's shoes, and tried not to think of how Alan must have felt when he did work it out.

He'd created the demon who could do that, who had brought human hearts to lay at his feet like a cat bringing its owner dead mice.

She could imagine what had happened after, the storm that had killed those two people, Alan and Nick both screaming until Alan's phone rang with her on the other end of the line. Now she knew why Nick was scared and Alan was ready to betray him.

"It wasn't fair," Jamie said, hesitating. "That they wouldn't see Alan."

"It wasn't fair," said Mae. "But that doesn't make you right."

Nick looked up at her then, and she was shocked by the stripped-down look on his face, blank as if every time she'd seen his face blank before, she'd been seeing a mask. This was his real face, and it was empty.

It might have been despair. Or he might not have been feeling anything at all.

"Did you ever think," Mae asked, her voice thin and small in the middle of this lush summer garden, staring into the demon's eyes, "that if Alan didn't love you any more, you could always make him?"

Nick's face stayed blank, as clean of expression as a skull, but past the memorial for the dead and above the summer leaves, there was suddenly a tree of lightning painted in silent fiery brushstrokes against the sky

"No," Nick snarled, thunder in his voice. "No, I did not."

"I didn't think so," Mae told him. "So that's the first step. Keep climbing."

Her phone rang. She grabbed it and saw that it was Sin calling.

"Excuse me, I have to—" she said, and sprinted off towards the trees.

She could see her whole city laid out before her as Sin's voice came rich and clear into her ear.

"I've got your army," she said. "You sure you know what you're doing?"

"Yeah," Mae told her. "Yeah, I'm sure." She laughed, her hand tight at the back of her neck. "It's good to – I'm glad to hear that. I could use some good news today."

"Two sixteen-year-old girls leading an army is good news?" Sin asked.

"Think about it this way," said Mae. "Joan of Arc was fourteen. Compared to her, we're kind of underachievers. Plus, I'm seventeen."

"Oh, in that case we'd better get on this before you're over the hill."

Sin laughed, the sound wild and a little reckless, the same way Mae felt, so glad to be doing something after feeling helpless for so long. Mae looked over to Nick sitting with his head still bowed at the foot of the statue, and Jamie leaning in towards him a little.

"You've got the demon signed onto this plan yet?" Sin continued.

"Not yet," Mae said. "But I will."

19

Treachery

PRETTY THING LIKE YOU SHOULDN'T BE WALKING HOME ALONE," Mae said as Alan emerged from the bookshop.

The windows behind him were already dark and the sun was slipping below the horizon, but Alan turned a golden smile on her. It lit up his whole face, like a beacon lamp in a window.

"Hey," she said, ducking her head because she didn't deserve that smile.

Because she'd come here with the full intention of doing everything she could to make Alan change his mind, so that when she told Nick they were setting up a trap for the magicians, his brother would be in on it. Nick would never have to know Alan had thought of betraying him.

It felt like dismissing what Alan had gone through in Durham as unimportant. It felt like betraying Alan, like choosing Nick.

Maybe it was.

"Haven't seen you around in a while," Alan remarked.

Mae had taken a week to finish school, to visit Sin and some of the people she'd collected, and to be cowardly about approaching Alan or Nick. But July was coming, and there was no time left to be afraid.

"I know," Mae said, and hesitated.

They left the little side street where the bookshop was hidden and came onto the high street, the shop fronts shimmering and the street itself in shadows, the evening sky inked shades of violet and coral.

"Nick told me," she continued quietly. "He told me and Jamie what he did in Durham. Alan, I'm so sorry."

She looked over at Alan. His head was bowed. Mae was forcibly reminded of the way his brother had sat when he told them, before he looked up with that terribly empty expression on his face.

"It was my fault," Alan said. "I was wrong to go there, and wrong to stay. I thought I could win them over, but it was selfish of me to endanger them like that. I wanted a chance with my family, but I didn't deserve it in the first place. I gave Nick the power to hurt them, and then I gave him the motive. It was my fault. But I'm going to fix it."

"Alan," Mae told him. "You can't."

"Mae. I have to."

She turned and faced him in the neon-lit twilight.

"You're risking your life and Nick's life on the word of a magician who has already tried to kill you and a demon who promised she'd get you both if you didn't give her a body. You can't give Liannan a body, and so you can't trust her. You can't leave Nick helpless to face the magicians. Nick will hate you. And that won't matter, because the magicians are going to murder you both."

"I don't think so," Alan said. "But I'm prepared to take that chance."

"Alan—"

They weren't even pretending they were going to walk on, that they weren't having a scene on the high street. They were standing in front of the Riddle sculpture, a little shielded from the view of curious pedestrians.

Mae doubted anyone would listen or spare them a second glance anyway. They would just see two teenagers breaking up.

"Mae. You didn't see, and you don't understand. My brother made four people love me. He made their heartstrings into puppet strings. Nobody in the whole world should have that kind of power," Alan said. "Least of all Nick."

"You shouldn't do it."

Mae heard her own voice shaking. Alan probably thought she was upset, caught up with fears for them and their fate at the hands of the magicians; the helpless little woman who would be staying at home wringing her hands and imagining horrors.

The only horror Mae was imagining was that of telling Nick that his brother was going to betray him.

Alan didn't know that the pleading note in her voice meant she was imploring him not to make her do it.

Mae did not stay standing this time. She sat on the edge of the Riddle sculpture, folded steel four times the size she was, all the sharp edges flowing together to form a razor point. Nothing had ever looked more modern, but every steel fold was inscribed with riddles taken from a book one thousand years old.

She closed her eyes and leaned her cheek against the evening-cool steel.

"Mae," Alan whispered, and Mae realised his face was very close to hers.

She opened her eyes and saw him there, one hand over her head, bracing himself against the sculpture. His eyes were on a level with hers, and the sky behind him seemed to be darkening to match them, the colours of sunset bleeding away to leave her with deep twilight blue.

"I heard you and Seb might not be getting along so well."

"You could say that."

Her whisper was so dry, it barely carried.

"I'm sorry that you're upset," said Alan. "But I'm glad he threw away his chance. And I have something to say."

She had the sudden childish impulse to shut her eyes, as if that would make him disappear, but she couldn't look away from him.

"Alan," Mae said, her voice breaking. "Don't."

"After my dad died, I looked everywhere for someone to love me. I used to sit on the bus and watch people, see if they looked kind, try to make them smile at me. I had a hundred dreams about a hundred different people, loving me." Alan's voice was low, but he didn't falter. He reached out and touched her hair, very gently, pushing it behind her ear. "Of all the girls I ever saw," he said, "I dreamed of you the most."

He leaned in then, when she was fighting the stupid, unreasonable impulse to cry, and kissed her. His mouth was warm, and she moved into the kiss instinctively.

It wasn't a deep kiss, but she found herself clinging to it, following his warmth, and trembling.

"Mae," Alan said, "will you go out with me? Don't answer now," he continued quickly, voice breaking in his haste. "Could you tell me on Saturday?"

Friday was the night of the Goblin Market.

"After all," he said, his mouth quirking, sweet and sad and a little rueful, "if you're right and I do die on Friday . . . I'm doing the right thing, I know I am, but I'm going to be scared. It would make me feel better to think that on Saturday, you might say yes."

It felt horribly, dangerously tempting to be wanted. Mae didn't know what she would say on Saturday.

She knew that on Friday, she was not going to let either of them die.

"I didn't think Alan would really go through with it," Jamie said.

He and Mae were sitting on the front steps of their house the next morning as Mae told him how trying to persuade Alan had gone, and about Alan asking her out. She had her hands clasped tight between her knees. Jamie was almost falling off the edge of the step, poking his nose into a vast red rose climbing the trellis.

There was a bee in it. Jamie was going to get stung if he wasn't careful.

"I know what Nick did was terrible," Jamie went on, his voice small. "But – Alan's meant to be on his side. I thought he would be, no matter what."

Mae wondered when exactly Jamie's allegiance had shifted so decisively from one brother to the other. She could remember a time when Jamie would have been unquestioningly on Alan's side no matter what the situation.

Nick kept taking things away from Alan without meaning to.

"Maybe he's tired of always being on Nick's side," Mae said. "It is kind of ruining his life, so far."

Jamie studied the depths of his rose. "I know you don't believe me, but we can trust Gerald," he said, his voice tripping over the name. "He's told me his plans. He isn't going to hurt Alan or Nick. But – but I wish Alan wasn't doing it, all the same. Nick's going to – he's going to be so angry."

Mae had left out the small detail of the Goblin Market army she was planning to lead against the magicians. She did not think Jamie would take at all well to the idea of Gerald being eliminated.

She also thought that if she could pull the wool over Jamie's eyes, Gerald would have no trouble doing the same.

When Jamie knew that Gerald would have killed them, he'd see that Mae had done the right thing. He would.

"I know," Mae said. "But I think— What the hell?"

She jumped to her feet at the sight of the figure running up their driveway towards them. He was staggering like a drunk and running at the same time, as if he was terrified of something behind him. For a moment Mae didn't recognise him, didn't know if he was young or old, just knew from the way he was running that something was terribly wrong. Her first thought was that this was an attack.

Her second thought was that it was Nick, and he knew the truth.

It was Seb.

He came closer, running and staggering, his eyes wide and wild and wet. He'd been crying, Mae thought with a feeling of intense shock. Seb, who acted so tough at school, who didn't even like being seen with his sketchbook.

For a moment he stood there blinking, as if he was dazed, as if he'd been running blind and was amazed to find himself at their door. Then he focused, and stood staring at Jamie.

"I don't want to do it again," he said. His voice cracked on "again", and he sounded sixteen for the first time since Mae had known him.

"Do what again?" Mae asked warily.

"Hey," said Jamie, the soft touch. "Are you – are you okay?"

Seb took another step and then another, still wavering in a way that was awful to watch, like someone walking on knives, and then tumbled forward on his hands and knees with his head in Jamie's lap.

"Uh," Jamie said. "I'm going to take that as a no."

He was Jamie, though, sweet to the bone, and after a moment he dealt with this exactly as Mae would have predicted, if she'd ever imagined that someone would come and have a nervous breakdown on their doorstep. He began, a little hesitantly, to smooth back Seb's ruffled brown hair.

Seb's shoulders heaved up and down convulsively.

"I didn't—" he said in a choked voice. "I didn't want to."

"No, no, of course not," Jamie said, casting a look at Mae. The look said, very specifically, What is he talking about? and Help!

Mae shrugged.

"I was committed," Seb said. "Laura said I was. I had to be. I didn't have anywhere else to go."

"Yes, you do," Jamie said instantly. "We know some people, Alan knows some people. That girl you met, Sin, she can help you. Alan will help you. If you don't want to do this, and Seb, believe me, you don't, I'll help you." He stroked Seb's hair with a little more confidence now. "Everything's going to be—"

Seb looked up, face like a drowning man breaking the surface when he'd thought he never would again. Jamie was bent solicitously towards him.

When Seb reached out it looked like the gesture of a drowning man too, his fingers locking around the back of Jamie's neck. Seb pulled Jamie's head down and kissed him on the mouth.

Mae started to think that she should maybe go inside.

Jamie jumped back as if Seb's mouth had conveyed an electrical charge.

"Um," he said. "Huh?"

"It was horrible," Seb told him. "I hated it."

"Look, I was caught off guard!"

Seb did not really seem to hear him, which as Jamie had descended to panicked babbling, Mae considered was for the best.

"It didn't seem like much at first," Seb said. "Just the demon, in the circle, and I didn't like it. I didn't like the way he laughed. Anzu. He said – he said he knew you."

"We had a thing," said Jamie absently, sounding as if he was not even listening to himself. "One of those things that end badly, where they never call, and also they mark you for death."

"It was just a tiny mark on some woman I was never going to see," Seb said, bowing his head again. Jamie automatically resumed petting him, looking a bit fraught. "What did it matter? And the power, the power felt—"

"I know," said Jamie. "I know. But it's okay, the Market people, they know how to take a first-tier mark off. Seb, it's going to be—"

"So I let him out again," Seb continued, hoarse suddenly. "And again. And nothing – nothing happened. I didn't even have to think about it. There was just the magic, and it was amazing and whatever the demon had done, really, it didn't have anything to do with me."

Jamie's hands stilled.

"Then I saw her," Seb said, heedless, words tumbling out like a man falling off a cliff with no way to check himself and no hope at all of being saved. "She was just this woman, she was small, she had brown hair, I'd never seen her before in my life. But she had these black eyes and there was this – this reptile feeling coming off her and this silence, this awful silence. She looked like a human, but she wasn't one. Not any more. And she looked at me and her tongue, it – it turned into a black snake and wriggled out from between her lips and Laura said" – Seb choked on horror – "Laura said, 'He says thank you.'"

There was a silence, thick and terrible. Then Jamie gave a full-body shudder. He pushed Seb violently away and scrambled to his feet, almost hurling himself at the door, and stopped at the threshold to look back at him.

His face was very pale.

"Don't you ever come near me again," he said.

"He wore a three-tier mark for weeks," Mae told Seb when the door snapped shut, the sound ringing out like a shot. "Every day he thought something like that was going to happen to him. You have to understand."

Seb's head came up and he stared at her, eyes widening and face flushing a slow, ugly red, as if he'd had no idea she was there at all.

"I'm sorry," he said huskily, and he got to his feet, still staggering a little. His jeans were dusty from the gravel. "I shouldn't – I'm sorry."

The black eye Nick had given him was gone. Mae didn't know enough about black eyes to guess whether it had vanished through time or magic. He was unmarked, the beautiful boy who'd smiled at her and stood by her when she was miserable, and he looked like he could barely stand.

This was what happened to recruits. This was what Gerald wanted to do to Jamie.

"You said you didn't want to do it again," Mae said. "Jamie was right before. We can help you. Come inside."

She started down the steps towards him, and he shied away like a terrified animal, hands up as if to ward her off or surrender.

"I made my choice," he said. "I'm wearing two of their marks. No matter where I go, they'll find me. And it's not like I want to go anywhere else. There's nothing for me anywhere else. It was stupid to come here. I'm sorry. Tell him I'm sorry."

Seb bolted. Mae was sure he just wanted to escape, but escape from them led straight back to Gerald.

She went into the hall and found Jamie curled on the bottom step of the flight of stairs.

"Hey," she said gently, and went over to her brother, sitting down on the step above him so she could rest a hand on top of his hair. Jamie leaned into her hip.

"Gerald's done a lot worse," Mae said quietly at last. "Why are you so mad at Seb?"

Jamie did not answer for a long moment, and when he did it was in a hushed whisper, like a child scared he was going to get into trouble.

"Because Seb's – Seb was just another kid at school who could do the same weird things I could. Then the magicians came and they were so – so in control, and the magic is so amazing, and he just said yes and yes and yes, and now he's a murderer. And I can see how it happened. I don't want to be like that."

"You won't be. You never could be."

She slid her arm around Jamie's shoulders, holding on tight, and felt him shaking.

"Also because Gerald is really nice to me, and Seb is a jerk," said Jamie. His voice kept trying to be light, and falling. "That shouldn't even matter, but I had a crush on Mark Skinner for years because he let me share his felt-tip pens, so my priorities are clearly very strange. And speaking of crushes, do I have sunstroke or did Seb just—"

"Yeah," Mae said.

Jamie paused, then asked thoughtfully, "Do you think he might have sunstroke?"

"Yes, a common effect of sunstroke," Mae said. "Headaches, hyperventilation, and kissing urges like crazy."

Jamie shut his eyes and sighed. "Well, that's just my luck."

"Lots of people would like to have someone tall, dark, and handsome around to love them sullenly and passionately," Mae said. "I read it in a book."

Jamie looked ill.

"Not me. I would like someone to express their feelings by being very, very nice to me all the time. And making me laugh. And then I would make them laugh too. And – and nobody would kill anybody."

"Oh, Jamie," Mae said.

She gathered him closer, his earring scraping her cheek, and he cuddled into her as if they were little again.

"Gerald says people would hate us if they knew about us," he whispered. "His family hated him."

"Gerald's an idiot," said Mae fiercely. "I love you. I do."

"The thing is," Jamie continued, low and miserable, "how can they help hating us, if we do things like this? We all seem to do it, and I love magic too. I don't want to be like that. But I don't want to be alone, either."

"You're not alone," Mae said into his hair.

"If," Jamie said, and hesitated. "If I told Mum, do you think she would hate me?"

"Don't tell Mum!" Mae burst out, her hold on him going tighter, horrified and protective. She felt as if she'd just snatched him back from stepping out in front of a bus.

Jamie went still against her, and then sagged.

They sat there together for a while in silence, Jamie's weight warm against her in the cold hall. Mae tried not to think of the fact that her army would be aiming to kill Seb, too. And he would deserve it.

Maybe she could get him out alive. Maybe Nick would forgive Alan. Maybe Jamie could even tell Annabel, someday.

"Not today," Mae amended at last.

Jamie gave a small nod and pulled away, no doubt to go and call Gerald, to talk to someone who really understood about magic and who would be very, very nice to him. Mae stayed sitting at the foot of the stairs, hugging her knees.

She'd kept telling herself that: not today, when she thought about telling Nick what Alan had planned for him.

But the Goblin Market was tomorrow.

It had to be today.

At first she thought the house was empty. The door opened at the touch of her hand and she walked in, calling out, "Nick? Alan?" and praying that Alan wouldn't be there.

No voice answered her. She went into every room and found them all deserted.

It seemed strange that they would go out and leave the door

unlocked, so Mae checked the garden in case Nick was there practising the sword.

Once she stepped outside, she saw the sky. Tendrils of cloud were spread across the blue dome, every cloud centred on this little house as if someone was playing cat's cradle with the whole sky.

Mae went back inside and headed for the attic. Once she was there she picked up the green copybook on the floor, dragged over the ladder in the corner, and climbed her way up to the roof.

Nick was sitting on the slant of the pebble-smooth grey roof tiles with clouds wrapped around his wrists like pale ropes. He looked over his shoulder and registered her with no apparent surprise.

Mae stood there looking down at the garden, where the sky was casting strange shadows, until Nick asked, "What do you want?"

She took the folded copybook, her excuse, out of her pocket. "I thought I might read to you."

Nick just shrugged, which she took as Yes, Mae, what an excellent idea, go right ahead. She smoothed out the copybook between her hands and opened it, seeing how few pages were actually left and not knowing when that had happened. She cleared her throat, told the Daniel Ryves in her mind not to let them down, and began to read.

Two days ago I left Alan and Olivia alone and went to the mountains with Nick for his eighth birthday.

We had a long drive, and I think he liked getting to ride shotgun for a change. Olivia usually gets the seat up beside me. As he stretched his legs out and enjoyed the room, it occurred to me that he was going to be tall, and for a moment I remembered Arthur. He was a big man, and he thought he was bigger than he was: I never needed to know about the magic to hate him.

"Growing up fast, kiddo," I said.

Nick glanced over from the passing cars to me with what I think was a glint of interest in those black eyes. "Will I be bigger than Alan?"

"Could be."

"Will I be bigger than you?"

"You never know your luck."

"It'll be pretty sad when Alan and I are both bigger than you," Nick said. "And you have arthritis."

"Oh, big talk from such a little man."

"We'll protect you from the demons when you're old and slow," he said. "As long as you stop trying to feed me broccoli."

I have a theory Nicky developed his smart mouth to stop Alan beaming at him every time he spoke. Nick doesn't like it when we make a fuss.

"Nice try, Nicky," I said, and he looked out of the window, lapsing back into his usual silence.

Alan wanted him to do something for his birthday. Something without Olivia. He looked up a father-son mountaineering expedition, and I think Nick quite enjoyed picking out a tent and supplies. He seemed less enthused once we were actually on our way.

"Alan might not be safe," he volunteered half an hour later. It startled me, as Nick generally waits for other people to start talking and then grudgingly responds.

"Hey," I said. "I promised you he would be, didn't I? He's safe, him and your mum. Let's just enjoy ourselves, okay?"

"Alan doesn't like to be left by himself," Nick said, still staring out of the window.

"Nicky, one of Alan's greatest ambitions in life is to be locked overnight in a library."

I spoke as patiently as I could, and he didn't pursue it. I thought he was just being crabby, the way he gets about early mornings and talking to strangers.

When we reached the camp, we had to introduce ourselves to the other father-and-son pairs. Nick was radiating coldness, and for a moment I was on their side, the human side, knowing how they must feel confronted with this monster child. I elbowed Nick's shoulder, and he glared at me.

"I'm Daniel Ryves," I said to a chorus of muttered greetings. "This is Nick."

I elbowed Nick again until he said hi, and then we set up our tent.

Mountaineering the next day was easier. Nick gets the hang of anything physical fast. I stood with a man called Jason watching the kids go down, and we talked a bit about having trouble with the tents and his son being alarmed by the sheep on the mountainside at night.

"Your boy was okay, I imagine," he said.

"Not much disturbs Nick."

"Yeah, well," he said, bridling a bit, as if I'd implied something about his child. "Seems to me – no offence – might be healthier for your kid if he did get a little bit more upset about things."

I looked down to the foot of the mountain. The other kids were still making their way down. Nick was already done, and glowering as the instructor tried to help undo his harness.

"Seems to me like my kid kicked your kid's ass."

It wasn't a clever thing to say. I used to be good at that, good at being one of the guys, but it gets harder to seem normal as time goes on. Unlike my Alan, I did not grow up with the certainty that I had to live a lie. And being a father means there is always, always someone else to think of.

They say a wife is flesh of your flesh and bone of your bone, but Olivia was able to leave with no sign that the separation from me was in the least painful, let alone like surgery. It's true with children, though. If my children are twisted, I twist with them. Normality is no longer an option.

That night Nick slipped away from the campfire when I was getting us some marshmallows to toast. I found him sitting at the edge of a cliff, looking down into the shadows and hollows that would have been a green valley by day.

"Hey, Nicky," I said, and did not reach out for him. It wouldn't have been safe, not with the way he instinctively recoils. "Come away from the edge."

"This is stupid," he said. "All these people are stupid."

"Give them a chance, Nick."

"I don't want to," he said, face bone white in the moonlight, looking up at me with those gleaming eyes.

He looked like a little goblin out in the wild, and then in another shift of moonlight like something half monster and half a magician I hate, as distant from humanity as all nightmare creatures must be.

"Alan doesn't like this," Nick said. "He'd like us to go home."

"Yeah?" I asked, and I reached out a hand. Not to touch him, just ready to catch him if he lost his balance. "Well, then.

Maybe we should pack up. We don't want your brother to be unhappy, do we?"

Nick helped me pack up, and we drove home through the night. I thought Nick might fall asleep. He gets comfortable in cars and falls asleep easily when we have to run, while Alan always spends those nights awake, pale and strained for days afterwards. I would've carried him in to bed.

He didn't sleep. He stared out of the window, calculating miles.

"This is a stupid car," he said at length. "It should go faster."

"That would be against the law, Nicky."

I got fixed with a baleful stare. "That's stupid."

Alan came running to the window when he saw the car outside. I saw the gleam of a knife in the lamplight, and I had to stop and concentrate on a simple act like turning off the car engine, my heart clenching because my son knows always to grab for a weapon first and look for the threat later.

"What happened?" he asked as he came running outside. "Did something go wrong? Are you all right? Did you not enjoy it? Why are you home?"

"It was stupid," said Nick. "And you're stupid too. It was your idea."

Alan looked at him, shocked and a little hurt. The tension was gone from Nick's body for the first time in two days. I seldom get to understand Nick better than Alan does, but I'd been the one there to see him trying to use a language that will never be quite familiar to him to tell me about feelings he isn't even comfortable having. I could look after them both, for a while.

"We brought you a giant bag of marshmallows, Alan,"

I said, and hugged him as I went by. "Don't start complaining, or we won't share."

The boys toasted marshmallows over our toaster, which is now irredeemably ruined, and Nick fell asleep on the countertop. I think he had a pretty okay birthday, in the end.

I went up to check on Olivia, who was sleeping, and then I sat down and wrote this. I don't even know why. I do not know what meaning this diary I started years ago has, or why I keep being drawn back to it.

Maybe just to record the boys, like a photo album, like a memento of a baby's first step and a pressed curl of their hair. It doesn't seem right to leave a record of Nick's first word and Alan's first gun, but a record has to be true. I don't know what truth will mean to Alan by the time he reads this, or if Nick will ever be able to read it and understand anything I was trying to say, but I wanted to put real feeling down here. So that they could open this book if they ever wanted to, and know beyond doubt or death what they meant to me.

This is not the story I meant to write, not the apology I wanted to give or an explanation that would make everything worthwhile.

But one thing is very clear to me now. I am writing this for both my sons.

Mae paused. There was no line drawn beneath the words, as there usually was when Daniel finished an entry, but the rest of the pages were blank.

"He never wrote any more," Nick said, toneless. "He died that winter."

"He really loved you," said Mae. "In the end. That's what he meant. That's what he wanted you to understand. He really loved you."

"And then he died."

Mae bit her lip, not sure if she was feeling frustration or grief for a man she'd never even met, for his stupid, stubborn son who had not known how to say he missed someone then and had never learned.

"He got a lot wrong, didn't he?"

Nick's head came up. "What?"

"Half monster and half magician," Mae said. "What way is that to think about someone you love? You didn't want to go on that trip. He shouldn't have taken you. He should have done better."

"My dad did his best!" Nick snarled. "It wasn't – the way he—"

He lost control of words and glared hatefully up at her, radiating coldness, the monster child all grown up.

"It was all really complicated," she said softly. "It's still really complicated. So if Alan did something to you – something that felt like coming into that room with your cradle in it, holding a knife – you could understand that it doesn't mean he hates you. He still—"

"What are you talking about?" Nick asked, even colder than before but suddenly in control, wielding his words like a weapon. "What has Alan got to do with this?"

"Nick, I want you to listen to me."

Nick was on his feet suddenly, uncoiling in a lethally fast movement and coming at her. Mae backed up fast, but she was on a roof with nowhere to go.

"What do you know?" he demanded.

His hair had gone wild around his face, like a writhing

crown of shadows. Mae realised that the wind had really picked up an instant before the cold hit her, scything through the thin material of her shirt. She shuddered, feeling the chill run all through her, like an icy knife sliding in and then stripping the flesh from her bones.

"He's going to betray you."

"He's not!"

"Nick," Mae said. "He is. He told me so."

Clouds twisted, tipping the world from shadows to sickly light and back again. Nick's voice turned like a striking snake.

"You're lying."

The storm was rising all around them, rising with this house as a nexus. Mae felt her hair fly straight up from her neck in a blast of cold wind.

"I'm not lying!" she shouted. "Nick, he told me. He had me call up Liannan so he could ask her if he could trust the magicians to trap you and strip you of all your magic. He told me when we were coming home from the Goblin Market that none of his reasons for freeing you were good enough. That no reason could have been good enough!"

Lightning slashed through the storm-dark clouds, as if someone was wielding a flaming sword and could cut through the sky like a curtain, leave it hanging and torn.

"He didn't," Nick growled, the words just barely words and not incoherent sounds of rage and pain. "He wouldn't, he—"

"He said he'd lie to trap you," Mae insisted, the storm stealing words from her lips as she spoke them, refusing to be afraid before she made him believe. "He said he was willing to take the chance that the magicians might murder you both. He said that nobody in the world should have the kind of power you do. He said, least of all you."

Thunder shattered the heavens with one blow. Lightning captured the whole sky in a net of blinding, terrible light. The wind hit Mae on all sides so she staggered away from Nick, her eyes smarting, and found herself at the very edge of the roof. Her toes were already over the edge, the drop to concrete tilting and grim before her. Vertigo hit sickeningly in the pit of her stomach, and she forced her suddenly heavy legs back up the slope of the roof just as another gust of wind struck.

"Nick!" she shouted. "Stop it! It's going to be okay. I've got a plan."

Nick looked in her direction, head tilting at a strange, unsettling angle, like a bird of prey.

"What else did he say?"

There was an edge to his voice like a sharpened sword, like the whine of an arrow through the air.

"It doesn't matter," said Mae. "None of it matters, Nick."

He laughed and turned his back on her still laughing, a wild, horrible sound that made the sky shudder with fracturing light. The clouds split and suddenly it was raining, not summer rain but cold sheets of water that gleamed silver and gold in the lightning and then went dark, drops landing so hard on Mae's skin that they stung. The cascade almost drove her to her knees.

She lunged at Nick instead, grabbing his arms, her fingertips sliding on his wet skin until she dug them in and pulled to turn him around. He didn't budge for a moment, immovable as a rock, then he whirled on her.

"Maybe none of it does matter," he told her. "And what happens to you then?"

"You've been warned now," said Mae. "There's an army of

Goblin Market people. When Alan takes you to the Goblin Market, when he tries to lure you into a magicians' circle—"

"When he—" Nick said, and laughed again with a catch in it.

The wind was screaming in her ears now. If she hadn't been so close to Nick, she wouldn't have been able to hear him. She could barely see him, the rain lashing gleaming needle points into her eyes, but she hung on tight to his arms.

"Don't go into the circle," Mae shouted at him, his face a pale blur above her. "Stay outside and fight with us. And we'll kill the magicians, and – and Alan will see he was wrong. He'll be sorry. Nick. Listen to me."

Nick leaned in and whispered in her ear, "Why?"

"Because I know what I'm doing," she said. "Because everything's going to be okay. I know you're upset—"

"Why?" Nick said again, his voice tearing the way the lightning was tearing at the sky. He slid his wet face against Mae's, so she felt the bridge of his nose and the cruel curl of his mouth against her cheek, as he demanded softly, "Why should I care? If – if – what you're saying is true, then I don't. If what you say is true, there's no reason at all to try and keep up the pathetic pretence that I could ever be anything like human."

There were lightning strikes now. Mae could see, over Nick's shoulder, in her rain-dimmed vision, that there was a tree burning.

He was going to kill somebody.

"Stop this," she said through clenched teeth, and slid her hands to his shoulders.

She tried to shake them, but he was stone under her hands, as if he was right and nothing about him was human at all.

Nick said, low and almost amused, "No."

"Don't you think you're being a little—" Mae began, and then Nick touched her. His palm hit her throat, strong fingers around her neck, then his hand slid around to the nape of her neck, tilting her head back.

"Don't you think you should be a little concerned, Mae?" he asked. "You with your lovely demon's mark. I'm done playing human. Just imagine what I could do to you."

The rain wasn't in her eyes any more. Nick was leaning over her instead, water slipping from his hair, breath coming in slow, shuddering pants. There was something watchful and terrible in his eyes.

The whole city could burn.

He was standing too close because he wanted her to be scared. He was waiting for her to run or to surrender.

She didn't plan on doing either one.

Mae stepped forward and caught his hand, and Nick started and made to pull away. She hung on, tangling their wet, cold fingers together, not letting him make them any demon terrifying any human. She knew him, had heard his true name, read his father's diary, held his hand before. They knew each other.

He stopped trying to pull away and just looked down at her.

Mae sucked in a breath of stormy air.

Then she reached up to curl her fingers tight into the soaked material of Nick's T-shirt.

"Okay," she whispered. "I'm imagining a few things."

Nick made a gasping, hurt sound and leaned in, his face half sliding and half scraping against hers, catching a little where he needed to shave, starting a slow, warm, prickling feeling crawling down her rib cage. Then his mouth caught hers, her lips parting, remembering the precise feel of his mouth against hers, and every nerve ending she had felt touched with lightning.

The whole city could burn, and for a moment she didn't care.

She was kissing Nick, he was kissing her, it was Nick again at last. Mae's back hit the wet roof tiles and she pulled him down with her, hands knotted in his wet hair, his mouth hot and demanding on hers, lips curling the way she remembered them. She'd memorised his mouth.

"Shhh," she said, frantic, between kisses. "Nick. It's all right."

It was so different from the first time. She'd been concerned about him then, too, but it hadn't been this wild, intangible thing, she hadn't felt her heart beating like a frenzied bird trapped in her chest.

"Shhh," she said against the corner of his mouth, and ran a hand up along the centre of his chest, flat muscle under soaked cotton. Her fingers caught on the talisman and the scar beneath it.

He almost smiled, though the smile twisted in on itself and disappeared. "Mavis," he said, his voice scraping away from the edge, and she told herself she didn't like it.

He was calmer now, she thought, and he might listen. She should pull back, deal with him calmly, be in control.

He kissed her again, sharing a shuddering breath from his open mouth to hers, his body pressing her down against the storm-washed roof tiles, and Mae kissed him back. She was burning hot in the middle of a storm, so hot she was shaking with it.

"Shhh," she said, nosing blindly along his cheek, kissing the sharp corner of his jaw and then sliding her mouth down the pale rain-slick line of his throat.

He didn't make sounds like other boys did, so she had to pay attention to every little detail in the small lightning-soaked space between them. She bit down on the curve where his neck sloped into his collarbone, tasting the warm rainwater pooled there and the cool skin beneath, and felt him tense above her.

"Come here," he ordered, and she pressed her lips against his throat and smiled.

Nick peeled the wet material of her shirt away from her skin, fingers sliding under the collar, and ran the shocking-cold metal of his ring along her mark. Mae arched up into him, and he caught her mouth and the small sound she made, his teeth running along the line of her lower lip.

"I have a—" Mae whispered into the slow, hot kiss, drunk on Nick all around her. She was tempted to thump her head against the roof tile in a desperate effort to clear it, but instead she kissed Nick some more. "I – oh God – I have a plan."

Her plan had not been to push the drenched cotton of his shirt up so she could run a hand up his ribs, skating over the leather band where he kept a knife hidden, but it was happening anyway. Nick was sitting up a little, she was levering herself up on her elbows to help him, to strip his shirt off so she could have wet smooth skin under her hands.

"This is becoming a habit of yours, Nick," Alan's voice said coldly from the skylight, and they both froze.

"Don't let me interrupt," Alan continued, and disappeared down the ladder before Mae had even registered the expression on his face, though she could tell from the tone of his voice that it couldn't have been good.

Mae swore between gritted teeth, and Nick bolted backwards, lunging away from her and towards the skylight. She pressed her forehead against the heel of her hand and cursed herself silently and at length. She was so stupid, how had she done this, and after what Alan had said to her on the high street. How he must feel now.

She scrambled to her feet and went for the ladder, making her way shakily down it, legs not working particularly well, as she heard Nick thundering down the attic stairs.

"Alan!" he shouted, but there was no answer back, not even a shout.

Mae was stumbling down the stairs to the hall when Nick caught Alan in the kitchen, the door open and the fluorescent lights on. Alan was standing beside the kettle, which he'd switched on. He looked pale and determinedly casual.

Nick had hold of the kitchen counter. The way he was gripping it and the fact that he was dishevelled and soaked to the skin combined to form the impression of a drowning man.

"Alan," he said, "I want to talk."

Mae was at the foot of the stairs now, making her way slowly to the kitchen door. She wasn't sure if she could help by getting involved. She couldn't leave the explaining to Nick, but she couldn't blame Alan if he did not want to look at her right now.

Apparently Alan didn't want to look at his brother, either. He was staring down at his empty cup.

"You do?" he asked Nick, his voice clipped. "Well, that's new and different for us. What do you want to say?"

Nick looked at him, eyes glittering under his wet fall of hair. Every muscle in his body looked tense, and Mae remembered what she had told Nick, realised how much he might hate Alan at this moment, and waited with her mouth gone dry to hear what Nick had to say.

Low and cold, Nick said, "Betray me."

Alan's head snapped up. "What?"

"Betray me," Nick said again, still in that terrible toneless demon's voice, hands clenching on the kitchen counter so hard Mae thought it would break. "Turn me over to the magicians, take the magic, do whatever you think you need to do, I do not care. But don't leave."

She'd had it all wrong, Mae thought, feeling numb all over. She'd known Nick was afraid of something, learning fear the way she'd described it: feeling paralysed even though you know you have to act, because you're sure that if you even move, the most terrible thing you can think of will happen.

She just hadn't understood.

From the look on Alan's face, he hadn't understood either.

"Oh, Nick," he said in a soft, amazed voice. "No."

He limped the few steps towards his brother, then reached out. A shiver ran all the way through Nick, as if he was a spooked animal about to bolt, but he didn't bolt. Alan's hand settled on the back of his brother's neck, and Nick bowed his head a little more and let him do it.

"No, no, no," Alan said in his beautiful voice, turning it into a lullaby, soothing and sweet. "Nick. I would never leave."

Mae had no place being there right now, so she closed the kitchen door softly and walked home.

Outside it was still dark, but the tattered storm clouds were curling around one another almost gently, the storm calmed, the sky full of possibility.

The rain had stopped.

20

The Demon's Price

MAE WOKE ON THE DAY OF THE GOBLIN MARKET TO THE sound of her phone ringing by her ear. It was Sin, freaking out about cover for her people. Mae sat up in bed, grabbed her laptop, and got some maps of Huntingdon Market Square up onscreen.

"Look, Sin," she said. "Think. The square's in the middle of town. There are houses on every side of it! Well, one side's a church, but you take my point. There is absolutely no chance that the magicians won't be shielding themselves. Trust me, I saw the Aventurine Circle do this on the Millennium Bridge. They'll be giving us cover. All we have to do is use it."

"And if they decide to take it down?"

"They'd expose themselves as well as us," said Mae. "It's going to be fine."

"It's not," Sin told her quietly. "People are going to die. I think it's worth it, to eliminate the magicians. You're not Market, though. Not yet. Can you handle people dying because of your plan?"

Mae rubbed at her eyes with the heel of her hand, fuzzy morning vision coalescing to St Leonard's fragile Gothic spire outside her window, stretching up into a clear blue sky.

"I don't know," she said quietly, and shut her eyes. "I guess we'll have to see."

Sin was silent for a moment. Then she abruptly switched topics. "The demon's agreed to the plan?"

"Yes," Mae said automatically, because if she even hesitated, Sin would know something was wrong and call the whole thing off.

Then she actually had to think about it. Nick had definitely not agreed, but she had told him and he hadn't said no, he'd just had the Nick equivalent of a nervous breakdown with the weather. He'd seemed amenable after that, but that might have just been because Nick was generally agreeable with people trying to pull all his clothes off.

He'd told Alan to betray him, but he didn't want Alan to do it. Mae thought of the way Alan had looked at Nick after Nick told him. She thought the odds were pretty good that Alan didn't want to do it either.

There was a very good possibility that Nick had told Alan about her plan, and they were both on her side now.

She might want to check before she bet people's lives on it, though.

"So there's a fence on one side of this marketplace?" Sin asked. "Do you think it'll be a good size to put my archers behind?"

"Uh, archers?" Mae said. She wondered if this was a secret second stage to their plan. Step one: defeat evil. Step two: enact Robin Hood play.

"Guns don't always work," Sin reminded her patiently.

"Bow and arrow's better than any throwing dagger. You can pick off magicians at your leisure."

"Can you shoot a bow?" Mae inquired, curious and a little thrilled at the notion.

"Yeah," said Sin. "But I like my knives better. I'm not much for leisure."

"I'd like a lesson someday."

"If we win this one," Sin said, "you can have anything you want. You'll be down here by seven, right?"

"At the latest. See you then."

Cambridgeshire was four hours away, and it was after eleven now. She had to call Nick. Mae hung up on Sin and keyed in the N to get Nick's number from her contacts list right away.

Nick had his phone turned off.

Alan had his turned off as well.

Mae scrambled out of bed and ran to her wardrobe so she could get dressed and get to Nick's house. The mirrored door covered in her stickers presented her with a wild-eyed girl whose pink hair looked like a rosebush gone rogue.

Well, she could brush her hair after the battle. She found jeans and a Dorothy Parker T-shirt that said MIGHT AS WELL LIVE and went down the stairs, hopping on first one foot and then the other as she tied her laces.

She stopped mid-hop when she heard her mother's voice coming from the parlour.

"James, I don't have all day," Annabel said irritably. "In fact, I didn't even have this lunch hour. I had to put off a round of golf with Elizabeth, and who knows when she'll be able to fit me into her schedule next?"

"Okay, Mum," Jamie said. "But – but I had to tell you this now. I have a schedule too."

"Elizabeth is a judge. They tend to have less time on their hands than the average teenage boy. You aren't even in summer school, despite the fact that I left several excellent brochures in your room. And on the hall table. And beside the fridge."

"Maybe I'm not the average teenage boy," said Jamie, very quiet, and Mae turned and ran back up the stairs into the parlour.

Annabel looked up from her seat. She was sitting with a glass of iced water in her hand, and she gave Mae a glance that took in her hair, her T-shirt, and the obvious fact that she'd just rolled out of bed, and then gave her a small smile that was probably against her better judgement.

"Good morning, Mavis."

"Jamie, don't do it," said Mae.

"Did anything weird ever happen around me when I was a baby?" Jamie asked. "Stuff breaking. Things flying through the air."

"There was that one nanny who had episodes," Annabel admitted. "But after two months we let her go, James, and you were only three. I doubt you were traumatised by the experience."

Jamie took a deep breath and said, "I wasn't traumatised. I was responsible."

"Jamie, don't do this," Mae begged him. "Not today."

"Mae, you don't get to choose," said Jamie, not even looking at her. "I need to know that Gerald's wrong. I need to know that she – that she won't—"

He was standing against the mantelpiece, back straight and thin against it, like a soldier who expected to be shot. Mae couldn't argue with him any more. She could only go to the mantelpiece so she was standing with him, because somebody had to be standing with him. He had to know she was with him, always.

"I love you," Jamie told Annabel. "I'll always love you. No matter what."

Annabel went suddenly vivid red in both cheeks, as if she had been slapped, but she said nothing.

"Didn't you ever wonder if – if there was something different about me?"

"Didn't we already have this talk when you were thirteen?" Annabel asked, sounding a little helpless. "I told you not to worry about it. Sometimes I do wish you would use less hair product."

"Mum, please," Jamie said desperately.

"James, I do not know what you want!"

Jamie looked across the room at his mother, his face white and strained. He looked like a gambler betting money he did not have.

"I want you not to hate me because I can do this," he said, and lifted a hand.

Annabel's water glass went flying out of her hand. The sunlight streaming through their gauze-curtained windows hit the glass and made the ice sparkle. Jamie gestured and the glass spun around in midair, glinting and lovely for a moment, such a simple thing, and Mae saw Jamie's face lighten, saw him glow with the belief that magic could be beautiful.

"Is this some kind of trick?" Annabel asked, her voice very cold, each word distinct, as if she was cutting her sentences apart with ruthlessly wielded silverware.

"No," Jamie said. "It's magic. I can do magic."

"James, is this a joke? I find it tasteless in the extreme."

Annabel's voice wavered as she looked at the glass and registered the extremely obvious lack of wires or pulleys. The hand she had been using to hold the glass finally seemed to accept that it was gone, and tightened into a fist.

"What else do you want me to do?" Jamie asked, and the glass fell to the carpet, not breaking but spilling ice. He raised a hand to the mirror over the mantel and it broke in half, a fault line fracturing the reflected room and putting Jamie and his mother on two different sides.

That was what made Annabel jump to her feet. She was unsteady for a moment, as if the heels she was always comfortable in had suddenly failed her.

"Stop it!"

"Tell me, Mum," Jamie demanded, his voice going uneven. "How do you feel about me now?"

The curtains were moving, twitching back and forth on the curtain rod like live snakes. The mirror was fracturing into glittering crazy-paving, about to fall to pieces.

"I said stop it!" Annabel ordered. "Stop behaving like a circus freak!"

Everything went still.

"Well," said Jamie, cool as his mother had ever been. "I guess you answered that question."

Annabel walked briskly back to her chair and picked up her briefcase, her hands fumbling a little to close the catch.

"I have had enough of this nonsense, James," she said, straightening up. She still looked shaky on her heels, but her face was pale and resolved. She and Jamie suddenly looked very alike. "I won't – we can discuss your punishment later. I don't know – I need to get back to work. I never want to see you do anything like that again!"

"Like what, Mother?"

Annabel's mouth quivered for a moment and then set. "I wonder if Elizabeth might still be up for golf," she said. "I am sick of wasting my time here."

"Annabel," Mae said. "Please, Annabel—"

Annabel looked scared, as if she thought Mae might start breaking things with her mind as well. She ran out of the door and across the landing, heading down the stairs and back to her uncomplicated life, where things like this did not happen.

Mae felt frozen until the sound of Annabel's car engine broke her trance and made her run again, down the stairs, to make her go back to Jamie, to make her take it back.

The car was already going down the driveway, so Mae ran after it and thumped it. Annabel did not look behind her. As far as Mae could see, her mother did not even check the side mirror. The car just accelerated, Annabel was that desperate to escape her kids and all their weirdness. Mae lost her head and tried to run after it, to chase her and catch her and keep her.

She stopped running when the car hit the main road towards the city, and sat in the grass of the crescent with her head on her knees. Annabel had never gone before, not really, not like Roger. She had always kept her distance but never left.

Mae got to her feet and walked back up the hill to her house as soon as she realised that they had both left Jamie alone.

When she pushed open the front door, she heard Gerald's voice coming from the direction of the kitchen.

She hesitated, then kept pushing the door open, but much more gently, and slipped inside.

Gerald wasn't looking in the direction of the door. He was sitting on one of the stools at the counter, sandy head tilted towards Jamie. Jamie was leaning against the kitchen surfaces with his arms wrapped around himself.

"I know it hurts, Jamie," Gerald said. "I'm sorry it hurts. But it won't keep hurting. The pain goes away. I promise."

Jamie gave a jagged little laugh.

"Jamie, look at me," Gerald commanded softly, and Jamie pulled his fixed gaze from the floor and looked. "I promise you," Gerald told him, serious.

Jamie's face softened, still sad but a little comforted and more than a little adoring.

Mae moved, barely letting her feet touch the floor as she did so, gentle and quiet as a shadow. She slipped up the stairs and into her room, inching her bedroom door open lest even a creak let Gerald know he and Jamie were not alone.

Nothing seemed to teach Jamie not to leave the door of his heart always open, not to believe people when they acted as if they liked him. Mae went to her chest of drawers and pulled open the second drawer.

She drew out the knife she had killed one magician with from underneath a folded shirt.

She'd dreamed about this knife, hated the thought of it, never wanted to use it again. Now the hilt fitted against her palm and everything was simple. She still hated the knife.

But she was perfectly prepared to use it.

Mae slipped the knife into her pocket and went to make her way down the stairs again, but she was stopped short by the sight of Gerald and Jamie, who had relocated to the hall. She hit the floor so she was hidden by the stair rail and watched, one hand in her pocket gripping the knife.

She could run down and help Jamie in time. Gerald wouldn't be expecting her to have a weapon.

Jamie did not seem in need of defence at the moment, though. Gerald's hand was cupped under his elbow, guiding but not forcing, and when Jamie stepped away, Gerald let him do it.

"I don't want to go back to the house."

"I think some of the other magicians could really help you," said Gerald. "Ben's brother and he tried to keep in touch for a while. I want to be able to help, Jamie, but I don't have the experience."

"You never wanted to see them again?"

"The magicians came and got me when I was eleven years old," Gerald said. "And God, Jamie, I was so glad to go."

Jamie looked up at him, eyes luminous with sympathy, and Gerald gave him a little pained smile.

"But a lot of the other magicians were like you. They had families who were well-meaning, or started out well-meaning, who tried not to be afraid, or pretended everything was all right. It didn't last. They'll always be scared of you. They'll always end up hating you, because you have more power than they do. Everything's about power in the end."

"I don't think so," Jamie said, but not angrily. He was looking up at Gerald as if he wanted to help him, to convince him, and of course Gerald would be able to see that and use it.

"No?" Gerald asked. "Then why does she hate you? Just because you're a circus freak?"

Jamie flinched as if he'd been hit.

"She had no right to say that to you," Gerald continued. "She has no rights left over you at all. She's not your mother any more. We're your family now. I'm your family now. I won't let anything hurt you ever again."

Why couldn't Annabel have said something like this? Mae thought, and was deeply and terribly angry with her, with

Gerald, even with Jamie for looking at Gerald with his heart in his eyes and on his sleeve, out in the open where Gerald could see it and play with it to win.

"We're going away, after we neutralise the demon."

Jamie frowned. "Nick."

"Sure," said Gerald. "This place where Arthur hatched his plot and where the child that wasn't a child was born, where it all went wrong, it's the place to end things, but I want my Circle to have a fresh start. We're going to go to Wales. I want you to come with me."

"What?" Jamie said, and almost smiled, an expression born more of nervousness than pleasure. "I can't—"

"Can you stay here?" Gerald asked him softly. "Will she want you here?"

"She's my mother!"

"And obviously, she loves you very much."

The light above them, shaped to look like a candelabra, rang out like a dream catcher in the wind, bulbs chiming in their metal cases. Gerald looked up as the sounds went faint as the far-off peals of a bell, and then looked back at Jamie.

"Don't you see?" he asked, his voice tender. "You don't belong here. You belong with me."

Jamie looked at Gerald with longing, and then looked away. "We could go to Wales and do magic, and everyone would be kind to me. Things would be beautiful, and I'd have so much power—"

"Yes."

"And we'd still send demons over the mountains to murder people."

"Nobody would make you do anything you didn't want to do. You could take all the time you need to get used to—"

"The idea of killing people?" Jamie asked, and he put a hand to his mouth and laughed behind it, terrible and muffled. "No. There's something you never understood, Gerald. You never had a chance."

Mae began to move, slowly, still crouched, to the top of the stairs. She was poised to leap up and run.

"You wanted me to like you," Jamie went on, softly. "Well, I do. I really do. You tried to make me like magic. And I do now, I finally do, so thank you for that. But I know where leaving with you leads. I could never hurt someone else so I could have magic. I don't care what happens to me. I won't come with you."

The front door slammed open with a bang. The lights began to rattle and swing. Mae stood up as Gerald grabbed Jamie's wrist, and Jamie made a small, agonised sound.

There was something moving below the surface of Jamie's arm, spreading from the point where Gerald's hand was, as if he'd changed Jamie's veins into lines of barbed wire.

"You'll change your mind."

"Gerald?" Jamie asked, his voice breaking.

Mae should have realised when Laura threw the spell at Jamie, and not Gerald. Of course there was a catch to the protection Gerald had given him. He was safe from everyone's magic but Gerald's.

"I don't intend to leave you here with these people so they can eat you alive or Celeste can snap you up. I don't intend to leave you at all," Gerald said. He didn't look friendly now, his eyes lit up electric blue and their house going mad around them. "You'll thank me later."

Jamie's breaths were coming out like sobs. He lifted a hand, and Gerald laughed down at him.

"You don't have enough power. Maybe one day."

"Let me go!"

Jamie ended with a scream that sounded torn out of him by the roots. Gerald was walking backwards towards the open door, dragging Jamie with him.

Mae gave up on waiting for Gerald to turn his back and just hurtled down the stairs, brandishing her knife.

She knew it was a mistake when Gerald saw her over Jamie's head and she remembered how she had been frozen once before, been tossed aside as if she could not possibly be a threat, and thought that once she was neutralised there would be nobody to help Jamie at all.

Before Gerald could do more than look at her with wide, shocked eyes, he let Jamie go and fell to the floor.

Annabel lifted her golf club over her head and hit Gerald with it again. She looked like an avenging angel with a truly excellent tailor.

"Get away from my son," she snapped to Gerald's unconscious body, and stepped over him without faltering for an instant in her mile-high heels.

"Mum," Jamie gasped, and flew to her, burying his face in the shoulder of her suit, arms around her waist and almost lifting her off her feet.

"James," said Annabel, sounding desperate and awkward and patting him on the back with the hand that wasn't holding the golf club. "Who is that man? What's happening? I shouldn't have – I shouldn't have left, that was a very badly judged move on my part, it won't happen again. Mavis, is that a knife?"

"Um," Mae said, and pocketed it. "Maybe?"

"Guns don't always work," Jamie muttered, muffled into her shoulder.

"Ah," said Annabel faintly. "Indeed."

"We can't call the police," Mae said. "They can't do anything against magic."

Annabel raised an eyebrow. "Of course not. Besides, my friend Cora is on the force; she would think I'd started using drugs. Is there anyone who might understand what is going on here?"

"There's Nick and Alan," Mae began.

The memory of where she'd been headed before she overheard Jamie's confession hit her like an earthquake. Mae grabbed for her phone and tried calling Nick's number again. It was still turned off.

It was past two o'clock.

"Annabel," said Mae urgently. "You have to drive me to Huntingdon."

"Cambridgeshire?" Annabel said, sounding more amazed than outraged. Mae had almost expected her to point out that she had a meeting, but she didn't. She patted Jamie's back again, seeming resigned to the fact that he wasn't letting go of her. She even let her hand rest on his shoulder once she was done. "Why do we need to go there?"

"Well, first of all, this guy is going to wake up soon, and we shouldn't be here when he does. And second, there's something I need to do. This guy – he's the leader of a whole bunch of magicians who are attacking Jamie and Nick, and I have a plan to deal with them, and everything's going to happen in Huntingdon Market Square, and I have to be there."

"You have a plan to deal with them?" Jamie asked incredulously, pulling away from Annabel a little and staring. "Oh my God, of course you do."

"I have to get there quickly," said Mae. "Mum, please. I

know you're confused. I know this all seems crazy. But if I don't get there, people will die."

Annabel seemed to come to a decision. She pulled away from Jamie completely and made for the stairs. "I suppose you can explain yourself in the car, Mavis. Excuse me while I fetch something."

"Fetch what?" Mae asked, wary.

Her mother glanced back over her shoulder, her perfect poise restored, and said, "Since guns don't work and the police can't be involved, I thought it might be a good idea to bring my sword."

When Annabel and Jamie were both already in the car, Mae lingered beside Gerald and pulled out her knife.

It glinted in her hand, sharp and bright in the shadows of the hall, and she remembered how it had felt to slide it into a man's body. The resistance the body had given her, how unexpectedly tough the flesh and muscle had been, came back to her like the dark ghosts of old dreams.

And she still had to do it. Mae knelt down on the cold floor of her home and tipped Gerald onto his back. He looked younger than she was used to thinking of him, scarlet mark at his temple and mouth soft with sleep, just a boy not much older than Alan.

She raised the knife.

Gerald's eyes snapped open, violently blue in the shadows. Mae sprang up and away from him before he could get his bearings, throwing herself out of the door and into the back seat of the car.

"Drive!" she shouted, and Annabel drove with a churning rattle of gravel, making it through the gates. They raced away from the magician and towards the battle.

They were on the M42 motorway by the time Annabel seemed to feel she had a firm grip on the world of magic, and by then Mae was panicking.

They weren't going fast enough. There had been a breakdown that caused a traffic jam and lost them too much time, and Annabel refused to even hit the speed limit on the grounds that being stopped by the police would hold them up longer.

Logic was not really holding up for Mae when the sun seemed to be racing her and winning. It dipped behind a cloud bank, and all she could see in the golden haze of sun and cloud was Sin and the Goblin Market people who had trusted her.

She kept trying to call Nick and Alan.

By the time she got to the hundred and thirtieth iteration of *"The number you are calling is not available. Please try again later."* she was frustrated enough to smack the back of the seat.

"Mavis," Annabel said warningly.

"If you'd let me learn to drive, you wouldn't have to be here, and I'd be there already!"

"If I'd let you learn to drive, I would never have seen you again," said Annabel. "You would have driven off to Glastonbury and lived up a tree or something."

Mae didn't know how to handle this new idea of Annabel, who was hardly ever around herself, wanting her daughter at home. So she snorted. "I could get some guy to drive me to any tree in England. I know you were just being mean because you never liked me."

It was meant to be funny, but it didn't come out sounding that way.

"I did like you!" Annabel said in a very sharp voice. "I know I never did it right. Roger said that I was an unnatural mother and that was why you were both turning out so . . . original, and I just wanted to get back to work because I knew what to do there. I didn't know what to do with a baby. It wasn't your fault, though. It wasn't either of your faults. It was mine."

"Hey, Annabel," Mae said, and punched her mother's shoulder. "Hey. Get a grip. I don't like babies either." She paused and thought for a moment. "Is that why you called me Mavis?"

"I don't understand," Annabel told her. "Mavis is a beautiful name. It always suited you."

"Did you call me James because it was beautiful too?" Jamie inquired, looking at his mother radiantly. He'd been looking at her that way ever since she showed up with the golf club of great justice.

"No, dear, that was after your great-uncle James, and then the wretched man left all his money to the whales anyway."

"Oh," said Jamie. "That's kind of cool, being named after an environmentalist." He paused. "I should try not to leave lights on so much."

It was almost a nice moment, and it was so ridiculously easy, nobody keeping any secrets and none of them angry with one another, but then Mae noticed that the sun was painting the clouds orange instead of gold, and she tried Nick's number again with a fresh and terrible burst of panic. Her breath was coming short, and she had to rest her forehead against the back of her mother's seat and swallow down fear in slow, careful gulps.

"This Alan Ryves character, he had no business telling you his plans," Annabel said. "It wasn't fair of him."

"Oh no, Mum," said Jamie anxiously. "Alan is great, you'll see."

"I don't trust men everybody likes," Annabel said in a dark voice. "Being nice isn't the same as being good."

"Yeah," Jamie said, arms crossed over his chest and eyes dark. Mae reached out and touched his sore wrist carefully, and he smiled. "I'm starting to get that now. But you're wrong about Alan. Some people think that being nice is a substitute for being good, or – or they're so messed up they think being nice is the same. Alan knows the difference. He just tries really hard to be nice, because he's afraid that he's not good at all."

Mae had to get back to taking deep, slow breaths because she thought of the terrible mistake Alan could be making right now, trying so hard to be good because he couldn't believe he was.

A terrible thought struck her. If Alan told Nick that he was sorry and he wouldn't do it, Nick would believe him. Nick had practically begged Alan; he would be happy to believe anything Alan said.

And if Alan was lying and trapped Nick in the circle anyway, what would Nick do?

Mae clutched the back of her mother's seat so hard that she felt her bones start to vibrate in time with the jolting of the car.

"Please," she said, holding on. "Annabel. Please hurry."

They sped over the medieval bridge that led to Huntingdon. The sun had slipped so far down that on one side of the narrow stone bridge the river was lost to shadows, the waters swirling past deep and dark and cool. It was twenty minutes past seven.

Annabel drove as close as she could to the market square and then murmured something about finding a parking space. Mae just flung open the car door and leaped out while it was still moving. Annabel stopped the car in the middle of the street, and she and Jamie rushed after her without even bothering to shut their doors.

Annabel was trying to hide her sword under her suit jacket without much success. People were staring . . .

And then they weren't. There were no people, as if the whole town had forgotten as one that these streets and this square had ever existed. The deserted street they were racing down seemed darker than the busy street they had left, as if light was lost with memory, as if they were running into oblivion, and Mae didn't even care as long as they got there in time.

Along the gold-starred fence she went, past the church that looked like a castle with stained-glass windows wide as doors. She almost ran into Sin, standing tall and dark at the corner of the fence.

"I'm sorry," she gasped out softly. "My brother – I couldn't—"

Sin's face was so stern it seemed medieval, like the old bridge or the church behind her, like an ebony carving over the black silk of her shirt. A bow and a quiver of arrows were strapped to her back.

"Doesn't matter," she said with despair cold as stone, and Mae looked past her to see the market square.

The square of Huntingdon town was more like a lopsided triangle, hemmed in by the church on one side and a vast domed building that had to be the town hall on the other. It was paved with herringbone bricks that looked deep red in the darkening evening and scarlet in the floodlights surrounding a sculpture of a thoughtful soldier.

Dead centre of the red triangle was a magicians' circle, already shimmering with power.

Nick was inside it with his black head bowed, his shoulders tense, as if he wanted to spring in a thousand different directions at once and could not move. He was already trapped, already betrayed.

She was too late.

The Obsidian Circle was massed behind the statue, in front of the town hall. Through the floodlights and the shimmer of magic, Mae could make out Gerald's and Laura's faces; every magician was watching the demon with glittering eyes, waiting for his downfall.

Even Seb at the back looked flushed and excited, carried away with victory.

Alan and Merris Cromwell, standing on opposite sides of the magicians' circle from each other and far away from Gerald and his followers, did not look victorious.

Mae, clinging to the black bars of the church fence as if they were the bars of her prison, could not see Merris's face. Alan was farther away but lit by the white glow of magic; he looked intent. The floodlights were streaming brightness behind him, and he was casting a long shadow.

From his shimmering trap, from the crackling heart of magic, Nick was staring at his brother.

"Liannan," Gerald said softly, the only voice in that nighttime square. "Liannan, we have caught a traitor for you. Come bind him. Wrap him in thorns. Give him a heart and shatter it like ice. Show him what you do to those who turn against their own kind!"

Liannan came like light, magic forming her shape against the night as if she had been written in by stars. It hurt to look at her, and then the dazzle dimmed so that Mae could make out the red of her hair, which seemed today to be blending with shadows, like blood in night waters, and the cruel curve of her mouth.

It still hurt to look at her.

"Look at you," Liannan whispered, sliding her hands up Nick's arms to his shoulders in an embrace that drew blood. "My darling. What a fool you are."

Nick did not even look at her.

She put her mouth to his ear and said with a delighted laugh, "How you're going to suffer."

Liannan stepped away from Nick and surveyed him like a warlord of old might have looked over some beautiful bleeding captive, with appreciation for her prize and her own prowess in winning it.

"You want to be Nicholas Ryves?" she asked. "So be it."

She lifted one of her knife-sharp hands. Light came bright and sharp from her upraised hand, like tame lightning, and it crawled up Nick's body and wound him in chains.

The chains had jagged edges, like the shapes of lightning bolts Mae had seen in pictures, hurled down from above by angry ancient gods. Nick was bleeding from a dozen places and his breath was coming in sharp, controlled pants that said he was in pain.

His eyes were still fastened on Alan. There was no warmth in those eyes, no capacity for forgiveness or understanding.

That inhuman gaze never wavered.

"I bind you to this body, Nicholas Ryves, to live within its limits and die its death," said Liannan, and a whip of lightning curled around Nick's neck as she laughed. "However soon that death may come."

She was almost dancing around Nick, slowly, bone-white feet flashing below a swinging skirt. She stopped dancing for a moment to stand on her tiptoes and speak in Nick's ear again.

"You are at my mercy," she told him. "And you know exactly how much I have of that."

Then she turned away from him and began to walk along the periphery of the circle, hair streaming. She was looking at Alan as she passed him, at Merris, at the magicians.

"I bind your powers to the exact limits agreed on in our bargain," she declared, and Nick's lightning chains flickered out like candles, leaving him bloody in the dark. "Now," Liannan said, lifting her chin, "I want out of this circle. I have kept our bargain, and I want my reward."

Gerald raised a hand, and the boundaries of the circle, the ghosts of the stones that formed the true obsidian circle, vanished. The magic began to recede like the tide.

"You have kept our bargain," he told her carelessly, his eyes on Nick. "And you will be rewarded. You'll get a body for this."

Liannan gave him a wolf's grin.

"Oh, I hope so," she said. "But I wasn't talking to you."

The magic was dwindling and Liannan with it, her bright, cruel beauty paling like a ghost about to disappear at dawn.

"One thousand nights of life," she said, closing her eyes and reaching out her hand.

"One thousand days of life," said Merris Cromwell. She reached into the dying heart of magic and grasped Liannan's hand. The demon's icicle fingers stabbed straight through, coming out the other side of Merris's palm like bloody prisms showing a thousand different shades of scarlet.

Merris screamed. And Liannan vanished, melting away into shadows from the feet up, the last thing to disappear the icicles piercing Merris's hand, leaving behind only a third-tier demon's mark in the hollow of her palm.

Merris's spine arched as if it was breaking and being reformed, her hair flying out in what seemed to be a sudden wind. It settled back over her shoulders shot with red. Like blood in night waters.

When she lifted her face, her eyes were black.

Beside Mae in the darkness, Sin made a small sound and buried her face in her hands.

"You haven't answered me," Liannan remarked in a torn, crackling version of Merris Cromwell's voice. "Have I kept our bargain?"

She looked straight across the darkness where the circle had been, past Nick.

"You have kept our bargain perfectly," Alan told her. "How do you like your reward?"

Liannan laughed at the look on the magicians' faces. She lifted her arms like a dancer, enjoying the new body, taking steps that looked like a dancer's steps.

Merris's body looked less like Merris's body every passing moment, the face growing young and smooth around those night-dark eyes. Liannan unwrapped the shawl from around her shoulders, and Mae noticed for the first time as its crimson folds fluttered to the ground that it was not held in place by Merris's talisman brooch.

"The magicians were offering me bodies I would not have to share," she said, drawing closer to Nick. "But I don't mean to complain. I trust you'll be grateful, Hnikarr."

"Sharing with Merris means the body lasts," Alan said, smiling at her nerve. Liannan laughed delightedly back at him. "And there are other benefits to a willing host. How do you like the voice?"

"Maybe I'll learn to sing," Liannan in Merris said, already dancing.

She circled Nick, her hand outstretched but not quite touching Nick's bloody arm as she went by. Her fingers looked longer than they should have in the floodlights, casting a pale shadow like the ghosts of her icicles, and then she went to stand before Alan.

"What can I say?" she asked him, watching him as if he was some amazing new game.

Alan kept smiling at her. "Whatever you like."

"Alan Ryves, it was a pleasure doing business with you," Liannan told him. "Feel like making another bargain with me so that I'll help you fight? I wouldn't ask for much. Just a little, little thing. Nothing you couldn't spare."

The magicians all went tense. Gerald glanced back at them, warning, and none of them moved or spoke a word.

"I think I've made enough bargains with you," Alan said.

"You may live to regret that," Liannan told him, and she put long, ice-pale hands on Alan's arms, leaned up, and kissed him. She looked at him as if she was fond of him and added, still smiling, "Then again, you may not live."

Alan just nodded. Liannan whirled away, black and crimson dress flaring with her mingled hair, shadows and blood, back to Nick.

"I told you I'd be on your side if I got an offer," she said. "A warning, though. Anzu won't be happy. Be careful. He knows how to hurt you. He knows you almost as well as I do."

"And you know me so well," said Nick, speaking for the first time. His voice was low and rough. It sounded far less human than hers.

"I think so," Liannan whispered. "Come away with me.

There's a wood outside, and a town full of people to play with. Come and be mine again."

"No," said Nick. "I have these people to deal with first."

He looked at Alan again, cold and intent, his attention like a single-minded avalanche, impossible to escape or survive.

Liannan just laughed at him, carefree and unchained. "Come and be mine later, then," she said, and spun away.

She came straight for the side street where they were crouching. Mae felt Sin flinch and lean against her for sheer animal comfort, both of them staring at Liannan with huge, terrified eyes as she went by. Liannan cast them an amused look, obviously highly entertained by Sin's horror and pain, and blew a kiss as she passed.

She was gone. There was only one demon left standing in the market square.

"Liannan seems to feel she got a fair price in your little bargain," Nick said to Alan, his voice terribly quiet.

He advanced on Alan like a predator, prowling with his eyes empty of anything but hunger.

"Later," said Alan quietly.

"No," Nick snarled.

He stopped in front of Alan, close enough to cut his throat. His stare was a challenge now, his voice out of control, ragged at the edges, consumed with fury.

"We discussed this last night. I'm a demon," Nick murmured to his brother. "And that means my cooperation comes at a price. I want it. Now."

Alan shut his eyes, as if he did not want to see the blow coming. "All right."

Nick, don't, Mae thought, curled up tight between Sin and

her mother, limbs frozen, heart going far too fast. Oh Nick, please don't.

Nick slid to his knees.

The magicians were moving now, puzzled and muttering. Even Gerald looked uneasy, confused and lost. Nick curled his hand around the back of Alan's knee. There was a moment of stillness, as if everything had been paused so the world could change.

Then Nick was on his feet, moving fast and light as a cat in the night, barely seen before he appeared where he wanted to be, which was beside his brother.

Alan moved to align himself with Nick and face the magicians. He moved smoothly with his weight on both legs, without a trace of pain.

"That was your price?" Gerald demanded, more bewildered than angry. "That was what you wanted, in exchange for all your power? What good is—"

Nick interrupted him by snapping his fingers. The shadows lingering around the edges of the floodlights in the square writhed and took shape at the demon's command, became two wavering creatures made of darkness, shadow panthers that came slinking into the light and winding around the brothers' legs.

I bind your powers to the exact limits agreed on in our bargain, Liannan had said.

The bargain she had made with Alan, when Mae had called her up and left them alone together. Not Gerald.

The bargain Alan had told Nick about last night, after Mae had left.

Nick smiled a demon's smile, slow and ravenous. "Who said anything about all my power?"

21

Bitter Fruit

M AE SAW THE EXACT MOMENT THAT FURY CRASHED THROUGH Gerald's patience and shattered it. He lifted a hand, and wind went blasting in Nick and Alan's direction. The other magicians took their cues from him and the murmurs of spell casting were suddenly all around, half the circle drawing back for what Mae guessed was a spot of demon summoning, the other half advancing with magic in their hands. Nick and Alan drew their weapons.

"Now," said Mae, and grabbed Sin's shoulder for emphasis. "Go and alert your archers. Tell the rest of them to come out in the open."

Sin's voice sounded faint and stunned, but there was a smile in it. "If you go out," she said, "they'll follow you."

Mae blinked. "Right." She stood up and dusted off her jeans, looking helplessly at Jamie and Annabel, who stood up with her. "Right, then," Mae said, and strode out into the market square.

Emerging from their places on the side streets at the other

two points of the triangle came the Goblin Market: the woman who sold wind chimes, the man at the knife stall who'd tackled a customer, the necklace-selling pied piper with the gleaming dark eyes. The piper wasn't holding up a trinket made of human bones this time, though. He was holding a bow and arrow, which he loosed into the midst of the magicians.

That was another signal, apparently. From the black fence surrounding the church, the gardens and towering trees, and the very roof of the church itself, there was suddenly a rain of arrows.

The magicians erupted into a counter-attack. A small storm front was rising in front of them like a force field, and in the storm were crows croaking wildly to one another and being tossed about in the wind like leaves. From the centre of the Obsidian Circle there sprang a wolf.

Mae took out her knife, which was seeming a bit inadequate just now, and braced herself for the onslaught.

One of the shadow creatures at Nick's feet leaped for the wolf. Alan shot a crow.

The Ryves brothers moved to join the forces of the Goblin Market.

It took Mae a minute to realise that the three newcomers were being guarded: that she, Jamie, and Annabel were being pushed to the back of the fray.

It made sense. All Mae had was a knife, and Jamie didn't even have that.

There was a flurry of snarls and yelps under their feet, then in the jostling, fighting crowd Mae suddenly saw faces that couldn't have possibly been there, her father and her friends from school, and Jamie called out, "Mum, Mae, they're illusions, don't pay attention to them," and Annabel struck out at one leering magician's face only to find her sword went clean through him and was parried by Nick.

"All of you, get behind me right now!"

"No, they need me," Mae argued.

"They needed you to make a plan," said Nick. "They may have even needed you to lead them into this square. But they do not need you to be at the front of a fight, because you don't know how to fight and you'll just get in everybody's way!"

He slashed at a crow and connected, bringing it down in a mess of blood and feathers. A pale girl with no eyes rushed for Mae, but Jamie raised his hand and she dissolved into the wind with a sound like a sigh.

Nick raised a hand and the storm died around them, so they could see four people – then five, and then six—coming at them from the narrowest side street, to the right of the town hall.

Only they weren't people, Mae saw in a burst of magic light behind them. They were demons, eyes like black jewels shining and perfect in ruined faces. The bodies they were using were dead.

"Surprise zombies," Jamie said faintly. "Fantastic."

"Not really a party until someone brings the surprise zombies," said Nick, and charged them.

The bodies moved too slowly to be much of a challenge, Mae saw, bile rising in her throat as Nick hacked his way through them, too fast for their fumbling, grasping hands to touch him, sword slicing through dead flesh and dark fluids. She saw Annabel go in after him; her impeccably behaved mother with a sword in hand and her blonde hair falling wild about her shoulders, cutting down the dead.

Mae felt violently proud and violently ill at the same time.

Nick spun and beheaded the body Annabel was fighting,

flashing her a savage, gleeful smile. Annabel gave him a nod.

Nick lunged in, sword just to Annabel's left, inches away from her side, sinking the blade into a dead body and carving its stomach out. He whirled away from the pieces of the dead that were now littering the square and performed a tight circle around Mae, Jamie, and Annabel, protective but restless as well, looking for his next challenge.

The arrows had stopped hailing in from overhead; Mae thought that the Market might have run out. She couldn't see how many magicians were down, but judging by the chaos all around them, it wasn't many.

"Alan could probably have organised this better," she said.

Nick flicked her a look. "Alan couldn't have organised this at all," he said. "Who would've trusted him? He's not a leader any more than I am. You two did fine."

"Illusion," Jamie's voice said behind them. "Illusion, illusion, disgusting illusion, eurgh."

Mae found herself smiling. Praise meant a lot more when the guy couldn't lie to you. "I'd like to see you being a war leader."

"Oh, yeah," said Nick. "My battle cry would be 'For blood, vengeance, and my undeniable good looks!'"

"I've heard worse," Mae said, and heard worse: heard the scream of insects, a high buzzing that made her think of plagues of locusts, of the fury of gods.

The magicians weren't gods, though, and these weren't locusts. They weren't any kind of insects Mae had ever seen before, more like nightmares of insects thought up by someone who had never seen any but had heard horror stories, flying spidery things with bristles and too-big red eyes.

"How was your summer?" Jamie asked nobody in particular.

"Well, I was eaten by insects from hell, and it was all downhill from there."

Nick lunged and reeled Jamie in by his shirt collar, hand on the back of his neck, and Jamie made a face and shut his eyes for a moment. When he opened them, there was a curving shimmer of silver in the brown irises, like the reflection of a scythe.

The nightmare buzzing died. The insects dropped out of the air.

Jamie was suddenly breathing shudderingly hard, as if he'd just run a race. His skin looked waxy, and he had to lean against Annabel's shoulder to stay upright. Nick looked a little pale himself.

"I can't give you enough power," he said. "You don't have the magician's sigil. I don't know how—"

"Try me," Mae said. "I have a mark, so maybe—"

She didn't finish her sentence. Nick reached out to her, though, and Mae felt the magic rush through her as if the mark was a lock with a key in it, opening, as if her body was a channel with water crashing through it, sparkling and sweet and changing everything.

She lifted a hand, and a crow flying at her head suddenly stopped as if it had hit a wall, screeched and slid limp to the ground. And she knew that the magic was all gone, so quickly, leaving her a shaking and empty vessel.

"You're not a magician," Nick said, dragging her out of the way as another storm hit, shielding her with his body. "It's like – it's like filling a cup or filling a lake, there are different magic capacities."

His eyes turned to Jamie, thoughtful, but before he could do a thing, the wolf that was really a magician came leaping at them, shreds of shadows in its teeth and a friend behind it. They hit Nick full in the chest, and his sword went flying.

Mae started towards him, but then there was another dead thing lurching at Jamie and Annabel, and Annabel was still trying to hold Jamie up. Mae ran to them instead, her shoes sliding on mess she refused to look down at, and grabbed Jamie so Annabel could swing.

"Mum is kind of badass," Jamie said into Mae's shoulder. "Where's Nick?"

Mae glanced around and saw Nick thump a wolf in its snarling face with his elbow, and then palm a dagger. "He's punching wolves."

"Good, good," said Jamie. "I know he likes to keep busy."

Mae looked across the nightmarish whirl that the market square had become and saw Alan at last, in the front wave nearest to the magicians, fighting to get to them with a knife in one hand and a gun in the other. She saw him hit someone in the face with his gun, so she presumed he was out of bullets.

They could lose, she thought, and then heard the moan slide out between Nick's clenched teeth when the second wolf got its claws in his shoulder to the bone. Mae and Jamie let out a curse at about the same moment and ran to Nick just as he slit its throat.

Mae pushed aside the wolf, which was turning back into a dead man even as she touched it, and bumped heads with Jamie as they both bent over Nick. He stared up at them from the bloody bricks, eyes wide.

"Do you think his eyes are all pupil?" Jamie asked desperately, patting Nick on the shoulder that wasn't wounded. "It's kind of hard to tell."

"I'm fine," Nick snarled, and shut his eyes.

"Mae, he is not fine!" Jamie almost yelled, and Mae scrambled to her feet.

"Oh God," she said. "Alan's down. Alan's *down* – I can't see him. I think he could be—".

"What?" Nick rasped.

Mae looked down and saw Nick struggle up on one knee. He glared up at her and then got painfully to his feet, a knife in either hand. There was blood running down his arm, his shoulder was a mess, and his mouth was set in a grim, determined line. "Where's Alan?"

"Oh, Alan's fine," said Mae, nodding to where Alan was throwing himself at the magicians again. Sin was beside him now, and the rest of the Goblin Market was behind her. "I was lying so you'd get up. Sorry about that."

Nick laughed, spun, and stabbed something. "Don't be sorry. I've just decided lying's kind of sexy."

Mae laughed too, but it was nervous. Nick was bleeding too much and not healing himself, he probably couldn't heal himself, and he was going to slip in his own blood soon if he kept trying to move as if he wasn't hurt.

Annabel was slowing down too. She stumbled, and Mae had to run and bring her knife down hard, almost severing a dead man's hand at the wrist so it would not touch her mother.

"Where's your brother?" Annabel panted, struggling to her feet.

Mae looked over at Jamie and saw him standing to one side of Nick, just before another stumbling demon went for Nick's throat and Nick went down again. Mae cursed and began to struggle back towards them, a hundred illusions and enemies in her way and Annabel shouting her name.

The dead thing's head came half off under Nick's knives,

415

and then Jamie was pulling it off Nick, who was really down this time. Mae could see a lot more blood.

"Nick!" she screamed, and Alan's head turned.

He left Sin's side and started to fight his way backwards through the crowd, the knives in his hands running blood, and he was running too.

It was too late, though. Jamie was kneeling at Nick's side and Mae saw the white, strained look on his face before he bowed his head over Nick's again, saying something lost in the sounds of battle.

Alan stooped and picked up Nick's fallen sword, and he was suddenly carving his way towards them, passing Mae without acknowledging her at all except by clearing a path for her to follow him.

Alan dropped to his knees by Nick's side just as Jamie got to his feet. The sword fell carelessly out of his hands and he touched Nick's hair, his fingers coming away crimson and slick with fresh blood.

"Nick," said Alan, and his voice broke on the name. "Oh, God. What have I done?"

A man rushed at Nick and Alan, one of the magicians and not an illusion, Mae was almost sure, going for them at their weakest moment. Mae stepped in, stopping his rush cold, and shoved her knife in below his ribs as hard as she could.

She'd been right. He wasn't an illusion, he was a man.

He was the second man she'd killed. Mae looked into his slack, surprised face, the weight suddenly sagging on her knife, and she wanted to cry or scream.

She shoved him and he toppled backwards, a heap of bones and flesh, with the ugly gracelessness of death. She'd wanted this battle. That meant she had to take what came with it.

"Hey," Nick said, his whisper a thread of sound in all the screaming noise of battle and yet somehow catching her ear all the same. "You were holding that sword like it was a big dagger. Never let me see you do anything like that again."

Alan made a sound that was torn roughly between a sob and a laugh.

The world went still.

Mae turned away from the brothers on her right and her mother on her left to find the source of all that stillness, the storm calmed as if it had never been, all the illusions suddenly night air. Above the bloodstained square there was suddenly nothing but stars.

The Obsidian Circle had stopped, hands up and magic arrested in their palms. One of them was a jaguar, and even it had gone still.

The only thing moving in the square was Jamie.

"Drop the helpless act," he said in a pleasant, reminiscing voice. "Isn't that what you said to me?"

"Um," said Seb.

The night was so clear, the air suddenly crisp as winter. Mae found herself caught by Jamie's eyes.

They were not brown, not even brown with a scythe-bright gleam. They were filled with the silvery shimmer of magic, making his eyes a scintillating wash of light. He looked blind.

On the side of his jaw there was a black demon's mark, shadows crawling and burning against his pale skin.

A magician with a demon's mark, not a magician's mark, and power flooding through it.

Mae heard her own voice in her head. *Nick could use Jamie as a channel for his power. It would help him to have a – a pet magician.*

"And you said, you could be so much more," Jamie told Gerald.

Gerald didn't look scared the way Seb had, for Jamie or for himself. He stepped forward.

"You can be so much more."

Jamie blinked at him, reptile-slow.

"You're like me," Gerald went on, low and coaxing. "You're a magician. You know whose side you're really on."

Jamie looked back at Mae with her bloody knife, Alan with his bloody hands in his fallen brother's hair. Mae followed Jamie's gaze and saw Nick stirring, obviously healed before her magician brother had got to his feet.

"Not yours," Jamie said. He lifted a hand, and the Obsidian Circle magicians fell against the side of the town hall like dolls hurled against a playroom wall.

Nick scooped up his sword and Alan took out his knives again, and Mae and Annabel joined them on either side. They all moved to stand behind Jamie.

Mae sought for Sin and found her, long knives in her hands and her silk shirt torn. She raised her eyebrows as if to say, What are you waiting for?

"Join up," Sin snapped, and the Goblin Market stood with the demon and the traitor and the magician as one.

Gerald got to his feet slowly, the other Obsidian Circle magicians rising slowly around him, their eyes wary. Seb stayed down, his wrists propped on his knees, watching Jamie.

"I wish it didn't have to be this way," Jamie told them, his luminous, terrible eyes travelling across every face in the Circle, and back to Gerald's. "I can't kill you."

"I could," Nick volunteered.

The Goblin Market seemed to agree with Nick, drawing in

closer, a tight, angry knot. Jamie glanced around at all of them and hesitated; he seemed to be on the verge of stepping back.

Then Gerald knelt on the ground.

"That's right," he called. "Come here."

Climbing over bodies and slipping through warriors' legs, his footie pyjamas stained with blood and the foul ooze of dead things, came Sin's little brother, Toby. He walked right into Gerald's arms.

Gerald straightened, holding the child's chubby hand out palm up and speaking a few words.

The world changed again, an illusion dissolving like mist in the sun, and they all saw the mark.

The mark was black and terrible in the hollow of that baby's little hand: it looked like the magician's sigil, but not quite enough like it. It showed a hand, forming a fist around someone else's heart.

Gerald must have invented two different marks. A variation on the magician's mark, which drained power from people instead of circles, and this one.

"This is the magician's version of the demon's mark," Gerald said, his eyes on Sin. "I have complete control over anyone who wears it."

He'd put the mark on Toby at the Goblin Market. He'd handed the baby over to Mae when he had no further use for him.

"I hold this child's life in the palm of my hand," Gerald said in a clear, carrying voice. "My Circle is walking out of here tonight."

"Toby," Sin said in a strangled voice, reaching for him. "How—"

"I wouldn't," Gerald advised. "I called the child here. I can make him go anywhere I want him to go. I could make him walk off a cliff. I could have him possessed. I could stop his breath with a thought. Have your people stand down."

"Get back!" Sin commanded.

But the Market could taste blood. They finally had magicians at their mercy, and Sin was not the leader yet.

"The child's as good as dead anyway," said Matthias the piper, his bow still strung. "It's not like he's ever going to take it off."

"Matthias!" Sin exclaimed, but there was a murmur of agreement around the square.

"And we don't want a leader who can be blackmailed!"

Toby started to cry, his soft, wailing voice rising above the slanted roofs of the buildings around the market square. Jamie gave Mae a look she couldn't read, not with his magic-hot eyes, but then his hand sought hers and she realised he was horror-struck.

"I take no pleasure in this," Gerald told Jamie, but Jamie continued to look as sick as Mae felt.

The piper was right, though. Mae could see no way to make Toby safe.

Sin stood with her back straight and her knives still drawn, her mouth trembling.

"Kill them," said Matthias, and the crowd surged.

Alan said, "Wait."

He came forward, made it almost to Gerald and the baby in a few long strides, and then Toby gave a long cry of pain. Alan stopped, hand outstretched.

"What good is the child to you?" he asked, his voice wrapping sweetly around every word, less guiding than simply making you want to follow him. "You can hear them. They'll kill you anyway. You need a better hostage than that."

He slanted a dismissive look at Toby's small head. Gerald was starting to look thoughtful.

"You need collateral to control the demon," Alan said, and he turned his hand palm up, reaching out the other for the baby. "Hand over the baby. Transfer the mark. You can have me."

"Alan," Nick said in a terrible voice. "Alan, no."

He started forward, knocking down everyone in his path.

"Now," Alan commanded, and Gerald reached out and clasped his hand.

It was over that soon. The baby was held gently in Alan's arms, and the mark was branded on his palm.

"Shhh," Alan murmured to the child, who was quieting already in his arms. "You're safe now."

He took two steps towards Sin and put her brother in her arms. She accepted him almost numbly, her face blank but her arms going around Toby tight.

Alan did it just in time, an instant before Nick reached him and spun him around, one hand clenching tight on Alan's shoulder. For a second Mae thought Nick was going to punch him.

Nick held on for a moment, in a tight grip that looked more like violence than anything else, and then he turned to Gerald.

"I'm going to make you sorry," he whispered in that demon's voice, like chains settling on your hands and feet, like a chill getting so deep into your blood it would never leave and you would never be warm again. "I'll make time longer, just so you can suffer in it. I'll never let you die. You'll live to the end of the world, crawling, bleeding, begging, wishing you had never even thought of touching my brother."

Gerald didn't answer in words, but Alan gave a short scream between his teeth and sank to his knees, and Mae knew exactly how much pain he would've had to be in before he let Nick hear that.

When Alan rose, he almost staggered. For a moment that seemed normal, and then Mae remembered he was meant to be healed now.

"Your brother was whole for all of five minutes," Gerald said. "Was it worth handing over any of your power for that?"

Nick shivered in one tight, controlled burst, as if someone had hit him.

"My ring," Gerald commanded.

Nick yanked it off his hand and threw the silver circle to the ground at Gerald's feet. He did not look away from Alan.

"Yeah," said Gerald, stooping to pick it up and sliding the bloodstained ring onto his finger. "I think we'll go now."

"Who said you could go?" asked Matthias. "Now you don't even have a child of the Market. Let the traitor die."

"It's worth a sacrifice," said a woman Mae remembered from the chimes stall. Alan looked at her, his face startled, and she turned her eyes away. "It's one life," she said. "We were all willing to risk ours."

The square seemed to turn upside down as Nick snarled, tipped into a darker world. Everyone shivered as the wind rose. Mae saw her breath on the air like a dragon's.

"You dare," Nick said softly.

The Market people cleared a space around the demon now, unity dissolving, tables turning, only a few of them left standing with Nick. Alan, Mae, Jamie, Annabel. And Sin, trembling, with the child in her arms.

"Wait," Sin said, sounding uncertain. They paid her no attention.

"Wait, you idiots!" Mae shouted. "Let's give the magicians a chance to surrender." She let her eyes move significantly to Jamie. "We've seen how useful they can be."

There was sudden murmuring among the Market people. Mae did not think they sounded largely in favour of the idea, but at least they were talking. Seb uncurled from the ground, green eyes alight.

"You must be joking," Gerald scoffed, but Mae saw that a couple of the other magicians looked thoughtful.

"I for one think it's an excellent idea, Gerald," said Celeste Drake, moving from the shadow of the church with the Aventurine Circle behind her. "Why don't you surrender to me?"

The Market people flowed back towards Nick and Jamie, towards them all. They were united again, trapped between two magicians' Circles.

Celeste paid them no heed at all. She sailed forward, serene as a china swan on a glass lake, until she was standing before Gerald with her hands held out to his.

"I told you that you would reconsider my offer."

Gerald regarded her coolly. "And you told me you'd take everything I had."

"True," Celeste admitted. "But in light of other contributions you can make . . ." Her eyes slid to Alan. "I'll make you the same offer I made before. Will you take it? Last chance."

"I will," said Gerald, and put his hands in hers.

"Circle of my circle," Celeste said. "You are mine, and your marks are mine, and your magicians are mine. I will brand you with the sigil of the Aventurine Circle, and no loyalty will come before your loyalty to me."

"I'm yours," Gerald told her, his head bowed.

"And your enemies are mine," said Celeste, her icy grey eyes sweeping the Goblin Market army. "And you will be leader of the Circle when I die. The bargain is struck. Do any of you dare stand against the Aventurine Circle?"

Everyone stood silent. There were just too many magicians, Mae thought. There was Helen the magician with her swords bright in her hands, Gerald with his marks: the union Mae hadn't wanted and hadn't planned on. Even with Nick and Jamie both, there were far too many to fight. Celeste wasn't likely to start fighting until she had the Obsidian Circle safely branded as hers.

The battle was lost. Their best chance for survival was to stay quiet.

Celeste turned away, and Gerald started after her. For a moment Mae thought it was over.

Then Gerald stopped beside Jamie and said, "Come with me."

Jamie stared at him.

"You know you have to now, don't you?" Gerald asked. "Now you've had power. All you want is more. Come with me."

Jamie kept staring, mouth a tender, hurt shape, still a little in love despite everything.

"Okay," he said.

"What?" Mae shouted.

She surged forward, but Annabel got there first, her sword a blur of light and then a line of steel held between Jamie and Gerald.

"You're not taking him," said Annabel. "He's mine."

There was a ring of steel on steel.

Helen of the Aventurine Circle had lunged forward, and now her blade was kissing Annabel's. They stood looking at each other. Annabel lifted her chin, defiant, and Helen's lip curled.

"You're wrong," she said. "He belongs to us now."

Mae thought Helen would turn away then, and she did.

First she lunged in and drove her sword to the hilt in Annabel's chest. Annabel made a small sound, more incredulous than pained, her body crumpling on the blade. Helen slid her sword free and swung back into line with the other magicians.

Annabel tumbled to the ground on her back.

"Mum," Jamie said, his voice small and terrified, and he dived to his knees by her side. Mae didn't know why there was a clawing in her chest, didn't know why her mouth had gone dry, when Jamie was going to heal her. When Annabel was absolutely fine.

She did not look fine. Their mother was lying with her smooth blonde hair fanned out on the bloodstained bricks. Blood was trickling from one side of her mouth, was a spreading pool on her white blouse, and her eyes were staring wide and sightless into the clear night sky.

Mae made a low, hurt sound in the back of her throat. Jamie's hands, frantically patting and searching, had gone still.

"Mum," Jamie repeated, panicked, as if he was searching for her, as if he had lost her and could not find her, as if she was not right there. "Mum, please, please. Mum."

And without Mae making the decision to kneel down, there she was on the bricks, on her hands and knees beside her brother.

She was making that low, wounded sound again, her hands on Annabel, shaking her and shaking her until Jamie pulled at her wrists.

"Mae," he said, crying, close to her ear. "Mae, don't. She's – she's—"

She was crying too. He was nothing but a blur of magic-hazed eyes and demon's mark, and then he was holding on to her, clinging around her neck the same way he'd clung to their mother this afternoon.

"Hush," Mae said, her voice sounding oddly distant in her own ears. Jamie's tears were slipping down her neck. She had to be strong for him. She smoothed her palm down her brother's shivering back, down the line of his spine. "Hush," she whispered again. "I know she's dead."

The Goblin Market was camped out in Portholme Meadow, not so far away from the town. It was, Mae vaguely remembered, the largest meadow in England. It was also, she realised dimly, quite beautiful. The caravans and tents of the Goblin Market took up only a tiny bright space of all the lush greenness, and all around them in the early morning were the sounds of birds singing and trees whispering to one another.

Mae was lying alongside Jamie in a red tent, watching the shadowy patterns the leaves cast on the fabric. She was trying not to move, trying not to wake Jamie after he'd cried himself to sleep, but she couldn't sit among all those strangers whispering condolences to her. She just lay there, watching the shadows move.

She didn't even know what they had done with the body.

"You do realise you're as good as dead," Nick said from

outside the tent. "With that mark on you. Gerald's playing with you like a cat with a mouse. He just wants us to think about what happens next. You're already crippled again."

"I don't mind that," Alan said gently. "It was you who minded."

Nick laughed with a razor edge to it. "Oh, you like being in constant pain."

"The leg's part of who I am by now. It just happened—"

"Because of me!"

"Yes," Alan told him, and Nick was suddenly, terribly silent. "Being your brother is dangerous," he continued. "It was a risk I took, it was something I chose. I changed myself and the world to keep you. And you were worth it."

"And if Gerald kills you," Nick ground out. "If he does worse."

"Then you were still worth it."

There was silence then, and no shifting of shadows. Alan didn't even try to reach out to Nick.

"You are so stupid," Nick grated out at last. "I hate you sometimes. I hate you. And I don't know how to save you!"

"Shhh," said Alan. "Don't wake Mae and Jamie."

Nick made a low, awful sound, like the snarl of a nightmare monster, and then his shadow retreated.

Mae climbed slowly to her feet and emerged from the tent flap into the hot sun.

"I'm already awake," she said. "What did they do with the body?"

Alan, standing like a lone guard by their tent, said, "They're taking her to Mezentius House."

"Why?" Mae asked, prepared to be outraged at anything. "My mother – she wasn't possessed."

427

"There's a graveyard there," Alan told her very softly, as if he was terribly sorry for her. "In case you or Jamie ever want to visit it."

"I never will," said Mae. "Never."

They couldn't report Annabel's death, though, couldn't show the police the body of a woman murdered with a sword without all having to face inquiry. The only alternative was tipping Annabel into the river with the rest of the dead. Mae shut her eyes and made a strangled sound, trying to banish that thought, of these people throwing her mother in the river.

Alan spoke while she had her eyes shut, his voice soothing and terribly sad for her; exactly the right voice. "Okay."

It made her mad. Her eyes snapped open.

"I don't want to go out with you," Mae hurled in his concerned face.

It felt as if there was a live animal scrabbling inside her throat, trying to draw blood. She was terrified she was going to cry.

She raged instead. "You played me. You asked me out to fool Gerald. You made sure that I wouldn't say no before the night of the Market. You never intended to betray Nick for an instant. You just wanted me to tell Jamie you were going to do it, so Jamie would tell Gerald and Gerald would believe him because it was coming from the mouth of Alan's girlfriend. It was a filthy thing to do."

Alan turned his face away from her a little. There was a river stretching by the side of the camp, the waters tranquil and gleaming in the dawn light, hovered over by strange dragonflies.

"I know it was," Alan said quietly.

"You couldn't have trusted me?" Mae whispered.

"I could have. I didn't," Alan whispered back. "It was easier and safer to lie. I'm sorry."

He'd probably been sorry the whole time he did it, but he'd still done it, heard what was wrong with Merris and worked out how to use that, got Mae to call up Liannan so he could strike a bargain with her and lie to her about what the bargain was, kissed her and lied, lied and lied and lied.

"You could have broken my heart," said Mae. "And you wouldn't have cared."

Alan smiled a crooked, hurt little smile. "I couldn't have broken your heart," he told her. "You never liked me enough for that."

Of all the girls I ever saw, I dreamed of you the most.

Mae swallowed and let her eyes slide shut for another moment. "I liked you a lot," she told him. "I think – I think maybe you could've had a chance with me. But you lied."

"Thanks for saying so," Alan said, as if he meant it. And as if he didn't believe her. He sounded sad, but resigned; he must have grown fairly used to the idea of losing her while he was lying to her.

Mae opened her eyes again and saw his narrow, pale face, his wonderful twilight eyes, and she reminded herself past the rage and pain that he had taken that mark last night. That at any moment he could be tortured, or possessed, or killed. His whole life hung on a magician's whim, and he had done it for a child he hardly knew, for a child who belonged to the Market that hated him as a traitor and a girl who hated him because he was crippled.

He had lied to her, the girl he'd wanted to love, cold-bloodedly and relentlessly, for weeks. And then he'd done one of the noblest things she had ever seen.

She could feel the shaking inside her, starting low in her stomach and building, but she wanted to hide it from everyone else. "Alan," she said. "You are crazy."

"See, that's why I started liking you," he said gently. "Because you're so smart."

Mae would've attempted a smile, but her face felt like it might crack. Alan looked as if he was trying to think of ways to speak to her, to touch her, to make her feel better, and she thought they might work and wanted to run.

"Mae," Jamie said tentatively, coming around the tent. "Can I talk to you alone?"

He looked flushed from sleep and tears, his spiky hair rumpled. He looked about twelve years old. Mae turned to him, as if he could pull her on puppet strings, desperate to do even the smallest thing for him.

"Of course, I'll go," Alan said. "I need to go and find a place where Nick and I can talk things out properly. Somewhere on the other end of the meadow, away from people."

Jamie smiled a wavering, falling-apart smile. "Or you could take a plane and have a conversation in the middle of the Sahara desert, possibly."

"Might be safest," said Alan. "Jamie, I'm so sorry."

"I know," Jamie said. "Alan, in case of – in case."

He hesitated and then went up to Alan and put his arm around his neck, having to go on his tiptoes to hug him because Alan was so tall. Alan did not hesitate for a moment, just put his arms around Jamie and held on.

"Thanks for everything," Jamie said at last, detaching and rubbing the back of his hand over his swollen eyes.

Alan looked at Jamie, puzzled and tender. "Everything's been my pleasure."

Then, being Alan and blessed with enormous tact, he looked at them both once more and just left, heading away from the Goblin Market camp and towards the hawthorn trees spreading broomstick-handle branches against the pale sky.

"Hey, you," said Mae, the words sticking in her throat.

Jamie looked at her, his eyes back to being dark again, being the exact mirror of hers. He reached out and she reached out, fingers curling in together and linked tight, and she wanted to promise him that nothing would ever hurt him again, that she would protect him, that she would always be there, always.

"I'm so sorry," he said. "It's all my fault. I thought if I went to London, I could help, no matter how strong Celeste's Circle will be now. I thought I could send word back. I wanted to help. But instead I – I killed—"

"You didn't," Mae said fiercely. "It was me who made the plan. If it hadn't been for me—"

"But you had to do it," said Jamie. "And I – I still have to go to London."

Mae felt her fingers clutch his, nails digging into the back of Jamie's hands.

"I have to go, Mae," Jamie insisted to her silence. "Alan's wearing a mark; we have to know what Gerald's planning to do to him. Celeste has got too many magicians, and control over Gerald's marks. She'll bring the war to us, and we'll need somebody behind enemy lines. And – and we have to work out a way to bring the Circles down. Did you see some of the magicians? They wanted to surrender. They can't keep thinking that the Circles are the only way, and killing people until they don't even remember that it's wrong. Someone has to do this. And I'm the only one who can. Will you be okay?"

He looked at her, hanging on to her just as hard as she was

hanging on to him and biting his lips, scared and struggling and in pain and still trying to do the right thing. Her Jamie.

Mae tipped her forehead against his and held on for just a little while longer. "Yeah," she promised him. "I'll be okay."

They stood like that until Jamie said, "Nick," and Mae said, "Huh?" and then stepped back as Jamie said, "Nick. Over here. Nick!"

Nick was striding past the tent, clearly intent on finding Alan again, but at Jamie's call he checked himself and came striding over to them. Someone had found him a new shirt, as the old one had been ripped in two and soaked in gore, but beneath the clean cotton his whole body looked tense and exhausted.

"What?" he asked.

Jamie let go of Mae's hands with one last, clinging press. "I'm really sorry about this," he said. "I know that you're upset about Alan and you don't know what to say to me about – about anything, and this is the worst time to try and talk to you. But I'm going to the Aventurine Circle so I can help Alan and all of us, because I'm the only one they'd let in. So there isn't any other time I can talk to you. I just wanted to say that you were a great friend. I'm really glad you asked me. I'm really glad we did that. And you can go and find Alan now. You don't have to say anything at all."

Jamie stood a careful distance away from Nick and spoke carefully too, anxiously, trying to get it just right.

He was seeing these moments as his last chance to get things right, Mae thought, sick and aching. In case he died somewhere in London, among enemies.

"What?" said Nick, and scowled. "What are you talking about? Don't be an idiot. You're not going anywhere."

"I am," Jamie told him sturdily.

"You want revenge for your mother?" Nick asked, and Jamie flinched. One of Nick's hands closed in a fist and then loosened. He took a breath. "I'll get it for you," he said. "Tell me what you want, and I'll make it happen. You don't have to go anywhere and get your idiot self killed."

"Okay, can you pass yourself off as a magician and gain Gerald's trust and pass us information about Celeste's plans and save all the magicians who want to be saved?" Jamie asked. "Because if so, awesome. I shall stay here and eat pie."

Nick blinked at Jamie. "I was thinking more in terms of killing someone."

Jamie's smile this time was still wavering, but it almost looked real. "I know. But this is something I have to do. So I'm going to go do it. You take care of yourself, Nick."

Jamie started to back away and his eyes left Nick, turning back to Mae.

"Hey," Nick said abruptly, and tossed something at Jamie's head.

Jamie caught it, fumbling it a bit, and then almost dropped it when he saw the rough carvings on the bright handle and worked out what it was.

"A knife, Nick?" he asked piteously. "I feel so betrayed."

"It's a magic knife," Nick said. "I made it myself."

"I don't want to seem ungrateful when you have given me this thoughtful, homemade and totally terrifying gift," Jamie told him. "But you can't imagine that I'm going to use it."

"Just to hold someone off. Just remember what I taught you," said Nick. "Just buy a little time so I can come and get you. Jamie. I'll come and get you."

"Nick," Jamie said. "I know. Thank you for my scary knife."

He looked down at the knife, a bit helplessly, and then put it in his pocket. Then he started across the meadow in exactly the opposite direction to Alan, along the side of the river.

"Also," Nick added curtly, "I'm sorry about your face."

Jamie looked over his shoulder, and touched the demon's mark crawling along his jaw with the back of his hand. "Sorry about saving all our lives by doing something you had to do?"

"Oh no," Nick said blandly. "I just meant, you know. Generally."

Jamie stared at him, shocked, and laughed. It was a real laugh, helpless and sweet, and Mae memorised it in case he died. Jamie by the river at dawn, laughing.

His eyes caught Mae's and he stopped laughing. His gaze simply held hers.

You and me against the world. Mae nodded at him, and Jamie turned and walked slowly away down the river. He squared his thin shoulders as he went, and the gesture almost broke Mae's self-control, but she had to be standing up and looking all right if he turned around.

"Don't leave," she ordered Nick between her teeth. If Jamie turned around, he would see that she wasn't alone. She watched Jamie go until even when she squinted against the dazzle of the sunlight on the water he was nothing but a tiny black speck, and then the speck was lost. "Okay," Mae said at last. It was all over. Jamie was gone. "Okay, you can go now."

Nick nodded, his head dipping briefly. His hair was such a dense black it looked dusty in the sunlight, the light glancing off it and forming white around it. The shape the light formed was jagged and nothing like a crown.

"That woman," he said. "Helen. I could have killed her on the bridge in London. I didn't. I thought – it was meant to be a human sort of gesture, sparing your enemies. Showing mercy. I got it wrong. I wish I'd killed her. Then Annabel would be alive instead."

Hearing her name was like a blow to a wounded place. Mae wanted to be blind suddenly, to be deaf and dumb and blind so they couldn't tell her about it and she wouldn't have to talk about it and she wouldn't have ever seen it, her mother's empty eyes staring up into the night sky.

"It wasn't your fault," she said numbly.

"No," said Nick. "But I'd like her to be alive. Not just for you, and Jamie. I'd – I liked her, I think."

Annabel, always walking so perfectly in her high heels, her sword flashing in the midnight garden.

"Just go away," Mae said, turning away from him, from his face, which was perfect and cold and uncomprehending, always.

"Mavis," Nick said, and then stopped.

Annabel had thought that Mavis, that horrible nightmare of a name, was beautiful. She'd given Mae that name because she thought it was beautiful. Mae's face felt too tight; her eyes were hot and swimming, and then they were running and her nose was running a bit too.

"Go away," she repeated, almost gasping out the words.

There was only silence, so for a moment she thought he had gone. Then she heard him say, "No," his voice deep and terribly close.

Nick put his arms around her. He moved slowly and awkwardly, but once he was done she was wrapped in strong arms, held against his chest. He was big and solid and warm all around her, and she found herself holding on to his shirt, holding tight in both clenched fists as if she was about to start beating on him. She was standing on her tiptoes, but he was taking most of her weight; she was pressing her face against his collarbone. It would be all right to hit him or to shriek or to do anything she liked.

This time yesterday morning Annabel had known nothing about magic. She'd had a day to learn, to show fear and grace, and then no more days.

Mae was just howling, screaming through her teeth, getting tears and snot all over Nick's shirt. They were going to put her mother in the ground out by Mezentius House, and the alternative had been putting her in the river.

Nick's arms were like iron bars around her. He wasn't murmuring soothing words or stroking her back, nothing like the demon in her dream, nothing like a human would have done in his place, but he wasn't letting go, either.

"Mavis. Mae," he said at last. "I don't know. You have to tell me. Is this right?"

"Yeah," Mae said into his shirt, her voice breaking, and she cried without screaming, just leaning into him and smelling cotton and steel. It was awful and heartbreaking and she was exactly where she wanted to be, here, with him, in these arms and no one else's, and she finally understood why she had kept coming back and why she'd kept acting like a crazy person, her plans always collapsing and nothing making sense. She got it now.

She was kind of in love with him.

It had never happened to her before, and he would not have even the slightest idea how to love her back.

She was too tired and broken apart to deal with that now. She just rested, her eyes shut and leaning against him, exhausted and almost glad. She loved him, and he was here.

It was tempting to try and fall asleep standing up,

measuring his steady breaths against her own, but by then she figured she was calm enough, and she owed it to him to step away.

"Thank you," she said. It came out sounding very formal. "I'm going to find Sin now. You can go after Alan."

Nick nodded, looking down at her. She looked back up at those strange alien eyes, that cruel mouth, and her heart turned over in her chest as if he had flipped it like a coin to show a new surface.

"We're going to sort this out," she promised him. "We're going to get Jamie back, and we're going to make Alan safe. We are."

Except there was no way to make Alan safe. Gerald could do whatever he wanted to him, anytime he liked, and Nick would have to watch.

Nick shifted, the line of his shoulders too tight, fury and helplessness on his face for one murderous moment, and then he nodded again.

"Tell me about your plan sooner next time. You're the war leader, aren't you?" he asked, and waited for her to nod. "So lead."

Mae watched him turn and go in the direction his brother had gone, stalking him like a predator.

"Yeah," she said softly to herself. "Sounds like a plan."

Mae didn't want to lie to Nick, so she went to find Sin, weaving through the narrow green pathways between the caravans and tents.

Sin was sitting in a deck chair with baby Toby in her lap, long brown legs hooked up over the side with her feet tucked into the place where the chair legs bisected. She was talking to Merris Cromwell.

Merris looked the same to Mae, except for her dead-black

eyes. The measured, approving smile she gave Mae was entirely her own. Mae could not see a trace of Liannan in her by day.

"Mae," Sin said with her vivid, welcoming smile, with passionate, determined sympathy. "Come and sit with us. I was just telling Merris how amazing you were."

"Indeed she was."

Sin looked gorgeous and carefree this morning, her torn silk changed to a loose cotton top and a denim skirt that left her legs bare. Her brother and her leader had been saved. She'd got what she wanted.

Only she caught Mae's hand as Mae went by, her fingers curling soft as a secret against Mae's palm, and Mae liked her too much to hate her now.

Celeste's war would crash down on Sin's head too. They had to be united, the way they had been for a moment in that market square.

"I hear that you were the one who formulated the whole plan," said Merris. "I hear that you were the one who tried to hold the force together by suggesting the magicians surrender. In fact, it seems you showed a great deal of initiative Cynthia here did not."

Sin stopped smiling.

Mae frowned at Merris. "Sin did great. She got all those people together. I could never have done it without her."

"Yes," said Merris. "She showed all the hallmarks of a very fine lieutenant. But it occurs to me that what this Market needs is someone independent and intelligent."

Sin's dark eyes were suddenly blazing with fury and hurt. Mae just felt fury. She barely knew this woman, but she was in no mood to see one of her friends put down like this for no reason.

"I have only three years," Merris said, her voice suddenly almost sweet, like the chiming of bells at the Goblin Market. "When I go, I want to be absolutely sure that my Market is in the best possible hands. From now on, I think I will be looking at you as well as Cynthia, trying to determine which of you should become leader of the Market in my place." She paused. "That is, if you want the job."

Mae looked around at all the colours of the Market, and thought of the night-time square, the feeling of a plan when all the pieces fell smoothly together, how terrible it felt to be useless. Jamie had made a plan and had gone to carry it out.

She needed to do something, and she had loved the Goblin Market from the very first time she had seen it.

"Oh yes," she said hoarsely. "I want it."

Merris rose from her chair, more lightly than a woman of her years should have been able to. Mae found herself lost in those demon-dark eyes.

"Excellent. Time will tell," Merris said, "which of you is up to the challenge. I look forward to finding out."

Mae and Sin found themselves staring at each other, a coldness slipping between them for the first time since the easy start of their friendship. Mae was not surprised to find herself suddenly assessing Sin's strengths and weaknesses, trying to think of ways to undermine one and exploit the other.

Sin's eyes were narrowed, cool: surveying her new rival, the impostor.

And then Mae remembered how kind Sin had been to her, and Sin might have remembered that Mae's plan had almost worked, or even what had happened to her mother. Sin looked away, through the twisting path of tent flaps and hanging lanterns, to the rolling expanse of the meadow. There were two dark figures against the horizon and the hawthorn. Nick and Alan, Mae thought, picturing Nick's look of helpless fury, were having a fight.

She knew how it would go. Nick would rage and Alan would lie, and neither of them would ever leave.

"Well, look at it this way," said Sin. "At least we're not being stupid enough to fight over a guy."

"That's true."

"Well. Let the best woman win."

Sin shut her eyes, taking a moment to relax in the sunshine spilling warm over the meadow, light touching the tips of the grass blades with honey. Mae tried not to think about Alan's heart in the hands of magicians or about Jamie friendless in their midst. She tried not to think about love or loss.

She looked around at the Goblin Market spread like a feast before her, and thought of war. She thought about winning.

"Yeah," Mae said. "Sounds like a plan."

ACKNOWLEDGEMENTS

Someone very wise once told me the second book is harder than the first: if the last one took a village, this took a city. But luckily I had a wonderful city to hand, and to thank!

Thanks to Kristin Nelson, agent extraordinaire, and the whole fabulous team at the NLA.

Thanks to Karen Wojtyla, otherwise known as the mistress of my soul, who, ably supported by Emily Fabre, stopped me babbling and using Terrible Romantic Clichés. Thanks to my UK editor, Venetia Gosling, who quite agreed with her, and my copy editor, Valerie Shea, who agreed with both of them!

Thanks to Simon & Schuster in their entirety, both in the US and in the UK, and to all my lovely foreign publishers as well. Your amazing support of the first book means that I trust you all absolutely with this one!

Thanks to Nicole Russo and Anna McKean, for organising the best US tour ever, and Scott Westerfeld for making every day of it fun. And to Kathryn McKenna for going around England with me, and the whole publicity team at S&S UK! Thanks to all the librarians and booksellers I met and have yet to meet – it's an honour and a privilege!

Thanks to Saundra Mitchell, who read the second draft and told me I would get there, and to Justine Larbalestier, who read the fourth draft and told me I had.

To Team Castle: Ally Carter, Jennifer Lynn Barnes, Sarah Cross, Carrie Ryan, Diana Peterfreund, Robin Wasserman,

Maureen Johnson, Holly Black, and Cassandra Clare, in memory of kittens, murders, and snickerdoodles.

To the S Club, Susan and Sinéad, due to much writing and more cupcakes.

To the Clique, who know who they are and keep me sane(ish).

To my friends and family, who showed up at events, cheered me on, and (shockingly) still answer the phone when I call, despite suffering through all that.

Thanks to Natasha, who never stops believing, and Jenny, who wishes we both would.

And thank you so much to the fans of The Demon's Lexicon, whose response to the book has awed and delighted me. The emails, the art, getting to meet and talk to you guys – I would still write if nobody read the books, but you all make it ten times more fun.